Stephen Gray was born in Cape Town in 1941 and was schooled at St Andrew's College, Grahamstown, and the University of Cape Town, from where he went to Cambridge University to complete a masters degree in English in 1964. While at Cambridge for a short time he was an editor of *Granta*. He lectured at the University of Aix-Marseilles and at the University of Iowa, where in the Writers Workshop he took a masters in Creative Writing. Since 1969 he has lived and worked in Johannesburg where he is Professor of English at the Rand Afrikaans University.

He is a novelist (*Local Colour*, 1975, *Visible People*, 1977, and *Caltrop's Desire*, 1980), and a poet whose volumes include *Hottentot Venus* (1979). He has worked in theatre, most recently with *Schreiner: A One-woman Play*, presented by the Market Theatre. He has edited a dozen collections of writing from Southern Africa, and published a literary history, *Southern African Literature: An Introduction* (1979). His research interests include comparative studies and historiography.

The Penguin Book of
Southern African Stories

» «

EDITED BY
STEPHEN GRAY

PENGUIN BOOKS

Penguin Books Ltd, 27 Wrights Lane, London w8 5TZ (Publishing and Editorial)
and Harmondsworth, Middlesex, England (Distribution and Warehouse)
Viking Penguin Inc., 40 West 23rd Street, New York, New York 10010, USA
Penguin Books Australia Ltd, Ringwood, Victoria, Australia
Penguin Books Canada Ltd, 2801 John Street, Markham, Ontario, Canada L3R 1B4
Penguin Books (NZ) Ltd, 182–190 Wairau Road, Auckland 10, New Zealand

This selection first published 1985
Reprinted 1985, 1986, 1987

Selection and Introduction copyright © Stephen Gray, 1985
The Acknowledgements on page 328 constitute an extension of this copyright page.
All rights reserved

Printed and bound in Great Britain by
Cox & Wyman Ltd, Reading

Typeset in 9/11½ Linotron 202 Plantin by
Rowland Phototypesetting Ltd
Bury St Edmunds, Suffolk

Contents

» «

CONTENTS

Introduction

» «

This collection is the first attempt on a large scale to compare systematically the various literatures of Southern Africa, to interfile them with reference to common experiences. The Contents page shows no sectioning of 'English South African literature' in one camp, 'Afrikaans literature' in another, and 'Black indigenous literature' in yet another kraal of its own. In not following traditional divisions, in starting from the proposition that all are integral parts of a far larger organization, one which is hospitable to the sprawling habits of literature itself, some of the extent and interconnectedness of literatures on this subcontinent can become apparent.

It is also a first to posit a larger literary geography than has been the case when anthologizers have addressed one or another of the literatures of the Africa South nexus. Previously the focus has been too narrow (Zulu literature) or too wide (new literature in English in Africa), or it has been theme-centric (the literature of Apartheid) or schooled (Black protest literature). The groupings into which historiographers have bunched areas of the literature have been many; none hold water entirely, none are self-sufficient and discrete. So here is a fresh attempt to push back the boundaries to the full extent of a functioning reality. This means, in terms of modern geography, South Africa, Lesotho, Botswana, Swaziland, Namibia, Zimbabwe and Malawi are included – they might arguably be described as one literary region which, through long trading in its history, its publishing and its educational practices, has more defining properties in common than the traditional differences and divisions. Call it 'Southern Africa' – I mean that as a literary field, and not as any constellation of current national states.

The boundary has also gone back in time. It is worth niggling about just how old literature in Southern Africa is, for, as far as literary histories go, Europe is usually held to be the aged one, and Africa the stripling. Not so in the local version, however; if as the anthropologists tell us Africa is the cradle of humankind (and the Transvaal is where the first language walked and talked), the timescale that holds Thomas Pringle and Andrew Geddes Bain as founding fathers of the European strain of the literature in the 1820s is indeed dealing with the last few seconds of a day which has been extremely long.

Although committed to paper only in the 1860s, the story with which this collection begins is at least pre-Christian. The text that describes the arrival of mortality among humans is an appropriate starting point for this literature, at least as venerable as any Western sacred text. At least, our writers have found it so.

This Southern Africa, huge in terms of time and space, happens currently to be dominated, but not entirely controlled, by South Africa – once the old Cape of Good Hope, one day surely to be Azania. It is currently difficult to get past the situation that South Africa is both the industrial giant of the region and its most noted violator of human rights. Those twin, not unrelated, circumstances are what the literature is ultimately about, and it evades neither issue. Accordingly much criticism of the literature of Southern Africa is alert to these two crucial factors – it has irremediably sold out to business interests in books, or is overtly partisan, battling the texts through to liberation. Neither circumstance, some of the time, is to the advantage of the literature itself. A more formal empiricism might release the answers as to why a particular work may be the way it is at any particular moment, and how such a continuum of moments builds into a literary polysystem, with its past, its present and its future.

In this collection, this line is followed through with reference to one form only – the story in prose. Call it 'short fiction', for many of the pieces here are significantly different from what is customarily described as the 'short story'. Short fiction as a literary mode has played a long and central role in all the sub-literatures of Southern Africa, and appears to have been serviceable in many situations: in autochthonous, pre-contact literature, particularly in Khoisan literature before 1800, as the vehicle for myth and fable; in black literature in indigenous languages, particularly in the nineteenth century, as the vehicle for legend and folklore; in colonial literature of the same period in European languages, as the vehicle for fireside tales; and, not to put too fine a point upon it, many of these are absorbed into the form of the written short story of modern times during the twentieth century. 'Myth', 'fable', 'legend', 'folklore', 'tale' and 'short story' are not mutually exclusive terms – if this collection has a thesis at all, it is that these categories of short fiction interdepend and co-exist in Southern Africa, and that all remain available to the writer always. Where the developmental model for other literatures rather assumes that the one form of short fiction supersedes the next and the next, with a growth towards sophistication and maturity being implied in this process, in Southern Africa there has not been that sifting and processing of one dominating tradition over time that has taken place in, say, the British or the American short story to produce a fixed model of trends. Here all categories of short fiction are practised at the same time: from Johannesburg, where the publication of a collection of orthodox short stories in English is praised at a launching party, it is possible to travel north to Pretoria (where the same will be happening in Afrikaans), to Mafikeng for fireside tales, to the Okavango for Khoisan myth, and on to Zimbabwe for, say, legend, or to the Transkei for, say, folklore. This is not a matter of atomized, different literatures, but of a few days of driving across an existing, functioning literary totality.

There are many orthodoxies, perspectives, uses for short forms. Who is to say that one use is more valid than another? Much nationalist literary thinking – the point is almost too obvious to make – insists on beaconing off this plethora of small groups into separate (imaginary) nation-states, supposedly each with its own unique literature contained generally and, for the sake of literary-critical convenience, within a strict language barrier – hence, Venda literature, Xironga, Northern and Southern Sotho, Shona literature, Afrikaans literature and the English (mixed-bag) strain. But, while perhaps being ethnographically sound, in literary terms this is a divide-and-rule tactic devised to lend pre-eminence to the work written in languages of European origin. It is not hierarchies that should be maintained, but cross-sections that should be taken – the comparison now.

As a result of the contiguity of language resources, Southern Africa has produced – the point is not a wild polemical one, but merely common sense – a high degree of polymath writers; the literature itself has thrived most in challenging, some would say incongruous, interface situations. The result has not been absorption and domination, but always response and transformation. No one literary practice has yet been reduced to extinction; every literary practice has been subject to adaptation. That has been the habit and the dynamic of the literature all along – a process of blending, reworking, making newly meaningful.

If there is one common shift that has taken place within the last century and a half, it is the general movement from oracy to literacy. (Xhosa was first rendered in print in 1823; the first Afrikaans poems began to appear in the 1860s; Malawi published its first literary book as late as 1969.) A special feature of Southern African literature, *even today*, is that exceptionally high proportions of stories are told, rather than written. Exceptionally high proportions of Southern African stories, recorded by literate authors of course, are about preliterate characters. I am not suggesting that the *writers* are mostly literate 'whites' and the *characters* mostly preliterate 'blacks', for the evidence of the work itself is not in favour of any such facile polarization. The battle for literacy is fought on many fronts, and the subcontinent remains one on which after, in some entrepots, up to five centuries of occupation, most of the population still cannot read or write. This was as true for Sol T. Plaatje's Gokatweng as for Herman Charles Bosman's Oom Schalk. Literary activity in orthodox Western forms is still a somewhat elitist affair, confined to a relatively small readership. Yet the shift from the spoken to the written persists as our major event.

The writers of this literature themselves, it seems to me, have never stayed small and elitist, though. Plaatje, for example, who wrote in Tswana, English and Afrikaans, saw it as part of his general mandate to act as a go-between, providing works for blacks to learn white literary codes and, at the same time, for whites to learn black codes. Eugène N. Marais, who was equally at home in Afrikaans and English, when he adapted the tales of Outa Hendrik, his San informant of 1913, and inserted them into Afrikaans literature, was providing children's texts which introduced his new readers to print as well as to oral history. Today, with his satirical fables in English, a writer like Es'kia Mphahlele is still performing the same function, introducing his audiences to the techniques of written composition as he draws on the resources of the deep past. Even Nadine Gordimer's story here is an implied commentary in one mode of another mode, in this case a hearsay article.

In this whole transaction – which I would maintain is the major and longstanding event of the subcontinent – the writer has always played a pivotal role, at the point where oral experience phases into the written, where the world of print and books and packaging receives the language of the environment. This, when all is said and done, is the essential theme of works otherwise as unalike as A. C. Jordan's 'The King of the Waters', Pauline Smith's 'The Schoolmaster', D. B. Z. Ntuli's 'Once in a Century', Bessie Head's 'The Lovers' and Elsa Joubert's 'Milk' – all stories which feature the writer as transcriber and shaper, as amanuensis of the spoken word.

Translation, also, is a major characteristic of the literature, for where languages rub shoulders in the marketplace (even if they do not in the academy) the writer misses out if he or she is not able to work in simultaneous transmission. I can state categorically that not one of the writers represented here is restricted to a tradition of monolingual resources; in the given situation, to attempt to be linguistically pure would be unthinkable. Some writers write in more than one language, most have a working knowledge of even more. Therefore it is wholly natural that the literature flourishes on transpositions and adaptations, as the instant a literary idea travels across language it emerges re-animated, newly valid, recontextualized. The complexity with which this interchange has occurred in the literature is too great to chart here; suffice it to say that to the simple process of sources and influences by which literature generates itself in a monoculture must be added the factor of translation which here has been creatively generative in a particular way. Nor should this process of translation be understood merely as the act of rendering a lesser-known language into a more accessible one; for writers in a contact situation it has worked in the reverse direction with reliable frequency as well.

Yet this collection appears in English. Most of the items are originally written in English, some by writers who would not choose English as their preferred language (R. R. R. Dhlomo, for example). By this I do not at all mean to suggest that Southern African literature is really English literature transposed to around African Capricorn, where it has aestivated into some new areas of experience, some new tropes that, yes, can be accommodated after all in the metropolitan model for English overseas in the old ex-colonies. No underhand co-opting of the whole into English is intended.

While it is true that English has served well as a first or second language for the majority of the writers of the territory demarcated by this collection since at least 1800, English has by no means always proved the obvious or only language-medium to choose: the intended readership has often not been English-speaking. English has proved good for business, somehow suspect for literature; too newly imported for grass-roots experience, too internationally generalized for catching the grit of what really is being said and felt. But the power and usefulness of English to reach outside the confines of the region, the ghettos of the local mind, remains pre-eminent; and most writers' work which has travelled beyond the borders of Southern Africa has travelled in English, and attendantly in forms which are acceptable to metropolitan English readers. Olive Schreiner made it out of here with the first colonial novel of importance in English a century ago, and William Plomer, Doris Lessing, Alan Paton, Es'kia Mphahlele, Nadine Gordimer, Bessie Head, Elsa Joubert and others have followed. But what is acceptable and meaningful in London and New York at any one time is not therefore automatically useful and meaningful here, and not necessarily in the same ways, either. Here writers have kidded themselves for a long time that success overseas, inevitably in English, is the ultimate accolade and vindication of their activities; but the truth might well be that the context from which they spring, and ultimately into which they feed back, is more decisive. Consequently in this collection I am suggesting that the vital context is here – a literary subcontinent of the imagination that accepted its multifarious unity as a norm from way back when, and rejoices in the most daring acts of syncretism and synthesis, far more important as a whole than any individual talents or key works which might have emerged from it.

So I have selected without much regard for 'reputation' and 'standing', and have consciously avoided previous anthologizers' typical favourites, the few 'chestnuts' that are frequently reprinted as if they were all there is to be discovered. Possibly most of what follows will be unheard of, even to the most assiduous scholar of the literatures; I trust that it will not remain that way.

And the fact that this collection is in English, or translated into English, seems almost fortuitous now. The true history of Southern African literature occurs between these stories, in the cut and jump the reader's mind makes adjusting from one small encounter to the next. I hope that, as the writers themselves tell their tales, fragment by fragment, the shape of the mosaic of which they are all part will become apparent. It is a unique one, seen whole.

Stephen Gray
Johannesburg, 1985

The Origin of Death

» «

TRANSLATED FROM THE NAMA BY W. H. I. BLEEK

The Moon, it is said, sent once an Insect to Men, saying, 'Go thou to Men, and tell them, "As I die, and dying live, so ye shall also die, and dying live."' The Insect started with the message, but whilst on his way was overtaken by the Hare, who asked: 'On what errand art thou bound?' The Insect answered: 'I am sent by the Moon to Men, to tell them that as she dies, and dying lives, they also shall die, and dying live.' The Hare said, 'As thou art an awkward runner, let me go' (to take the message). With these words he ran off, and when he reached Men, he said, 'I am sent by the Moon to tell you, "As I die, and dying perish, in the same manner ye shall also die and come wholly to an end."' Then the Hare returned to the Moon, and told her what he had said to Men. The Moon reproached him angrily, saying, 'Darest thou tell the people a thing which I have not said?' With these words she took up a piece of wood, and struck him on the nose. Since that day the Hare's nose is slit.

Dove and Jackal

» «

FRANK BROWNLEE

COLLECTED FROM THE XHOSA

Of all the birds there is none quite like the dove; all her ways are gentle and she believes evil of none.

Jackal is a person full of tricks and cunning.

One day Dove, perched on the branch of a tree, was watching her three little children, who nestled together in their house made of sticks. She was singing softly to the children when Jackal passed beneath the tree. Hearing Dove's song he sat down and looked up; seeing Dove he said, 'Good day, child of my younger sister.'

Dove replied, 'Good day to you, my uncle.'

Jackal asked, 'What are you doing up there, Dove, and what is the meaning of your song?'

Dove said, 'I am singing to my children so that they may rest peacefully in our house of sticks.'

Jackal said, 'Your song, Dove, is very beautiful. How many children have you?' Dove said there were three.

Jackal ran round about to see if anyone was looking; then he returned to his place below the tree. He said, 'Dove, you have a large family. I am very hungry; throw down one of your children for me to eat.' Dove said she could not think of doing that, as each of her children was equally dear to her.

Jackal became abusive; he said, 'Can you, a person whose ways are said to be all gentleness, sit up there with three fat children while a person below is starving? Just look at my ribs, how they stand out with hunger.' Jackal drew in his breath so as to make his ribs stand out sharply.

Dove said, 'I am very sorry for you, Jackal, but my children are dear to me, and I will not throw one down.'

Jackal, beginning to weep, lay down and said, 'Dove, are you going to sit up there with three fat children while a person dies before your eyes?' Jackal lay down and began to whine and weep.

Dove said, 'Go to your place, Jackal, and obtain your food where you are used to obtaining it.'

At that Jackal sprang up in a rage. He said, 'You little thing up there, are you insulting me while I tell you of my great hunger? I have dealt very patiently with you, but now my patience is finished. Unless you throw down one of your children I will climb your tree and eat up not only your children but also you and your house of sticks.'

Dove became frightened at this. She was so frightened that she forgot that Jackal was unable to climb a tree. So to save her other two children and her house and herself she threw down one of her children.

Jackal ate that child, and after he had done so he ran round about to see if anyone was looking; then he came back to his place under the tree. He began to weep and whine; the tears flowed from his eyes. He lay down on the ground and made as if he were about to die. Then he looked up to where Dove was sitting. 'Oh, Dove,' he said, 'I am dying of starvation, help me. How many children have you?'

The Dove replied, 'I have only two, two, two.'

Jackal said, 'Oh, kind Dove, throw just one more to me so that I shall not die.'

Dove replied, 'No, no, no, I have only two, two, two.'

Jackal said, 'Have you forgotten of my forbearance towards you? I said I would climb up the tree and eat you and your children and even your house of sticks if you did not throw down one of your children – throw down just one more so that I may not die of hunger.'

Dove said, 'I have only two, two, two.' Jackal ran round to see if anyone was looking; then he came back and said, 'Dove, make ready for your end, I am coming up the tree to eat your children and you and even your house of sticks.'

Dove was so much afraid that she threw down a second child. Jackal ate it and sat still for a while; then he ran round about to see if anyone was looking.

He came back to his place under the tree and said, 'Dove, help me, I am dying. Throw down just one more of your children, otherwise I must lie down beneath your tree and pass away. How many more children have you?'

Dove replied, 'Just one, just one, just one. If you must die, you must die.'

Jackal said, 'Now, Dove, you have insulted me very sorely; I have borne much from you. Unless you throw down that child, I will climb up your tree and eat your child and you and even your house of sticks.' As he said this Jackal rushed up to the stem of the tree and made as if he were climbing.

Dove, being so frightened, forgot that Jackal could not climb a tree and threw down the last of her children. Jackal ate it and after he had run about to see that no one was looking went on his way.

Dove, looking upon her empty house of sticks, sang mournfully, 'Woo, Woo, Woo,' as she sat upon a branch of the tree. As she was singing sorrowfully to herself, Ndwe, the blue crane, came stalking along. When he heard the song of Dove in the tree, he looked up and said, 'My youngest sister, why this song of mourning; what has made you sad?'

At first all Dove could say was, 'Woo, Woo, Woo.' Then she said, 'Jackal has been here – Woo – he asked me to throw down one of my children – Woo – and then, when he threatened to eat us all, I threw down a child – Woo – he again threatened us and I threw down a second – Woo, Woo – he threatened a third time and I threw down my third and last child – Woo, Woo, Woo.'

Crane stood still for a long time looking up at where Dove sat. He walked slowly this way and that, then he stood still under the branch where Dove was sitting. He turned his head sideways, so that one eye was looking up and one was looking down; he lifted his wings and replaced them carefully upon his back as is the manner of cranes when in deep thought; then he said, 'My youngest sister, I grieve with you in the loss of your children, but you were safe in your place high up in that tree. Who was it told you that a jackal could climb a tree?'

Dove answered, 'Woo, Woo, Woo, it was Jackal who said he would climb our tree; in my fear I had forgotten that he was no climber, Woo, Woo, Woo; it is through my foolishness that my children are no more.'

'My little sister,' he said, 'it is not altogether foolishness that has lost you your children: it is your simpleness that has brought you this sorrow. I will see to it that Jackal is dealt with.' So saying, Crane strode off with long steps. He adjusted his wings as is the way of cranes when considering a matter. His steps were slow and he was deep in thought. A sudden rustling in the undergrowth startled him. He spread his wings ready to rise, when he saw that it was Jackal who had caused him to start. So he adjusted his wings as though he had been spreading them for the purpose of flying. Jackal seemed to have been running fast and far, for his tongue was lolling from his mouth and saliva dripped from its red tip.

Crane stood silent and turned his head sideways so that one eye looked upwards and one down upon Jackal as he crouched in the undergrowth.

Jackal, panting, said, 'Goo-goo-good day, grandfather, this meeting is unexpected.' At the same time he drew his dripping tongue into his mouth, but had to extend it again to allow himself to breathe freely.

Crane regarded him closely, with head on one side, and said, 'What hasty journey has brought you to this stage of exhaustion?'

Jackal drew in his tongue, which was lolling at the side of his mouth, and swallowed slowly, but found he had again to extend it. He answered between his pantings, 'I have a wife and family of three at my home in the rocks, ha, ha, ha. One of my children required tender food – ha, ha, ha – and I have been seeking it – ha-ha, he-he. Hence am I breathless and weary, but excuse me, grandfather, I see that a storm of rain is threatening. I must get back to my house.'

Crane said, 'If you must get back to your house it would be as well for you to go at once – you people who travel upon the ground travel slowly; for us who fly, a long distance is as nothing.'

Jackal, seeking in some way to please and flatter Crane, said, 'Kwowu! you of the long wide wings, I have always envied the bird people to whom distance is nothing.'

Crane said, 'Meet me at this place tomorrow at this time. As I have taught many of my children, so will I teach you to fly.'

Jackal, thanking Crane for his promise, agreed to be at that spot the next day and withdrew, disappearing in the undergrowth.

The next day Jackal and Crane met at the appointed place. Crane walked up and down with long, slow steps; Jackal sat at the edge of a thicket. Crane said, 'If you, Jackal, wish to learn to fly, you must do all that I tell you.' Jackal agreed to that. Crane said, 'Do you see that mimosa tree with the gum dripping from it? Go to that tree and rub yourself all over with gum.'

Jackal went to the tree and rubbed the whole of his body with gum and returned to Crane, saying, 'This business of learning to fly is not pleasant; all my hair sticks together in a very uncomfortable way.' Crane said nothing, but began to pluck feathers from himself and stick them into the gum with which Jackal was covered, till his whole body was covered with feathers. Then Crane took one of the long feathers from his tail and stuck it on to Jackal's tail.

Jackal was very much pleased at his own appearance. He walked about on his hind legs and waved his front legs, saying, 'Kwowu! today I am a bird; long distances will be as nothing to me.' He tried to fly but found he could not, so he went to Crane saying, 'What trick is this? You have made me into a bird, but yet I am unable to fly.'

Crane said, 'You are in too much of a hurry, I have still to teach you to fly in the same way that I teach my children. You must get upon my back and I will take you high up in the air. When I tell you to fly you must get off my back and fly. That is how I teach my children.'

Jackal said nothing. He sat down and looked up into the sky and looked at Crane.

Crane said, 'If you look at me in that insulting way I will not teach you to fly.'

Jackal said, 'Pardon, Chief, I meant no insult; I was just trying to measure the height of the sky.'

In the end Jackal got upon Crane's back, and when he had settled himself there firmly, Crane spread his wings and rose; he flew up and up, and still higher. At last he said, 'Now, Jackal, make yourself ready to fly.' Jackal looked down. He was so high up that the women hoeing in the fields below looked like little ants and their huts looked like brown ticks.

Crane said, 'When I say "fly" you must jump off my back and fly. Now fly, Jackal.' At the same moment Crane withdrew himself from under Jackal. Jackal moved his legs in a way that he thought was flying, but only feathers came out, feathers came out and feathers came out, so that there was a long trail of feathers behind him as he fell. He looked down and saw women hoeing in the fields below. He shouted, 'Heyi, women, remove your hoes so that I may not fall on them.' The women, hearing a voice from the skies, were frightened and threw down their hoes and ran away. Jackal fell upon the hoes with a great crash, and there he died.

The King of the Waters

» «

A. C. JORDAN

TRANSLATED AND RETOLD FROM THE XHOSA

It came about, according to some tale, that Tfulako, renowned hunter and son of a great chief, was returning home with his youthful comrades after a hunt that had lasted many days. On a misty night, they lost their way in the forests, and when the next day dawned, they found they were travelling on a wide plain of bare, barren land that they had never seen before. As the day strengthened towards midday, it became very hot. The youths had plenty of baggage – skins and skulls of big game, carcasses of smaller game as well as their clothes and hunting equipment. They felt hungry and thirsty, but there was no point in camping where there were no trees, no firewood, and no water. So they walked on wearily, their baggage becoming heavier and heavier, their stomachs feeling emptier, their lips dry, and their throats burning hot with thirst.

At last, just as the sun was beginning to slant towards the west, they suddenly came upon a fertile stretch of low land lying between two mountains. At the foot of the mountains there was a grove of big tall trees surrounding a beautiful fountain of icy-cold water. With shouts of joy the youthful hunters laid down their baggage on the green grass in the shade and made for the fountain. They took turns stooping and drinking in groups. Tfulako was in the last group, together with his immediate subordinates. When he knelt and bent down to drink, the fountain suddenly dried up, and so did the stream flowing from the fountain. All the youths fell back, startled. They exchanged glances but said nothing. Tfulako stood a little while gazing at the fountain, and then he motioned his subordinates to come forward, kneel and bend down again. They obeyed his order, and the fountain filled and the water began to flow as before. Tfulako stepped forward, knelt beside them, but as soon as he bent down to drink, the water vanished. He withdrew,

19

and the water appeared again, and his comrades drank their fill. Tfulako walked silently back to his place in the shade, and from there he gave a signal that all must draw near.

'Comrades,' he said, 'you all saw what happened just now. I assure you I don't know what it means. You all know me well. I've never practised sorcery. I don't remember doing any evil before or during or after this hunt. Therefore I've nothing to confess to you, my comrades. It looks as if this matter has its own depth, a depth that cannot be known to any of our age-group here. However, I charge you to go about your duties in preparation for our day's feast – wood-gathering, lighting of fires, flaying of carcasses, and roasting – as if nothing had happened. We'll feast and enjoy ourselves, but before I leave this fountain, I must drink, for we don't know where and when we'll find water again in this strange land.'

The youths went about their assigned duties, some flaying the wild game, some collecting wood, some kindling the fires, some cutting off titbits from the half-flayed carcasses and roasting them, so that while the main feast was preparing the company could remove the immediate hunger from their eyes, and stop their mouths watering. Tfulako tried to eat some titbits too, but this aggravated his thirst. So he went to stand some distance away from his comrades and watched the fountain. It had filled again, and the water was streaming down the valley as it had been doing when they first came upon this strange place.

When the main feast was ready, he joined his comrades as he had promised, but found it impossible to eat because of his burning throat. So he just sat there and joined in the chat, trying to share in all the youthful jokes that accompanied feasting. The meat naturally made all of them thirsty again. So once more they took turns drinking from the fountain. Once more Tfulako came forward with his own group, but once more the fountain dried up as soon as he bent down to drink.

There could be no doubt now. It was he and he alone who must not drink, he alone who must die of thirst and hunger, he, son of the great chief. But what power was it that controlled this fountain? He moved away from the fountain and thought deeply. He had heard tales of the King of the Waters who could make rivers flow or dry at will. He concluded that the King of the Waters, whoever he was and whatever he looked like, must be in this fountain, that this King must have recognized him as the son of the great chief, that this King must have resolved that the son of the great chief must either pay a great price for the water from this fountain or die of thirst. What price was he expected to pay? Then suddenly he turned about, walked up to the brink of the fountain and, in sheer desperation, called out aloud: 'King of the Waters! I die of thirst. Allow me to drink, and I will give you the most beautiful of my sisters to be your wife.'

At once the fountain filled, and Tfulako bent down and quenched his thirst while all his comrades looked on in silence. Then he had his share of meat.

After this the whole company felt relaxed, and the youths stripped and bathed in the cool stream to refresh themselves for the long journey before them. Tfulako took part in all this and enjoyed himself as if he had forgotten what had just happened. Towards sunset, they filled their gourds with water from the fountain, picked up their baggage and resumed their journey home. On the afternoon of the fourth day, they were within the domain of their great chief and, to announce their approach, they chanted their favourite hunting-song:

> Ye ha he! Ye ha he!
> A mighty whirlwind, the buffalo!
> Make for your homes, ye who fear him.
> They chase them far! They chase them near!
> As for us, we smite the lively ones
> And we leave the wounded alone.
> Ye ha he! Ye ha he!
> A might whirlwind, the buffalo!

So Tfulako and his comrades entered the gates of the Royal Place, amid the praises of the bards and the cheering of the women.

Tfulako took the first opportunity, when the excitement over the return of the hunters had died down, to report to his people what had happened at the fountain. No one, not even the oldest councillors, had any idea what the King of the Waters looked like. Most of them thought that since he lived in the water, he might look like a giant otter or giant reptile, while others expressed the hope that he was a man-like spirit. But everybody, including the beautiful princess, felt that this was the only offer Tfulako could have made in the circumstances. So they awaited the coming of the King of the Waters.

One afternoon, after many moons had died, a terrible cyclone approached the Royal Place. On seeing it, the people ran quickly into their huts and fastened the doors. As it drew nearer, the cyclone narrowed itself and made straight for the girls' hut where the beautiful princess and the other girls were, but instead of sweeping the hut before it, as cyclones usually do, this one folded itself and vanished at the door.

When calm was restored, the girls discovered that they were in the company of a snake of enormous length. Its girth was greater than the thigh of a very big man. They had never seen a snake of such size before. This then, they concluded, must be Nkanyamba, King of the Waters, come to claim his bride. One by one the girls left the hut, until the princess was left alone with the bridegroom. She decided to follow the other girls, but as soon as she rose to go the King of the Waters unfolded quickly, coiled himself round her body, rested his head on her breasts and gazed hungrily into her eyes.

The princess ran out of the hut with her burden round her body and, without stopping to speak to anybody at the Royal Place, she set out on a long, long journey to her mother's people, far over the mountains. As she went, she sang in a high-pitched, wailing voice:

> *Ndingatsi ndihumntfan' abo Tfulako,*
> *Ndingatsi ndihumntfan' abo Tfulako,*
> *Ndilale nesibitwa ngokutsiwa hinyoka, nyoka?*

Can I, a daughter of Tfulako's people,
Can I, a daughter of Tfulako's people,
Sleep with that which is called a snake, snake?

In reply, the King of the Waters sang in a deep voice:

> *Ndingatsi ndimlelelele ndinje, ndinje,*
> *Ndingatsi ndimlelelele ndinje, ndinje,*
> *Ndingalali nesibitwa ngokutsiwa humfati, fati lo?*

Long and graceful that I am, so graceful,
Long and graceful that I am, so graceful,
May I not sleep with that which is called a woman, a mere woman?

And so they travelled through forest and ravine, the whole night and the following day, singing pride at each other.

At nightfall they reached the home of the princess's mother's people. But the princess decided to wait in the shadows for a while. When she was sure that there was no one in the girls' hut, she entered there unnoticed and closed the door. Then for the first time she addressed herself directly to her burden:

King of the Waters, mighty one!
Sole possessor of the staff of life!
Thou that makest the rivers flow or dry at will!
Saviour of the lives of thirsty hunters!
Thou that comest borne on the wings of mighty storms!
Thou of many coils, long and graceful!

By this time, the King of the Waters had raised his head from its pillowed position and was listening. So the princess went on: 'I am tired, covered with the dust of the road and ugly. I pray you, undo yourself and rest here while I go announce the great news of your royal visit to my mother's people. Then I shall also take a little time to wash and dress myself in a manner befitting the hostess of the greatest of kings, Nkanyamba the Mighty, Nkanyamba the King of the Waters.'

Without a word, the King of the Waters unwound himself and slithered to the far end of the hut where he coiled himself into a great heap that almost reached the thatch roof.

The princess went straight to the Great Hut and there, weeping, she told the whole story to her uncle and his wife. They comforted her and assured her that they would rid her of the Nkanyamba that same night, if only she would be brave and intelligent. She brushed away her tears immediately and assured them that she would be brave and determined. Thereupon her mother's brother told his wife to give orders that large quantities of water be boiled so that the princess could have a bath. While these preparations were going on, he took out some ointment and mixed it with some powders that the princess had never seen before. These he gave to his wife and instructed her to anoint the whole of the princess's body as soon as she had had her bath. Then the princess and her aunt disappeared, leaving the head of the family sitting there alone, grim and determined.

When they returned, the princess looked fresh and lovely in her nkciyo. She had stripped herself of most of her ornaments. All she had were her glittering brass headring, a necklace whose pendant hung delicately between her breasts, a pair of armlets, and a pair of anklets.

'Your aunt has told you everything you are to do when you get there?' asked her mother's brother, rising to his feet, as they came in.

'Everything, malume,' replied the princess, smiling brightly.

'You're sure you will not make any mistake – doing things too hastily and so on?'

'I'm quite cool now, malume. You can be sure that I'll do everything at the right moment.'

Then the head of the family produced a beautiful kaross, all made of leopard-skins, unfolded it, and covered his sister's daughter with it. 'Go now, my sister's child. I'm sure you'll be more than a match for this – this snake!'

The princess walked briskly back to the girls' hut. Once inside, she threw off the kaross and addressed the King of the Waters: 'King of the Waters! Here I stand, I, daughter of the people of Tfulako, ready for the embrace of Nkanyamba, the tall and graceful.'

As she said these words, she stretched out her beautiful arms invitingly to the King of the Waters.

This invitation was accepted eagerly, but when the King of the Waters tried to hold her in his coils, he slipped down and fell with a thud on the floor. Smiling and chiding him, the princess once more stretched out her arms and invited him to have another try. He tried again, but again he fell on the floor with a thud. Once again the princess stretched out her arms encouragingly, but again the King of the Waters found her body so slippery that for all his coils and scales he could not hold her. This time he slipped down and fell with such a heavy thud on the floor that he seemed to have lost all strength. He could hardly move his body, and all he could do in response to the princess's invitation was to feast his eyes on her beautiful body.

'It's my mistake, graceful one,' said the princess, lowering her arms. 'In my eagerness to make myself beautiful for the King of the Waters, I put too much ointment on my body. I'll go back to the Great Hut and remove it immediately, then I shall return and claim the embrace I so desire.'

With these words, she picked up her kaross, stepped over the threshold, and fastened the door securely from outside. Her uncle and aunt were ready with a blazing firebrand, and as soon as she had fastened the door, they handed it to her without saying a word. She grabbed it and ran round the hut, setting the grass thatch alight at many points, and finally she thrust the firebrand into the thatch just above the door. The grass caught fire at once, and the flames lit the entire homestead.

No sound of any struggle on the part of the King of the Waters in the burning hut. He had lost all power. No power to lift his body from the ground. No power to summon the wings of mighty storms to bear him away from the scorching flames. The King of the Waters was burned to death.

Everything happened so quickly that by the time the neighbours came, nothing was left except the crackling wood.

'What happened? What happened?' asked one neighbour after another.

'It's only one of those things that happen because we are in this world.'

'Is everybody safe in your household?' they asked.

'Everybody is safe. It's a pleasant event, my neighbours. Go and sleep in peace. When the present moon dies, I'll invite you all to a great feast in honour of my sister's beautiful daughter here. Then will I tell you all there is to tell about the evil we've just destroyed.'

The following morning the head of the family rose up early and went to examine the scene of the fire very carefully. He found that although the body of the Nkanyamba had been reduced to ashes, bones and all, the skull was intact. He picked it up and examined it. Then he collected some wood, piled it on the ashes and set fire to it. He then picked out the brains of the Nkanyamba from every little cranny, and let them fall on the fire. Then he scraped the inside of the skull, removing every little projection and making it as smooth as a clay pot. All the matter removed fell on to the fire and burned out completely. He took the skull indoors and washed it thoroughly with boiling-hot water, and then rubbed it thoroughly with the remnants of the grease and powder that had been used by the princess on the previous night.

Meanwhile the princess was in a deep sleep, nor did she wake up at all until the early afternoon. Her aunt had given orders that no one was to go into the hut where she was sleeping, except herself, for a whole day and night. So, after putting the Nkanyamba's skull away, the head of the family went about his daily duties and kept away from his niece's hut. But on the following morning, as soon as he knew that the princess was awake, he went to see her, taking the skull with him. The princess shuddered a little when she saw it.

'Touch it, child of my sister,' said her uncle. 'Touch it, and all fear of it will go.'

The princess touched it, but noticing that she still shuddered, her uncle withdrew it, sat beside her and chatted a little.

Later in the day, the head and mistress of the house discussed the condition of the princess. They agreed that her cousins could enter her hut and sit and chat with her as long as they wished, but that she must remain in bed until all signs of fear had disappeared. So every morning her uncle took the skull to her and made her handle it. When he was quite satisfied that she did not shudder any more, he told his wife that the princess was now ready to get up and live normally with the rest of the family.

One day the head and mistress of the family were sitting and chatting with the princess in the Great Hut when the princess casually rose and walked across the floor, took the Nkanyamba's skull down from its place on the wall and turned it over and over in her hands, while all the time she carried on with the conversation as if not thinking about the skull at all. The two elderly people exchanged glances, nodded to each other and smiled.

'Now I can see she's ready to go back to her parents,' said the head of the family as soon as he and his wife were alone. 'She doesn't fear that skull any more now. It's just like any other vessel in the house. So we can proceed with the preparations.'

Two—three days passed, and a great feast was held in honour of the princess. All the neighbours came, and the head of the family told them the whole story of Tfulako's promise to the King of the Waters, and what happened thereafter. The neighbours praised the princess for her bravery and thanked their neighbour on behalf of the parents and brother of the girl. The uncle then pointed out five head of cattle that he was giving to his sister's child to take home. Then one after another his well-to-do friends and neighbours rose to make little speeches, thanking him for the gift to his sister's child, and adding their own 'little calves to accompany their neighbour's gift', until there were well over two tens of cattle in all. After each gift of a 'little calf', the princess kissed the right hand of the giver. Then it was the uncle's turn to thank his neighbours for making him a somebody by enriching so much the gift that his sister's child would take home with her.

The village mothers had withdrawn to a separate part of the homestead, and while the men were making gifts in cattle, the women were making a joint present consisting of mats, pots, bowls and ornaments of all kinds. When these had been collected, the head of the family was asked to accompany the princess to come and see them. Some of the elderly mothers made little speeches, presented the 'small gift' to the princess on behalf of the whole motherhood, and wished her a happy journey back home. Both the head and the mistress of the family thanked the mothers.

Before the festivities came to an end, the young men of the village sent spokesmen to their fathers, reminding them that the princess would need an escort.

'We know that very well,' said one of the elderly men with a smile. 'But you can't all go. And let me remind you that those of you who are going will have not only to drive the cattle but also to carry all those pots and other things that your mothers have loaded the princess with.'

'We understand, father,' replied the chief spokesman. 'We are ready to carry everything. We have already agreed too that it would be fitting that the princess be escorted by those of the age-group of her brother, Tfulako.'

'You've done well,' murmured some of the men.

A few days later, while the princess was being helped by her aunt to pack her belongings, the head of the family brought the beautiful kaross that the princess had worn on the night of the killing of the Nkanyamba. The princess accepted it very gratefully and embraced her uncle for the wonderful gift. Then he produced the Nkanyamba's skull and would hand it over to her.

'What am I to do with this thing, malume?' asked the princess, much surprised.

'It's yours,' replied her uncle. 'It was you who carried the King of the Waters all the way from your home village so that you could destroy him here.'

The princess received the skull with both hands, thanked her uncle, looked at it for a little while and smiled.

'I know what I'll do with this,' she said as she packed it away.

'Aren't we going to be told this great secret?' asked her uncle.

'In truth it's no secret to you two,' replied the princess. 'Some day, some day when my brother Tfulako becomes the chief of our people, I'll give this to him to use as a vessel for washing.'

'You have a mind, child of my sister,' remarked her uncle.

'Why do you say that, malume?'

'Because that was exactly what I hoped you would do with it.'

It was a pleasant journey for the princess and her male cousins and other young men of her brother's age-group. They did not take their journey hurriedly, for they must allow the cattle to graze as they went along. They themselves camped and rested whenever they came to a particularly beautiful place. They sang as they travelled and, among other songs, the princess taught them the songs that she and the King of the Waters had sung to each other in these same forests and ravines. She sang her high-pitched song, and the young men sang the song of the King of the Waters in a chorus.

When they approached the Royal Place on the afternoon of the third day of their journey, they started to sing this song aloud. The song was heard and immediately recognized by all those villagers who had heard it on the day of the cyclone. The princess's voice was recognized as hers, but the many deep voices remained a puzzle.

No one had seen Tfulako run into his hut to grab his spears and shield, but there he was, standing alone near the gate, shading his eyes in order to have the first glimpse of the singers who were about to appear on the horizon.

When the singers and the herd of cattle came in sight, he concluded that his sister was in the company of the Nkanyamba she loathed, together with a whole troop of followers driving the customary bride-tribute of cattle.

'What!' he exclaimed, blazing with anger. 'Does this mean that my sister has been burdened with this hateful snake all this time? I'm going to get my sister free!' And he took one leap over the closed gate.

'Wait, Son of the Beautiful!' shouted the councillors. 'You're going into danger. Wait until they get here.'

'I'll never allow those snakes to enter this gate. I don't want any of their cattle in the folds of my fathers. If no one will come with me, I'll fight them alone. Let him bring all the nkanyambas in the world, I'll die fighting for my sister.'

And he ran to meet the singers.

Before he had reached them, however, all the hunters of his age-group were with him. For the women of the Royal Place had raised the alarm, and it had been taken up by other women throughout the village, and from one village to another, so that in no time all the youths had grabbed their spears and shields and followed the direction indicated by the cries of the womenfolk.

The singing suddenly stopped, and there were bursts of laughter from the princess's escort.

'Withhold your spears!' shouted one of them. 'The enemy you're looking for is not here. That which was he is now ashes at Tfulako's mother's people. Here's Tfulako's sister, beautiful as the rising sun.'

And the princess stepped forward to meet her brother who had already leapt forward to meet her. They embraced with affection.

'Forgive me, my father's child,' said Tfulako, deeply moved.

But the princess would not allow her brother to shed a tear in the presence of other young men. She laughed, disengaged herself and stepped away from him.

'Forgive you what?' she asked. 'Forgive you for giving me a chance to prove that I am the worthy sister of Tfulako, killer of buffaloes?'

Before Tfulako could reply, she started to sing his favourite hunting-song, altering the words to suit the event. By this time, the youths of the two groups had mingled together in a friendly manner. As soon as they took up the song, she pulled out the Nkanyamba's skull and, holding it high, she led the march into the village and through the gates of the Royal Place:

> Ye ha he! Ye ha he!
> A mighty whirlwind, the Nkanyamba!
> Fasten your doors, ye who fear him.
> They chase them far! They chase them near!
> As for us, we scorch the cyclone-borne
> And we carry their skulls aloft.
> Ye ha he! Ye ha he!
> A mighty whirlwind, the Nkanyamba!

The Unreasonable Child
to Whom the Dog Gave its Deserts;
or, A Receipt for Putting Anyone to Sleep

» «

TRANSLATED FROM THE DAMARA BY W. H. I. BLEEK

There was a little girl who had an eïngi (pronounced 'a-inghi', some kind of fruit). She said to her Mother, 'Mother, why is it that you do not say, "My first-born, give me the eïngi"? Do I refuse it?'

Her Mother said, 'My first-born, give me the eïngi.' She gave it to her and went away, and her Mother ate the eïngi.

When the child came back, she said, 'Mother, give me my eïngi?' but her Mother answered, 'I have eaten the eïngi!'

The child said, 'Mother, how is it that you have eaten my eïngi, which I plucked from our tree?' The Mother then (to appease her) gave her a needle.

The little girl went away and found her Father sewing thongs with thorns; so she said, 'Father, how is it that you sew with thorns? Why do not you say, "My first-born, give me your needle"? Do I refuse?' So her Father said, 'My first-born, give me your needle.' She gave it to him and went away for a while. Her Father commenced sewing, but the needle broke; when, therefore, the child came back and said, 'Father, give me my needle,' he answered, 'The needle is broken;' but she complained about it, saying, 'Father, how is it that you break my needle, which I got from Mother, who ate my eïngi, which I had plucked from our tree?' Her Father then gave her an axe.

Going farther on she met the lads who were in charge of the cattle. They were busy taking out honey, and in order to get at it they were obliged to cut down the trees with stones. She addressed them: 'Our sons, how is it that you use stones in order to get at the honey? Why do not you say, "Our first-born, give us the axe"? Do I refuse, or what do I?' They said, 'Our first-born, give us the axe.' So she gave it them, and went away for some time. The axe broke entirely. When she came back she asked, 'Where is the axe? Please give it me.' They answered, 'The axe is broken.' She then said, 'How is it that you break my axe, which I had received from Father who had broken my needle, which I got from Mother who had eaten my eïngi, which I had plucked from our tree?' But they gave her some honey (to comfort her).

She went her way again, and met a little old woman eating insects, to whom she said, 'Little old woman, how is it that you eat insects? Why don't you say, "My first-born, give me honey"? Do I refuse or not?' Then the little old woman asked, 'My first-born, give me honey.' She gave it her and went away; but presently returning said, 'Little old woman, let me have my honey!' Now the old woman had managed to eat it all during her absence, so she answered, 'Oh! I have eaten the honey!' So the child complained, saying, 'How is it that you eat my honey, which I received from the lads of our cattle, from our children who had broken my axe, which had been given me by Father who had broken my needle, which was a present from my Mother who had eaten up my eïngi, that I had plucked from our tree?'

The little old woman gave her food, and she went away. This time she came to the pheasants, who scratched the ground; and she said, 'Pheasants! how is it that you scratch the ground? Why do not you say, "First-born, give us food"? Do I refuse, or what do I?' They said, 'First-born, give.' So she gave to them, and went away. When she came back and demanded her food again, they said, 'We have eaten the food.' She asked, 'How is it that you eat my food, which I had received from a little old woman who had eaten up my honey, that I had got from the lads of our cattle who had broken my axe, which had been given me by my Father who had broken my needle, which was a present from my Mother who had eaten my eïngi, which I had plucked from our tree?' The pheasants, flying up, pulled out each one a feather and threw them down to the little girl.

She then, walking along, met the children who watched the sheep. They were plucking out hairs from the sheep-skins. So she asked them, 'How is it that you pull at these skins? Why do not you say, "First-born, give us the feathers"? Do I refuse, or what do I?' They said, 'First-born, give us the feathers.' She gave them and went away, but all the feathers broke. When she returned and said, 'Give me my feathers,' they answered, 'The feathers are broken.' Then she complained, 'Do you break my feathers which I received from the pheasants who had eaten my food, which had been given me by a little old woman?' They gave her some milk.

She went again on her way, and found their own handsome dog gnawing bones. She said, 'Our dog, how is it that you gnaw these bones?' The dog answered, 'Give me milk.' She gave it him, and he drank it all. Then she said to the dog, 'Give me back my milk.' He said, 'I drank it.' She then repeated the same words which she had spoken so often before; but the dog ran away, and when she pursued him, he scampered up a tree. She climbed up after him, but the dog jumped down again on the other side. She wanted to do the same, but could not. Then she said, 'Our dog, please help me down.' He answered, 'Why did you pursue me?' and ran away, leaving her up the tree.

'That is enough,' say the Damara.

Little Reed-Alone-in-the-Whirlpool

» «

EUGÈNE N. MARAIS

TRANSLATED FROM THE AFRIKAANS BY DAVID SCHALKWYK

The first messenger in Gammadoekies was the little yellow Bushman, Reed-Alone-in-the-Whirlpool.

His pa's pa, old Heitsi Eibib, gave him this name while he was still in carrying-skins. He could run so fast that the dust would swirl about his heels in little whirlwinds; and at full pelt, then he became a small dull streak in the middle of the track.

Then came the great danger to Gammadoekies. That night old Heitsi Eibib held a council-of-war, for great was their distress. He even had old Rockrabbit-One-Eye called to sit in, and he was so old that his jaw was worn away and his eyes pinched almost wholly shut.

The whole night they sat around the fire in the depression in the dry river-bed, and it was finally old Rockrabbit-One-Eye who put together the Great Word. And at the red dawning of day they called Reed-Alone to carry the message to Rooi Joggom.

And as he arrived he heard the young women crying in the grass huts: 'Hot-'tgorra! Hot-'tgorra!' And the men were so afraid that their toenails clattered and the sweat fell from their bodies in hailstones. Each one would have been able to snuff out the fire with one breath.

And when the day turned pale, he dashed off from Gammadoekies. In his left hand he carried his instruments, and with his right fist he beat upon his forehead: a blow of the fist for each word of the message – then he could not forget it.

The last words of his Old Pa had been: 'Beware of Nagali: she will waylay you with her many tricks; her magic is strong. If you put a foot wrong, your

32

body will be drawn as taut as the string of the great stringed instrument, the ramkie!'

When the sun stood on high they could still see the little whirlwinds turning under his feet on the furthest ridge, but Reed-Alone was himself merely a dull streak along the track.

Then Rockrabbit-One-Eye said: 'Arrie! There are sparks in the wolf's tail!' For it was he who had thought out the great word.

And when Reed could no longer see his own shadow, he looked ahead along the track. And there he saw a thin little Bushman maid. She stepped slowly across the road in a few dancing steps. 'Arrie, sister,' Reed exclaimed, 'can you dance?'

'Brother!' she said, 'what will you put on the anthill?'

'These instruments cannot be bettered,' said Reed, and he laid them on the anthill. 'And what do you have, sister?'

She drew the blue lace of beads from around her neck and put that down. And then they raced off into the veld. They remained neck and neck as far as the third anthill, but from there the maid began to dance rings around him, and she swept in a great half-moon back towards Gammadoekies. And Reed wanted to shout: 'This way, my sister! This way!' but his breath failed him, and she danced so fast that she blew the words right from his mouth. And Reed's heart sank, and he thought: 'I will sprint that way and save my instruments.' But as he darted away he saw the little brown maid dancing way ahead of him like a cloud scudding on the mountain-top; and while he was still far away she swept up the instruments and recovered her beads. And he heard her laughing, and she called out to him: 'I'll always outstrip you, my boy. I'll give Nagali your regards.' And when she danced away he saw that all the time it had been the whirlwind from the great desert.

And he said: 'Hot-'tgorra! the string of the great ramkie!' for the sun was sinking and Rooi Joggom is far away!

And he raced away once again, but now he no longer repeated the message, for the sorrow of the instruments filled his heart.

And he streaked along the track as far as the Middelberg Pass. And then he noticed, beside the loose rock to the left of the track, a Bushman sitting, and as he ran he heard the sallow companion call: 'What sorrow causes my brother to drag his feet today?'

And Reed-Alone stopped next to him. 'Can my brother run?' he asked.

'The young women of Jakkalsdraai have told me so,' said the sallow Bushman.

And Reed's heart was afire within him, for he had never met anyone who could so much as breathe his dust.

'Shall it be to the top of the pass?' Reed-Alone asked.

'Heitse!' said the sallow Bushman, 'baboons run up mountains. No, my friend, let it be to the sharp rock,' and he pointed back down to the bottom of the valley, and they took their marks. And as they darted away the sallow Bushman slipped away from Reed. And Reed shut his eyes, and he gave it all he had. And when the earth felt level beneath his feet, he looked up once more, and he saw the sallow Bushman as a tiny cloud of dust away ahead on the track. And when he passed his hand across his eyes he saw that it was Nagali's little antelope, her Oribi. And he put his hand to his mouth and his heart turned to water within him. And he whirled about and leapt up the mountain, and all he could say was: 'Father of my father!'

It was dark before Reed-Alone reached the banks of the Moetmekaar drift, and there he stopped again for the first time. As the lightning struck, he cried: 'Heitsi! Nagali is making light to find me out!' and he hid himself.

He could hear the roar of the dark waters from afar, for the river was wild, and ahead of him in the drift he could see the gleam of the twilight, like the tail of a fish, swirling in the whirlpool.

'It's across or the string of the ramkie!' Reed-Alone said, and he stepped into the water.

And on the other side, on the bank, was old Nagali's kierie, made from the bitter-pit tree, and Reed heard her scornful laughter. And then he said: 'Heitse, sister! We'll be talking to each other face to face in a while. I am master here.' And right there he had the great mishap. He had forgotten the news which had come to Gammadoekies that Nagali had finally obtained the magic stick which made her master of the crocodile.

And as Reed-Alone entered the dark waters, and began to feel them eddy, he sang the counter-charm:

'I'll hold here and you hold there,
O you Yellow Beings, hold your share.'

But it was in vain. On the other side, against the bank, he saw the whirlpool before his feet, and crossing seemed impossible. And then he noticed, right next to him, the big sweet-thorn log with one of its ends in the shallow water. Slowly he clambered on to it, peering to the place where Nagali's bitter-pit kierie lay, and he chortled delightedly into the hollow of his palm. And then he felt the sweet-thorn log stir beneath him, and move beneath him, and he clawed at it with every nail, and three times he called his great-grandfather's great name. But all in vain. He heard the bitter-pit kierie call out: 'So, my boy, who's master now?'

But he had forgotten the answer.

Then he became aware that it was Nagali's crocodile; and the next moment he found himself on the sand-bank from which he had started, but he was unaware of this.

And once more he dashed away, beating on his forehead again, and again he recalled Heitsi Eibib's message, and he shot into the night. And ahead of him he saw the great fire, and he stopped amongst them just as the red day dawned, and he began to recite his message. But before he was half-way through it, they grabbed him, and then he realized that he was back in Gammadoekies, and that the one who had him by the left leg was his very own grandfather.

And Heitsi Eibib said to Old Rockrabbit-One-Eye: 'We must draw him more tautly than the string of the great ramkie.'

And then they put out the little flame of Reed-Alone-in-the-Whirlpool.

Hannie's Journal

» «

ANTHONY DELIUS

EXPEDITION AGAINST THE FETCANI
BY HANNIBAL HAMPTON
DEDICATED TO MY FATHER
MY AUNT MARGARET
MY SISTER ELIZA-JANE
AND COUSIN FREDDIE

Monday (some time in June), Camp at Kafirs' Drift:

Here we are with ten other campaigners, including the four Bowkers –
preserve us! – and long Mr Pete Goffen lying stretched out alongside me like
that picture of a knight on his sepulchre, his nose to heaven and dead to the
world. And here am I using my saddle as a desk and an old tent spike as a
candlestick and, with the help of a bit of starlight, for there's no moon here
tonight and the bush is crowded round us black as pitch, composing myself to
set down our day's adventures. Well there's not much to say about it, except
we spent it riding through deeper and deeper bush, and listening to the
opinions of the Bowker brothers. They say, for they all seem to speak at once
sometimes, that we are riding out to face the whole Zoolah army from the
north with General Shaka leading them. I here ventured an opinion of my
own, that good generals don't ride out in front of their forces, but keep in the
rear to direct the battle. But one Bowker is of the opinion I am a poor ignorant
fool if I think uncivilized Kafirs and Zoolahs have the same notions of
fighting as the Frenchies and the English. He – don't ask me who, for all
the Bowkers look as alike as watermelons to me – begs leave to inform me
in any case Zoolah chiefs have witch-men who promise to make them
invisible to bullets. So you can see we do not want for brilliant conversation.
Goodnight.

Wesleyville

Arrived here in great style after crossing four rivers – the Fish, the Beka, the Kayskama, the Chalumna. Made much welcome by Martha and Jack. Old Martha has certainly grown a bit more buxom but Jack is as lean as ever, though his beard is a bit longer and scragglier. Anyway Martha is still a great provider – Pete and I haven't ate so well since we left the Ridge two days ago – and they've both been uncommon hospitable to all of us, even the Bowkers, for you got to be uncommon Christian to be courteous to them. As Pete remarks, he'll probably shoot a Bowker long before he shoots a Zoolah. Martha says of us, 'My, you're quite young men now!' and Pete says, 'Well, Sis, what did you expect us to be?' All the same she is greatly delighted we are here. So are young Robert and Mary, they're quite big now, and little Jennie's nearly 2 years and loves Pete heartily. They have a fine stone house of their own and there's a bigger one where the Shaws stay. And there's a schoolhouse of sorts where we all stay and a church, of course, and beyond that where the Christian Kafirs stay in their huts. The Shaws are away, and Jack's a bit alarmed about this. Mrs Shaw is staying with other missionaries at Butterworth, but the Revd Shaw's gone even farther north to see some descendants of white people who were wrecked.

Major Dundas has rode in and given us a lecture on discipline. He says, 'I'm depending on you young English fellows to be an example of discipline to the Boers. These Dutchmen are bonny fighters, but short on discipline.' Then he distributes us each a pocketful of beads and buttons for buying food on the way, mostly cattle. If we've got any over, says the Major, we can buy ourselves a herd of cattle on the way back – but not going forward for, according to the Major again, cattle play the very devil with offensive military operations!

Wednesday (I think it's July now)

The Boers rode in today, and Dries with them, so we are three now, and practically outnumber the Bowkers. The big chief hereabouts came to look us over. He's called Pato, quite a stylish chap, not as tall as some of the Kafirs I've seen, about the same height and build as old Koba. He was dressed in a full rig-out, all sorts of birds' feathers in his hair, a fine kaross cloak with leopard-skin facings, and riding an indifferent horse too. He had with him his brother, Kungwe, who they say ruled these people – they're called the Amagunukwebe – after the Boers killed the old chief and Pato was not old enough to become chief.

Chief Pato was very polite, but I could see him staring at our little party of English and Boers and saying to himself, 'Well, by my sacred ancestors, if that's all they got to go off and fight the Zoolahs and Fetcani, I had better set about thinking how to defend myself.' But he kept a brave smile.

Thursday, Butterworth mission

Crossed three more rivers, the Buffalo, Gunabee, and Kay, and arrived at another of Mr Shaw's Methodist missionary stations. We are now in the territory of the biggest Kafir chief of all, Hintsa. Some tremendous hills coming here and all round dotted with round Kafir houses, hundreds and hundreds of them in clusters and ones and twos. Don't notice many cattle about, and Dries says they probably hide them because of the rumours of Zoolahs and Fetcani being about. Mrs Shaw and the other wives were very kind to us, but we could see they were worried by the whereabouts of Revd Shaw in these dangerous times. As for our Major, there is nothing for it but we ride on, striking north-west to the sources of the Bashee River and Chief Faku's country of the Pondo, and it's hard, cold ground for a bed tonight again.

Friday, Hintsa's Place

Pete's on watch, and I'm next – but frightened to close my eyes less I see again some of the sights I saw today.

But the day started off very beautiful. As we rode from early morning the country got more splendid, and often away in the distance there were green hills with brown huts along them, like brown pimples on green flesh, and farther on were the Amatola mountains some say are special holy places of the Kafirs, full of deep kloofs and woods. But the most remarkable sight I saw I thought first was a long line of clouds on the horizon, no thicker than a tick-bird's feather. As the day warmed up – for it's perishing cold here of a morning first thing – I saw that it was snow, lying along mountains miles and miles away. 'That's the Drakensberg – Dragon's Mountain,' says Dries. 'They go on for thousands of miles up Africa and the tail of the river Nile runs out of its other end.' The Kafirs, says Dries, think it's full of spooks and they call it Quathlamba, Place of the Spirits, and they never go there for fear spooks will catch them.

But later that morning we saw some very different sights. It makes me sick even now to write of the sights we saw. Heads and arms and limbs lying about the place, some with bits of flesh still on, others half gnawed, infants with heads beaten to bloody pulp and covered with those horrible blue flies, a body ripped open and two vultures pulling at a long bit of innards between them like any two starlings fighting over a worm. And the smell rising in the bright sunlight was frightful.

We heard other things even more frightful than we saw. Oom Hennie Rademeyer, the leading Boer with us, rode forward with some of his party and found a number of villages in much the same condition. They also found one of the attackers who'd been left for dead among the corpses. This man said he was sorry so many had been killed, but he came from a place beyond the mountains where people had become cannibals, there was so much killing among the tribespeople of men and so little grain planted. They came for food. He died soon after they found him. The Boers think there must be more than one lot of attackers.

We rode hard for King Hintsa's Great Place. There's thousands of huts here, and thousands of people all come to stare at us and thieve anything they can – they got a sack of fresh bread Mrs Shaw gave us practically the moment we came in. Hintsa's sent off for his councillors so the Major can talk with them tomorrow. My eyes feel tired now, and my body too, but I have no desire to close them. Here comes Pete in from watch. We're more concerned with thieves from our allies than Fetcani or whoever it is.

Saturday

Today we all sat in a great clearing in front of Chief Hintsa's Great Place, and debated about what to do next. At least, the most of us sat together behind the Major and the two Boer elders. The Major did all the talking (with words of advice from the Boers). One of the Major's two Hottentot aides, Karools, translated. And the sight before us was truly awesome – the great man himself, Chief Hintsa, in a magnificent kaross and a fine feather on his head, a big fellow with his black skin gleaming with some oil or fat, behind him all his councillors, and behind them it seemed about half the whole Kafir nation. At least some were absent because we could see in the distance women working in the fields and gardens with hoes, and some boys minding cattle – but I don't think there was a grown man absent from the gathering. Well, the Major was soon asking the Chief why he was not preparing to defend himself, and the Chief pointed out that the place was already crowded with warriors gathering to beat off the Fetcani. Then it emerged it was the Kafirs' neighbours, the Tambookeys, who had been most severely mauled by the invaders and lost villages and people and thousands of cattle. The Major said that he had passed through Chief Pato's country, but had not heard there of any call for forces from that chief to help. The chief councillor asked very scornfully, 'Why should the son of the blood of Tshiwo turn to the son of the mere creature of Tshiwo?' But soon after this mysterious argument the Chief himself stepped in again and it was reasonably quickly decided we must ride to the chief of the Tambookeys, Vusani; and, if he will get a force together, Hintsa's people will join him and us to advance against the Fetcani, which all say are some sort of Zoolahs, either fleeing from others or an advance party. In any case it seems expected of us that we will bear the main brunt of the fighting. So later we set off, with fifty of Hintsa's warriors.

It's cold enough now to make me creep so close to the fire I fear for burning my journal as I write in it.

Sunday

Long before we reached Chief Vusani's Place early today we met people going south with their pots, reed sleeping-mats and cattle. When we came to the Chief's it was a scene of confusion, everybody swarming about the place, groups of warriors with their bundles of assegais and cow-hide shields, all very aimless and very disorderly, and plenty of shouting. But in the middle, very dignified and looking as if he had just won a great battle, the Chief himself, with a whole crest of warrior's blue-crane feathers on his head and a cloak of silver jackal-skin wrapped around him. As soon as we saw him he started up with a long complaint about the number of his cattle the Zoolahs had taken.

Finally at last it is agreed that messages are sent back to Hintsa that we advance together. But as it's Sunday today the Boers say we must now make the best to observe the Sabbath, and have a decent dinner at least, so the Major asks the Chief for an ox for his men. But the Chief looks very doleful and says the Zoolahs have had all his good cattle.

The Major turns blue and red in the face by turns and shouts, 'I'll not be fobbed off by some skinny old cow that's nothing but sores, bones and gristle!' So there's more argument and we get a fairly presentable ox at last, for a handful of beads. After supper Pete falls very thoughtful, so Dries and I offer a penny for his thoughts.

'Why,' says Pete, 'I was calculating, if it takes all that argument to get a slice of beef, how many years will it take each of us to get that small herd the Major promised?'

Monday

It rained last night, and our trees dripped on us, and this morning the wind is very keen, but no message likely from Hintsa's place before afternoon. One of the Boers comes and tells Dries they have seen a sea-cow pool near, and that sea-cow meat is very tasty and would we like to come and shoot some, to lay by for meat, for it might not be easy to come by as we move forward. We went with them to higher up the river (the Bashee) where it's broad and very sluggish – and there's four hippo heads just above the water, eyes, nostrils and little ears flicking. We fired several volleys at them but we seemed only to hit one.

Then the Major arrived roaring like a lion. 'Where the devil in hell do you think you'll get fresh powder and shot?' he cries at the top of his lungs. 'By God, I hope when you've several thousand Zoolahs coming down on you, you don't find your pouches empty!'

Tuesday

Messages have now come from Hintsa that they will meet us beyond the Bashee and advance on the Zoolahs. I'm very excited at the thought my first battle must be tomorrow or the next day, and a bit frightened too.

Wednesday

Crossed the Bashee just as dawn was coming and set out for our rendezvous. Around us are Tambookeys moving at a slow jogtrot to the whooping and chanting of their witchdoctors – strange men in skins, with bones and all sorts of dried roots hanging about them. All the time they keep up this whooping and angry yelling and dancing and whirling and sometimes the warriors answer them in chorus. Just after midday we were met by Hintsa's people.

Now again we are trying to sleep, with a great din of singing and dancing going on all round us, and mock fights in the firelight and drumming and stamping on the ground, so everything seems to be shaking slightly with it all. I said to the Major, 'Don't these people ever sleep? They'll be too weary from dancing and singing to fight the next day.' But the Major says Kafir constitutions are different from ours, and need to be greatly excited before they go into battle. If they slept now all their courage might drain away, and by tomorrow they could all have slunk off home.

Friday

The morning after our great victory!

I must start at the beginning of it all. It was not even light yet when the scouts came back with news the Zoolahs were quite near. A great quiet falls upon our force, us and the Kafirs and Tambookeys alike, for now I think it occurs to all of us that the Zoolahs, who had beat all tribes for hundreds of miles around, are a different proposition to anything any of us came against before.

It was rather a misty morning, and when we first saw the Zoolahs we thought they were a row of bushes half-way up a hill – but it soon came on us they were too orderly for bushes, and then someone said, 'It's them! There they are!'

Everything stopped, even I think for one moment my heart. About a thousand Zoolahs stood together in three or four lines barring our way up the hill. They just stood there silent, looking down at us. Not a Tambookey or Kafir stirred. I had the strangest feeling that even the sky above us had fallen silent. The Zoolahs stood still as black statues. But I had no feeling to cut and run, as I feared I would have. I was glad to have Pete and Dries and even the Bowker brothers near me, but I was also curious to know what I would do next, what we would all do next. So with everybody there I sat on my horse and stared. As we did so my memory seemed to go right back on its own, and I remembered, suddenly very clear, sitting on Papa's shoulders in St Peter's Field before we left England.

Then one of the Zoolahs steps forward from the middle of them, a lot of finery on his head and ankles, brandishes his great stabbing assegai, and gives a huge yell at us. You could hear it roll away in the valley round us. At once one of the witchdoctors on our side leaps forward, raises his bunch of assegais forward to heaven in one hand and his magic stick in the other, and screams a stream of insults and curses. Next minute on every hand there is a rattling and muttering, and I see every warrior round me is beating his shield with his spear. And a rumbling and rattling comes back to us from the Zoolahs up the hill. Nobody stepped a yard out of line, the Major sat gravely on his horse, we all sat gravely on our horses, and the great rattling and rumbling went on all round, and the distant rattling of the Zoolahs came down to us.

Then a messenger comes to the Major from the Chiefs, can't we fire a few shots at the Zoolahs. But the Major sends back his answer pretty sharply, why don't the Tambookeys and Kafirs do some attacking? All the time our two forces are standing there clattering and rumbling at each other. But at last our Major says in an annoyed tone, 'Oh very well, then,' and shouts to us, 'Party will advance a hundred paces.' A great hush comes over our side, and then over the Zoolahs, and there's only the sounds of our horses clicking and stumbling forward.

'Halt!' shouts the Major. 'Take aim, fire high, fire!' And a ragged volley is fired – and as if it had nothing to do with it, one man falls among the Zoolahs, and another bends double, screaming.

'Right, my brave lads,' shouts the Major, 'reload to give them another!' But suddenly the Zoolahs are running up the hill, and there's a great roar from the Kafirs and Tambookeys and they're racing up the hill after them, and the air is thick with assegais.

Off we go, riding like mad for the top of the hill, the Major yelling, 'Keep line; keep your eye on me.' But as soon as we've got to the top we see the Kafirs and Tambookeys have run into a real fight, for just over the hill is a bigger force of Zoolahs and our men have run into them pell-mell.

'Follow me,' hollers the Major. 'Make for the flank and fire down their lines.' So off we go again behind the Major. And now it becomes all jumbled up, like a very windy day when everything seems flapping and voices come through to you in rags and patches. 'Steady yourselves,' the Major shouts. 'Fire at command.' Fire. Reload. Fire. Reload. Fire. And we see consternation among the Zoolahs as the men beside and behind them begin to fall, or scream with wounds, and they look back to us, and round at their own, and they see confusion there too, and Kafirs and Tambookeys and assegais pouring in from the front now, and the Major all the time shouting, 'Now take it in turn, half load, half fire.' Fire! Fire! Fire! and next the Zoolahs are beginning to stream away towards the woods across the little valley, dragging dead and wounded with them as they go.

'Don't charge, don't charge,' shouts the Major, 'let the Kafirs do that.' So we rode through to the main battlefield and looked at some of the dead Zoolahs left behind – Kafirs and Tambookeys running past had jabbed their assegais into them and the dead were a sorry sight. It was strange, they were not dead men to me as they were dead enemies – yet I did feel a pang for them at last. One of the Boers, looking down, says, 'These all look thin, starved – I thought the Zoolahs were big fellows.'

'Nobody looks his best when he's dead,' says the Major.

But soon we had other business to attend to, for the Tambookeys had found their cattle hidden just inside the woods and next thing it's Kafirs and Tambookeys chasing cattle all over the place, and the Zoolahs forgotten. All except some women with children who come running to us to say Tambookeys and Kafirs are killing them in the woods. We handed them over to the Chiefs to look after, though we had our doubts, and wondered what would become of them. We were quite relieved to see them alive later that day.

Next day

I gave up writing about our victory because my hand got cramped with so much writing and only my saddle for a desk. But I must tell you about our great victory celebration. At sunset we set out back to Tambookey Great Place, convinced the Zoolahs were in full retreat, and had had enough of our guns. The Kafirs and Tambookeys did not stop to say thank you or by your leave, but went rushing past us with as many cattle as they could manage. I swear if the Zoolahs had come back again they would have kept going off with the cattle just the same and left us to fend the Zoolahs off as best we might. We finally slept outside Vusani's big kraal – and there was no welcoming committee to see us in, not so much as a dish of sour milk or Kafir beer.

The next morning some of the Boers said to the Major, where's all the cattle he was to be given for a feast. The Major goes stumping off and he comes back later cursing something horrible, saying he hopes the Zoolahs come back and subjugate the whole Tambookey nation, and Vusani with them. Later Chief Vusani sends us two skinny old cows long past their prime, chased by an old man and a boy. Well, you should have seen our Major's face, like a rising full moon it was, but we had to make do with the beasts. We slaughtered them to make a feast for ourselves, and one of Vusani's wives comes by to bring us some beer, and says she can't understand why we are having this separate feast, because all the preparations are for a great feast the next night, to celebrate the great victory of the Tambookeys over the Zoolahs. But the Major says, he hopes they enjoy their feast by themselves, for the next time the Zoolahs come around they can beat them by themselves. 'Tell that to your husband, Madam,' and he said this so fiercely that the Boers nearly rolled on the ground laughing at him, and it was hard for us to keep a straight face as Mrs Vusani Number Three or Four went off, looking mighty puzzled. Well, that was my first battle and victory celebration.

Monday

I wrote so much about the battle that I feared I would have no ink left. We are on our way back, covering much the same ground again. Only incident worth mentioning is a tremendous row between the Major and his two Cape Corps aides. For when we came to set up camp tonight, the Major found he seemed to have a bag of brass buttons and another of beads missing. After questioning them both, the Major is satisfied that it is Hendrik and has tied him up to a tree for the night. He says we will court-martial him in the morning. And so to sleep, for we are all dog-tired.

Tuesday

We held the court this morning, and Hendrik lied most desperately. When he was finally tied to the tree and the other Cape Corps man, Karools, ordered to give him 25 with the sjambok, and blood ran down his back and he began to scream and cry, I began to feel sorry for the poor Tot. We took him at the Major's orders and threw him in a nearby sea-cow pool to cool off, and all his clothes after him. At last the fellow gets out the other side and stands there and screams at the Major, 'Waar's my pay!'

'You've got your pay, and if I ever catch you again you'll get more of it!'

Then Hendrik yells out horrible curses on the Major and his mother and all his relations. At last he is gone, staggering and stumbling off into the veld, and we could hear his screeching and shouting back at us for quite a time.

'What happens to him now?' I asked Karools.

He says, 'Oh, he'll go and dig up where he's buried what he stole and buy himself some nice fat cows and perhaps a Kafir wife.'

We rode on again but about midday a messenger comes up with us from Grahamstown to say Colonel Somerset's also set out to repel the Zoolahs, but with a big force and is camped on the Kay.

Thursday

Well, here's a surprise. We've said goodbye to the Major and the others, and are remaining with Colonel Somerset and his force tonight. Sorry to see the others go, for we got quite fond of them, even the Bowker brothers. The Major made quite a speech to Pete and me as he left. He said, 'You are good young fellows, steady as two rocks, boys, and you'll do brave things if you live long enough.' But I have to relate why we are here, in this very pretty spot just above the Kay drift, watching a party of elephant spray themselves, instead of riding back home. Dries will convey you our messages when he rides past.

When we came up to this camp yesterday it was nearly midday. We waited around while the Major goes in to see the Colonel in his tent, and we hear quite a lot of argument, and the Colonel saying, 'That's the devil of it, man. You can't be certain.' And the Major comes out to us a little later and says that me and Pete are to go and see the Colonel.

So in we went to the Colonel, and he is sitting at a camp table with a map spread on it. I know that long ago we all thought he was very haughty, but Pete and I quite took to him, and he appeared most friendly, even with his tangle of eyebrows and great bush of a moustache. He talks to us for a while and says the Major has a high opinion of us, and we look likely lads – and then he says, 'You may think I'm flattering you both to some purpose, eh? Well, I am!' and he laughs as if he's made the greatest joke in the world. And he says, too, that the Major thinks there's no need for us to do what he's asking us, for the Zoolahs have now retreated. This might very well be so. 'The Zoolahs may be gone,' he says, 'but to have fled after a few score killed, that doesn't sound like Zoolahs from what I've heard of them.'

He wants us to ride forward to a Boer he knows who lives in Kafir country and would have the most reliable information on what Zoolah forces are approaching or retreating. This is a Mr Roggeburg.

Pete asks, 'Is he a missionary, Colonel?'

The Colonel gives a great snort, hara, and cries, 'Anything but! In fact he's a deplorable beggar. But he lives in Hintsa's country and he knows everything that goes on from the border to Shaka's place.'

We leave first thing tomorrow. The Colonel has to ride back to Grahamstown on some matter. We are to report to him there. I asked the Colonel's aide to take this journal, and if we get lost or something, he is to give it to Papa.

Thursday

Back in Grahamstown, unharmed, but with bad news. Mr Roggeburg says there is a big Zoolah force still coming on. So the Colonel sets off first light tomorrow, and takes us with him. I've got my journal back and must tell you about this Boer, Roggeburg.

We got to Butterworth to find Mr Shaw and his family have already gone back to Wesleyville. Mrs Shrewsbury then gave us a Christian Kafir, Jonathan Bleku, to escort us to show us where Roggeburg lives. Our guide, at last, became very reluctant to take us nearer to Roggeburg's place and he stayed on at a village close by, and sent us on with a boy who got lost approaching the place, rather circling round it until he nearly got us shot. For Roggeburg leapt out on us with two other Kafirs and they levelled their guns at our heads before we knew where we were. Our little guide nearly died of fright.

Roggeburg listened to us with a great deal of suspicion until I had explained our mission to him. He is a great big fellow, with shoulders like a bull and rather shabby leather clothes. Pete's a good six feet three but he seemed almost reedy beside Roggeburg's bulk. Add to that tangled yellow hair and a heavy face the colour of burnt brick, with two bits of blue glass in for eyes, and you've got a sight anybody might be frightened by. We sat with him outside a big hut in a sort of Great Place like a chief's, but more in straight lines, I mean the other huts were – and we could look down by the light of sunset to a little river and the sea with a beach curving along it. We watched all this fade while Roggeburg gave us some beer. A big, splendid-looking Kafir woman brought it to us – she was almost as big as Roggeburg himself – but he did not present us to her. He told us most unpleasant news about the Zoolahs and their Chief, whom he called Oo-Shaka. He assured us that a big Zoolah army was coming down chasing another group Oo-Shaka had ordered to be wiped off the face of the earth, and would perhaps give Chief Faku's Pondos a rough lesson, too. He felt it a wise precaution for Colonel Somerset and some force to advance to Hintsa's northern borders as a reminder to the Zoolahs to go no further. Then having delivered himself of this, Mr Roggeburg bade us farewell. We gaped at this and Pete blurted to him, could we not rest the night there, for our horses were already weary with travelling all day.

He stared at us, grunted, and then took us to a hut at the bottom of the row, and left us, to rub down our horses and feed them with some fodder one of his men brought us. We were just preparing to go to bed with empty bellies ourselves, when Roggeburg comes out of the dark with an invitation to dine with him – on Kafir beer, stiff mealy-corn porridge, meat and gravy. He drank just like a Kafir, smacking his lips over the beer, and giving a groan of pleasure after a good swig of it. He falls at last to praising the excellence of all things Kafir. 'This beer, this tyalli,' he cries, holding up half a calabash full in front of the fire, 'none of your thin English brew can compare with it! Why, it's a food, too, and doesn't eat up a man's stomach like that red Cape brandy!' We ate hearty but drank as little as we could, intent on staying friends – but Pete nearly finishes everything, by asking, 'How long have you lived like this, then?'

Like a gun-shot Roggeburg shouts, 'Like what?' and we can see his blue, bloody eyes blaze at us across the fire.

'Well, it seems such a free life,' I say quickly.

He bursts out: 'Yes, it is free and I'm free, living as God meant a man to do! And the others don't do it because they are a lot of cowards. But in their hearts they envy us – me, and Coenrad Buys who took over Gaika's mother, and all the others who got away from the Bible and the double-bed.'

We still kept quiet, and he stares at us waiting for us to say something – and at last he shouts at us: 'You think the English are different, hey?' He offers an opinion that we are beardless snot-noses who have seen nothing in our lives yet. And that we had only to go fifty miles or so to the north to see descendants of an English officer and his daughters wrecked on these shores last century. Yes, says Roggeburg with relish, that fine English officer, a general he'd heard it said, married a whole row of Kafir wives, and married off his daughters to local chiefs, and settled down to live as a Kafir among Kafirs fully content, and never made the smallest attempt to get back to England. And today, says Roggeburg, their descendants, except for a certain lightness of colour, are as much Kafirs as their neighbours, and have long forgotten to be Christian Mense. And we were to mark his words that many English and even more Boers would do likewise, when they stopped being frightened of the Bible, missionaries, mothers, grandmothers and so forth.

We said we were sure it was all very interesting but we had a hard day's riding to do. So we'd be off to bed, thank you. At which he jumps and grabs his gun and levels it at us over the fire and bellows, 'That's what you want, is it? Lay a finger on one of my women and I'll blast you both to hell, for I can shoot like a cat in the dark!'

At which Pete says, getting in a temper too, 'So can I, Mr Roggeburg!'

Then there's nothing for it but I have to put a small coal from the fire at one hundred paces and Roggeburg misses it hopelessly in three shots, and Pete puts it out with his first, though by then it was burned down till you could scarce see it. 'I see you can handle your weapons,' says Roggeburg with much respect, 'but don't try to handle my women!'

So we went off to sleep and left before dawn the next morning. There was no one out to bid us farewell. I said to Pete as we rode off, 'Old Roggeburg was so impressed with your shooting, Pete, I was afraid he was going to give you one of his wives!'

'I thought of that myself,' says Pete, 'and I nearly missed deliberate.' We rode back like fury with our news about the Zoolahs.

Monday, 24 August

Altogether about 1,000 of us or more, very different to the scratch lot under Major Dundas, a taste of real military life. Camped tonight on a long slope coming down to the Bashee again. Mr Roggeburg came into camp and greeted me and Pete like old friends, and then went for a long confab with the Colonel. Messages from Vusani and Hintsa about big Zoolah forces approaching.

Listened to an argument between an officer of the 55th and Captain Aitchison of the Cape Mounted Rifles. This officer had made some slighting remark about the value of the Totties as soldiers, and Captain Aitchison said by God he would rather have Totties at his back in this sort of war than any great clumsy clanking red dragoon. Totties, he said, knew their Kafir, could think like him, and were quick as terriers through the bush. And he gave it as his opinion that, for all their discipline and bravery, the 55th were cumbersome 'as old bulldogs in red flannel'.

Tuesday

Great to-do, having conferences with Chiefs Hintsa and Vusani, and also Chief Faku of the Pondo to the North. Whenever Pete and I weren't running messages for the Colonel up and down the camp we stayed to listen what was being said. There's a promise made to have 12,000 Kafirs and Tambookeys on the march to the Bashee tomorrow. Chief Faku's a big man, very cheerful in spite of what's happened to his people, very calculating too, always watching very sharp even when he is laughing. I mean he is supposed to have lost half his people and cattle in a fight with the Zoolah vanguard – or Gwame or Fetcani, some say one, some say another – and yet here he is with his big face and little waggling beard as jolly as at a beer-drink.

All are agreed that there's a big force on the Umtata and more following after. By this evening the plain around was filling up with Kafirs, dancing round their fires to get their courage up. The CMR men watch them, very supercilious about their only having assegais, and the few with guns hardly knowing which end the bullet comes out.

Friday

Pete and I have now fought in our second big engagement, the Battle of Umbulumpeen. And I'm pleased to tell you we won – though no thanks to our Tambookey, Kafir and Pondo allies. First we saw of the Zoolahs was what seemed a small group drawn up on the ground just before the forests. Captain Aitchison rode up with a small detachment to tell them to surrender and retire back to Zoolah country – but they mocked and jeered at him, and began to rush at him with their stabbing spears. So Aitchison fell back with his Hottentots, stopping to fire and then ride back and stop and fire again until the CMR lines were regained. Then all fired. Soon the red line of the 55th advanced, extended, and fired a volley into a rushing line of Zoolahs. The charge of the Zoolahs seemed to wither, then another line rushed out of the forest – crash from the 55th, bang-bang-bang from the CMR, screams, yells and shouts from the Zoolahs, and another line is rushing forward from the trees. Suddenly it's as if somebody has struck a gong as big as the sky and there's a high whistling over us – 'It's the artillery!' shouts Pete. Soon it's all a mighty fury of sounds – Voom! Voom! Crash! Bang-bang-bang! Shrieks of cannonballs and yells, taunts and screams of Zoolahs!

As soon as it was clear the Zoolahs were faltering, in went the Pondos and the Kafirs, raining down assegais upon the Zoolahs and charging in a mass, screeching their heads off. 'What cowards!' says Pete. But a Hottentot soldier standing near laughs, 'If we can do it for them, why should they run in and get killed?' I suppose he was right, but it's not very admirable.

Soon there's a most dreadful row in among the trees and terrible screeching and wailing, and word comes back there's bloody butchery going on, even among women and children. The Colonel sends us flying down there. The sight that met us was truly pitiful. Whole families of Zoolahs, fathers, mothers, children and babes all clubbed to death. You should have seen and heard the Colonel when we told him – purple with rage. 'Get those damned cannon here!' he cries. And the next minute he has them levelled at another mass of Hintsa's Kafirs running into the forest, first two balls over their heads, and when they did not stop, two bang in the middle of them. They stopped then all right, shouting and shaking their assegais and fists.

One of the Chiefs comes rushing up and says what are we doing, and the Colonel says, 'By God, I'll give you all the same medicine as I gave the Zoolahs if this killing doesn't stop!' The Chief says, 'They would have done it to us!'

Then the Colonel says that whatever the Kafir customs are, the custom of the English is to spare the enemy after a battle, and not to harm women and children, and as the English forces won this battle for them, this must be respected. So the leaders said it was not their custom to harm women and children either, but these Zoolahs had killed whole villages full of people, and had eaten them too as far as some reports went, and how could the people's vengeance be restrained.

'Either you'll restrain it,' says the Colonel, 'or I'll restrain it, and I'll do it with the big boom-booms even if I have to blow half your people to glory to teach them some humanity.'

So the killing was brought to an end, at least where it was possible for the Colonel to hear about it.

Today there's been rumours too that these people were never Zoolahs at all, but the Fetcani or Gwame people, all running away from the Zoolahs. Captain Aitchison told the Colonel his CMR men believe Faku and Hintsa have tricked him into attacking these people, for they have heard that the real Zoolahs would not be travelling with wives and children but all men in proper regiments. And to speak true the women and children and the few men we have brought here are very thin and starved-looking. But the Colonel will have none of it but we have won a fine victory and secured the peace of the frontier.

Saturday

Mr Roggeburg has come in again, and tells the Colonel of mysterious reports he hears that the main Zoolah force has turned back, or been defeated by another tribe on the way. Chiefs Vusani, Faku and Hintsa have again come to see the Colonel, and give him their word that the Zoolahs or Gwames or who they may be will be given mercy, according to English custom. The main danger is passed, and our main forces are to go back. Most pleased of all is Chief Faku, his big face shining and his little beard waggling as he talks to the Colonel – promises to treat the prisoners he takes 'like my own children'. Beside him Hintsa is much more dignified and serious, and I for one would be more ready to take his word. But still some of the women and children, whose men have been killed or have disappeared, are going to be sent back to the Colony, though what they are to do there nobody can say.

Tuesday, Wesleyville

Arrived here with party taking the women and children to the Colony. Colonel thanked us for our help and said we could go. We were sorry to say farewell, though glad to go home at last, and the Colonel was courteous to us

always and when we went he said, 'Tell your fathers they have good cause to
be proud of you. One day they'll have to find their officers among you young
fellows here, and I'll recommend you for a commission any time you should
ask me.' But later Peter said to me what I was thinking at the time, that eight
weeks of this kind of life has been enough, and I wouldn't like to be at it
forever, even to be a Colonel.

Here we met Mr and Mrs Shaw again as well as spending the evening with
Martha and Jack, whom we enthralled with our military exploits. Mr Shaw
says to me, for he was off somewhere in the morning, 'I wish your father
would pay us a visit one day. When I first came here he was very doubtful it
would be any good.' He said it very quietly but I am sure he would very much
welcome a visit from Papa. So would Jack and Martha, too, and no doubt
Pete's little nephew and nieces.

Thursday
   Back home and end of Journal.

Gokatweng and the Buffaloes

» «

TRANSLATED FROM THE TSWANA BY SOL T. PLAATJE

Gokatweng Gaealashwe is chieftain of the Bakwena people at Molepolole. He is a Bechuana who has travelled a great deal on foot, on horseback, in waggon, by rail, and by sea and river boats. He has even been as far as Egypt, the land of the Pharaohs.

He has hunted elephants and lions, he has seen all kinds of things, and some of the stories of his experiences seem almost too strange to be true. The following is one of them. He says:

'We were a party of Bakwenas returning from the mines in Rhodesia, and journeying to Gwelo to take the train back to the Bakwena country. In the forest we came across what looked like the tracks of a herd of cattle, mixed up with the tracks of donkeys, and we wondered what kind of cattle it could be so very far away from human habitations. While we were wondering, some Matabeles appeared who were following that track. They said it was not oxen and donkeys, but buffaloes and zebras. As I was anxious to see what a buffalo was like, we diverged from our road and went with the Matabeles. We went on until we arrived at a post station, where the horses of the mail-coaches used to be changed.

'The two men in charge of the horses were white men. They took guns and mounted and went with us. When we arrived in the depths of the forest, we found a large herd of young buffaloes. The white men went in front and prepared to shoot. The Matabeles said: "Now the white men are going to put their foot into a hornet's nest; so look for some strong trees and climb up them. Anyone who doesn't climb up a tree will not see his mother again (this year)." The white men in front put a bullet into the herd, and one of the calves screamed. The sound instantly roused the mothers of the herd far away in the forest.

'While we were sitting among the branches of the trees, we saw a cloud of dust; it grew until it seemed to reach the clouds in the sky; then the Matabeles said: "They are coming." The cloud of dust approached. Soon a herd of buffaloes emerged from the forest, galloping towards the calves. The white men then mounted their horses and fled.

'When the buffaloes approached the calves, a bull left the others and chased the white men. But in spite of every effort on the part of the horses, we were astonished to see the buffalo overtake them, rush in between them, pass them, and finally turn round to rejoin the others. All this happened so quickly that we thought the buffalo had done nothing; it had, however, caused considerable damage.

'When the buffalo turned back, one of the horses fell with its rider. We climbed down the trees, and found that the buffalo had torn the horse's side with its horns while it was running. It crushed the calf of the man's leg, but fortunately did not break any bone. The horse, however, died.

'We placed the wounded man on the remaining horse and conveyed him to his station, and proceeded on our journey.'

The Outspan

» «

J. PERCY FITZPATRICK

'There is no art in the Telling that can equal the consummate art of the Happening!'

It was a remark dropped by a forgotten someone in a prospector's hut one night, years and years ago, when we had exhausted snakes and hunting, lucky strikes and escapes, and had got away into coincidences. One of the party had been telling us an experience of his. He was introduced on the day he arrived to a man well known on the fields. It seemed quite impossible that they could have met before, for they compared dates and places for ten years back, and yet both were puzzled by the hazy suggestion of having seen the other before and, in our friend's case, of something more definite. His remark to the other was: 'I can't help feeling that I saw you once in a devil of a fright somewhere – or dreamt it, I suppose!'

But this first feeling faded quickly away, and was utterly forgotten by both. Later on they shared a hut near Rimer's Creek, and afterwards, when houses came into vogue, they lived for several years together, while the first impression was lying buried, but not dead.

One day, in the process of swapping yarns, the other man was telling of the 'narrowest escape he ever had' – and all due to such a simple little mistake. A ticket collector took the tickets at the wrong end of a footbridge. Instead of collecting them as the passengers from the train *went on to* the bridge, he took them as they were *going off*. The result was that the crowd of excursionists was too great for the little bridge, and it slipped between the abutments, carrying some two hundred people into the river below, the narrator being one of them. It was then that the dormant idea stirred and awoke – jumped into life – and our friend put up his hands as he had done fifteen years before, when the little bridge in Bath dropped, and gasped out: 'My God! you were the other chap that hung on to the broken rail! *That's* where we met!'

That was what prompted the forgotten one to say after we had lapsed into silence: 'There's no art in the Telling that can equal the consummate art of the Happening!'

And I only recall the remark because it must be my apology for telling plain truth just as it happened.

When a man has spent some years of his life – the years of young manhood they generally are – in the veld, in the waggon, or tent, or Bush, it is an almost invariable rule that something which you can't define germinates in him and never entirely dies until he does. When this thing – this instinct, feeling, craving, call it what you will – awakens, as it periodically does, it becomes a madness, and they call it trek-fever, and then, as an old friend used to say, 'You must trek or burst!' There are many stories based on trek-fever, but this is not one of them; and if you were to ask those who know them or, better still, get hold of any of the old hands, hard-headed, commonplace, unromantic specimens though they might be, who have lived in the veld – if you gave them time to let it slip out unawares – you would find that every man jack of them would have something to say about the camp-fire. I do believe that the fascination within the fascination is the camp-fire in veld life, with its pleasant yarn-swapping, and its long, pregnant, thoughtful silences, no less enjoyable. The least loquacious individual in the world will be tempted to unfold a tale within the circle of a camp-fire's light.

Everything is so quietly, unobtrusively sociable, and subjects are not too numerous in the veld, so that when a man has something apropos or interesting to tell, he commands an appreciative audience. Nobody bores, and nobody interrupts. Perhaps it is the half-lazy preference for playing the listener which everyone feels that is the best security against bores and interruptions.

The charm of the life is indescribable, and none who have tasted it ever weary of it, ever forget it, or cease to feel the longing to return when once they have quitted it.

It was in '91, the year after the pioneers cut their way through the Bush, with Selous to guide them, and occupied Mashonaland. We followed their trail and lived again their anxious nights and days, when they, a small handful in a dense Bush, at the mercy of the Matabele thousands, did not know at what hour they would be pounced on and massacred.

We crossed the Lundi, and somewhere beyond where one of their worst nights was passed we outspanned in peace and security, and gossiped over the ruins of ancient temples and the graves of modern pioneers. There were half a dozen of us, and we lay round the fire in lazy silence, too content to speak, simply *living* and drinking in the indescribable glories of an ideal African night.

It was someone knocking his pipe out and asking for the tobacco that broke the long silence, and the old Barbertonian, who had had to move to release the tobacco, looked round with the air of wanting someone to talk to. As no one gave any sign, he asked presently: 'Are you chaps asleep?'

'No!' came in clear, wakeful voices, with various degrees of promptness.

'I was just thinking,' he said, refilling his pipe slowly, 'that this sort of thing – a night like this, you know, and all that – although it seems perfection to us, isn't really so perfect after all. It all depends on the point of view, you know. A night like this must be a perfect curse to a lion or a tiger, you know.'

'Your sympathies are too wide, old man,' said the surveyor. 'Chuck me a light, and console yourself that your predatory friends do well enough when others are miserable. Take a more human view.'

'If you want an outlet for your native sympathy, you might heave me out a cushion,' suggested another. 'I've made a pillow of a bucket, and got a dent in my head. The thick cushion, old boy, and I'm with you so far as to say that the lions have a jolly hard time of it with so much fine weather.'

The Barbertonian lighted up his pipe and threw the cushion at the last speaker.

'H'm!' he grunted between puffs. 'I was really thinking of it from quite a human standpoint – the view of that poor devil who got lost here two months ago. Now, *he* couldn't have thought much of nights like these. Do you think he mused on their beauty?'

'Oh, I heard something of him,' said one. 'Lost for forty days in the wilderness, wasn't he? I remember. The coincidence struck me as peculiar.'

'Yes, it was odd in a way. He was just "forty days and forty nights". He went out with a rifle and five cartridges to kick up a duiker along the riverbank here, and somehow or other got astray towards sundown, and lost his head completely. Five cartridges, seven matches, no grub, no coat, no compass, and no savvy! That's a fair start for a forty days' picnic, isn't it?' he resumed. 'Well, he fired off all his cartridges by dark, trying to signal to his camp, and then threw away his rifle. Fact! He broke the heads off two matches – he was shaking so from fright – before he realized that there were only seven altogether. But as he had nothing to cook, it didn't really make much difference whether he had matches or not.'

'What, in winter time, and with lions about?'

'Yah! Well, you get used to that. It was a bit frosty, and sometimes wet, and at first the lions worried him a lot and treed him several nights; but he says that that was nothing, while the sense of being lost – dead, yet alive – remained.

What's that? Live? Oh, he doesn't know himself how he lived, but we could pretty well tell by his condition when we found him. We were out shooting about five miles downstream, and on one of the sandy spits of the river we saw fresh footprints. Nigger, we thought, as it was barefoot. We wondered, because there were no kraals near here, and we had seen no cattle spoor or footpaths. I was on top of the bank every minute expecting a duiker or Bush buck to make a break out, and – I tell you – I don't know when I got such a start – such a *turn*, I should say – as when I caught sight of a white face looking at me out of an ant-bear hole. Great Caesar! there was something so infernally uncanny, wild, and hunted in the look that I instinctively got the gun round to cover him if he came at me. When the others came up, he crawled out, stark naked, sunburnt, scratched, shock-headed – still staring with that strange hunted look – came up to us and – laughed! We led him back to our camp. He could tell nothing, could hardly understand any of our questions. He was quite dazed. His hands were cut and disfigured, the nails were worn off with burrowing for roots. We went to his den. It was a big ant-bear hole under an old tree and among rocks – a well-chosen spot. He had burrowed it out a bit, I think, and in a sort of pigeon-hole or socket in the side of it there were a few nuts, and round about there were the remains of nuts and chewed roots, stones of fruit, and such things. I never could understand how it was that, being mad as he certainly was then, he had still the sense – well, really it was an instinct more than any knowledge – to get roots and wild-fruits to keep body and soul together!'

'A suggestive subject, truly,' said a man who had more millions to his credit than you would expect of a traveller in Mashonaland. 'A man starving within rifle-shot of his friends and supplies. Helpless in spite of the resources that civilization gives him, and saved from absolute death by a blessed instinct that we didn't know was ours since the days of the anthropomorphic ape! H'm! You're right, Barberton! He couldn't have thought much of the beauties of the night, and, if he thought at all, he must have placed a grim and literal interpretation on the *Descent* of Man when he was grubbing for roots with bleeding, nail-stripped fingers or climbing for nuts without a tail to steady him!'

Among us there was a retired naval man, a clean-featured, bronzed, shrewd-looking fellow, who was a determined listener during these camp-fire chats; in fact, he seldom made a remark at all. He sat cross-legged, with one eye closed – a telescope habit, I suppose – watching Barberton for quite a spell, and at last said, very slowly, and seemingly speaking under compulsion: 'Well, you never know how they take these shocks. We picked a man up once whose two companions had lain dead beside him for days and days. Before he became delirious, the last thing he remembers was getting some carbolic acid from a small medicine-chest. His mates had been dead two days then, and he had not the strength to heave them overboard. I believe he wanted to drink the carbolic. Anyway, he spilt it, and went off his head with the smell of carbolic around him. He recovered while with us – we were on a weary deep-sea-sounding cruise – but twice during the voyage he had short but violent returns of the delirium and the other conditions that he was suffering under when we found him. By the merest accident our doctor discovered that it was the smell of carbolic that sent him off. Once – years after this – he nearly died of it. He had had fever, and they kept disinfecting his room; but, luckily for him, he became dangerous and violent, and they had to remove him to another place. He was all right in a few days.'

'Do you believe that a man could live out a reasonably long lifetime in the way that "forty days" chap lived? I suppose he *could*, eh? Shoo! Fancy forgetting the civilized uses of tongue and limbs and brain! It seems awful, doesn't it? And yet men have been known to deliberately choose a life of savagery and barbarism – men whose lines had been cast in easy places, too!'

'That's all very well,' said Barberton. 'Now you are speaking of fellows settling down among savages and in the wilds voluntarily, and with certain provisions made for emergencies, etc., not of men *lost*.'

'Even so, a man must deteriorate most horribly under such circumstances.'

'Well,' said Barberton contemplatively, 'I don't know so much about that. It all depends upon the man. Mind you, I do think that the end is always fiasco – tragedy, trouble, ruin, call it what you like. We can't throw back to barbarism at will. For good or ill we have taken civilization, and the man who quits it pays heavy toll on the road he travels, and, likely enough, fetches up where he never expected to.'

The man who wrote for the papers smiled.

'I know,' he said with kindling eye – 'I know. It was just such a case you told us of at Churchill's Camp the other night. A man of the best calibre and training goes wild and marries two – mark you, *two*! – Kaffir women, and becomes a Swazi chief, and then the drama of the –'

'Drama be damned!' growled Barberton. 'It was one case out of twenty of the same sort.'

Barberton was nervously apprehensive of ridicule, and hated to be traded and walked out for effects.

'I was up on the Transvaal–Swazi border in '86,' said the millionaire. 'I remember you told me something of them then. It was a warm corner, Swaziland, then – about the warmest in South Africa, I should think. Eh?'

'You're right. It was. But,' said Barberton, turning to the correspondent, 'you were talking of men going amok through playing white nigger. Well, I can tell you this, that two of my best friends have done that same trick, and I'd stake my head that better men or more thorough gentlemen never trod in shoe-leather, for all their Kaffir ways.'

'Do you mean to say,' asked the millionaire, 'that you have known men settle down among natives, living among them as one of themselves, and still retain the manners, customs, instincts, habits of mind and body, even to the ambitions, of a white man?'

'No – well, I can't quite say that. Their ambitions, as far as you could gauge them, were a Kaffir's; that is, they aspired to own cattle, and to hunt successfully, but – And yet I don't know that it is right to say *that* even, because in almost every case these men get the "hanker" for white life again sooner or later. The Kaffir ambition may be a temporary one, or it may be that the return to white ways is the passing mania. Who knows, anyway? From my own experience of them, I can say that the return to their own colour almost invariably means their doom and ruin. I don't know why, but I've noticed it, and it seems like – like a sort of judgement, if you believe in those things.

'And you know,' he said, after taking a few pulls at the pipe again, 'there's a sense of justice in that, too. Civilization, scorned and flouted, being the instrument of its own revenge! If one could vest the abstract with personal feelings, what an ample revenge would be hers at the sight of the renegade – sick-hearted, weary, and shamefaced – coming back to the ways of his youth and race, and succumbing to some one part of that which he had despised and rejected *in toto*!'

Barberton generally became philosophic and reminiscent on these fine nights. Someone would make a remark of pretty general application, and he would sit up and wag his old head a few times in silence; then, from force of habit, examine his pipe and knock it out on the heel of his boot, and then out would lounge some reminiscence in illustration of his philosophy.

It was generally introduced by a long-drawn, thoughtful, 'We-ll, you know, I've always thought there was something curious about these things.' He would have another squint down the empty bowl of the pipe and ask for the tobacco. There would be a couple of grunts, and then, as he lighted up, he would say, between puffs, 'I remember, in '78, up at Pilgrim's', or, 'There was a fellow up Barberton way in '86.'

This night he sat in tailor fashion, with an elbow socketed in each knee-bend, and his hands clasped over the bowl of his pipe.

'One of the rummiest meetings I ever had,' said he, smiling thoughtfully at the recollection, 'was in the Swazi country in '85. Did I ever tell you about Mahaash and the Silver Spur?'

He gave a gurgling sort of chuckle, and puffed contentedly at the big-bowled briar.

'There were two of us riding through the Swazi country, and making for the landing-place on the Maputa side. We had had a row with the Portuguese about some cattle that the niggers stole from us. A couple of the niggers got shot, of course, during the discussion, and we had to quit for a while and take a rest on the Lebombo. But that's nix! When we got to the Komati, we were told that there was a white man on the Lebombo whose Kaffir name was Sebougwaan. That's the name the niggers give to a man who wears an eyeglass or spectacles. We were jogging along doing our thirty miles a day, living on old mealies roasted on a bit of tin, and an occasional fowl – Swazi fowl, two to the meal – helped down by bowls of amazi – thick milk, you know. We used to sleep out in the Bush every night, with a blanket apiece and saddles for pillows, and the horses picketed at our heads. Man, it was grand on nights like this! We were always tired and often hungry; but to lie there in the peace and stillness of the Bush, to look up at the stars like diamond dust against the sky, and not care a damn for anything in God's world, why – why – I call that living! All those months we had no knowledge of the outer world. As far as we were concerned, there might as well have been none. We had one book, *The Ingoldsby Legends*. If anyone could have seen me reading Ingoldsby by the light of the fire, and have heard every now and then the bursts of laughter over "The Jackdaw of Rheims" or "The Witches' Frolic", and others, his face would have been a study, I expect.

'However, I was telling you about Mahaash. Mahaash was a big induna, and had about five to seven thousand fighting men. He used to konza to Umbandine, but paid merely nominal tribute, and was jolly independent. He was the cleverest-looking nigger I have ever seen. Small, thin, and ascetic-looking, with wonderfully delicate hands, clear features, and lustrous black eyes. Really, he gave one the idea that he saw through everything, or next to it, and though he said very little, he looked one of the very determined quiet ones. We had to pass his place to get to Sebougwaan's, and, of course, had to stay the day and pay our respects. His kraal was on top of the highest plateau, near the Mananga Bluff. It lay on the edge of a forest, and the road – an aggregation of cattle-tracks – was very steep and very stony. You can imagine we were not overflush just then, and what puzzled us was what to give the chief as a present when he would accord us an interview. Rifles and ammunition we daren't part with, and we were mortally afraid they were just the things he would want to annex. Finally, it occurred to us to present him with one of my chum's silver spurs. Heron didn't favour this much. He said it would likely cause trouble; but I put that down to his disinclination to spoil his pair of swagger spurs. Only the day before our arrival the chief had purchased a horse; he had sent to Lydenburg for it, and it was the first they had ever seen in that part of the country – which seems odd when you think that the chief's own name, Mahaash, means "the Horse". However, to proceed. We got word next day that the chief would see us, and after the usual hour's wait we had our indaba, and presented the silver spur. I must say he viewed it very suspiciously – very! – and when we showed him how to put it on, he gave a slow, cynical smile, and made some remark in an undertone to one of his councillors. I began to agree with Heron about the unwisdom of giving a present so little understood, and would gladly have changed it, but that Mahaash – who was of a practical turn of mind – sent a man for our horses, and bade us ride with the "biting iron" on. We gave an exhibition of its uses which pleased him, and we, too, felt quite satisfied – for a moment! But things didn't look quite so well when he announced that he was going to ride his horse, and he desired Heron to strap the spur on to his bare foot. It was no use hesitating – we had to trust to luck and the chances that a skinny moke such as his was would take no notice of a spur; besides which, Heron, with good presence of mind, jammed the rowels on a stone and turned most of the points. It was no good, however. The chief had never been astride a horse before; he was hoisted up by a couple of stalwart warriors. Once on, he laid hold of the mane with both hands, and gripped his heels firmly under the horse's belly. I saw the brute's ears go flat on his neck. The two supporters stepped back. Mahaash swayed to one side, and, I suppose, gave a convulsive grip with the armoured heel. There was a squeal and scuffle, and a black streak shooting through the air with a red blanket floating behind it. The chief bounced once on the stony incline, shot on for another ten feet, and fetched up with his head against a rock. I can tell you that for two minutes it was just hell let loose. We dropped our rifles – we always carried them – and ran to the chief. I believe if we had kept them they'd have stuck us, for there were scores of black devils round each of us, flashing assegais in our faces, and yelling: "Bolalile Inkos! Umtagati umtagati!" – "They have killed the chief! Witchcraft! witchcraft!" But in another minute we saw Mahaash standing propped up by several kehles, and holding one hand to his head. He steadied himself for a moment, gave us one steady, inscrutable look, and walked into his private enclosure.

'For four days we remained there – prisoners in fact, though not in name. Nothing was said about leaving, but our guns and horses were gone, and we were given a hut to ourselves in the centre of the kraal. We didn't know whether Mahaash was dead, dying, or quite unhurt. We didn't know whether we were to be despatched or set free, or to be kept for ever. On the morning of the fifth day we found our horses tied to the cattle kraal in front of our hut, and a grey-headed induna brought word to us that Sebougwaan, for whom we were looking, lived not far from there along the plateau. We took the hint, and saddled up. As we were starting an umfaan brought a kid, killed and cleaned, and handed it to me – a gift from the chief; and the old induna stepped up to Heron with a queer look in his wrinkled, cunning old phiz, and said: "The chief says, 'Hamba gahlé' ('Pleasant journey'), and sends *you* this."

'It was the silver spur.'

Barberton had another squint at his pipe, and chuckled at the recollection of the old nigger's grim pleasantry.

'But I was telling you about that white man on the Bomba,' he resumed. 'Well, we weren't long in making tracks out of Mahaash's kraal, and as we dodged along through the forest, following a footpath which just permitted a man on foot to pass, we realized how poor a chance we'd have had had we tried to escape. Every hundred yards or so we had to dismount to get under overhanging boughs or trunks of fallen trees or networks of monkey-ropes. The horses had got so used to roughing it that they went like cats, and in several places they had to duck under the heavy timber that hung, portcullis fashion, across the dark little pathway. This was the only way out at the back of Mahaash's. In front of him, of course, were the precipitous sides of the Lebombo Range.

'We went on for hours through this sort of thing, hardly seeing sunlight through the dense foliage; and when we got out at last into a green grassy flat, the bright light and open country fairly dazzled us. Here we met a few women and boys, who, in reply to our stock question, gave the same old reply that we had heard for days: "Sebougwaan? Oh, further on ahead!"

'We just swore together and like one man, for we really had reckoned to get to this flying Dutchman this time without further disappointments. We looked around for a place to off-saddle, and made for a koppie surrounded by trees.

'Heron was ahead. As we reached the trees, he pulled up, and with a growing grin called to me, "I say, just look here! Here's a rum start!"

'It was clearly our friend Sebougwaan. He was standing with arms akimbo, and feet well set apart, surveying critically the framework of a house he was putting up.

'He had a towel round his loins, and an eyeglass screwed tightly into the near eye. Nothing else.

'We viewed him *en profile* for quite a while, until he turned sharply our way and saw us. It was one of the pleasantest faces in the world that smiled on us then. Sebougwaan walked briskly towards us, saying: "Welcome, gentlemen, welcome. It's not often I see a white face here. And, by-the-by, you'll excuse my attire, won't you? The custom of the country, you know, and 'In Rome –' Well, well. You'll off-saddle, of course, and have a snack. Here, Komola! Bovaan! Hi, you boys! Where the devil are they? Here, take these horses and feed them. And now just 'walk into my parlour'. Nothing ominous in the quotation, I assure you."

'He bustled us around in the jolliest manner possible, and kept up a running fire of questions, answers, comments and explanations, while he busied himself with our comfort.

'It was a round wattle-and-daub hut that he showed us into, but not the ordinary sort. This one was as bright and clean as a new pin. Bits of calico and muslin and gay-coloured kapelaan made curtains, blinds and table-covers. The tables were of the gin-case pattern, legs planted in the ground; the chairs ordinary Bush stools; but what struck me as so extraordinary was the sight of all the English periodicals and illustrated papers laid out in perfect order and neatness on the table, as one sees them arranged in a reading-room before the first frequenters have disturbed them. There was also a little hanging shelf on which were five books. I couldn't help smiling at them – the Bible, a Shakespeare, the Navy List, a dictionary, and *Ruff's Guide*.

'They say that you may tell a man by his friends, and most of all by his books; but I couldn't make much out of this lot, with one exception. I looked at the chap's easy bearing, the pleasant, hearty manner and torpedo beard, and concluded that the Navy List, at any rate, was a bit of evidence. However, he kept things going so pleasantly and gaily that one had no time in which to observe much.

'Lots of little things occurred which were striking and amusing in a way, because of the peculiar surroundings and conditions of the man's life rather than because of the incidents themselves. For instance, when we owned up that we had had no breakfast, we found ourselves within a few minutes enjoying poached eggs on toast, and I felt myself grinning all over when the Swazi boy waited in passable style with a napkin thrown carelessly over one shoulder. Surely a man must be a bit eccentric to live such a life as this in such a place and alone, and yet take the trouble to school a nigger to wait on him in conventional style.

'I thought of the peculiar littleness of teaching a nigger boy that waiter's trick, and concluded that our friend, whatever his occupation might be, was not a trader from necessity. After breakfast he produced some excellent cigarettes – another fact in the nature of a paradox.

'We were making for the landing-place on the Tembe River, and had intended moving along again that day; but our host was pressing, and we by no means anxious to turn our backs on so pleasant a camp, so we stayed overnight, and became good friends right away.

'I was quite right. He had been in the navy many years, and had given it up to play at exploring. He said he had settled down here because there was absolute peace and a blissful immunity from the ordinary worldly worries. Once a week a native runner brought him his mail letters and papers, and, in fact, as he said, he was as near to the world as he chose to be, or as far from it.

'He had a curious gold charm attached to a watch-chain, which I saw dangling from a projecting wattle-end in the dining-hut. I was looking at this, and puzzled over it; it seemed so unlike anything I had ever seen. He saw me, and, after putting us to many a futile guess, told us laughingly that he had found it in one of the villages they had sacked on the West Coast. I don't know what sort of part he took in these nasty little wars, but I'll bet it was no mean one. We listened that night for hours to his easy, bright, entertaining chat, and although he hardly ever mentioned himself or his own doings, one couldn't but see that he had been well in the thick of things, and dearly loved to be where danger was. Now and then he let slip a reference to hardships, escapes and dangers, but only when such reference was necessary to explain something he was telling us of. What interested us most was his description of General Gordon – "Chinese Gordon" – with whom he appeared to have been in close contact for a good while. The little details he gave us made up an extraordinarily vivid picture of the soldier-saint, the man who could lead a storming-party, a forlorn hope, with a Bible in one hand and a cane in the other; the man who, in the infiniteness of his love and tenderness, and in the awful immutability of his decision and justice, realized qualities in a degree which we only associate with the Deity. I felt I could see this man helping, feeding with his own short rations, nursing, and praying with, the lowliest of his men, the incarnation of mercy. But I also saw him facing the semi-mutinous regiment of barbarians, and, with the awful passionless decision of fate itself, singling out the leaders here and there – in all a dozen men – whom he shot dead before their comrades, and turning again as calm and unmoved as ever to repeat his order, which this time was obeyed! I pictured this man, with the splendid practical genius to reconquer and reorganize China, treasuring a cutting which he had taken from what he verily believed to be the identical living tree from which Eve had plucked the forbidden fruit. Surely, one of the enigmas of history!'

'Do you mean to say that's a fact?' asked the millionaire, as old Barberton paused.

'As far as I know, it certainly is. Our friend told it as a fact, and not in ridicule, either, for he had the deepest reverence and regard for Gordon. He assured us, moreover, that Gordon was once most deeply mortified and offended by a colleague of his treating the matter as a joke and laughing at it. Gordon never forgot that laugh, and was always constrained and reserved in the man's presence afterwards.

'I wish I could remember a hundredth part of our host's anecdotes of well-known people, descriptions of places and of peoples, accounts of travels and adventures. He seemed to know everyone and all places. It was three in the morning before we thought of turning in. After breakfast we saddled up and bade adieu, but our friend walked along part of the way with us to put us on the right path. He was carrying a bunch of white Bush flowers – a curious fancy, I thought, for a man clothed in a towel and an eyeglass. I remarked on the beauty of the mountain flowers, and he held up the bunch.

'"Yes," he said, "they are lovely, aren't they? Poor old Tarry! He was my man – the only other white man that ever lived here. He was with me for many years, and died here two summers back – fever contracted on the Tembe. Poor old fellow! I fixed him up on the bluff yonder. He used to gather these flowers and sit there every day of his life looking out towards Delagoa, wondering if we would ever quit this place and get a sight of old Ireland again. I take him a bunch once in a while. Come up and see where a good friend lies."

'We left the horses and climbed up the rough path, and looked at the unpretentious stone enclosure and the soft slate slab with a rough-cut inscription:

PADDY TARRY'S REST!
Are ye ready?
Aye, aye, sir!

'Our friend leaned over the low stone wall and replaced the faded wreath by the fresh one.

'We left him standing there on the ridge, clear-cut above the outline of the mountain, and took our way down the rough cattle-path that wound down to the still rougher, wilder kloof through which our route lay. I remember so well the way he was standing, one foot on a projecting rock, arms folded, until we were rounding the turn that took us out of sight. Then he waved adieu.

'We had unpleasant times on that trip to the Tembe. We met all the murderous ruffians in that Alsatia, and they were all at loggerheads, thieving and shooting with both hands. However, we got out all right after months and months of roaming about, owing to the trouble about those Kaffirs, and I think we had both forgotten all about Sebougwaan by the time we fetched up in Lydenburg again. There was always something happening in that infernal outlaw corner of Swaziland to keep the time from dragging!

'My chum went off to his farm; but I had no home, and took the road again with waggons, and loaded for Barberton at slashing fine rates. I got there just as the Sheba boom was well on. Companies were being floated daily, shares were booming, money flowing freely. All were merry in the sunshine of today. No one took heed of tomorrow. Speculators were making money in heaps; brokers raking in thousands.

'You know how it is in a place like that. After you have been there for a few hours, or a day or two, you begin to notice that one name is always cropping up oftener than any other; one man seems the most popular, important and indispensable. Well, it was the same here. There was always this one name in everything – market, mines, sport, entertainment – any blessed department. You can just imagine – at least, you can't imagine – my surprise when I found that my naked white Kaffir sailor-friend, Sebougwaan, was the man of the hour. I couldn't believe it at first, and then a while later it seemed to be the most natural thing in the world; for, if I ever met a man who looked the living embodiment of mental, moral and physical strength, of good humour, grace and frankness – a born king among men – it was this chap.

'I met him next day, and he seemed more full of life and personal magnetism than ever. After that I didn't see him for three or four days; you know how time spins away in a wild booming market. Then somebody said he was ill – down with dysentery and fever at the Phoenix. I went off at once to see him. I couldn't believe my eyes. He was emaciated, haggard, with black-ringed eyes sunk into his head, and so weak that he couldn't raise his arm when it slipped from the bed. He spoke to me in whispers and gasps, only a word or two, and then lay back on the pillows with a terrible look of suffering in his eyes, or occasionally dropping the lids with peculiar suddenness; and when he did this the room seemed empty from loss of this horrible expression of pain.

'I stood at the foot of his bed, and didn't know what to do or say, and didn't know how to get out of a room where I was so useless. This sort of thing may only have lasted a few minutes, or perhaps half an hour – I don't know; but after one long spell he opened his eyes suddenly and looked long and steadily into mine, sat bolt upright, apparently without effort, lifted his glance till I felt he was looking over my head at something on the wall behind me, and then raised both arms, outstretched as though to receive something, and, groaning out, "Oh, my God! my poor wife!" dropped back dead.'

There were five intent faces upturned at Barberton as he stopped. The rosy glow of the fire lighted them up, and the man nearest me – the millionaire – whispered to himself, 'Good God! how awful!'

'Well, who was he? Did you –' began the man who wrote for the papers.

Barberton looked steadily at him, and with measured deliberation said: 'We never knew another word about him. From that day to this nothing has ever been heard to throw the least light on him or what he said.'

Far away in the stillness of the African night we heard the impatient half-grunt, half-groan of the lion. Nearby there was a cricket chirping; and presently a couple of the logs settled down with a small crunch, and a fresh tongue of flame leaped up. Barberton pumped a straw up and down the stem of the faithful briar, and remarked sententiously: 'Yah, it's a rum old world, this of ours! I've seen civilization take its revenge that way quite a lot of times – just like a woman!'

No one else said a word. Now and then a snore came from under the waggon where the drivers were sleeping.

The dog beside me gave some abortive whimpers, and his feet twitched convulsively – no doubt he was hunting in dreamland. I felt depressed by Barberton's yarn.

But round the camp-fire long silences do not generally follow a yarn, however often they precede one. One reminiscence suggests another, and it takes very, very little to tempt another man to recall something which 'that just reminds him of'.

It was the surveyor who rose to it this time; I could see the spirit move him. He sat up, stroked his clean-shaven face, closed the telescope eye, and looked at Barberton.

'Do you know,' he began thoughtfully, 'you talk of chaps going away because of something happening – some quarrel or mistake or offence or something. That is all a sort of claptrap romance, I know – the mystery trick, and so forth; but I confess it always interests me, although I know it's all rot, because of a thing which happened within my own knowledge – an affair of a shipmate of mine, one of the best fellows that ever stepped the earth, in spite of the fact that he was a regular Admirable Crichton.

'He was an ideal sort of chap, until you got to know him really well, and found out that he was cursed with one perfectly miserable trait. He never – absolutely *never* – forgave an injury, affront, or cause of quarrel. He was not huffy or bad-tempered – a sunnier nature never was created; a more patient, even-tempered chap never lived – but it was really appalling with what immutable obstinacy he refused to forgive. In the instances that came under my own notice, where he had quarrelled with former friends – not through his own fault, I must say – nothing in this world, or any other, for that matter, could influence him to shake hands or renew acquaintance. His generosity and unselfishness were literally boundless, his courage and fidelity superb; but anyone who had seen evidence of his fault must have felt sorrow and regret for the blemished nature, and must have been awestruck and frightened by his relentlessness. Death all round him, the sight of it in friends, the prospect of it for himself, never shook his cursed obstinacy; as we knew, after one piece of business. He got the V C for a remarkable – in fact, mad – act of courage in rescuing a brother officer. The man he carried out, fought for, fought over, and nearly died for, was a man to whom he had not spoken for some years. God knows what the difference was about. This was their first meeting since quitting the same ship, and when he carried his former friend out and laid him safely in the surgeon's corner of the square, the half-dead man caught his sleeve, and called out, "God bless you, old boy!" All *he* did was to loosen the other's grip gently, and, without a word or look at him, walk back into the fight. It seems incredible – it did to us; but he wouldn't know him again. He had literally wiped him out of his life!

'This trait was his curse. He was well off and well connected, and he married one of the most charming women I have ever met. For years none of us knew he was married. His wife was, I am convinced, as good as gold; but she was young, attractive, accomplished and, in fact, a born conqueror. Perhaps she was foolish to show all the happiness she felt in being liked and admired. You know the long absences of a sailor. Well, perhaps she would have been wiser had she cut society altogether; but she was a true, good woman, for all that, and she worshipped him like a god! None of us ever knew what happened; but he left wife and child, settled on them all he had in the world, handed over his estates and almost all his income, and his right to legacies to come, went out into the world, and simply erased them from his mind and life.

'That was a good many years ago – ten, I should think; and – I hate to think it – but I wish I was as sure of tomorrow as I am sure that he never recognized their existence again.'

The surveyor shuddered at the thought.

'He was a man who could do anything that other men could do. He was best at everything. He was loved by his mates, worshipped by his men, and liked and admired by everyone who met him – until this trait was revealed. Others must have felt as I did. When I discovered *that* in him, I don't know whether I was more frightened or grieved. I don't know that I didn't stick to him more than ever – perhaps from pity, and the sense that he was his own enemy and needed help. I have never heard of or from him since he left the service, and yet I believe I was his most intimate friend. Oliver Raymond Rivers was his name. Musical name, isn't it?'

Barberton dropped his pipe.

'Good God! Sebougwaan!'

The Woman's Rose

» «

OLIVE SCHREINER

I have an old, brown, carved box; the lid is broken and tied with a string. In it I keep little squares of paper, with hair inside, and a little picture which hung over my brother's bed when we were children, and other things as small. I have in it a rose. Other women also have such boxes where they keep such trifles, but no one has my rose.

When my eye is dim, and my heart grows faint, and my faith in woman flickers, and her present is an agony to me, and her future a despair, the scent of that dead rose, withered for twelve years, comes back to me. I know there will be spring; as surely as the birds know it when they see above the snow two tiny, quivering green leaves. Spring cannot fail us.

There were other flowers in the box once: a bunch of white acacia flowers, gathered by the strong hand of a man, as we passed down a village street on a sultry afternoon, when it had rained, and the drops fell on us from the leaves of the acacia trees. The flowers were damp; they made mildew marks on the paper I folded them in. After many years I threw them away. There is nothing of them left in the box now, but a faint, strong smell of dried acacia, that recalls that sultry summer afternoon; but the rose is in the box still.

It is many years ago now; I was a girl of fifteen, and I went to visit in a small up-country town. It was young in those days, and two days' journey from the nearest village; the population consisted mainly of men. A few were married, and had their wives and children, but most were single. There was only one young girl there when I came. She was about seventeen, fair, and rather fully-fleshed; she had large dreamy blue eyes, and wavy light hair; full, rather heavy lips, until she smiled; then her face broke into dimples, and all her white teeth shone. The hotel-keeper may have had a daughter, and the farmer in the outskirts had two, but we never saw them. She reigned alone. All the men worshipped her. She was the only woman they had to think of. They talked of her on the 'stoep', at the market, at the hotel; they watched for her at

70

street corners; they hated the man she bowed to or walked with down the street. They brought flowers to the front door; they offered her their horses; they begged her to marry them when they dared. Partly, there was something noble and heroic in this devotion of men to the best woman they knew; partly there was something natural in it, that these men, shut off from the world, should pour at the feet of one woman the worship that otherwise would have been given to twenty; and partly there was something mean in their envy of one another. If she had raised her little finger, I suppose, she might have married any one out of twenty of them.

Then I came. I do not think I was prettier; I do not think I was so pretty as she was. I was certainly not as handsome. But I was vital, and I was new, and she was old – they all forsook her and followed me. They worshipped me. It was to my door that the flowers came; it was I had twenty horses offered me when I could only ride one; it was for me they waited at street corners; it was what I said and did that they talked of. Partly I liked it. I had lived alone all my life; no one ever had told me I was beautiful and a woman. I believed them. I did not know it was simply a fashion, which one man had set and the rest followed unreasoningly. I liked them to ask me to marry them, and to say, No. I despised them. The mother heart had not swelled in me yet; I did not know all men were my children, as the large woman knows when her heart is grown. I was too small to be tender. I liked my power. I was like a child with a new whip, which it goes about cracking everywhere, not caring against what. I could not wind it up and put it away. Men were curious creatures, who liked me, I could never tell why. Only one thing took from my pleasure; I could not bear that they had deserted her for me. I liked her great dreamy blue eyes, I liked her slow walk and drawl; when I saw her sitting among men, she seemed to me much too good to be among them; I would have given all their compliments if she would once have smiled at me as she smiled at them, with all her face breaking into radiance, with her dimples and flashing teeth. But I knew it never could be; I felt sure she hated me; that she wished I was dead; that she wished I had never come to the village. She did not know, when we went out riding, and a man who had always ridden beside her came to ride beside me, that I sent him away; that once when a man thought to win my favour by ridiculing her slow drawl before me I turned on him so fiercely that he never dared come before me again. I knew she knew that at the hotel men had made a bet as to which was the prettier, she or I, and had asked each man who came in, and that the one who had staked on me won. I hated them for it, but I would not let her see that I cared about what she felt towards me.

She and I never spoke to each other.

If we met in the village street we bowed and passed on; when we shook hands we did so silently, and did not look at each other. But I thought she felt my presence in a room just as I felt hers.

At last the time for my going came. I was to leave the next day. Someone I knew gave a party in my honour, to which all the village was invited.

It was midwinter. There was nothing in the gardens but a few dahlias and chrysanthemums, and I suppose that for two hundred miles round there was not a rose to be bought for love or money. Only in the garden of a friend of mine, in a sunny corner between the oven and the brick wall, there was a rose tree growing which had on it one bud. It was white, and it had been promised to the fair-haired girl to wear at the party.

The evening came; when I arrived and went to the waiting-room, to take off my mantle, I found the girl there already. She was dressed in pure white, with her great white arms and shoulders showing, and her bright hair glittering in the candlelight, and the white rose fastened at her breast. She looked like a queen. I said 'Good-evening,' and turned away quickly to the glass to arrange my old black scarf across my old black dress.

Then I felt a hand touch my hair.

'Stand still,' she said.

I looked in the glass. She had taken the white rose from her breast, and was fastening it in my hair.

'How nice dark hair is; it sets off flowers so.' She stepped back and looked at me. 'It looks much better there!'

I turned round.

'You are so beautiful to me,' I said.

'Y-e-s,' she said, with her slow Colonial drawl; 'I'm so glad.'

We stood looking at each other.

Then they came in and swept us away to dance. All the evening we did not come near to each other. Only once, as she passed, she smiled at me.

The next morning I left the town.

I never saw her again.

Years afterwards I heard she had married and gone to America; it may or may not be so – but the rose – the rose is in the box still! When my faith in woman grows dim, and it seems that for want of love and magnanimity she can play no part in any future heaven; then the scent of that small withered thing comes back – spring cannot fail us.

The Schoolmaster

» «

PAULINE SMITH

Because of a weakness of the chest which my grandmother thought that she alone could cure, I went often, as a young girl, to my grandparents' farm of Nooitgedacht in the Ghamka valley. At Nooitgedacht, where my grandparents lived together for more than forty years, my grandmother had always young people about her – young boys and girls, and little children who clung to her skirts or were tossed up into the air and caught again by my grandfather. There was not one of their children or their grandchildren that did not love Grandfather and Grandmother Delport, and when Aunt Betje died it seemed but right to us all that her orphans, little Neeltje and Frikkie and Hans, Koos and Martinus and Piet, should come to Nooitgedacht to live. My grandmother was then about sixty years old. She was a big stout woman, but as is sometimes the way with women who are stout, she moved very easily and lightly upon her feet. I had seen once a ship come sailing into Zandtbaai harbour, and Grandmother walking, in her full wide skirts with Aunt Betje's children bobbing like little boats around her, would make me often think of it. This big, wise and gentle woman, with love in her heart for all the world, saw in everything that befell us the will of the Lord. And when, three weeks after Aunt Betje's children had come to us, there came one night, from God knows where, a stranger asking for shelter out of the storm, my grandmother knew that the Lord had sent him.

The stranger, who, when my grandmother brought him into the living-room, gave the name of Jan Boetje, was a small dark man with a little pointed beard that looked as if it did not yet belong to him. His cheeks were thin and white, and so also were his hands. He seldom raised his eyes except when he spoke, and when he did so it was as if I saw before me the Widow of Nain's son, risen from the dead, out of my grandmother's Bible. Yes, as if from the dead did Jan Boetje come to us that night, and yet it was food that I thought of at once. And quickly I ran and made coffee and put it before him.

When Jan Boetje had eaten and drunk my grandparents knew all that they were ever to know about him. He was a Hollander, and had but lately come to South Africa. He had neither relative nor friend in the colony. And he was on his way up-country on foot to the goldfields.

For a little while after Jan Boetje spoke of the goldfields my grandmother sat in silence. But presently she said: 'Mijnheer! I that am old have never yet seen a happy man that went digging for gold, or a man that was happy when he had found it. Surely it is sin and sorrow that drives men to it, and sin and sorrow that comes to them from it. Look now! Stay with us here on the farm, teaching school to my grandchildren, the orphans of my daughter Lijsbeth, and it may be that so you will find peace.'

Jan Boetje answered her: 'If Mevrouw is right, and sin and sorrow have driven me to her country for gold, am I a man to be trusted with her grandchildren?'

My grandmother cried, in her soft clear voice that was so full of love and pity: 'Is there a sin that cannot be forgiven? And a sorrow that cannot be shared?'

Jan Boetje answered: 'My sorrow I cannot share. And my sin I myself can never forgive.'

And again my grandmother said: 'Mijnheer! What lies in a man's heart is known only to God and himself. Do now as seems right to you, but surely if you will stay with us I will trust my grandchildren to you and know that the Lord has sent you.'

For a long, long time, as it seemed to me, Jan Boetje sat before us and said no word. I could not breathe, and yet it was as if all the world must hear my breathing. Aunt Betje's children were long ago in bed, and only my grandparents and I sat there beside him. Long, long we waited. And when at last Jan Boetje said: 'I will stay', it was as if he had heard how I cried to the Lord to help him.

So it was that Jan Boetje stayed with us on the farm and taught school to Aunt Betje's children. His schoolroom was the old waggon-house (grandfather had long ago built a new one), and here my grandmother and I put a table and stools for Jan Boetje and his scholars. The waggon-house had no window, and to get light Jan Boetje and the children sat close to the open half-door. From the door one looked out to the orange grove, where all my grandmother's children and many of her grandchildren also had been christened. Beyond and above the orange-trees rose the peaks of the great Zwartkops mountains, so black in summer, and so white when snow lay upon them in winter. Through the mountains, far to the head of the valley, ran the Ghamka pass by which men travelled up-country when they went looking for gold. The Ghamka river came down through this pass and watered all the farms in the valley. Coming down from the mountains to Nooitgedacht men crossed it by the Rooikranz drift.

Inside the waggon-house my grandfather stored his great brandy casks and his tobacco, his pumpkins and his mealies, his ploughs and his spades, his whips and his harness, and all such things as are needed at times about a farm. From the beams of the loft also there hung the great hides that he used for his harness and his veldschoen. Jan Boetje's schoolroom smelt always of tobacco and brandy and hides, and when the mud floor, close by the door, was freshly smeared with mist it smelt of bullock's blood and cow dung as well.

We had, when Jan Boetje came to us, no books on the farm but our Bibles and such old lesson books as my aunts and uncles had thought not good enough to take away with them when they married. Aunt Betje's children had the Bible for their reading-book, and one of my grandfather's hides for a blackboard. On this hide, with blue clay from the river bed, Jan Boetje taught the little ones their letters and the bigger ones their sums. Geography also he taught them, but it was such a geography as had never before been taught in the Platkops district. Yes, surely the world could never be so wonderful and strange as Jan Boetje made it to us (for I also went to his geography class) in my grandfather's waggon-house. And always when he spoke of the cities and the wonders that he had seen I would think how bitter must be the sorrow, and how great the sin, that had driven him from them to us. And when, as it sometimes happened, he would ask me afterwards: 'What shall we take for our reading lesson, Engela?' I would choose the fourteenth chapter of Chronicles or the eighth chapter of Kings.

Jan Boetje asked me one day: 'What makes you choose the Prayer in the Temple, Engela?'

And I, that did not know how close to love had come my pity, answered him: 'Because, Mijnheer, King Solomon who cries, "Hear thou in heaven thy dwelling-place, and when thou hearest forgive", prays also for the stranger from a far country.'

From that day Jan Boetje, who was kind and gentle with his scholars, was kind and gentle also with me. Many times now I found his eyes resting upon me, and when sometimes he came and sat quietly by my side as I sewed there would come a wild beating at my heart that was joy and pain together. Except to his scholars he had spoken to no one on the farm unless he first were spoken to. But now he spoke also to me, and when I went out in the veld with little Neeltje and her brothers, looking for all such things as are so wonderful to a child, Jan Boetje would come with us. And it was now that I taught Jan Boetje which berries he might eat and which would surely kill him, which leaves and bushes would cure a man of many sicknesses, and which roots and bulbs would quench his thirst. Many such simple things I taught him in the veld, and many, many times afterwards I thanked God that I had done so. Yes, all that my love was ever to do for Jan Boetje was but to guide him so in the wildnerness.

When Jan Boetje had been with us six months and more, it came to be little Neeltje's birthday. My grandmother had made it a holiday for the children, and Jan Boetje and I were to go with them, in a stump-cart drawn by two mules, up into a little ravine that lay beyond the Rooikranz drift. It was such a clear still day as often happens in our Ghamka valley in June month, and as we drove Neeltje and her brothers sang together in high sweet voices that made me think of the angels of God. Because of the weakness of my chest I myself could never sing, and yet that day, with Jan Boetje sitting quietly by my side, it was as if my heart were so full of song that he must surely hear it. Yes, I that am now so old, so old, was never again to feel such joy as swept through my soul and body then.

When we had driven about fifteen minutes from the farm we came to the Rooikranz drift. There had been but little rain and snow in the mountains that winter, and in the wide bed of the river there was then but one small stream. The banks of the river here are steep, and on the far side are the great red rocks that give the drift its name. Here the wild bees make their honey, and the white wild geese have their home. And that day how beautiful in the still clear air were the great red rocks against the blue sky, and how beautiful against the rocks were the white wings of the wild geese.

When we had crossed the little stream Jan Boetje stopped the cart and Neeltje and her brothers climbed out of it and ran across the river-bed shouting and clapping their hands to send the wild geese flying out from the rocks above them. Only I was left with Jan Boetje, and now when he whipped up the mules they would not move. Jan Boetje stood up in the cart and slashed at them, and they backed towards the stream. Jan Boetje jumped from the cart, and with the stick end of his whip struck the mules over the eyes, and his face, that had grown so dear to me, was suddenly strange and terrible to see. I cried to him: 'Jan Boetje! Jan Boetje!' but the weakness of my chest was upon me and I could make no sound. I rose in the cart to climb out of it, and as I rose Jan Boetje had a knife in his hand and dug it into the eyes of the mules to blind them. Sharp above the laughter of the children and the cries of the wild geese there came a terrible scream, and I fell from the cart on to the soft grey sand of the river-bed. When I rose again the mules were far down the stream, with the cart bumping and splintering behind them, and Jan Boetje after them. And so quickly had his madness come upon him that still the children laughed and clapped their hands, and still the wild geese flew among the great red rocks above us.

God knows how it was that I gathered the children together and, sending the bigger boys in haste back to the farm, came on myself with Neeltje and the little ones. My grandfather rode out to meet us. I told him what I could, but it was little that I could say, and he rode on down the river. When we came to the farm the children ran up to the house to my grandmother, but I myself went alone to the waggon-house. I opened the door and closed it after me again, and crept in the dark to Jan Boetje's chair. Long, long I sat there, with my head on my arms on his table, and it was as if in all the world there was nothing but a sorrow that must break my heart, and a darkness that smelt of tobacco and brandy and hides. Long, long I sat, and when at last my grandmother found me, 'My little Engela,' she said. 'The light of my heart! My treasure!'

The mules that Jan Boetje had blinded were found and shot by my grandfather, and for long the splinters of the cart lay scattered down the bed of the river. Jan Boetje himself my grandfather could not find, though he sent men through all the valley looking for him. And after many days it was thought that Jan Boetje had gone up-country through the pass at night. I was now for a time so ill that my father came down from his farm in Beaufort district to see me. He would have taken me back with him but in my weakness I cried to Grandmother to keep me. And my father, to whom everything that my grandmother did was right, once again left me to her.

My father had not been many days gone when old Franz Langermann came to my grandparents with news of Jan Boetje. Franz Langermann lived at the toll-house at the entrance to the pass through the mountains, and here Jan Boetje had come to him asking if he would sell him an old hand-cart that stood by the toll-gate. The hand-cart was a heavy clumsy one that the roadmen repairing the road through the pass had left behind them. Franz Langermann had asked Jan Boetje what he would do with such a cart? And Jan Boetje had answered: 'I that have killed mules must now work like a mule if I would live.' And he had said to Franz Langermann: 'Go to the farm of Nooitgedacht and say to Mevrouw Delport that all that is in the little tin box in my room is now hers in payment of the mules. But there is enough also to pay for the hand-cart if Mevrouw will but give you what is just.'

My grandmother asked Franz Langermann: 'But what is it then that Jan Boetje can do with a hand-cart?'

And Franz Langermann answered: 'Look now, Mevrouw! Through the country dragging the hand-cart like a mule he will go, gathering such things as he can find and afterwards selling them again that he may live. Look! Already out of a strap that I gave him Jan Boetje has made for himself his harness.'

My grandmother went to Jan Boetje's room and found the box as Franz Langermann had said. There was money in it enough to pay for the mules and the hand-cart, but there was nothing else. My grandmother took the box out to Franz Langermann and said: 'Take now the box as it is, and let Mijnheer give you himself what is just, but surely I will not take payment for the mules. Is it not seven months now that Jan Boetje has taught school to my grandchildren? God help Jan Boetje, and may he go in peace.'

But Franz Langermann would not take the box. 'Look now, Mevrouw,' he said, 'I swore to Jan Boetje that only for the hand-cart would I take the money, and all the rest would I leave.'

My grandmother put the box back in Jan Boetje's room, and gave to Franz Langermann instead such things as a man takes on a journey – biltong, and rusks and meal, and a little kid-skin full of dried fruits. As much as Franz Langermann could carry she gave him. But I, that would have given Jan Boetje all the world, in all the world had nothing that I might give. Only when Franz Langermann had left the house and crossed the yard did I run after him with my little Bible and cry: 'Franz Langermann! Franz Langermann! Say to Jan Boetje to come again to Nooitgedacht! Say to him that so long as I live I will wait!'

Yes, I said that. God knows what meaning my message had for me, or what meaning it ever had for Jan Boetje, but it was as if I must die if I could not send it.

That night my grandmother came, late in the night, to the room where I lay awake. She drew me into her arms and held me there, and out of the darkness I cried: 'Grandmother! Grandmother! Is love then such sorrow?'

And still I can hear the low clear voice that answered so strangely: 'A joy and a sorrow – a help and a hindrance – love comes at the last to be but what one makes it.'

It was the next day that my grandmother asked me to teach school for her in Jan Boetje's place. At first, because always the weakness of my chest had kept me timid, I did not think she could mean it. But she did mean it. And suddenly I knew that for Jan Boetje's sake I had strength to do it. And I called the children together and went down to the waggon-house and taught them.

All through the spring and summer months that year, getting books from the pastor in Platkops dorp to help me, I taught school for my grandmother. And because it was easy for me to love little children and to be patient with them, and because it was for Jan Boetje's sake that I did it, I came at last to forget the weakness of my chest and to make a good teacher. And day after day as I sat in his chair in the waggon-house I would think of Jan Boetje dragging his hand-cart across the veld. And day after day I would thank God that I had taught him which berries he might eat, and which bulbs would quench his thirst. Yes, in such poor and simple things as this had my love to find its comfort.

That year winter came early in the Ghamka valley, and there came a day in May month when the first fall of snow brought the river down in flood from the mountains. My grandfather took the children down to the drift to see it. I did not go, but sat working alone with my books in the waggon-house. And always on that day when I looked up through the open half-door, and saw, far above the orange grove, the peaks of the Zwartkops mountains so pure and white against the blue sky, there came a strange sad happiness about my heart, and it was as if I knew that Jan Boetje had at last found peace and were on his way to tell me so. Long, long I thought of him that day in the waggon-house, and when there came a heavy tramping of feet and a murmur of voices across the yard I paid no heed. And presently the voices died down, and my grandmother stood alone before me, with her eyes full of tears and in her hand a little damp and swollen book that I knew for the Bible I had sent to Jan Boetje . . . Down in the drift they had found his body – his harness still across his chest, the pole of his cart still in his hand.

That night I went alone to the room where Jan Boetje lay and drew back the sheet that covered him.

Across his chest, where the strap of his harness had rubbed it, the skin was hard and rough as leather. I knelt down by his side, and pressed my head against his breast. And through my heart there ran in farewell such foolish, tender words as my grandmother used to me – 'My joy and my sorrow . . . The light of my heart, and my treasure.'

Outa Sem and Father Christmas

» «

TOON VAN DEN HEEVER

TRANSLATED FROM THE AFRIKAANS BY
BARBARA MACKENZIE

Sweets were by now only a lingering memory and meat no more than a word to set the mouth watering. Three times a day it was Kaffir corn and ground acorn coffee; the Kaffir corn however boasted some trifling variations: first Kaffir corn porridge, then stamped Kaffir corn, and finally extra stiff Kaffir corn porridge.

'Ag, Outa Sem,' Jannie had lamented, 'I would so like a nice bit of meat, or a spoon of syrup over my porridge or a little sugar in my coffee!'

Jannie's father and brothers were away on commando, and he had been left behind alone on the farm under the care of Aia Koema, an elderly Griqua maidservant, and her husband Outa Sem.

One day when Jannie had been repeatedly sighing for the fleshpots of Egypt, Outa Sem, succumbing to his wry sense of humour, fried a piece of an old leather strap and deluded him into believing it was sheep's tripe. It smelt delicious, but when he bit into it, Jannie grimaced in such unutterable disgust that Outa Sem fell flat on his back, kicking his legs in the air in an ecstasy of delight. Unhappily for him his transports were of brief duration, for Aia Koema appeared on the scene and made short work of her lord and master. She descended on him with such fury that it was quite a time before he ventured into the kitchen again. However, old Sem was the kind one couldn't keep down for long, and when he fell into disgrace he always cast about for some means of reinstating himself.

That evening when Jannie was sitting as usual in front of the kitchen hearth, Outa Sem opened the conversation with his customary dramatic exordium. 'Stephanus, Johannes, Jacobus, Kastrol, and can you tell me what day tomorrow is?'

At his baptism Jannie had not been given a single one of those names, but Outa Sem's air of solemnity was enough to excite an immediate response.

'No, Outa Sem.'

'Well bless my soul; you mean to tell me, my Basie, that you really and truly don't know?'

'No, Outa Sem.'

'Stephanus!' – in a stern, admonishing tone – 'protect and save us, you are no better than an ignorant heathen! Aren't you ashamed of yourself?'

'Yes, Outa Sem; but what day is it then?'

'It is Christmas Day, the day on which our Blessed Saviour, the Lord, is going to be born.'

'But, Outa Sem! Surely He was always there; He made heaven and earth; then how can He be born only tomorrow?'

'Look, my Basie, it's great and wonderful things those, way above the heads of most big people; don't you start bothering about them yet awhile – one day when your beard starts sprouting, Outa Sem will explain it all to you.'

The time flew happily by as they sat recalling Christmas festivities of past years – the fun and excitement, and the mighty slaughtering, and the colossal roasts, and the Christmas presents, and old Sem was almost in tears at the thought of the fine tot of brandy he would have to do without.

Just before he said good night old Sem remarked: 'My Basie, I'm going to lie in wait for old Father Christmas tonight. Seems like to me he's trying to dodge coming to our farm; but I'll get him here for sure if I have to haul him along by his beard this very night! And you with not a stocking to your name. Well then, just hang this grain-bag at the end there of your bed tonight – only let me get my hands on him and there'll be a present for you – or there will be trouble for someone, big trouble!'

When Jannie woke up next morning he lay still, his thoughts idly wandering, till suddenly the discussion of the night before came back to him. Like a flash he was out of bed and pouncing on the sack. Yes, a sort of lump there! What was it? A mouth-organ? A clasp-knife? Gee, but it's something big – too big for a mouth-organ or a clasp-knife! He thrust his hand into the sack, shut his eyes tight and groped around. Goodness, how funny the things felt. He dragged them out: a little bottle of sugary honey, then a few pieces of sweet mealie-cane cut in lengths, and finally a giant of a guinea-fowl! And Jannie voiced his delight so exuberantly that Outa Sem and Aia Koema came running in to share in the jubilation.

About eleven o'clock that morning the guinea-fowl began to send forth a heavenly odour – so delicious that Jannie could not bear to stay outside any longer. However, he was not wasting his time on mere olfactory bliss, for while he was watching Aia Koema's activities his jaws were busy dealing with the sweet cane. Just then in walked Outa Sem, stooping under a yoke, at each end of which swung a bucket of spring water with a wreath of willow twigs in it to prevent spilling. He stopped dead and his nostrils blew in and out like the flanks of an exhausted horse.

'High-tigh-tigh, folks! It smells here very much as if you'll be able to eat till you burst today if you don't look out!'

'Yes, Outa Sem' – Jannie's words came tumbling over each other – 'oh thank you, thank you ever so much, Outa Sem, for going to fetch Father Christmas. But, Outa Sem, where did he find the presents?'

'At the back of the moon – that's where one finds all sorts of things.'

'But tell me, Outa Sem, how did you manage to get him here? Was it a battle to the death?'

Old Sem unhooked the buckets and placed them on the kitchen bench. Then with the eye of an expert he first made an estimate of the degree of goodwill that prevailed in Aia Koema's direction. Only then did he lower himself comfortably on to the bench and let out a sigh: 'Aighty-ty, my Basie, perhaps if Aia Koema won't mind giving me a little something to wet my whistle, I'll try to get it working.'

Without a word Aia Koema poured him out a mug of the acorn coffee.

'Child of your father, it was no joke getting that old Father Christmas here, no, by golly it wasn't! For donkeys' and donkeys' years he has been driving a team of crack reindeer drawing his carriage, and he skims over the earth so that his wheels only just graze the top of a steep hill every now and then. Now as you know, his old transport road here runs right along the lowest part of the Rooikops ridges, but the scent of his trail lies only on the tops of the mountains close by. And how was a poor old Outa Sem like me to manage to follow his spoor and catch him single-handed? So I took a few sheaves of young barley to tempt his reindeer, and a terrapin to make them jib if perhaps I got them on the leeward side, and my sling to back up my words just in case the old chap became unreasonable and lost his temper with me. Then I trotted off way over there towards the Sugarbush hills, where it's quite high up, to see if I could catch a glimpse of the old fellow.

'But what do you know? I hadn't even crossed Deelfontein Nek when I spotted right in front of me on the road someone limping along with a sack on his back.

'At first I had it in mind just to shoot past him because I thought then it was only one of these Indian traders, but then it struck me you don't find Indians wandering about in the Transvaal any more these days. So I drew a little nearer in the moonlight and peered at him from under the brim of my hat –

and guess what! On my soul, if it wasn't old Father Christmas, his very own self.

'"Oh my goodness gracious, Baas Christmas!" I cried, "and how come the Oubaas travels tonight on Shanks's old pony just like a Jew trader? What's happened to the transport?"

'"Ag, my dear good old Outa Sem," answered Father Christmas and plumped down on his bundle for a bit of a rest so that his feet could cool off, "ag, my dear Outa Sem, ever since Golly Roberts came into the country, I've had nothing but worry, vexation and sorrow! The night before last I outspanned at Floors Venter's over there at Dwaalhoek, down near the Vaal River, and drove my reindeer in amongst his animals in the kraal – and to think it was my crack team too! Bad luck that just that very night one of Golly Roberts's columns of Tommies turned up to liquidate young Floors's beasties – I suppose you know old Tommy isn't too bright when it's a question of cattle. I was just going to give them a friendly hail but already it was all up with my reindeer!"

'Now, Sem my boy, I thought to myself, tonight you mustn't waste time standing and yapping; so I gave the bundle a few prods and said: "How 'bout a little something, Oubaas, for my Basie over at Rietfontein farm No. 144 – you know it, don't you, Oubaas, just a little bit this side of Daspoort? Isn't there perhaps something I could take him?"

'"Ag Outa Sem, my dear good chap, now I really am so sorry. The presents I brought specially for him are still lying in my carriage in Floors Venter's yard; they were too heavy to carry. There was a dapple-grey rocking-horse with red saddle and bridle; a black airgun – not one of these shiny tin affairs – with a few boxes of pellets; then there was a black-handled clasp-knife with two blades, a Rodgers, no less; there was . . . But what's the use of crying over spilt milk? Come, let's look if we can't find something for him here."

'Father Christmas shook out all his stock on the road and we gave the things a look-through: there were a few plugs of black tobacco and some rolls of chewing-tobacco; one or two little bottles of lavender water with bits of ribbon round the neck; a couple of pipes and a razor with a strop; there were tapes and lengths of whale-bone, lace and needle-cases. Old Father Christmas shook his head gloomily. "No, Outa Sem, I don't seem to have a thing here that will make your Basie's heart jump for joy."

'"But look now, Baas Christmas," taking my courage in both hands I put it to him, "couldn't we make a bit of a try for Vaal River again perhaps?"

'"What! with these poor old feet? Bless me, Outa Sem, I've only just come from there! How am I ever to manage it? I've still got to visit Heidelberg – and Boksburg – and Elandsfontein, and all that on my own two feet!"

'"Oh my goodness, Baas Christmas," I cried artfully, "but Baas will never in this world be able to manage that!"

'"Too true, too true!" groaned Father Christmas and sat down despondently on his bundle and rubbed his sore feet one against the other.

'"Now look here, Baas Christmas," I said ever so cunningly, "don't you lose heart, for where there's a will there's a way. You come along with me to my baas's farm just the other side of that craggy little hill, then I'll transport you and your stock just wherever you want to go. We've got tons of vehicles, animals, harness, everything there."

'When we reached here the dear old boy was proper mad because he saw at a glance that all our cattle and horses had joined the English army. I coaxed him ever so nicely: "Wait a bit, Oubaas, just a sec and you will see how a smart lad can make something out of nothing." Then I pulled the old spider carriage out of the clump of reeds where our Oubaas had hidden it from the Tommies – or loaned it out to the frogs. I pitched it upside down and whipped off the wheels. Then I slammed it full of nails, top and bottom, back and front, left and right, till it looked just like a young porcupine.

'To every nail I tied a thread of cotton, this one long, that one short and so on, and at the other end of each thread I fastened a dung-beetle. No time at all the grass was black with the swarm of creatures and they were piled one on top of the other like locusts on a broom-bush. They were kicking over the traces and tangling up the harness like a span of foolish young oxen. It wasn't long before old Father Christmas was muttering and grumbling; so I just had to soothe and coax him again. Didn't I know that where cattle are scarce the dung-beetles starve? So I went a little way off and then I was back with a long whipstock and a little pat of dung kneaded on to the end the way boys load their claysticks when they play.

'"Jump to it, Oubaas!" I shouted, "jump or you'll be left behind!"

'Father Christmas's trousers had barely so much as touched the seat when I stuck out the whip in front, and whirra-wirra, folks! What's going on? When the dung-beetles took the strain, the bottom of the old spider shot over the palmiet rushes so that they were almost flattened. I raised the tip of the whipstock ever so little and I swear to goodness the wings began to hum like a million bees all mad as mad! I lifted the whip just the least bit higher still and 'pon my soul you should have seen how the farm dropped away from under us, all sideways, and I couldn't make out a thing except the dam shining far off below us!

'We skidded to the left to pass a big heavy cloud and almost grazed the moon's left horn! Just for a joke I made a few sharp twists and turns; and then I also wanted to see if Father Christmas would get the wind up or take it all in his stride. But no fear! When I swerved round so that the old spider was practically lying on its side against the wind, the old boy gave such a shout of laughter that his mouth looked just like a bugle, and he yelled at me: "Sem! Sem, old so-and-so! By gum, Sem, you're a lad in a thousand! You're the champ, Outa Sem, the tops, the king of them all!"

'We loaded up at Floors Venter's, and before the moon had tucked itself away Heidelberg was behind us. At dorps and farms where there were still people living, we off-loaded presents, and the lighter the spider became the faster we flew through the air. By first cockcrow we were already streaking back home, just passing Nigel on our left.

'Now you know, a whole night's work like that can make one's cattle as hungry as wolves. It so happened that to the right of Heidelberg there was a bunch of hands-uppers and other old jokers who had been able to hang on to their cattle and I could see my team was beginning to be drawn downwards. Perhaps it was the pat on my whip getting too dried out by the wind. The first time we flew so low Father Christmas was delighted, and while we were skimming between Doors van Tonder's mealie patches, he was helping himself right and left to the sweet canes and piling them up on board. By gum, it was jolly to see how the old boy was enjoying himself. He was singing away for all he was worth into the wind that was plastering his beard flat against his cheeks.

'The sky was growing pink as we sailed over Jan Vermaak's great big bluegum trees and then, high-tigh-tigh folks, I tell you I got the biggest fright of all the frights of my life! And for why? Jan Vermaak's kraal was full up with red Afrikander cattle! The beetles must have spotted it right away because the humming from their wings rose up like a violin string that you've screwed to the limit, and they pelted straight for the kraal at top speed.

'"Up! Up!" yelled Father Christmas. "Climb, boys, climb!" I roared.

'Nothing doing! In the end I was holding the whip practically upright, but not a climb out of the beetles. The wall of the kraal was rushing at us like an express train! It got bigger and bigger and nearer and nearer and . . . wha-a-am!

'Cart upset? Cart upset my foot! Wirra-warra, but I ask you, folks, did Outa Sem see stars that time! We just hung on like a couple of monkeys. The first bounce of the old spider shot it up off the kraal wall and it whizzed as light as a bird right over the kraal, and at the second bounce it landed in the dunghill on the far side of the kraal's drain-hole; and when it bounced for the third time, Outa Sem swears to you it dropped right on top of Wildeals Koppie bottom up, and all I could see was Father Christmas's beard sticking out at one side, just like the tail feathers of a widow-bird caught in a trap.

'I put my shoulder right under the axle and heaved till my knees were all a-tremble. Out crawled Father Christmas on all fours and combed the dung from his beard with his fingers. And when I'd shoved over the spider so that it was right side up once more, bless me if I didn't see a huge guinea-fowl lying there that Father Christmas had landed on and squashed to death.

'But oh my golly, what a mess the things were in! The dapple-grey rocking-horse was as battered as Father Christmas – it looked just like a rotten mealie-cob that had been through a threshing machine. The red saddle and the bridle were in ribbons. The airgun was twisted like a corkscrew. As for the Rodgers clasp-knife, it had grown itself legs and vanished.

'When Father Christmas stood up, he rocked a little on his feet like a man who has taken more than a drop too much. Then he rummaged in the pocket of his coat and hauled out the bottle of honey; it wasn't even cracked because it must have landed right on top of the guinea-fowl. Then he put the honey, the sweet canes and the guinea-fowl all together, and said rather sadly: "Take these things, Outa Sem, my dear good fellow, and put them in your Basie's grain-bag with my compliments. Such a pity about the other fine presents, but as your own Oubaas always says, no use crying over spilt milk and what's done is done. You're a champ, Outa Sem, the tops, one of the best! It's fact and I don't deny it; in future you can go driving as much as you like, but you don't catch Father Christmas ever going with you again, because I've learned how much I can chew at one bite!"

'The last I saw of him, he was plodding over the Nek, away over there on the highway, hobbling all along side along, pretty much as the old song has it!'

The Rooinek

» «

HERMAN CHARLES BOSMAN

Rooineks, said Oom Schalk Lourens, are queer. For instance, there was that day when my nephew Hannes and I had dealings with a couple of Englishmen near Dewetsdorp. It was shortly after Sanna's Post, and Hannes and I were lying behind a rock watching the road. Hannes spent odd moments like that in what he called a useful way. He would file the points of his Mauser cartridges on a piece of flat stone until the lead showed through the steel, in that way making them into dum-dum bullets.

I often spoke to my nephew Hannes about that.

'Hannes,' I used to say. 'That is a sin. The Lord is looking at you.'

'That's all right,' Hannes replied. 'The Lord knows that this is the Boer War, and in war-time He will always forgive a little foolishness like this, especially as the English are so many.'

Anyway, as we lay behind that rock we saw, far down the road, two horsemen come galloping up. We remained perfectly still and let them approach to within four hundred paces. They were English officers. They were mounted on first-rate horses and their uniforms looked very fine and smart. They were the most stylish-looking men I had seen for some time, and I felt quite ashamed of my own ragged trousers and veldskoens. I was glad that I was behind a rock and they couldn't see me. Especially as my jacket was also torn all the way down the back, as a result of my having had, three days before, to get through a barbed-wire fence rather quickly. I just got through in time, too. The veld-kornet, who was a fat man and couldn't run so fast, was about twenty yards behind me. And he remained on the wire with a bullet through him. All through the Boer War I was pleased that I was thin and never troubled with corns.

Hannes and I fired just about the same time. One of the officers fell off his horse. He struck the road with his shoulders and rolled over twice, kicking up the red dust as he turned. Then the other soldier did a queer thing. He drew

87

up his horse and got off. He gave just one look in our direction. Then he led his horse up to where the other man was twisting and struggling on the ground. It took him a little while to lift him on to his horse, for it is no easy matter to pick up a man like that when he is helpless. And he did all this slowly and calmly, as though he was not concerned about the fact that the men who had shot his friend were lying only a few hundred yards away. He managed in some way to support the wounded man across the saddle, and walked on beside the horse. After going a few yards he stopped and seemed to remember something. He turned round and waved at the spot where he imagined we were hiding, as though inviting us to shoot. During all that time I had simply lain watching him, astonished at his coolness.

But when he waved his hand I thrust another cartridge into the breach of my Martini and aimed. At that distance I couldn't miss. I aimed very carefully and was just on the point of pulling the trigger when Hannes put his hand on the barrel and pushed up my rifle.

'Don't shoot, Oom Schalk,' he said. 'That's a brave man.'

I looked at Hannes in surprise. His face was very white. I said nothing, and allowed my rifle to sink down on to the grass, but I couldn't understand what had come over my nephew. It seemed that not only was that Englishman queer, but that Hannes was also queer. That's all nonsense not killing a man just because he's brave. If he's a brave man and he's fighting on the wrong side, that's all the more reason to shoot him.

I was with my nephew Hannes for another few months after that. Then one day, in a skirmish near the Vaal River, Hannes with a few dozen other burghers was cut off from the commando and had to surrender. That was the last I ever saw of him. I heard later on that, after taking him prisoner, the English searched Hannes and found dum-dum bullets in his possession. They shot him for that. I was very much grieved when I heard of Hannes's death. He had always been full of life and high spirits. Perhaps Hannes was right in saying that the Lord didn't mind about a little foolishness like dum-dum bullets. But the mistake he made was in forgetting that the English did mind.

I was in the veld until they made peace. Then we laid down our rifles and went home. What I knew my farm by was the hole under the koppie where I quarried slate-stones for the threshing-floor. That was about all that remained as I left it. Everything else was gone. My home was burnt down. My lands were laid waste. My cattle and sheep were slaughtered. Even the stones I had piled for the kraals were pulled down. My wife came out of the concentration camp and we went together to look at our old farm. My wife had gone into the concentration camp with our two children, but she came out alone. And when

I saw her again and noticed the way she had changed, I knew that I, who had been through all the fighting, had not seen the Boer War.

Neither Sannie nor I had the heart to go on farming again on that same place. It would be different without the children playing about the house and getting into mischief. We got paid out some money by the new Government for part of our losses. So I bought a waggon and oxen and we left the Free State, which was not even the Free State any longer. It was now called the Orange River Colony.

We trekked right through the Transvaal into the northern part of the Marico Bushveld. Years ago, as a boy, I had trekked through that same country with my parents. Now that I went there again I felt that it was still a good country. It was on the far side of the Dwarsberge, near Derdepoort, that we got a Government farm. Afterwards other farmers trekked in there as well. One or two of them had also come from the Free State, and I knew them. There were also a few Cape rebels whom I had seen on commando. All of us had lost relatives in the war. Some had died in the concentration camps or on the battlefield. Others had been shot for going into rebellion. So, taken all in all, we who had trekked into that part of the Marico that lay nearest the Bechuanaland border were very bitter against the English.

Then it was that the rooinek came.

It was in the first year of our having settled around Derdepoort. We heard that an Englishman had bought a farm next to Gerhardus Grobbelaar. This was when we were sitting in the voorkamer of Willem Odendaal's house, which was used as a post office. Once a week the post-cart came up with letters from Zeerust, and we came together at Willem Odendaal's house and talked and smoked and drank coffee. Very few of us ever got letters, and then it was mostly demands to pay for the boreholes that had been drilled on our farms or for cement and fencing materials. But every week regularly we went for the post. Sometimes the post-cart didn't come, because the Green River was in flood, and we would most of us have gone home without noticing it, if somebody didn't speak about it.

When Koos Steyn heard that an Englishman was coming to live amongst us he got up from the riempies bank.

'No, kêrels,' he said. 'Always when the Englishman comes, it means that a little later the Boer has got to shift. I'll pack up my waggon and make coffee, and just trek first thing tomorrow morning.'

Most of us laughed then. Koos Steyn often said funny things like that. But some didn't laugh. Somehow, there seemed to be too much truth in Koos Steyn's words.

We discussed the matter and decided that if we Boers in the Marico could help it the rooinek would not stay amongst us too long. About half an hour later one of Willem Odendaal's children came in and said that there was a strange waggon coming along the big road. We went to the door and looked out. As the waggon came nearer we saw that it was piled up with all kinds of furniture and also sheets of iron and farming implements. There was so much stuff on the waggon that the tent had to be taken off to get everything on.

The waggon rolled along and came to a stop in front of the house. With the waggon there were one white man and two kafirs. The white man shouted something to the kafirs and threw down the whip. Then he walked up to where we were standing. He was dressed just as we were, in shirt and trousers and veldskoens, and he had dust all over him. But when he stepped over a thorn-bush we saw that he had got socks on. Therefore we knew that he was an Englishman.

Koos Steyn was standing in front of the door.

The Englishman went up to him and held out his hand.

'Good afternoon,' he said in Afrikaans. 'My name is Webber.'

Koos shook hands with him.

'My name is Prince Lord Alfred Milner,' Koos Steyn said.

That was when Lord Milner was Governor of the Transvaal, and we all laughed. The rooinek also laughed.

'Well, Lord Prince,' he said, 'I can speak your language a little, and I hope that later on I'll be able to speak it better. I'm coming to live here, and I hope that we'll all be friends.'

He then came round to all of us, but the others turned away and refused to shake hands with him. He came up to me last of all; I felt sorry for him, and although his nation had dealt unjustly with my nation, and I had lost both my children in the concentration camp, still it was not so much the fault of this Englishman. It was the fault of the English Government, who wanted our gold mines. And it was also the fault of Queen Victoria, who didn't like Oom Paul Kruger, because they say that when he went over to London Oom Paul spoke to her only once for a few minutes. Oom Paul Kruger said that he was a married man and he was afraid of widows.

When the Englishman Webber went back to his waggon Koos Steyn and I walked with him. He told us that he had bought the farm next to Gerhardus Grobbelaar and that he didn't know much about sheep and cattle and mealies, but he had bought a few books on farming, and he was going to learn all he could out of them. When he said that, I looked away towards the poort. I didn't want him to see that I was laughing. But with Koos Steyn it was otherwise.

'Man,' he said, 'let me see those books.'

Webber opened the box at the bottom of the waggon and took out about six big books with green covers.

'These are very good books,' Koos Steyn said. 'Yes, they are very good for the white ants. The white ants will eat them all in two nights.'

As I have told you, Koos Steyn was a funny fellow and no man could help laughing at the things he said.

Those were bad times. There was drought, and we could not sow mealies. The dams dried up, and there was only last year's grass on the veld. We had to pump water out of the boreholes for weeks at a time. Then the rains came and for a while things were better.

Now and again I saw Webber. From what I heard about him it seemed that he was working hard. But of course no rooinek can make a living out of farming, unless they send him money every month from England. And we found out that almost all the money Webber had was what he had paid on the farm. He was always reading in those green books what he had to do. It's lucky that those books are written in English, and that the Boers can't read them. Otherwise many more farmers would be ruined every year. When his cattle had the heart-water, or his sheep had the blue-tongue, or there were cut-worms or stalk-borers in his mealies, Webber would look it all up in his books. I suppose that when the kafirs stole his sheep he would look that up, too.

Still, Koos Steyn helped Webber quite a lot and taught him a number of things, so that matters did not go as badly with him as they would have if he had only acted according to the lies that were printed in those green books. Webber and Koos Steyn became very friendly. Koos Steyn's wife had had a baby just a few weeks before Webber came. It was the first child they had after being married seven years, and they were very proud of it. It was a girl. Koos Steyn said that he would sooner it had been a boy; but that, even so, it was better than nothing. Right from the first Webber had taken a liking to that child, who was christened Jemima after her mother. Often when I passed Koos Steyn's house I saw the Englishman sitting on the front stoep with the child on his knees.

In the meantime the other farmers around there became annoyed on account of Koos Steyn's friendship with the rooinek. They said that Koos was a handsopper and a traitor to his country. He was intimate with a man who had helped to bring about the downfall of the Afrikaner nation. Yet it was not fair to call Koos a handsopper. Koos had lived in the Graaff-Reinet District when the war broke out, so that he was a Cape Boer and need not have fought. Nevertheless, he joined up with a Free State commando and remained until peace was made, and if at any time the English had caught him they would have shot him as a rebel, in the same way that they shot Scheepers and many others.

Gerhardus Grobbelaar spoke about this once when we were in Willem Odendaal's post office.

'You are not doing right,' Gerhardus said; 'Boer and Englishman have been enemies since before Slagtersnek. We've lost this war, but someday we'll win. It's the duty we owe to our children's children to stand against the rooineks. Remember the concentration camps.'

There seemed to me to be truth in what Gerhardus said.

'But the English are here now, and we've got to live with them,' Koos answered. 'When we get to understand one another perhaps we won't need to fight any more. This Englishman Webber is learning Afrikaans very well, and some day he might almost be one of us. The only thing I can't understand about him is that he has a bath every morning. But if he stops that and if he doesn't brush his teeth any more you will hardly be able to tell him from a Boer.'

Although he made a joke about it, I felt that in what Koos Steyn said there was also truth.

Then, the year after the drought, the miltsiek broke out. The miltsiek seemed to be in the grass of the veld, and in the water of the dams, and even in the air the cattle breathed. All over the place I would find cows and oxen lying dead. We all became very discouraged. Nearly all of us in that part of the Marico had started farming again on what the Government had given us. Now that the stock died we had nothing. First the drought had put us back to where we were when we started. Now with the miltsiek we couldn't hope to do anything. We couldn't even sow mealies, because, at the rate at which the cattle were dying, in a short while we would have no oxen left to pull the plough. People talked of selling what they had and going to look for work on the gold mines. We sent a petition to the Government, but that did no good.

It was then that somebody got hold of the idea of trekking. In a few days we were talking of nothing else. But the question was where we could trek to. They would not allow us into Rhodesia for fear we might spread the miltsiek there as well. And it was useless going to any other part of the Transvaal. Somebody mentioned German West Africa. We had none of us been there before, and I suppose that really was the reason why, in the end, we decided to go there.

'The blight of the English is over South Africa,' Gerhardus Grobbelaar said. 'We'll remain here only to die. We must go away somewhere where there is not the Englishman's flag.'

In a few weeks' time we arranged everything. We were going to trek across the Kalahari into German territory. Everything we had we loaded up. We drove the cattle ahead and followed behind on our waggons. There were five families: the Steyns, the Grobbelaars, the Odendaals, the Ferreiras and Sannie and I. Webber also came with us. I think it was not so much that he was anxious to leave as that he and Koos Steyn had become very much attached to one another, and the Englishman did not wish to remain alone behind.

The youngest person in our trek was Koos Steyn's daughter Jemima, who was then about eighteen months old. Being the baby, she was a favourite with all of us.

Webber sold his waggon and went with Koos Steyn's trek..

When at the end of the first day we outspanned several miles inside the Bechuanaland Protectorate, we were very pleased that we were done with the Transvaal, where we had had so much misfortune. Of course, the Protectorate was also British territory, but all the same we felt happier there than we had done in our country. We saw Webber every day now, and although he was a foreigner with strange ways, and would remain an Uitlander until he died, yet we disliked him less than before for being a rooinek.

It was on the first Sunday that we reached Malopolole. For the first part of our way the country remained Bushveld. There were the same kind of thorn-trees that grew in the Marico, except that they became fewer the deeper into the Kalahari that we went. Also, the ground became more and more sandy, until even before we came to Malopolole it was all desert. But scattered thorn-bushes remained all the way. That Sunday we held a religious service. Gerhardus Grobbelaar read a chapter out of the Bible and offered up a prayer. We sang a number of psalms, after which Gerhardus prayed again. I shall always remember that Sunday and the way we sat on the ground beside one of the waggons, listening to Gerhardus. That was the last Sunday that we were all together.

The Englishman sat next to Koos Steyn and the baby Jemima lay down in front of him. She played with Webber's fingers and tried to bite them. It was funny to watch her. Several times Webber looked down at her and smiled. I thought then that although Webber was not one of us, yet Jemima certainly did not know it. Maybe in a thing like that the child was wiser than we were. To her it made no difference that the man whose fingers she bit was born in another country and did not speak the same language that she did.

There are many things that I remember about that trek into the Kalahari. But one thing that now seems strange to me is the way in which, right from the first day, we took Gerhardus Grobbelaar for our leader. Whatever he said we just seemed to do without talking very much about it. We all felt that it was right simply because Gerhardus wished it. That was a strange thing about our trek. It was not simply that we knew Gerhardus had got the Lord with him – for we did know that – but it was rather that we believed in Gerhardus as well as in the Lord. I think that even if Gerhardus Grobbelaar had been an ungodly man we would still have followed him in exactly the same way. For when you are in the desert and there is no water and the way back is long, then you feel that it is better to have with you a strong man who does not read the Book very much, than a man who is good and religious, and yet does not seem sure how far to trek each day and where to outspan.

But Gerhardus Grobbelaar was a man of God. At the same time there was something about him that made you feel that it was only by acting as he advised that you could succeed. There was only one other man I have ever known who found it so easy to get people to do as he wanted. And that was Paul Kruger. He was very much like Gerhardus Grobbelaar, except that Gerhardus was less quarrelsome. But of the two, Paul Kruger was the bigger man.

Only once do I remember Gerhardus losing his temper. And that was with the Nagmaal at Elandsberg. It was on a Sunday, and we were camped out beside the Crocodile River. Gerhardus went round early in the morning from waggon to waggon and told us that he wanted everybody to come over to where his waggon stood. The Lord had been good to us at that time, so that we had had much rain and our cattle were fat. Gerhardus explained that he wanted to hold a service, to thank the Lord for all His good works, but more especially for what He had done for the farmers of the northern part of the Groot Marico District. This was a good plan, and we all came together with our Bibles and hymn-books. But one man, Karel Pieterse, remained behind at his waggon. Twice Gerhardus went to call him, but Karel Pieterse lay down on the grass and would not get up to come to the service. He said it was all right thanking the Lord now that there had been rains, but what about all those seasons when there had been drought and the cattle had died of thirst? Gerhardus Grobbelaar shook his head sadly, and said there was nothing he could do then, as it was Sunday. But he prayed that the Lord would soften Brother Pieterse's heart, and he finished off his prayer by saying that in any case, in the morning, he would help to soften the brother's heart himself.

The following morning Gerhardus walked over with a sjambok and an ox-riem to where Karel Pieterse sat before his fire, watching the kafir making coffee. They were both of them men who were big in the body. But Gerhardus got the better of the struggle. In the end he won. He fastened Karel to the wheel of his own waggon with the ox-riem. Then he thrashed him with the sjambok while Karel's wife and children were looking on.

That had happened years before. But nobody had forgotten. And now, in the Kalahari, when Gerhardus summoned us to a service, it was noticed that no man stayed away.

Just outside Malopolole is a muddy stream that is dry part of the year and part of the year has a foot or so of brackish water. We were lucky in being there just at the time when it had water. Early the following morning we filled up the water-barrels that we had put on our waggons before leaving the Marico. We were going right into the desert, and we did not know where we would get water again. Even the Bakwena kafirs could not tell us for sure.

'The Great Dorstland Trek,' Koos Steyn shouted as we got ready to move off. 'Anyway, we won't fare as badly as the Dorstland Trekkers. We'll lose less cattle than they did because we've got less to lose. And seeing that we are only five families, not more than about a dozen of us will die of thirst.'

I thought it was bad luck for Koos Steyn to make jokes like that about the Dorstland Trek, and I think the others felt the same about it. We trekked right through that day, and it was all desert. By sunset we had not come across a sign of water anywhere. Abraham Ferreira said towards evening that perhaps it would be better if we went back to Malopolole and tried to find out for sure which was the best way of getting through the Kalahari. But the rest said that there was no need to do that, since we would be sure to come across water the next day. And, anyway, we were Doppers and, having once set out, we were not going to turn back. But after we had given the cattle water our barrels did not have too much left in them.

By the middle of the following day all our water had given out except a little that we kept for the children. But we pushed on. Now that we had gone so far we were afraid to go back because of the long way that we would have to go without water to get back to Malopolole. In the evening we were very anxious. We all knelt down in the sand and prayed. Gerhardus Grobbelaar's voice sounded very deep and earnest when he besought God to have mercy on us, especially for the sakes of the little ones. He mentioned the baby Jemima by name. The Englishman knelt down beside me, and I noticed that he shivered when Gerhardus mentioned Koos Steyn's child.

It was moonlight. All around us was the desert. Our waggons seemed very small and lonely; there was something about them that looked very mournful. The women and the children put their arms round one another and wept a long while. Our kafirs stood some distance away and watched us. My wife Sannie put her hand in mine, and I thought of the concentration camp. Poor woman, she had suffered much. And I knew that her thoughts were the same as my own: that after all it was perhaps better that our children should have died then than now.

We had got so far into the desert that we began telling one another that we must be near the end. Although we knew that German West was far away, and that in the way we had been travelling we had got little more than into the beginning of the Kalahari, yet we tried to tell one another lies about how near water was likely to be. But, of course, we told those lies only to one another. Each man in his own heart knew what the real truth was. And later on we even stopped telling one another lies about what a good chance we had of getting out alive. You can understand how badly things had gone with us when you know that we no longer troubled about hiding our position from the women and children. They wept, some of them. But that made no difference then. Nobody tried to comfort the women and children who cried. We knew that tears were useless, and yet somehow at that hour we felt that the weeping of the women was not less useless than the courage of the men. After a while there was no more weeping in our camp. Some of the women who lived through the dreadful things of the days that came after, and got safely back to the Transvaal, never again wept. What they had seen appeared to have hardened them. In this respect they had become as men. I think that is the saddest thing that ever happens in this world, when women pass through great suffering that makes them become as men.

That night we hardly slept. Early the next morning the men went out to look for water. An hour after sun-up Ferreira came back and told us that he had found a muddy pool a few miles away. We all went there, but there wasn't much water. Still, we got a little, and that made us feel better. It was only when it came to driving our cattle towards the mudhole that we found our kafirs had deserted us during the night. After we had gone to sleep they had stolen away. Some of the weaker cattle couldn't get up to go to the pool. So we left them. Some were trampled to death or got choked in the mud, and we had to pull them out to let the rest get to the hole. It was pitiful.

Just before we left, one of Ferreira's daughters died. We scooped a hole in the sand and buried her.

So we decided to trek back.

After his daughter was dead Abraham Ferreira went up to Gerhardus and told him that if we had taken his advice earlier on and gone back, his daughter would not have died.

'Your daughter is dead now, Abraham,' Gerhardus said. 'It is no use talking about her any longer. We all have to die some day. I refused to go back earlier. I have decided to go back now.'

Abraham Ferreira looked Gerhardus in the eyes and laughed. I shall always remember how that laughter sounded in the desert. In Abraham's voice there was the hoarseness of the sand and thirst. His voice was cracked with what the desert had done to him; his face was lined and his lips were blackened.

But there was nothing about him that spoke of grief for his daughter's death.

'Your daughter is still alive, Oom Gerhardus,' Abraham Ferreira said, pointing to the waggon wherein lay Gerhardus's wife, who was weak, and the child to whom she had given birth only a few months before. 'Yes, she is still alive . . . so far.'

Ferreira turned away laughing, and we heard him a little later explaining to his wife in cracked tones about the joke he had made.

Gerhardus Grobbelaar merely watched the other man walk away without saying anything. So far we had followed Gerhardus through all things, and our faith in him had been great. But now that he had decided to trek back we lost our belief in him. We lost it suddenly, too. We knew that it was best to turn back, and that to continue would mean that we would all die in the Kalahari. And yet, if Gerhardus had said we must still go on we would have done so. We would have gone through with him right to the end. But now that he as much as said he was beaten by the desert we had no more faith in Gerhardus. That is why I have said that Paul Kruger was a greater man than Gerhardus. Because Paul Kruger was that kind of man whom we still worshipped even when he decided to retreat. If it had been Paul Kruger who told us that we had to go back we would have returned with strong hearts. We would have retained exactly the same love for our leader, even if we knew that he was beaten. But from the moment that Gerhardus said we must go back we all knew that he was no longer our leader. Gerhardus knew that also.

We knew what lay between us and Malopolole and there was grave doubt in our hearts when we turned our waggons round. Our cattle were very weak, and we had to inspan all that could walk. We hadn't enough yokes, and therefore we cut poles from the scattered bushes and tied them to the trek chains. As we were also without skeis we had to fasten the necks of the oxen straight on to the yokes with strops, and several of the oxen got strangled.

Then we saw that Koos Steyn had become mad. For he refused to return. He inspanned his oxen and got ready to trek on. His wife sat silent in the waggon with the baby; wherever her husband went she would go, too. That was only right, of course. Some women kissed her goodbye, and cried. But Koos Steyn's wife did not cry. We reasoned with Koos about it, but he said that he had made up his mind to cross the Kalahari, and he was not going to turn back just for nonsense.

'But, man,' Gerhardus Grobbelaar said to him, 'you've got no water to drink.'

'I'll drink coffee then,' Koos Steyn answered, laughing as always, and took up the whip and walked away beside the waggon. And Webber went off with him, just because Koos Steyn had been good to him, I suppose. That's why I have said that Englishmen are queer. Webber must have known that if Koos Steyn had not actually gone wrong in the head, still what he was doing now was madness, and yet he stayed with him.

We separated. Our waggons went slowly back to Malopolole. Koos Steyn's waggon went deeper into the desert. My waggon went last. I looked back at the Steyns. At that moment Webber also looked round. He saw me and waved his hand. It reminded me of that day in the Boer War when that other Englishman, whose companion we had shot, also turned round and waved.

Eventually we got back to Malopolole with two waggons and a handful of cattle. We abandoned the other waggons. Awful things happened on that desert. A number of children died. Gerhardus Grobbelaar's waggon was in front of me. Once I saw a bundle being dropped through the side of the waggon-tent. I knew what it was. Gerhardus would not trouble to bury his dead child, and his wife lay in the tent too weak to move. So I got off the waggon and scraped a small heap of sand over the body. All I remember of the rest of the journey to Malopolole is the sun and the sand. And the thirst. Although at one time we thought that we had lost our way, yet that did not matter much to us. We were past feeling. We could neither pray nor curse, our parched tongues cleaving to the roofs of our mouths.

Until today I am not sure how many days we were on our way back, unless I sit down and work it all out, and then I suppose I get it wrong. We got back to Malopolole and water. We said we would never go away from there again. I don't think that even those parents who had lost children grieved about them then. They were stunned with what they had gone through. But I knew that later on it would all come back again. Then they would remember things about shallow graves in the sand, and Gerhardus Grobbelaar and his wife would think of a little bundle lying out in the Kalahari. And I knew how they would feel.

Afterwards we fitted out a waggon with fresh oxen; we took an abundant supply of water and went back into the desert to look for the Steyn family. With the help of the Sechuana kafirs, who could see tracks that we could not see, we found the waggon. The oxen had been outspanned; a few lay dead beside the waggon. The kafirs pointed out to us footprints on the sand, which showed which way those two men and that woman had gone.

In the end we found them.

Koos Steyn and his wife lay side by side in the sand; the woman's head rested on the man's shoulder; her long hair had become loosened, and blew softly in the wind. A great deal of fine sand had drifted over their bodies. Near them lay the Englishman, face downwards. We never found the baby

Jemima. She must have died somewhere along the way and Koos Steyn must have buried her. But we agreed that the Englishman Webber must have passed through terrible things; he could not even have had any understanding left as to what the Steyns had done with their baby. He probably thought, up to the moment when he died, that he was carrying the child. For, when we lifted his body, we found, still clasped in his dead and rigid arms, a few old rags and a child's clothes.

It seemed to us that the wind that always stirs in the Kalahari blew very quietly and softly that morning.

Yes, the wind blew very gently.

The Cloud Child

» «

STEPHEN BLACK

I once told a stranger that I had never been on the top of Table Mountain, nor half way up it, although born and brought up in Cape Town. He looked as though he thought I was not speaking the truth. So some months ago I went up, not on foot, I confess, but still to the top. When the mules were rolling in the sand and bracken I took a stroll round the reservoirs and came across a child who was obviously a European, although as brown as many a Cape boy. He was a shy youngster, with ragged hair on his head, and no boots on his feet; dressed in a pair of old knickers and a woollen shirt. Naturally I was surprised. It seemed an astonishing thing that a bare-headed and bare-footed child should be on the top of Table Mountain at seven years of age, while I had not got up there until well on the way to thirty. But it was still more astonishing to find that the boy had never been down the mountain. He had lived in the clouds all his life.

'I was born over there,' he said, pointing to a house at the end of the reservoir. This was after I had overcome his shyness by letting him see a trout line prepared. Presently I pulled out a speckled beauty of at least twenty ounces, and looked at it with some pride. 'I never catch them,' remarked the boy simply. He looked at me in a rather pitiful way, and I could see a tear gathering in each of his eyes as I pulled the hook from the mouth of the wriggling fish. 'I like to watch the fish in the water,' he went on. 'To see them leap, and twist in the sun.'

I put away the fishing tackle, feeling uncomfortable at the look in the child's eyes. 'What is your name?' I asked. 'Philip,' he answered, 'I am called Phil.' I asked by whom, perhaps stupidly. 'By Mother and Father,' he replied with an air of surprise. He did not know that there were children without parents.

'Tell me what you do here all day long.' It was incomprehensible to me that life on a mountain top could be anything but dull and dreary. We were walking away from the water now, and the trout was packed in my basket. Somehow I felt sorry I had caught it.

Phil started talking. He got up in the mornings, he said, and went among the pines that grew to the edge of the water to hear the doves coo. The home of every vink was known to him; they built their nests over the water. The Kaffir vinks were beautiful, and so were the suikervogels and swartkops. Then there was the valley where the disas grew, both red and blue. And clumps of everlastings stood higher than his head. There were skulpad and taaibosch bessies to be gathered, but Phil said he never troubled to pick flowers for they grew all around and looked better that way than in a tin fading. In the autumn there was the suikerbosch flower, loaded with syrup, which he collected in a jug for his mother to boil down to a delicious kind of treacle. Often he saw buck. They were not very wild, for nobody troubled them with guns or dogs. His dog's name was Mac, and at that time was with his father at the other end of the reservoir.

It was charming to hear this child of the clouds talk. He was so simple and earnest, and so unhuman. Most town children of seven are merely inhuman. Phil told me, as we walked to a point from which the town could best be seen, that at nights he loved to watch the red spreeuws flying home to the cliffs. They cried out mournfully, and only ate berries; whereas the white-tipped spreeuws sat round his father's cows all day, screamed loudly, and ate the ticks. When we reached the edge of the mountain I cried out with delight at what lay before me. The boy's eyes brightened too. 'I long to go down,' he said, 'do you?'

'I have been down,' I replied, feeling superiority for the first time that day.

'My father has too,' said Phil proudly, 'and my mother says she went down when I was a little boy. We are all going in the basket on the wire one day.'

The sight was the grandest I had ever seen, but people from abroad tell me that to see Table Mountain in the early morning from some miles out at sea is finer. But no impression can efface the one made by the sight from the summit. Far away were the mountains of Hottentot's Holland. All around was peace.

'When I was a little boy,' spoke the child, 'Mother used often to come with me here. She showed me the sea and the ships and the big white houses. But I want to see them close; they are so far away. Does that little ship sail over the sea?' he asked, suddenly pointing to a Castle liner that was steaming out. I told him it did, and that it was not a little ship, but a very big one. Still the ten-thousand-tonner looked small enough from there.

'I see the ships every day,' said the boy. 'They come just as the stars do each night and the flowers in spring; and they go like the birds to their nests. But why do they come and go? It must be a great trouble. And where do the stars go every night? I see them come as I go to bed; but when I get up in the morning they are gone.'

I had a good pair of glasses with me and took them out of my pocket. Phil should have a treat. He shall see the ships and the large white houses. But before I could speak, he said: 'It must be very beautiful down there. Can you always see the mountain? We often have big, wet clouds around us and then I can't see the ships or the houses. The clouds come over us, and the wind blows. Then Mother says I must stay in the house. What are those little things like dassies on the ground beside the sea?'

Below us on the white sands I could see that a crowd was gathered. 'Those are people,' I said.

'Oh,' he said.

The cloud child asked me many things. I told him of the trains which kept running backwards and forwards beneath pale clouds of smoke, and he was quiet for a long time. 'I want to see a train,' he said at length. 'But I love the big things that run round the mountain and the sea. Father says they are trams pulled by electricity. I don't know what electricity is, but the big trams are fine. They run up the mountain in the dark like moving stars. Mother says they run late at night, but I go to bed before that and see only two trams with stars. When I was a little boy I first saw them, and I thought they were stars that came with the night like the others. They went so fast, as the stars do when they travel. I am going to be very happy when I go down; I shall see all the things I love.'

'I hope so, Phil.'

Then eagerly he went on. 'I see lots of pretty little houses that move about. They go a little and stop a little. I know them all. Every night when I go to bed I think of the little houses on wheels, and say to myself, Dear God, give me one when I grow up, for Christ's sake. Amen! Look, look,' he cried suddenly, 'there is one now.'

I took out my glasses and while adjusting them saw a huge vehicle apparently drawn by four horses; but could not make out what it was, for the distance was too great.

'What is it, what is it? My house, my house that goes up and down! Oh tell me!'

I had a suspicion, but did not utter it. Instead I took a long look through the glasses, and saw a municipal dirt cart. But I did not tell the boy.

Fuel of Fire

» «

ARTHUR SHEARLY CRIPPS

I was lucky to get a lift. We had risen before the moon took to her bed, and the sun had left his. We were driving through green woodlands when the light grew clear around us. A little while ago their graceful trees had been ruddy or bronze doubtless. Now it was the turn of the hill-trees on the great koppie that we passed within a mile, to grow bronzed and to redden. For the month of November had only just come in. We outspanned in a valley where the new green of the grass had come already. No doubt a month ago it had looked very black and firescathed. Now the showers had brought kind healing and amendment. We made our morning Memorial together (being all of us Christians – bound on some sort of a Christian pilgrimage), and after that we breakfasted and smoked at ease while the mules grazed close by, and the driver boiled his pot, and fed it with meal, and stirred and ladled out, and ate in the fullness of time. My heart was very thankful. How much better and kindlier one's lot seemed now, fallen as it was once again in this fair ground of a country at peace in War-time. This countryside pleased me ever so much better than British East or German East – this Mashonaland. There to north I remembered without enthusiasm the tropical passions of the elements, I remembered rather miserably some of the things that a state of war had meant.

After breakfast, there was no hurry about our inspanning. But when we had once got off we were soon up level with the farmhouse on the hill's shoulder. We halted for friendship's sake, and waited for the cups of coffee that we were assured would be soon ready. Our host was Dutch-looking, but seemed British; I thought rather narrowly British in his sympathies. He discussed the War keenly and thoughtfully with my companion. He had two brothers in German East, I knew, and he was soon asking me about them. But our paths up that way had not converged. I could only tell him by hearsay about the main advance, wherein they had been sharing, and I had not. As I told, a dark handsome, gentle-voiced woman brought our coffee out. Soon a shy little girl put up her head round the corner of the stoep, and withdrew again. I jumped down to greet her. Then she agreed to come and shake hands with us both. Her father coloured up, and smiled as he told me of a great scheme. A lady in town had offered to board this child. So kind, wasn't it? She was of sturdy English make (her father's father was an Essex man, I had been told). Her hair and eyes were very dark: she looked ever so capable.

'Yes, very kind,' I murmured, but I was reflecting that the lady's kindness might not be so very ill-rewarded. The child might prove useful and cost little. She might give the sort of help that is apt to be useful and costly in a country like ours. 'Yes,' said the father smiling, 'and she may get to the day school that way, the lady says. We couldn't have nearly afforded to send her into town otherwise. But now she's got her chance of a regular school.' 'Oh, really,' said my friend. His kind ugly face looked none too pleasant as he said it, I remember noticing that.

Then he went to his mules to buckle up a strap somewhere. I was surprised to hear him cursing something under his breath. It was not his manner, I thought, to curse straps or mules. We said goodbye – a very cordial one – and then drove down towards the main road. It winds through a vlei towards the town. We had got almost to the big water-course so banked up in thirsty sand, when he told me what he was cursing. He repeated his words deliberately: 'Damn it to hell,' he said. I protested faintly till he made it clear to me what he was damning, then I recklessly endorsed his damnation. For he was not cursing Heaven or humanity; he was cursing that blessed Anglo-Dutch, or rather Dutch-English, institution of South Africa, the colour-bar. He had been told by one of the managers that should the father apply for admission to school on behalf of the child we had seen, he would be certainly refused. The father was really much too poor to send her away, he told me. 'They're ever so honest and hard-worked. They've put up a great fight on mealie meal against bad seasons. They've pinched hard for the child's poor little outfit. He's got into debt for it. He's a Britisher, and has got two brothers fighting. Very dubious, dark children have been admitted already, as presumably Dutch. Dutch and colonials rule the roost here. And to leave Christianity alone, where does British Imperialism come in? It's risking spoiling a life, and the life of such a decent kid.'

Thereat he certainly condemned guiltily, as he should not have condemned, Dutchmen and colonials – their churches, their social order, and their sanctimony. 'Thank God I was at plebeian Oxford,' he said, 'and was free to mix with coloured men. This is far more select, this dorp academy, with its elect Principal and its supermen-managers.' We nearly had a row about his language.

We came over a rolling down towards the commonage. 'They've kept free from fires here,' I said. 'Yes,' he said, 'but I'm doubtful if their vigilance pays, if their game's worth the candle, I mean if such absence of illumination is worth all their watching about.' 'It saves waste of life,' I said, 'animal and vegetable, if you can only keep the fires away.' I appealed to the wisdom of our laws as well as to the argument of mercy which appealed to me. 'And you get that sort of thing,' he said, pointing to the thick brown tufts of unappetizing feed. 'That's been going more than a year, hasn't it? "Oh for a wind and a fire," say I.' We passed over the commonage, which showed very black with recent fires. 'It looks rather knocked out,' I said. 'Yet not without hope,' he answered.

We were driving back about the same time next forenoon. A great fire was rushing wind-driven over that rolling upland. 'At last,' he said. I sighed. A mile further on we came into the smiling green vlei. 'This was black a while back,' he said. 'Doesn't the fire help a bit after all? Who wants that mouldy stuffy old feed – isn't it parabolic of that fusty Dutch-Anglo dorp and its prejudices? What are they meant for, and it? "Fuel of fire," say I.' I smiled indulgently. Since we had got into town things had happened. We had had our memorial services for the Dead that last night, and this same morning. It was the week of All Hallows and All Souls – a time that often tempts me to homesickness. One is apt to think of hazy, yellow-leaved, dreamy times in old England just about then – not to speak of old familiar faces. That night of the first Service was very starry, and the morning of the second Service was brilliantly clear, the rain seemed to be very far away for the time being. People had come at night rather well. Not to speak of one of the school managers having died quite recently, news of one of our police's death out scouting had leaked through from German East. I preached Paradise to that attentive congregation in the iron-roofed church that natives had been so discouraged from attending. I was glad one straggled into the back seats I had battled for, just to demonstrate one's principle of barring out the colour-bar. It was all very soul-soothing, thought I, that Memorial Evensong – the stars outside, and the golden evening brightening in the west of the hymn, and the lesson about white robes and palms – presumably of victory or harvest-homing. My friend waited for me outside under the lamp. 'Very fine,' he said in his grimmest way, 'the Anglican view of hopeful souls turned promiscuously into a sort of orchard and rose-garden with plenty of light to gild them, and rest to wrap them.' I smiled. 'True enough in its way,' I said. 'There's another side doubtless, yet the preaching of that doesn't appeal to me particularly. I don't want to work on people's apprehensions. But don't let me stand in your light.

You're a lay reader with a bishop's licence. You can preach and welcome tomorrow morning.' 'Trust me not to refuse,' he said. 'I don't want to play up to apprehensions exactly. I want to state what seem to me to be relentless laws of cause and effect, and to show the only way with any sort of hope in Christ that I happen by faith to see.' So he had preached that morning. He preached quite simply on the trying of every man's work, on the burning of flimsy work, on the saving of the workman, yet so as by fire. There was a small but select gathering in the Church of Saint Tertullian; two of the school managers even were there. Surely I had baited the trap, I thought guiltily as I looked upon them, by my over-amiabilities of the night before. Yet that side was true enough, the side I had preached. And was not this side also true in its way? The preacher seemed at first to be referring to my own obsession with the words 'resist not evil', my following of Tolstoy in my own evangel. He was warm in his commendation. 'And yet,' he said, 'let us remember a just God's resistance to evil. He resists and judges righteously, where we may neither resist nor judge. If we agree not to resist evil violently for Jesus' sake, yet ought we not to warn people of their God's unrelenting resistance? While we would not obscure the fear of our just God by fear of us unjust men, let us remember our just God!' He spoke of judgement and of purgation, of what seemed to be indicated hereafter by the stupidity and cruelty of people's prejudices in South Africa. He painted quite luridly the purgation he anticipated as likely for such as would dare to wreck a child's education, and possibly her life for a colour-scruple. He glowed and kindled. There was no mistaking his drift. He painted the fires of purgation. He painted, too, their presumable fuel, much as I believe old preachers limned the flames of hell and their denizens. 'And it may lengthen out into hell! Who knows?' he kept interjecting. 'Who knows but that that prejudiced spirit you play with may be a damned spirit after all, fuel for the fire that is not quenched, food for the worm that does not die?'

I could not have preached happily on his lines, but for all that I acknowledged that the thing might well be of God – this bizarre surprise at his preaching that was glassed in at least two of his listeners' eyes.

Did that sermon do any good? Let me anticipate! The child came into town as a half-time servant. Somebody's letter got handed up to the Administrator, and he made a request to the managers. The child was clearly European by predominance of race. They spent five hours of their precious time in discussion. The officials wanted to oblige the Administrator, and they had their way at last. But whether the child once admitted will have much of a time, I am inclined to doubt, should she pass into the Paradise of so select an academy. I heard an ominous story of the Dutch minister last week, how he had threatened a hiding to any child of his that spoke to this forlorn little girl, who seems hard up for playmates. I heard yesterday that one of my Church magnates had asked that the child should not come up to play with his own. Yet the fire of God has been preached, and I am willing to allow that the thing may have wanted doing rather badly in my amiable parish. Doesn't any real true Christian Peace Doctrine mean spiritual fire and sword? Doesn't it mean burning and fuel of fire as set against the confused noise and garments rolled in blood of earthly campaigns? Doesn't any real true Christian Imperialism mean the sword of the Spirit and the fire of the Gospel against South African Racialism? Perfect love casteth out fear, but what has Racialism to do with such a perfect love as will banish the fear of God?

After all, can any reasonable and lively Christian Faith avail to find any evangelically reasonable destination short of hell for South African Racialists dying in their Racialism save such place of purgation as my friend indicated? Yes, of course, God's prerogative of mercy in Jesus is limitless, but are these Racialists so merciful to little coloured children that they should obtain mercy without judgement from Jesus' judgement?

And if the purgative fire seem so inevitable, why not warn its prospective fuel?

Granted the Love of Jesus (Who was certainly what South Africans would call a Jew Boy, Who was possibly so dark that any dorp school would have hummed over His admission, Who enrolled Himself in that House of David – one of Whose ancestresses was the Hamitic Rahab apparently who took Ham's curse as well as Japheth's); granted that that Love is the one and only supreme motive for Christian Reform, yet for all that, facts are facts, and it may be kind to tell people into what fires the fires of Racialism threaten to merge themselves. On the whole, I am glad that our lay reader preached on that bright morning that over-gloomed sermon, preaching from my own soothing pulpit to my startled congregation. They did not seem to know what to make of it. But the preacher himself seemed quite unrepentant about it. He was talking to me about it that morning when we drove home again, he to his farm and I with him, to walk on to my mission. We outspanned in a very green valley, I remember, and sat long over roast monkey-nuts that his driver benignantly provided.

'The Lord put a word into my mouth,' my friend said quite firmly and simply. 'Was there not the cause – the cause of a child's career? Didn't our Saviour speak plainly as to the ugly analogy of the man drowned like a dog with a stone round his neck in the deep of the sea? Weren't His children in question when Jesus spoke; wasn't there a Christian child in question when I preached?'

I thought he made out something of a case for his position as a preacher of fiery doom. We were sitting on a beautiful green carpet. The Earth there had come through her bad time. Away on the hillside a black forbidding patch testified to the unpleasantness of the remedial stage. Away in the distance was a beautiful tree-shaded granite hill with much show of brown foliage and purplish underspaces. Just beside that hill the flames came driving (through the old last year's feed, I suppose). His eyes followed mine the way of the flames. 'Hurray!' he said heartily. 'Now we shan't be so very long surely after all. Don't you see the green grass on its way? It was a snug corner, verily, for the old dry stuff. Look, how the flames leap up in the thick of it! Not very juicy browse nor tasty feed, but fine for the fire; good for that, anyway. It was a snug corner, but at last the time was ripe when the fire came driving straight for it – the fire with the wind behind. "Which things are a parable,"' he said, his ugly sunburnt face twitching curiously, his eyes quite handsome, nay, even splendid with honest scorn. He was shaking his fist towards the prim little dorp that we had left behind over the ridges. 'No doubt but ye are the people,' he said, 'ye that have made the freedom of England and the franchise of Jesus of no effect by your tradition – your sacrosanct tradition. What's the good of the frowsy old stuff? It must be some good; what is it? It isn't very good pasture for sheep or horses, not to speak of dairy cattle, but it's noble food for fire, don't you think?

'There it lies-up so snug and sheltered and screened – the old dead survival – hidden in the prim little corrugated iron-roofed houses, and the narrow gumtree avenues, and the whitewashed Dutch tabernacle where they sing "Safe in the Arms of Jesus" (would you believe it?). But the time will come, it mayn't come in my day or in yours, but the time will come sure enough, when the Fire will trek dead straight for this old dead-ripe stuff – the Fire with the Wind behind. Then God have mercy on them whose work it was! For their work shall be burnt, aren't we sure of that? But as to they themselves being the sort to be saved so as by fire can we be so very sanguine? Meanwhile –'

The way he so humbly appealed to me for my opinion on that moot point, did much to conciliate me. He had not carried me with him all the while. He seemed to me a bit out of date, too like an ante-Christian prophet. Yet how my heart went out to him as he ended up so very abruptly with his 'meanwhile'. His voice broke queerly, and his eyes shone. 'Meanwhile – they may manage to give a child or two a rough passage. They've got pluck enough for that, the blighters, haven't they?' He turned away from me with a sort of a sob. 'The time'll come sure enough, but it's their time now, and they know it,' he said. 'God pity her!'

When the Sardines Came

» «

WILLIAM PLOMER

Quite ordinary people sometimes behave in an extraordinary way. A sudden mood will possess them, and drive them to cast off their closest ties, which they find a hindrance to the attainment of new and mad desires. Lifted to the heights, they have no more use for comfortable valleys, and forsaking reality, they embrace the air. At any rate, that was the case with Mrs Reymond.

On the South Coast of Natal, in the early nineteen-twenties, there was a charming and little-frequented retreat which showed few signs of becoming so spoilt, or should one say developed, as it is now. A road, for instance, now runs past Reymonds, with quite a quantity of traffic, and houses are going up here and there. But at that time the only means of communication with the outside world (beyond one or two paths that led off through the bush into the native reserve) was the tiny station known as Reymond's Halt, which never figured in timetables, but of which you caught a glimpse from the train. The line ran between the house and the sea, and everywhere was the characteristic thick bush. The house stood in a large clearing which had been converted into a pretty garden – a lawn, palms, poinsettias and so on. At the back were some grassy uplands called 'the farm', because Reymond ran a few cows, kept poultry, and maintained some fields of maize and a large vegetable garden, these things taking up much of his time. Yet he took things fairly easily. He was still under fifty, but the war had knocked him about rather badly. He was a quiet, harmless, equable sort of man, who took less interest in politics than most South Africans do – 'All governments are alike,' he used to say – and who, unlike many of his fellow countrymen, treated the natives with fairness and even kindness, and had a good name among them in consequence.

His wife was rather younger than himself, and people had said that their marriage was romantic, though it was probably no more romantic than most. They were childless, but obviously very happy together, sufficiently alike (in their taste for a quiet life, for example) and yet sufficiently different to get on well with each other. Reymond sought for himself the quiet interests of the 'farm' as if to forget the strenuousness of his earlier existence. His wife, on the other hand, finding things a little quiet down there, made some effort to keep in touch with the outside world. She read a certain amount, played a lot of tennis and a little Chopin, and took an interest in all sorts of things. She was not very well educated, and had not very good taste. Rupert Brooke and Omar Khayyám were her poets, the dust having settled on Ella Wheeler Wilcox, but she enjoyed the efforts she made towards improving herself and enjoying herself. The contrast in the natures of husband and wife made a pretty balance. Sitting in a long chair on the veranda he would listen to her with his pipe in his mouth, and when she had done talking he would ask her advice or tell her about this or that happening on the 'farm'. She always made a point of spending a day in Dunnsport once a week, partly for shopping purposes and partly to see her friends there. Reymond went to town less often.

They might almost have been taken for a model married couple, until a slight restlessness in Mrs Reymond's behaviour became noticeable. It seemed as if she no longer enjoyed her activities for their own sake but as an outlet for a kind of frustrated energy. As she was no longer a young woman, one might have expected her to be like her husband, contented and settled, but then she was not so old that there was really any reason for her to behave as if life had nothing more but repose to offer her. No, she was lively, and with only a hint of a foreshadowing of age about her, a certain dignity and resignation at times in her manner.

It was a young medical student called Edwards who had the best chance of observing her behaviour. A cousin of Reymond's, he came to stay for a couple of months because he had some reading to do for an examination, and wanted quiet. It was certainly quiet enough down there, and he soon fell into a regular routine, which was only broken by occasional dances and weekends in Dunnsport. After breakfast he used to go straight down to the beach with his books. He always went barefoot, first down the steps to the railway, all warm in the morning sun; then over the prickly cinders of the line; and then along the short, tunnel-like path through the bush to the sea. It was shady and sandy and uncannily silent in there, and one came suddenly out again to the sun and the sound of the waves. He used to work all the morning, then swim, then return to the house for lunch on the veranda, sleep awhile out of doors, and then go fishing (he never caught much) or walk along the line. If the weather was especially warm he had a second swim, usually worked again before supper, and spent the evening talking, or singing (rather badly) to Mrs Reymond's accompaniment, while her husband sat on the veranda smoking his pipe. Almost the only variants to this programme were visits to or from their neighbours, none of whom lived very near. And once Reymond took Edwards out shooting, but they came back very hungry and almost empty-handed, and Mrs Reymond laughed at them, with just a suggestion of bitterness in her gaiety.

It was wintertime, and the weather was nearly perfect, only sometimes a little windy. There was a sort of drowsiness in the air which was very peaceful and pleasant, and only marred by Mrs Reymond's slight uneasiness and by those trifling odds and ends of everyday troubles which tend, in isolated places, to become magnified into things of importance.

'I hope you'll still be here,' Reymond said to his guest once or twice, 'when the sardines come.'

The coming of the sardines, it seemed, was expected to take place at about the same time every year. It was the great annual event. Immense shoals (so Edwards was told) would pass slowly up the coast, close inshore, and pursued by innumerable seabirds and large predatory fish. At that time everybody stopped work and turned angler.

Edwards was still at Reymonds' when the sardines came. It was one day towards the end of June, a perfect day. Like most perfect things, it didn't last long, but a great deal happened in the time. There were no clouds and no waves. There was no wind. It was perfectly warm and still, and the sea undulated so lazily that the tides seemed to have lapsed, and the water was scarcely troubled at its edge. The sky above the horizon was a darker blue than the sea. At lunch-time the kitchen boy brought the rumour of the sardines' approach. An extraordinary atmosphere of tension and excitement was at once created, as often happens before some natural event, and all three seemed to have lost their appetites. Afterwards they noticed that the wind had got up a little, and the sea was no longer quite so calm, but this was usually the case in the afternoon.

At about two o'clock some dark stains were visible on the sea, rising and falling with the waves, the water round them disturbed, and birds wheeling overhead. A little later they heard voices from the beach and went down all armed with rods and nets and baskets. The servants had preceded them.

The sands, nearly always deserted, were now crowded with all kinds of people, men, women and children of all colours and ages. To the right and left, hundreds of fishing-rods rose into the air. Everyone was looking out to sea, and not very far out, for the dark patches, which were enormous shoals of sardines, had spread and spread, and coming nearer had become much larger. One could see distinctly the flashing of huge triangular fins and curving tails as the larger fish swam madly round their prey. One could also distinguish that most of the birds were gulls and gannets. Snow-white in the afternoon sun, the gannets fell like bombs, rising a moment or two later brown and wet from the waves, fish in beak. The tide, the current, the pursuers, and the inscrutable alliance of fate and nature, gradually drove the myriads of victims towards the beach, where excitement almost gave way to ecstasy. And when a wave at last drove the first edge of a shoal right up on the shore, so that in retreating it left a few silvery flounderers on the wet sand, a sudden movement ran right through the crowd, and an old Indian woman in a magenta skirt darted into the water with a basket. A moment later, and the sardines had really arrived. There was a certain poetic justice in the fact that nobody bothered about them – they had enemies enough already. No, the old hunter in the heart of man was after bigger game, and it was the pursuing fish that everybody wanted to catch.

The pitch of excitement was intense. It was the one mad day in the year. Not only were the sardines maddened with fear (or whatever in them corresponds to that feeling) of their pursuers, but the second fear now possessed them of being driven clean out of their element. As for the great fish-of-prey, the lust of the chase had driven them into such a frenzy that, with an utter disregard of consequences, many found themselves driven up by their own energy and the impetus of the waves right on to the beach, where their great metallic fins and steely tails grooved into the soft wet sand like the keels of ships that run aground in a fog. Until that moment their natural aversion to man had been in abeyance, and had they been able to consider him at all, they would no doubt have seen him simply as a rival. The air was thick with the wings and cries of birds, but they held a little more aloof than the fish.

Most remarkable of all was the behaviour of the crowd, which was very mixed. There were Indians and Mauritians from the sugar-mill a couple of miles away; Zulus from kraal and kitchen; poor whites and bywoners; people who rather fancied themselves, like the Scotch engineer from the mill, with his trousers now rolled up over the knees; one or two people of rather the same sort as the Reymonds; and a selection of the oddities who used to live in those parts, hidden away here and there in little houses in the bush along the coast. There was a gaunt woman, who was a vegetarian, lived by herself and did water-colours; an old Norwegian sailor who lived between the sun and the sea, wearing only a pair of khaki shorts, his torso burnt to the colour of rosewood and covered with fine gold hairs; and a family of Russian refugees – an old father who never left the house, a daughter who worked in Dunnsport, and a young son. Mrs Reymond and Edwards used to make jokes about these last, especially the son, a tall, fair young man with wild, elemental eyes. Indeed, they had given him the nickname of 'the bush-baby', calling him after the large-eyed galago, that strange creature of the woods. And the 'bush-baby', like almost everybody else round about, whom they knew either by sight or by repute, was of course on the beach on this day when the sardines came.

The excitement of the hour had already worked an extraordinary, an almost magical effect upon the minds of all these people – an effect as violent and as magical as upon the fish. Divided at all times by a thousand barriers, of race, of money, of caste, of class, of language, of pride and fear, but especially by various kinds of colour-bar – the Indians and natives living in mutual contempt, the 'coloured' people looking down on their darker neighbours, the whites and near-whites looking down on everybody else, and being, in consequence, for the most part mistrusted in their turn – divided like this at all times, they were now, quite surprisingly, all brought to a level. Just as enemies will unite in a common fear of a common danger, so they will sometimes be united by something which makes an appeal to any emotion as primitive as fear – by a promise, for example, of something for nothing. In this case, one rather heavy touch of nature had made the whole world kin.

Mingled with the sounds of splashing and dashing, the cries of birds and children, could be heard the hiss of lines being thrown, and the whirr of unwinding reels. Here and there a great fish was hooked, and rods could be seen bent nearly double, as if they might snap at any second, jerking spasmodically without a pause, as if they had a motor bicycle on the hook instead of a fish. Except in the case of the old Norwegian sailor, it was mostly out of the question for one person to manage one fish; to every engaged rod there were at least two fishermen; and it was even possible to see an Indian, a Zulu, a white and a half-caste all united in a single effort – a rare sight indeed in United South Africa.

It was not long before Mrs Reymond said to Edwards: 'Oh, look, Charles, there's the Russian bush-baby! And he's hooked a fish!'

There he was, a blond boy of less than twenty, in shorts and an open shirt, rather slender, with the large eyes of one who has learnt too young the meaning of hunger, and who has looked at death too near and too soon. He was staggering about in the sand, and looked almost as if he were doing some savage dance, straining every muscle to prevent himself being dragged into the sea, and to stop the rod, which was bent in the shape of a C and kicking like a sapling in a cyclone, from being jerked out of his hands or snapped in two. The servant who had come with him was holding him back by the waist, and two or three boys ran up to give a hand if needed. The whole effect was that instead of playing the fish they were being played by it.

Mrs Reymond was fascinated. She had eyes for nothing else. Her husband was busy some distance away, and had apparently not caught anything yet. As for Edwards, he had already landed a fair-sized fish, and had handed his rod over to the kitchen-boy. Mrs Reymond took no notice of either of them. Not even when a giant rock-salmon was caught by the naked hands of a group of children and dragged floundering out of the water, was her attention diverted. The Russian boy, or rather the Russian boy's fish, was gradually moving away to the left, away from the main scene of action, and Mrs Reymond moved too. Edwards couldn't make out what was interesting her so much. It seemed to him that a dozen tussles quite as remarkable were going on at the same time.

Important things in life often happen so suddenly and unexpectedly that they simply take one's breath away; if they happen in other people's lives, and one is only a spectator, it is often a little difficult to grasp, let alone convey, the exact reason for them, their details and consequences. All Edwards knew was that at that moment he felt quite certain that something important was going to happen and that it wasn't going to happen to him. On the left of the beach was a group of jagged rocks, to which the Russian was gradually getting nearer, and his supporters were excitedly warning him to try and avoid them. But the fish was wild and perhaps wise as well, and plunged determinedly on in the same direction. Occasionally it reared itself out of the water, and in the late light it looked, to the heightened imagination of the spectators, as big as a dolphin. A moment later the Russian boy sprang up on to a high rock, and with a very precarious foothold seemed in danger of falling. But still he held on. Edwards expected Mrs Reymond to say, 'Oh, isn't he plucky!' but she was far too intent to speak. He glanced back to see how far they had come from the crowd, when he heard her utter a sudden little cry, a most moving sound that seemed to come straight from her heart, and turning quickly round, he saw that the Russian boy had disappeared. She ran forward, her high heels sinking into the sand, and Edwards followed.

When they arrived at the rock the Russian boy was being lifted out of the water. His wet hair had fallen over his face, and he was bleeding horribly from the leg. By a miracle, the rod was neither broken nor lost, and a wiry Indian, up to his waist in eddying water, was holding it upright with all his strength, the butt end pressed against his hip. The Russian boy, the 'bush-baby', fainted from loss of blood. Fortunately both Edwards and Mrs Reymond (who had done some nursing during the war) knew what to do. When the flow of blood had been checked by a rude tourniquet, the boy was carried up to the house and laid, by Mrs Reymond's orders, on her bed. She looked round once for her husband, but he had been a good way off at the time of the accident, and not knowing what had happened was not yet back.

'Will you fetch the doctor, Charles?' she said, turning to Edwards. 'I'd rather you went than one of the servants.'

Edwards went. To reach the doctor meant a long ride through the reserve,

and he did not return with him until ten. (All that is changed down there now
– they have a telephone and a car and so on.) It appeared that the wound had
been caused by a sharp bait-knife, worn casually sheathless in the belt, but
there was also a slight fracture in the foot, caused by the fall. The consequence
was, it was decided that the patient should remain where he was, and he did. It
should be remarked that the fish was landed by the Indian; it was a 'springer',
rather over five feet long, the shape and colour of a torpedo. Before it was cut
up, the patient, the Indian and the splendid carcass of the victim were
photographed together by Edwards. Mrs Reymond was overjoyed.

'It was really you who caught it,' she said to her protégé.

Meanwhile Edwards went on with his work as usual, and Reymond went
every day to see the patient's old father and report progress. Like all Russians,
the old man was a great talker; like all Russian refugees, he let it appear that he
had had something to do with the Court; anyway, quite a friendship sprang up
between him and Reymond, whose visits to this new acquaintance grew
longer every day. So Mrs Reymond was left even more in touch with her
patient than she otherwise would have been.

The change that came over her during the following days was most
remarkable. All her restlessness seemed to have vanished, and she looked ten
years younger. She was sometimes silent for several minutes, which was
unlike her. And when she talked, it was about Boris – the progress of his cure,
what he had told her about his early life, what he had said about this, that or
the other. At times she was like a mother boasting of her child's cleverness,
and it is no exaggeration to say that at other times she was like a young girl
shyly praising a lover. When Boris was able to get up and hobble about with
crutches she was so pleased that it would not have been surprising to hear her
exclaim, 'See, he can walk!' Her continual pleasure was very evident, but she
was inclined to be brusque with her husband, and even (so Edwards thought)
to neglect him. And Edwards watched Reymond closely to see what effect this
was having on him, but that mild-tempered man seemed to remain exactly as
usual. Then one day, walking barefoot along the veranda, Edwards happened
to glance in at a window and saw Boris kissing Mrs Reymond. When he had
got over his surprise (which was not altogether a surprise) he wondered, being
rather young and foolish, if he ought to draw Reymond's attention to what
was going on. But fortunately he had enough sense to keep his mouth shut.

Boris soon gave up his crutches, and carried a walking-stick instead. He
and Mrs Reymond used to go for short walks together – very short walks, for
they often walked just down the garden, crossed the railway line, followed the
path through the bush and, seeking out some group of rocks on the beach, sat
in the shelter of them for hours at a time. When Boris was almost well again, it

became known that instead of going back to his father's cottage on the coast he was going to take up a job in Dunnsport. Two days before he went, Edwards happened to be passing through that silent tunnel of foliage between the railway and the beach and, trudging through the deep, dry sand, couldn't help overhearing voices coming towards him.

'So you see,' said Boris, speaking in his attractive foreign accent, 'that wouldn't really be possible . . .'

'But I shall *never* forget –' Mrs Reymond answered, and her voice was quite transfigured with emotion.

Edwards coughed, and as he came face to face with them made some bright remark about the weather. As far as his own observation went, that was about the end of the whole affair.

Boris duly left, and for a week or two it was plain that Mrs Reymond missed him grievously. Indeed, as if to hide the fact, she mentioned it casually more than once, and even pretended to joke about it. It would not be true to say that she was soon her usual self again. When she was resigned as far as she could be to the absence of Boris she seemed to have lost her former restlessness and, by contrast with her recent fervours, appeared definitely middle-aged. It was as if in the course of a few weeks she had made up the difference between her own age and her husband's, and a new peacefulness seemed to have asserted itself in their relationship, a mutual confidence. And then one day, during a walk along the beach, Reymond turned to Edwards and seemed about to speak. But it was plainly hard for him to do so, for he was not much of a talker at any time, and was quite unused to expressing his more intimate feelings.

'Oh, Charles,' he said, 'I want to explain to you something you mayn't quite understand.'

'Yes?'

'About my wife,' said Reymond, looking out to sea, 'and Boris.'

'Yes.'

'Why do you say "yes" like that? I suppose you have your own ideas . . . I suppose you wonder why I didn't do anything about it. That's just what I'm going to explain. Well, you know how things are with us, we have no children, and we don't see many people down here. Of course I don't mind that, but for my wife – for a woman, you know – it's not so nice. I could see for some time that she's been feeling it a bit. Of course she's not so used to a country life as I am . . . Well, I saw how it was after – well, after the sardines came. That boy just became everything to her. He was like a son and a friend and a sweetheart all rolled into one. Well, I'm not a terribly jealous man, but I can't say I altogether liked the look of things. But you see, if there's one thing I can't stand, it's when I feel that my wife's not happy. I thought it was better to let things run their course. I felt sure my wife would come down to earth again all right, and she did . . . Now I know nothing like that'll ever be likely to happen to us again. I dare say it's not so nice for a woman to feel that she'll soon be face to face with old age . . . And then you see, women are funny. She'd have been annoyed if she'd thought I wasn't jealous, and yet knowing that I *was* jealous somehow irritated her . . . Ah well, I'm sure it's all over now . . . I don't know why I've told you all this, except that I didn't want you to get wrong ideas into your head. And I must say it wouldn't have been any easier if you hadn't been here – triangles are apt to have sharp corners . . . And anyway, if you hadn't been here you'd have missed the sardines!'

'Which I wouldn't have missed for anything,' said Edwards. He longed to know how Mrs Reymond had justified her behaviour after Boris's departure – had she repented with tears? had everything been taken for granted? or what? – but he didn't like to say anything. Besides, he wanted to appear understanding, a man of the world, and tried to look the part in silence. In any case, they had almost reached the house, and Mrs Reymond was waving to them from the tea-table, which had been set on the veranda.

When Edwards left the South Coast his mind was quickly filled with his own affairs, but whenever he thought of the Reymonds he was haunted by that woman's voice saying 'I shall *never* forget . . .' and again he seemed to see her trying to hurry forward, her high heels sinking into the sand at every step, towards the last passion of her life.

The Death of Masaba

》《

R. R. R. DHLOMO

'Fellows, what do you think of this business of Masaba?'

'Yes, just tell us what happened.'

'Men, the boy is dying. I heard from Stimela, the boss-boy of the lashers, that Masaba fainted twice in the mine today. Stimela he ran to tell Boss Tom, who did not even want to listen to him, but only said: "Get away, there are lots of boys in the compound."'

'But what made Masaba faint in the mine?'

'Well . . . I saw that there was a mistake in his ticket. It was not stamped *ten days' light underground work*.'

The others they laughed when they heard the word 'mistake'.

'Clear out,' they cried, 'there is no *mistake* there! We old boys know well that if Masaba had been a white man there would have been no *mistake*. Didn't Boss Tom say "there are lots of Kaffirs in the compound"? If one dies, meaning Masaba, the Government will bring more. He said that after Stimela had told him, "Masaba is fainting, he cannot lash."'

The others were silent; each was busy with his own thoughts.

This affair was worrying their hearts a great deal. These men – they were five, sitting round a glowing bucket fire – had left their kraals for the mines, forced to do so by hunger and want. They left their homes knowing of the terrible accidents that occur below the surface of the mines. Their only hope was that the always-wise white people would be true to them and treat them well: safeguard them from underground dangers, and work them as people with equal feelings though their skins were black.

The working place where they were stationed was deep down on the 18th level. The heat on that level was terrible; so intense that unacclimatized boys were liable to get heat-stroke. Behind them a yawning, dreary shaft threatened their lives; while in front a naked, creaking rock rose sheer above them. From its grim, muddy face trickled drops of dirty, poisonous water.

Under these disabilities, with death everywhere beckoning, Boss Tom made them lash as though the Furies were after them. Here their half-naked bodies were bent unceasingly over the shovels. Even old lashing hands were seen staggering under the heat, and through the pangs of hunger. As these were their daily lot in life, they did not mind it at all, for they had infinite trust in their masters.

But today, when they saw Masaba, the victim of callous indifference, yes Masaba, their young fellow countryman, who was not even supposed to be placed on the lashing gang, their hearts were filled with blood. The first incident happened when they were shovelling madly. Masaba suddenly dropped down . . . and fainted.

Boss Boy Stimela ran and told Boss Tom: 'Nkosi, the boy Masaba has fainted. He can't lash.'

Boss Tom was greatly surprised when he heard that a 'Kaffir' could not do the job for which he was solely created, the handling of the shovel. He said to Steamer: 'What! Masaba can't lash? A bloody Kaffir . . . can't lash?'

'I know, sir,' replied Steamer, 'that Masaba faints as soon as he stoops to lash. I think he's not used to it yet.'

'Oh, kick him, Steamer.'

Steamer was, however, one of those fast-dwindling Boss Boys who, instead of 'waking up' Masaba with a kick, according to orders, went to him and said, 'Try and lash, boy. The Boss will hit you, say you're loafing.'

Poor Masaba went and threw himself at his master's feet.

'Nkosi, I am not used to lashing yet. I get so tired, sir, and my head aches so. My eyes get clouded and misty when I stoop to lash, sir. O, I beg you, sir; my good Boss, my father, give me another job until I'm used to this job of lashing. I will work well, sir. I will do anything for you, Boss. But lashing kills me, Boss, please.'

And he burst into tears, while his fellow workers muttered ominously under their breath.

It is difficult for a boy and his Boss to come to quick understanding down there. Because in the mine their language is different from ours. There their speech is made up of all those naked and revolting phrases that would shame the Prince of Darkness. Still muttering amongst themselves, they said, 'Masaba, isn't your ticket stamped?'

'I don't know,' sobbed Masaba. 'This is my first time to work in the Mine. I began work yesterday.'

'Hey, what's up there?' bawled Boss Tom, drawing nearer. 'If I get you talking again, Masaba, there'll be hell for you.'

'He is dying, sir,' cried Stimela in a strained voice.

It was then that Boss Tom uttered words seemingly innocent in his thoughts, but to natives' minds full of damning meanings. This thoughtless ganger who did not know the working of a native's mind said: 'There are lots of Kaffirs in the compound!'

The boys having digested these words bent once more over their shovels. A piercing cry stopped their labours. For, with a heartrending cry, Masaba fell with a sickening thud, knocking his head against a jagged piece of rock on the stope. Without delay he was carried to the surface and from there was hurried to the hospital. When his fellow countrymen heard that Masaba was seriously ill, they brooded.

'Lord Jesus, please save Masaba for his poor mother's sake. She will be left alone in this world.'

The next day, as they were changing from their wet clothes, a mine police boy entered their room: 'Er . . . er . . . Madoda the manager said I should come to tell you that Masaba is dead.'

When an inquiry was held over the death of Masaba, it was found that Boss Tom was guilty. For he had caused a new boy to lash before putting him first on light undergound work, as was the rule with new boys. Through his carelessness and indifference he had caused the death of Masaba.

'I say, fellows, if Masaba had died accidentally, it would not have mattered. But I hold that he was murdered. For his ticket was stamped: *Not to be employed on lashing.*'

'Hau, didn't you hear that Boss said to Stimela, "There are many Kaffirs in the compound"? Ho! Ho! You don't know the white people!'

And they went out to dig Masaba's grave.

Lonesome

》《

PETER ABRAHAMS

I had just arrived in Cape Town when I met her. But that's going too fast. See, on my way down I was happy till I came to the spot. It was a strange spot. I have often wondered since then why the train had to stop there. See, it had so much to do with me afterwards. I could not sleep for nights on end. I kept on thinking about it.

When I thought, I saw everything again. The few houses where the railway siding was. Deep in a valley . . . The earth was green when the train passed there. Beautiful and green. Little grass fingers stretched out to touch the sun. Just like human beings stretching out to touch something they don't know. Funny how people want things they don't know. But that's why it's so good to live . . . I hate philosophers sometimes. I know my friends will say, 'Oh, don't!' You see it's a crime. But I love crimes sometimes. That kind of crime. It's a crime to know so much, and to understand so much, like the philosophers.

What I mean is this. The doctor who delivers the woman of her child is doing a job. Just a job. If he's a new one, there is some excitement in it. But it's still just a job . . . But with you and me it's so different. It's the earth. Generations of earth. Centuries of earth. Timeless earth. It's the earth bursting loose slowly. Coming up and breaking up. Opening up. You know, like a ball of damp earth falling apart. And you see inside it. You see nothing. But it's beautiful to see it, although it's nothing . . . That is what philosophers miss. That's why I hate them sometimes.

The deep valley without the sun. It was early morning. The steward had brought a cup of coffee that was like muddy water. See, I travelled in the coloured carriage, and that is very far from the dining car. So it was muddy and cold . . . But I had had some worse things to drink in my life, and it was all right. I didn't even blame him for charging me a tickey for the cup of cold muddy water. I said, 'Thank you,' very decently, and smiled at him. He just looked at me and took the tickey and went out. I didn't even blame him for that. See, he was white. And you're everything in this country if you are white. Bishop, king, steward, bum, office boy, all of them. You are God's chosen child. Even Mrs Millin says it. She says we coloureds are 'God's step-children', and all the papers review her and say, 'Yea, yea.' So what do I say? Well, just nothing.

But it was beautiful in that little place. After the steward took the tickey and went out I sat down and gulped down the muddy water so I should not get bilious looking at it. It was better inside than out. My insides didn't have eyes, and so could not look at it . . . Then I looked out of the window . . . I should have looked at the houses of the railway officials living at that siding. I know what the houses of the Natives are without looking. I just know. I should have looked at the homes of the officials, but I did not. I looked at the houses of the Native workers who are workers. I say this because in this country you have WORKERS and Workers and workers. The one with the small w is the working-class worker. The one with the big W gets his orders from the one with all the big letters, and passes them on to those with all the small letters. So it's WORKERS and Workers and workers.

If you are fortunate enough to have a sickly-looking fowl-run you will know what I mean . . . Only your fowl-run is usually very well ventilated. These houses were not. Half a dozen or so pieces of corrugated iron. A pole. Usually a rotting tree-trunk. Wire. Rope. String. Rotting planks. Every type of junk . . . Nail these together and you have the houses I saw . . . But I wasn't shocked at all. I just wanted to refresh my memory.

See, it's like this everywhere in this country. You start off at Louis Trichardt or Pietersburg and you go down to Cape Town or Natal. And if you don't travel first, and pull down your blind to flirt with the young lady who got on at the last station, and look around you, and say, 'Poor black things,' and throw a penny when you see little native boys begging at the sidings, and pull down your blind again . . . Mostly you do these things. But *if* you do not do these things, you will see that everywhere things are like this. Dirt, Death stinking, squalor shouting at you. And you will wonder.

All the people in this country are so used to it all that they do the things I have said. Pull down their blinds. Flirt with the young girl who got on at the last station. Murmur, 'Poor black things.' Throw a tickey and laugh to see the little bags of skin and bone fighting for it.

Poor black things!

This is South Africa. The land of the white man. Stolen from the black man. He says so. I don't. I don't say anything of my own. I have no brain. Niggers are not supposed to have any brain here. It is a crime. Again, my friends say, 'No, you should not say such things. We are white, but we respect your brain. We treat you as our equal, don't we? You must not be a defeatist. Things will come out right. The whites in the country are learning to know that the blacks are as good as they are. You must do your share in educating them.'

Yes. But what am I? Am I a superman? Always understanding? Always doing the right thing? Always the perfect and understanding person? I am human, too. I want to live a sane and rational life. I do not want to work for things that will come when I perhaps am not here. Why should I work for a brave new world that I will not see? I think of the simple things of life, too.

These are the things I spoke to her about when I met her in Cape Town when I had just arrived.

She was good to look at. I think I was a little in love with her. Not really. Just because of the awful loneliness, I think. Somebody to sit with quietly. Somebody to talk to. Somebody to look at. I guess that made me imagine I was a little in love with her. Human sympathy. Understanding, and somebody to share a bit of myself with . . . But, comrade, you are a defeatist. You must not think of such things. You know that there is companionship in the Movement as far as that is possible.

As far as that is possible.

How far?

Again, I told her about the siding where the train stopped, and what the steward did, and how I looked at the shacks of the native workers, and I told her about the three types of workers.

She did not understand. I know she thought I was a little mad. That I was a defeatist. That I had sold out the Movement. Funny, huh? Well, it's true. The Movement. People living in shacks. People begging for a living.

Young intellectuals feeling utterly impotent.

They don't see. And they say, 'Don't, comrade; that's defeatism.' What do I care about defeatism when I am feeling lonesome? What do I care about anything when I need human companionship and sympathy and am told that all will be well *after the* . . .

What about a bit of *now*?

Nigger with a brain? Nigger thinking? No. I'm sorry to disappoint you. I'm scared to think. I will go mad if I think. Those others who are mad are thinking these things. They have passed them on to me. I told her these things. A little companionship. Not to discuss anything. Not to hear that I am a promising young writer for the Movement. Not to be told that they think my book is going to be good. Not these things. Not to be told that there is going to be a Mass Meeting and that I must give the crowd of my best.

What about a little bit of warmth? Someone to hold in my arms? Someone to love and lie down with when I am tired?

Young intellectual? Young fool would be better.

I told her these things. Sitting in a non-European café where we went so that it would be all right.

I was a little bit in love with her; or rather, with her company. She could understand, and could give me sympathy, and then interest me in the Mass Meeting. But I guess she wanted to get away to go to a show. So we rushed through the tea, and again she told me the Movement was doomed if young, intellectual leaders like myself were becoming defeatist. What did the comrades in the other countries do?

They at least had someone to talk to. Some woman to understand. Sex can be got in the street. But companionship is something like a religion. A God.

The green valley at the little siding where the train stopped . . .

The little hovels that refreshed my memory of my people . . .

The steward . . .

The nights spent in reading. Talking aloud to myself to hear *some* voice. Any voice. Even my own. Just not to be mad by morning.

Young intellectual!

God and the Movement. Must do something.

Do you know what it is to be a nigger in body? Sub-human. And in mind a person? That is what I call loneliness. But don't forget, I am not thinking. That is reserved for Europeans only. Niggers go to jail.

That spot . . . little niggers asking for a penny . . .

White man flirting with girl who got on at the last station.

Steward. Muddy water. Oh, God!

She was talking. What is the position like up north? How is work? To hell with work, and the position, and everything! Be a comrade! See, I am lonely. See, I have not spoken to a person for years. Either it's all about the Movement or all about nothing. Talk about *something*, for God's sake. Any bloody old thing.

That spot. Green valley in the mountains at a siding where the train stopped.

Years of utter loneliness.

The Movement.

A woman to talk to. A woman with brains who *can* talk; instead, she babbles silence.

Jesus. Nigger body. Animal body.

Human mind.

That spot. Muddy water. God and the nigger bodies with nigger brains. Wish I was like them!

Damned fool to have gone to college.

Not me speaking.

Do you know what I have been saying? Do you understand?

Don't be ashamed to say so if you do not. Millions have failed to.

It would be too good to be true, for you to understand.

Don't hide your smile of pity.

I understand . . .

Loneliness taught me.

The spot . . .

GOD!

Sebolelo Comes Home

» «

C. E. MOIKANGOA

TRANSLATED FROM THE SOUTHERN SOTHO
BY THE AUTHOR

Sebolelo, a woman of the baSuto, stood still considering the situation. There on the floor of the hut, snoring among the liquor he had vomited as he fell, lay the Xhosa husband who had thrashed her in his drunken rage.

'If I had known that married life was like this,' she thought, 'I would have remained in my father's and mother's home and been content to be called an old maid rather than be treated like a dog. My mother failed to tell me that married life was such a rotten affair.'

She took her baby, put it on her back and tied the strings of the skin carrier lest they become loose in her flight. She collected her personal effects and bundled them together to carry on her head. 'Remain like that, you useless dog,' she said. 'Remain rolling in that smelling filth you have vomited.' She set out, homeward bound. After giving the door her back she spoke again as if to someone, saying: 'My father and mother still love me. They have not driven me away from home.'

She walked as fast as her feet could carry her, quite alone in the night. She was by nature much afraid of the spirits but she forgot them all because of the suffering she had endured.

The baby she was carrying was the second-born, for she had had a miscarriage with her first child when five months pregnant.

After having walked a distance of about two miles she met a small party of men who returned from a marriage feast. She got a fright but summoned up courage like one who was prepared for any emergency. She recognized them by their voices. They, too, recognized her at once.

'Good night, Nonaese.'

'Good night, my fathers.'

'Where do you come from and where are you going at this time of the night?' asked Putsoe, the leader.

'I come from the village here and I am going to visit my home. It is a long time since I last saw my mother and father.'

'What is wrong that you should travel in the night and, worse still, alone?'

'I have chosen to travel in the night when it is still cool. And I want to reach home before sunrise.'

'Men, I have my doubts: this woman is deserting; no woman could be courageous enough to travel alone in the night like this. Has she been granted permission by the husband to visit her parents?' muttered Tilo. But they let her go.

Sebolelo walked faster for fear they might report to her mother-in-law and pursue her while she was still near. She was travelling on a bright moonlit night, such that one might see another while still at a good distance. As she walked along the road with her thoughts scattered, thinking of her home-in-law and frequently looking back, she heard the beating of drums: *Too-tooloo, too-tooloo, tooloo, tooloo,* and singing, although the latter was muffled and at low pitch. She stopped to detect the direction from which this came. She heard it clearly in the direction she was going and coming nearer and nearer. She was seized with a sudden fright. 'Oh, I die with my baby while away in the wild country!' said she. She looked about and saw a huge tree covered with thick foliage by the roadside but a little way off. She made for it, scrambled up, and found something like an old nest of a hammer-head among the branches where she settled down cross-legged with the baby on her lap. She looked about and listened carefully. She satisfied herself that the singing came from the direction she was travelling.

It was a crowd of men and women, and as they came nearer and nearer, the singing and the beating of drums became clearer and clearer.

The leaders carried a very tall banner that seemed as if it reached up to the clouds. This had some smaller things dangling on the sides – these made a ding-dong.

There were three drums. One was carried by the leaders, the second by those in the middle of the procession while the third was carried in the rear. It was a terribly long procession of men and women and as Sebolelo sat watching them, trembling with fear, she saw them swerve from the road and head straight for the very tree where she and her baby had sought refuge. These men and women moved and ran about stark naked!

Sebolelo was fully convinced that they were the sorcerers she had so often heard about from childhood but never could believe there were such people. 'Today I have seen them with my own eyes,' said she.

For quite a while they performed all sorts of strange and weird antics. After a time they commenced a ceremony of the Magic Wand which, it is said, is the last lesson to be learned by one receiving instructions in sorcery. By mere providence the child sank into a deep slumber.

A certain woman spoke and said: 'You, So-and-so, and So-and-so, lie on your stomachs near that small stone. You, So-and-so, and So-and-so, near that tuft of grass – each pair facing in a different direction. You, Khoarai and Homoi, lie down there on your sides facing each other and at the same time holding each other by the hands. You must all close your eyes.'

She took the magic stick which induces drowsiness and sleep, and said: 'I want you to look closely at this stick and carefully to note the difference between it and the one which makes one wake up.'

She fanned them with the magic stick and the couples on the ground all fell fast asleep. She then said: 'You, Hlabahlabane, shake Katse, try to make him wake up; hold him by the hands and drag him along; take and carry him on your shoulder.' He accomplished all this but it seemed as if he were handling a corpse. He at last burst out, saying: 'This man is dead.'

The instructress took another magic wand and said: 'This one is used for waking up. You must observe that these two sticks are exactly of the same length and thickness and are of the same colour; they are only different at the points. The one for waking the people up has a very small hole hardly noticeable at the thin end and has a sharp point.' She took it and fanned them, and they were all awakened but they were as if they could not tell what had happened during the time they were asleep.

Then the instructress said, 'You, Ma-Sebolelo, want to be initiated in sorcery. It is no play-game. One must be prepared to make a supreme sacrifice. The life of one's first-born is the true foundation.'

Sebolelo sat still as death in the branches above while the instructress continued to speak. But suddenly the child in her arms passed water up in the tree. The water trickled down: 'Drip, drip, drip, drip, drip-drip, drip-drip-drip, drip, drip,' upon them.

'Oh,' cried one below, 'it is already daybreak! The birds are passing water! Daylight has overtaken us. Let us go!'

They all rose up and left the place hurriedly. No sound of any kind was heard after their departure except the hooting of a stray owl only, the bird of sorcerers. They followed the same road by which they had come.

Sebolelo watched them until they had completely disappeared in the distance. There was neither the beating of drums now, nor any singing.

Sebolelo had two hearts. One said: 'Retrace your steps,' while the other said: 'Proceed homeward.' She thought to herself, 'Let me wait a little longer in the tree and suckle the baby. Perchance one of the crowd might return.'

True enough, she saw a woman come running back along the road. She reached the spot and looked about in search. In no time the lost article was discovered. 'I nearly lost something of value,' was the remark made. And the voice was of one well known to Sebolelo.

As she sat and meditated and questioned herself about all she had heard and seen she found herself in deep slumber, for sleep is an enemy which does not recognize even the foes with which one is surrounded. When she woke up she found it was daybreak. She climbed down the tree, put the child on her back, the bundle on her head, and was on the road homeward bound.

Sebolelo bestirred herself and reached her home at sunrise . . . the home where she lived in infancy, where she grew up as an uncircumcised girl and later as a setsoejane, a fully initiated girl . . . the home where she was sought in marriage and was finally married. She arrived when all yearned to see her.

Seipati, her younger sister, was seized with sudden fright when she saw her in the enclosure. She shouted: 'What? Our sister, Sebolelo!' The sudden exclamation called out those in the house. They squeezed each other at the door. Even the dogs rejoiced and seemed as if they were asking the question: 'Where have you been all this time?'

Her mother came out, greeted and kissed her caressingly. With a surprised look on her face she asked: 'Where do you come from in the night like this, Sebolelo, my child? Your father and I were already planning to ask your parents-in-law to grant you permission to pay us a visit to see this child you have, of whom we have been hearing but whom we do not know. What a handsome boy! What is his name?'

'Mother, Xhosa names are difficult! I do not know if you will be able to pronounce it. He has been named after one of the Chiefs of his father's people. He is named Sandile.'

'Come to me, Santile, my grandchild.' She then stretched out her hands, received the child and kissed it.

'What a good-natured child! He is unlike other children, he does not refuse people.'

His grandfather was the last to come out of the house. The noise woke him up. He greeted his daughter and asked the general conditions of life.

'Where are my friends, Mzondeki and Madlamini, how are they keeping?'

'They are all keeping well, my father.'

'Where is the rain at your place?'

'As for the rain, there is enough of it. It will be a year of plenty if hailstorms do not come to destroy the crops. And how are you, my father?'

'God has still His merciful hand upon us, my child. One who was seriously ill and almost died last month was Monaheng, the eldest son of our Chief. Nevertheless the Chief's doctor attended him and here we see him beginning to walk about. Rain we have none. We had a shower at the beginning of last month, we even planted a few garden lots. But the crops have been badly scorched by the heat and have perished. We shall have to go to assist in harvesting at our friends' place.'

He turned to his wife and said: 'Please give me that child here, Ma-Sebolelo, I would like to see him.' His grandmother passed the child over. His grandfather received him and kissed him on the cheek and remarked, 'What a weighty child! I wonder on what do you feed him! What a handsome Xhosa! He has taken after his people. They are a fine-looking set of people, but as for colour and nostril he is a complete picture of his mother.'

Ma-Sebolelo broke in, 'Ra-Sebolelo, the child about whom we have been planning has arrived with her baby whom we see for the first time. Is there no beast which could be slaughtered for their home welcome? This little boy is a Chief at his own home and should therefore be honoured.'

'Yes, it is true. He has visited his maternal home for the first time.'

When the cattle left the kraal next day Khunyeli, the red-spotted ox, the leader of Ra-Sebolelo's team, remained behind with outstretched legs on the open space in front of the kraal . . . the ox which was so dear to Ra-Sebolelo's heart that he had even composed a few lines of verse in his honour. In praising him, he would say:

'Khunyeli, the red-spotted of Ra-Sebolelo's,
He gave them no rest while in captivity by Batlokoa,
He bellowed a lamentable cry,
It is unworthy of Koeneng's beast to hear him cry in a strange village,
The cry released the cattle from captivity.
He was leading them when they entered the home village,
The Sotho beast, the god with moist nostrils.'

After skinning the beast the men cut off small pieces for roasting. The sweet smell of roasted beef summoned passers-by to the open space, for the ox had grazed on rich pastures and was fat to the hoof.

The women bestirred themselves among the pots, for they were cooking half of the animal as there were so many children in Ra-Sebolelo's home. Ma-Sebolelo went to the pots to dish out the meat in accordance with customary law. She then called her daughter to show her the dishes and give orders about them.

'You must listen carefully, my child. This dish belongs to the men at the khotla, your fathers, this one is your own father's, this one is mine, this one is your own, and this last one belongs to the children, the small worms of your own mother's house. I hope you have listened and noted them well. I am going to ask for some snuff from Mapotsane; that woman grinds and makes a very nice snuff.'

'Yes, my mother, I have followed well what you have told me,' and starting with the children's she pointed at each dish as she named them, ending with that of the men at the khotla.

The old lady went away and delayed a long time at her friend's place. After some time, however, she returned.

'I had thought I would come back soon, not knowing that Mapotsane would detain me with news. She is glad to hear you have arrived. She says she will come to greet you tomorrow. Today she is making a mat for her daughter-in-law who is about to be confined.

'Have you eaten your meat, my child?'

'No, my mother. I have just eaten the meat of a very fat chicken brought me by my paternal aunt, Mosili, immediately after you left, and the fat is still thick in my heart. I shall take my meat after I have suckled the child, a little later.'

'Bring my dish then, my child,' said the mother. 'I want to satisfy my craving for meat. You know that we have a taste of meat only when there are visitors like you.'

As she had not tasted meat for a long time she swallowed the pieces without even thorough chewing. But while there still remained one large chunk of meat with a piece of fat on it, they heard, 'Eh! Eh! Eh! Eh! Eh! Eh!' Ma-Sebolelo's eyes were turning round in their sockets!

Ra-Sebolelo was hurriedly summoned from the khotla.

'What is the matter?' he asked.

'Father, we do not know.'

'Hurry up and call the doctor. Tell him to come at once.' But before the messenger had even reached the doctor's place, the spirit had deserted the flesh.

'The doctor says he is coming.' While the messenger was still speaking, someone said: 'There he comes, the old Mampuru.' He came hopping slowly along . . . Mampuru the well-known expert, greatly respected for the achievements with which his name was associated.

'What is the matter?'

'We shall hear from you,' someone replied.

He took out a small package from his bag, untied it, took out a serokolo, chipped a piece off with his teeth, chewed it and then spat on the divining bones. They were already in his hands. He threw them on the ground and remained silent a few minutes, scanning them all the time, and then recited their praises, saying:

> 'Phalafala of Rakhatoe's,
> That hang over precipices, the field mouse suckling
> Propellers that move the immovable,
> Push them forward that they may be exposed.
> The story of sorcerers is never unfolded,
> Mampuru of Tsoene only unfolds such things,
> Monkey come down from the house top,
> Name them one by one, let us hear.'

'They would not be mine, Mampuru. The self-murderer is never sympathized with. Ma-Sebolelo has committed suicide with her own hands. A certain woman gave her a small package containing poison. Here is that woman, the bones point her out. These two monkeys speak. Here they face each other and are conversing.

'The old lady had been instructed to kill someone in order that she herself might be initiated into the art of sorcery by making use of parts from the body. That medicine has caused Ma-Sebolelo's death.'

He then collected the bones of the dead animals, the diviners of the living. He saluted all, saying: 'Remain in peace,' and was gone.

Mampuru returned home and left the people dumbfounded in sorrow.

'Is it not advisable that we call in another doctor,' remarked someone. Sebolelo was not in the least concerned. She was grinding red ochre.

'Thalane,' she said, 'bring me the selibelo you will find in the house, that I may mix the ochre for my body with fat from my father's beast. I want everyone to see that I am at my own home now.'

All present were surprised at her behaviour.

Meanwhile the body had swollen up and had changed colour; it was green like seawater. The mouth was wide open and foaming. The tongue was hanging out like that of a dog after having chased an animal in the hot sun. The eyes were protruding like those of an owl among the thick bushes in daytime.

Ra-Sebolelo was ashamed.

'Sebolelo,' said he, 'you make me feel ashamed indeed. We are in deep sorrow, mourning the death of your mother but to you it appears as if nothing serious has happened.'

'Father, it is indeed painful to me that you should find fault with me as a child who has no respect. If you knew what I know, you would not have said what you have been saying.'

'What is it that you know? Say it out that we too may hear and know it.'

'Fathers and Mothers, open your ears that you may understand well. You call in these doctors and yet you do not have any faith in them. Even if some may be untrustworthy, today, at any rate, this particular one has told the whole truth. The Ancestral Spirits can bear him witness – the Ancestral Spirits who live where there is neither rancour nor evil.'

There was dead silence; even those who were weeping wiped off the tears and listened attentively in order to follow what Sebolelo was saying in defence of her unseemly unconcern. She spoke as one whose toe was tied with a string.

She continued and said: 'I left my home-in-law soon after bedtime. It was about midnight when I crossed the stream Likhetlane. When I approached the huge tree on our side of the stream I heard some singing and the beating of drums. I stood still and listened. I saw a big procession of men and women coming along the road; it was clear we were going to meet. I said to myself, "Tree, you will have to be my father and mother today." I scrambled up the tree and found a nice place among the branches where I settled down and put the child on my lap. When I thought they were going past, they swerved and made straight for the tree where we were hiding. I was practically dead with fear. These men and women, who had put on nothing in front to take away the sense of shame, performed all kinds of magic. I saw the two short sticks with which people are fanned, either to sleep or to wake up. I also heard the instructions given as to how these sticks should be used. But I heard much more.

'After a long time a woman spoke and said: "You, Ma-Sebolelo, want to be initiated in sorcery. Sorcery is not a plaything. It demands and costs the life of a person." She then handed my mother a small package, saying, "One going in for this art must be prepared to make a supreme sacrifice . . . the life of one's first-born is the true foundation. Should Sebolelo eat, we shall go and exhume the body the night of the day of the burial and use the parts taken from her body to initiate you.

'"If you carry out my instructions without a single mistake," she said, "I can assure you nobody will ever go behind you. Here am I, I already have one hundred and forty-three victims under the ground and yet I am only forty-three years married. There is none of those well-known doctors who has been able to smell me out. Why? Because I was initiated into this art by sacrificing Moitsepi, my first-born, the child I loved most dearly.

'"I hope you have followed and caught well what I have been saying, my friend."

'The crowd dispersed when my child passed water in the tree. They left in a great hurry while I sat meditating and wondering at what I had just seen and heard. On looking up I saw one human figure come running along the road. She reached the spot, searched for something under the tree and discovered it. Then she followed the crowd, running. I knew who it was by appearance and by voice.

'While I sat in loneliness on the tree after the disappearance of that person, asking myself many questions, I fell fast asleep together with my little baby. When I awoke it was daybreak. I came down from the tree and took the road and reached home when the sun was just leaving the ground.

'I shall not worry you with the slaughtering of Khunyeli, with which you are all familiar. The meat was prepared and cooked. After the meat had been divided, my mother called me while I was busy working in the house to show me the dishes. She said she was going to Mapotsane's for some snuff. She ended with these words: "I do hope you are quite clear, my child."

'"I am quite clear, mother." I started naming the dishes one by one, pointing at each with my finger, commencing with that of the children and ending with the one which belonged to the men at the khotla.

'"You would not have been the child of my upbringing," said my mother when I finished pointing at them, "if you had made a mistake."

'At long last my mother returned and said to me, "Have you taken your meat, my child? Please bring me my dish, that I may satisfy the craving for meat. You know too well yourself that we only taste meat through visitors like you."

'There it is! You now see the result of the small package which my mother picked up under the tree. Do you still say the doctor is a liar and that another doctor should be called in?'

She continued and said: 'Some of those who were in that night-crowd are men and women living in this very village of ours and I can name them if needs be. The majority, however, were men and women living in the neighbouring villages.'

The woman to whom Ma-Sebolelo had gone for snuff, and others who had been in the crowd at night, suffered guilty conscience and thought their names would be brought out. They kept their eyes on the ground and could not look those present in the face.

* * *

Now Ra-Sebolelo was a man of some standing, highly respected in the village and throughout the country. He was a councillor at Chief Thuloane's khotla. He became confused in thought through what had befallen him. Nevertheless, he was compelled to report the matter to the Chief.

'Senokoane, hasten to the Chief,' said he, 'and tell him I have sent you to report the sudden death of Ma-Sebolelo. You must explain carefully the whole story as narrated by Sebolelo.'

Chief Thuloane was a minor Taung Chief who lived at Mpharane and was noted, not only for his hunting exploits, but also for justice in administering the law at his khotla. Cases of appeal from his decisions were very rare.

The messenger left in a great hurry, for the corpse had already gone bad and forced the people to leave the hut. Fortunately he found the Chief and the councillors at the khotla, hearing a case.

'Motaung!' said the messenger with the right hand in the air, thus greeting the Chief.

After a while a councillor whispered into the Chief's ear, telling him that there was a messenger at the khotla. The proceedings were suspended.

'Chief, I have been sent to you by Ra-Sebolelo to report the unexpected death of Ma-Sebolelo.'

'When did that happen?' asked the Chief. 'We saw Ma-Sebolelo go past there to Mapotsane's not long ago. We even saw her enter Mapotsane's door.'

'She passed away in the late afternoon, Chief, just after her return from Mapotsane's. I have been instructed to detail what happened so that the Chief may understand. Sebolelo arrived yesterday morning at sunrise from her home-in-law. It is she who has given us a full and clear account of what has caused her mother's death.'

Then Senokoane related the story of the night-crowd under the tree near the stream Likhetlane and of all that Sebolelo saw and heard. He explained how Ra-Sebolelo's ox, Khunyeli, was slaughtered, the cooking of the meat, the dishing out in accordance with orders given by the dead one. He told the Chief what the doctor, Mampuru, had revealed after throwing divining bones and how what he had said coincided with the story related by Sebolelo after he had left.

'Tell Ra-Sebolelo,' said the Chief, 'that I have received the sad news and I express my sympathy with him, his family, and all his blood relations. Nevertheless the corpse of that dog, that sorcerer and murderer of my people, must be dragged along, and thrown away on top of that hillock overlooking the village, so that the vultures and the flesh-eaters may satisfy their hunger. The body must not be buried in the usual way.'

Painful though the Chief's orders were, they had to be carried out.

'Tie the body with riems, drag it along and throw it away on top of that hillock,' commanded Ra-Sebolelo.

'There is no way of tying and slipping the body along the ground because it is already in a state of decay,' said Senokoane. 'The only way is to carry it on a stretcher, although I know we shall have broken the Chief's orders.'

'Carry it then on a stretcher, I shall bear the consequences,' said the owner of the body.

They carried her in turns. A very stout and heavy person was the deceased. They put the body down at the spot indicated and left it exposed.

As they departed, they saw the vultures already soaring above, high in the air. And when they entered the village the birds of prey were already sitting around the carcass awaiting the arrival of the black and bald-headed one, morena tlake, the king, to open the way for the commoners to satisfy their hunger. He arrived and went nearer, pulled out an eye, and then another, thus declaring the feast open. In no time there remained nothing but a skeleton, the ribs forming a sort of cage wherein bees could easily hive. The eye-sockets presented a spectacle terrible to look at.

The village dogs scared away the birds and moved about the carcass, gnawing at whatever remained of flesh on the skeleton. They, in turn, were driven away by the herd-boys on their arrival with their herds of cattle and flocks of sheep from the veld at sunset. After milking, and folding off the calves, they took hold of the skeleton with their whips and dragged it into a large pool where they usually watered their herds. Henceforth the pool received a new name and was called the Grave of Ma-Sebolelo.

The next day, all the dogs that had gnawed at the skeleton were found dead and decayed, pieces of flesh falling off when handled.

A messenger was sent to the mountain Matlakeng to see if anything had happened to any of the vultures.

A traveller left Tsotetseng for Pitseng. When he reached the khotla at Mpharane, he was so excited that he even forgot the usual preliminaries when men meet each other the first time. 'I have seen a most wonderful thing when I passed near Matlakeng! I found tens and tens of vultures dead at the base of the mountain. It seems to me they came rolling down the mountainside from the high cliffs above, judging by the feathers and the pieces of wings that remained on the mountainside. The smell is most unbearable. I have travelled far and wide but I have never seen anything like it!'

'What has killed those vultures is what has killed our dogs,' said Tsoeu, the most famous hunter at Mpharane. 'I have lost a most beautiful dog, a bloodhound named Phaphama, for which I paid the Chief seven sheep. Such a fast runner I have never seen. It did not run but flew like a bird. It fed my family, who were never without meat. I regarded it as my gun whenever we went out on a hunting expedition; these men here can bear me witness. I have suffered an irreparable loss. That woman's medicine is a very strong poison with which she will, I am afraid, exterminate the people. If I were the Chief I would force Sebolelo to bring out her name and then put her away.'

The traveller was taken round and shown the dogs where they lay dead and rotting. It was only then he realized what had caused the death of the vultures.

'I agree with you,' he said; 'you men should make the Chief realize the danger with which his tribe is threatened.'

And when the messenger who had gone to the mountain returned, he could not speak enough of the dead vultures and of their terrible smell.

'I have counted twenty dead, including morena tlake, the great chief who lay bald-headed, dead amongst his followers.'

'These poor birds, God's creatures, and our dogs, without doubt, are Ma-Sebolelo's victims,' said Tsoeu, who spoke with an aching heart when he thought of his beloved dog, Phaphama, and of all that had befallen the village since Sebolelo had returned to her home.

Once in a Century

» «

D. B. Z. NTULI

TRANSLATED FROM THE ZULU BY C. S. Z. NTULI

The children, grandchildren and the great-grandchildren sat on the grass in the shade. They all stared expectantly at MaMsomi, a very tall old lady. She sat and peered at them with her watery grey eyes. Her face was criss-crossed with wrinkles. When she smiled she revealed one solitary tooth. She had every reason to smile so broadly because her children had organized a great party to celebrate her estimated one hundred years of life on earth.

'What do you say, my children? You want me to tell you the story of the most memorable event in these hundred years I have lived?'

Her grown-up children – the organizers of the celebration – agreed eagerly. They knew that in the life of someone who had lived a hundred years, one particular event would probably stand out among all the others as the event of the lifetime. 'Don't tell us a fable, Granny,' said one of the grandchildren.

'There is no real-life experience that I have not told you about, my children. I have told you everything I could remember. If you want a story, let me tell you a fable. I certainly have not told you all the fables I know.'

'No, Granny. Please! Tell us a real story – something that actually happened to you. We don't mind even if some of us have heard the story before. It's very likely that it will be new to many of us. Please, Granny: the greatest event of your life.'

'That is quite true, my child.' The old lady stopped smiling. She knitted her wrinkled brow. 'Although I have told you about almost all the important events of my life, there is one which I have reserved through all the years. I told myself that I would tell the story of that event if the Creator allows me to live very long. Well, you say I have lived very long. So this, perhaps, is the right time for me to tell the story. It is a story of the most frightful experience I have gone through. In fact, I have always been trying hard to forget that terrible experience because whenever I thought of it I simply panicked. I feared that the whole thing would happen again just as suddenly as it did that awful afternoon long, long ago.'

The old lady coughed softly to clear her throat. She wiped her wrinkles with a new handkerchief. She peered steadily at the host of bright faces around her. They were all eyes and ears: even the tiny ones in their mothers' arms seemed to appreciate the distance in years between them and the grand old lady.

'This happened shortly after I had become a member of the Mlangeni family. I think it was only six months after I had arrived here. Then this thing happened to me. But . . . no! I mustn't tell you this story; if I do you won't sleep well tonight.'

Several young voices shouted together: 'No, Granny! Please tell us the story. We won't be scared.'

She knitted her brow again. This, certainly, was not just one of the fascinating stories she had told before. It was something unique, for Granny was not in the habit of taking wide detours to get at her stories. There was silence under the tree – a silence disturbed only by the gentle rustle of the leaves above.

'Mlangeni was not at home that day, and the little girl who had come with me on my wedding day had gone out to collect firewood. I was all alone, singing a little tune as I went about my household chores. All of a sudden, a hair at the top of my head gave a premonitory twist. I told myself it was nothing. The hair gave another twist. Then my whole scalp seemed to shrink and go cold, as if every hair on my head had stood on end. I stopped singing. The premonitory sensation spread over my whole body. I felt unsafe in the hut – as if a deadly being was about to pounce upon me. I put away the broom with which I had been cleaning the floor. I looked around. Could a snake have sneaked in? No. There was no snake in the hut. Was the thing stalking me from outside, then? I went to the door and peeped out. There was nothing directly in front of the hut. I looked right: nothing there. I looked left, and . . . there it was! To this very day, my children, it is a mystery to me why I did not drop dead in the doorway. There it was, standing perfectly still, but as menacing as a black mamba poised to strike . . .'

'What was it, Granny? A lion?'

'No, my child; something infinitely more terrible: a huge black man! He was pitch black, my children. He wore a loinskin and nothing else, and carried an enormous knobkerrie in his left hand. He did not move. He did not speak. He just glared at me with eyes as large as those of that bull over there. I was scared. I stepped out. For a moment I looked away from those eyes to see if there was anyone who could hear if I screamed. The world seemed to have been deserted. I thought of sprinting away, but a glance at those legs convinced me that the brute would run me down in a few strides. He was extremely fit, his great muscles bulging as if they would break through his black skin.

'I saw those muscles clearly when the hideous fellow began moving towards me, my children. Slowly he came nearer. He came nearer, and I noticed how ugly he was. He was ugly, my children, without a single redeeming feature. He came close to me with his nauseating, slimy ugliness. I trembled. I wanted to scream. He stopped only a few paces away from me. He glared at me, his barrel of a chest rising and falling. I noticed then how loud his breathing was.

'I opened my mouth to scream, but, to my greatest dismay, my voicebox would not function. I stood and stared at the black man. My heart was beating hard. For a single moment I shifted my eyes away from his, and in that instant he struck me a stunning blow with his knobkerrie.

'When I regained consciousness, my ears picked up a steady rumbling sound. I opened my eyes. A large snow-white sheet of water was hurtling down the face of a high precipice, to plunge with a roar into a large pool at the bottom of the cliff. I was lying near a waterfall. It was already after sunset. I tried to get up. I couldn't. My whole body was aching. Then I heard the croaking of frogs further down the river, where I could see reeds and swamps. I tried to think hard, but I could not recognize this place. I asked myself why I was there. Then I remembered. The black man! He was the last person I had seen. When I opened my eyes again – now my thinking was quite clear – I saw him. He was sitting on a stone, glaring at me exactly as he had done before he knocked me out. I was terrified. I thought about my in-laws. I thought about my father and mother. "What if they find me here?" I thought. What would happen to my name?

'The man just sat there, looking at me. He did not even wink. It was gradually becoming dark. I heard no noise other than the croaking of the frogs and the rumbling of the waterfall. I saw only the falling white water and the black man. I tried to get up but I could not move a single limb. It felt as if my whole body was paralysed.

'Now I could see only a faint outline of the black man's body against the deepening blackness of the night. The waterfall rumbled monotonously until my head began to reel. I just told myself I was not going to faint. The possibility of my captor falling asleep could not be ruled out. I looked up towards him, hoping that he might be dozing off already. My heart almost jumped out through my mouth. The black man's eyes were now glowing like two embers. I knew then that my predicament was much worse than I had thought. Once again I tried in vain to get up and scream for help.

'The rumbling waterfall was now a pale grey in the darkness. The fiery eyes were still staring at me. The embers gradually became two bright torches lighting up the whole place in front of the black man. I could see his knees and his knobkerrie.

'While I was trying hard to think of a way to escape, I heard a noise other than the sound of the waterfall and the frogs. It was a sound of many human voices. The noise gradually increased, showing that the people were coming nearer and nearer. As the volume of the voices increased, the dizziness that I had been feeling also increased. I felt as if I was being swung to and fro in the air. Now I could hear what those people were singing. I listened as if my life depended on hearing the approaching choir. Children's voices! They were singing and clapping their hands in time to the music. I listened. Now I could pick up the words of the almost unintelligible song:

'"Ha thithi, hathutha,
Shiya shiya hathithi, hathutha.
Kuyakhuya, hathithi, hathutha."

'The singing came closer. I did not see the singers, but I heard that they were now standing around me. The noise of the waterfall gradually became fainter while the singing grew louder: "Ha thithi, hathutha".

'All of a sudden a thunderous voice roared from where the black man was sitting: "We mean business, now, MaMsomi. You too must sing. Now!" To my greatest surprise, my voicebox functioned normally again. I began to sing with the unseen children. Slowly and hesitantly at first, I picked up the tune as the children sang. After a few repetitions, I was singing as well as the best of them and soon afterwards I was the leading singer: "Ha thithi, hathutha . . ."

'The song penetrated my mind, my heart and my soul, and I sang it with so much depth of feeling that I almost wept. I was fully conscious of everything that was happening – fully aware of what I was doing and why I was doing it. Even the dizziness had passed. My thinking was perfectly clear. I thought about your grandfather. I wondered what he was doing after finding that I had disappeared. My disappearance, I thought, must have been reported to the neighbours. A messenger must have been sent to my home. A search must have been launched.

'The man with the eyes of fire read my thoughts. He roared: "Don't you worry: I am in charge here. Today you will be transformed. I will decide what you shall become. You are no longer going to live the way you are accustomed to. I want you to be like those who are singing. Sing louder!"

'I sang at the top of my voice. Then the man himself began to sing in his deep bass voice. The fire came closer, and I knew what that meant: the black man was coming nearer. The movement of the fire showed that the brute was dancing. The children's voices were singing with increased vigour, throwing in a remark here and there in appreciation of the black man's performance. The eyes of fire came very close to me. I had no doubt in my mind then that my days of normal, human living were over. Tonight I was going to be changed into one of those semi-human beings of whose existence I had always refused to believe. The eyes of fire were boring down into my brain as the horrible fellow stood astride over my prostrate body. He was singing. I was singing. Everybody was singing: "Ha thithi, hathutha . . ."

'Suddenly I was seized by many coarse hands. I was lifted bodily off the ground. They sang on as they lifted me. I did not stop singing. The man sang even more vociferously. He spoke again: "My name is Bhodloza, the one who breaks things. You shall do my will." Then he sang. I was lifted higher . . . higher . . . right up, and then with a mighty heave the hands threw me into the pool. Just when I splashed on the water, the large knobkerrie landed with a thud on the top of my head. I lost count of space and time.

'When I came to, my body was in ice-cold water. I felt my body shrinking, becoming smaller and smaller. They were still singing: "Kuyakhuya, hathithi, hathutha."

'Ah, my children! When I say I am very old, I mean more than the age that can be counted in scores of years. I refer more to the variety, the depth and the intensity of the experiences I have gone through.'

There was silence among the children. The keen interest which had been aroused could be seen in their eyes. In most of the eyes, MaMsomi saw expressions of deep sympathy. They requested her to continue.

'It's difficult to go on, my children. I think I must not tell you the rest of what happened to me that night. It's too terrible. Even in my grave I won't forget it. In fact, as I did not die that night, I don't think I shall ever die. There are aspects of life which one can't believe until one comes to grips with the stark reality of those things. When you hear about diviners who spend long periods of time at the bottom of deep pools and still manage to breathe, you might think it's all old women's fables. It's easy enough to shake your head knowingly when you hear of water sprites or of exhumed corpses transformed into goblins, but when you . . . well, well! Let me go back to the story.

'My body was immersed in ice-cold water, and I felt it shrink. Then the whole body began to itch as if thousands of tiny ants were nibbling at my skin. In spite of everything that had happened, my mind was still perfectly clear. I remembered what the black man had said about being changed into something else, and I took a resolution: if he meant that he wanted to change me into a kelpy, then he was making a serious mistake. I was not prepared to change. I was going to remain an ordinary human being. The nibbling at my skin intensified. I intensified my resolution: I didn't want to change. I was not prepared to be separated from Mlangeni. Never!

'The singers were still at it. The black man's roaring bass was now singing the lead. The others were lisping as vigorously as ever, but their voices were becoming hoarse. Then the man spoke: "You are a hard nut to crack, MaMsomi. I am now passing you on to the next stage. You shall do my will." I felt the hands again. They pulled me out of the pool and carried me away, singing their song all the way. They carried me into a large cave. By the dim light of a fire which had been lit in the stinking cave I saw that there were many rows of human skulls, baboon skulls, dog skulls and skulls of several other strange animals. By the same light I saw – for the first time that long night – what type of creatures comprised the black man's choir. They had human form. Judging by the size of their bodies – all very short – one would have thought they were children, but their heads were those of grown-up people, both male and female. The males had little beards. They all wore skirts made of grass. They sang and danced very vigorously but they did not sweat.

'While I was still looking around in amazement, the black man came in. There was no more fire in his eyes. He went and sat by the fire. Then he began to sing. Once again he arrested my eyes with his. As he continued looking steadily into my eyes, my head began to reel again. The nasty smell was adding to my discomfort. The man spoke: "This is the end of the road, MaMsomi. As you already know, my name is Bhodloza. Nobody has ever resisted me at this stage. This is the final stage. You are a stubborn subject, MaMsomi. I am glad I got you. You will be very useful to me. Dance, you there! Sing!"

'The short creatures danced more vigorously than ever before. Now they had formed a single line. They moved around me as they danced and clapped their hands. The cave echoed to the sound of the singing voices, the stamping feet and clapping hands: "Hathithi, hathutha."

'The man then took what must have been one of a few large pieces of a broken clay-pot. From the tip of one of the firebrands he broke off a cinder into the piece of a clay-pot. He sprinkled some powder on the live cinder. A blue smoke rose from the burning powder. The man seized my head and held it face down over the rising smoke. He ordered me to inhale the smoke. When I did, I felt as if my head was splitting in two. All of a sudden my dislike for the gruesome cave was displaced by an ardent love for this place. I loved the dancing. I loved the black man. I felt a strong dislike for your grandfather. I wished I would never see him again. And for the first time since I had been knocked down in front of my hut, I stood up and joined the dance. I danced.

Even on my wedding day I had not danced like this. I only wished I could become as short as the others. But as far as the singing was concerned, I had every reason to be satisfied with myself. My beautiful soprano rose loud and clear as I led what must have been the best rendering of our great song:

> '"Ha thithi, hathutha
> Shiya shiya hathithi, hathutha
> Kuyakhuya, hathithi, hathutha."

'That, my children is the most memorable experience in the hundred years I have spent on earth.'

'What happened next in the cave, Granny? I see you are still very tall,' asked one of the listeners. 'How did you escape?'

The ancient one smiled. 'You and your questions! It's time to eat now. Bring all the soft delicacies that don't require any chewing. Then I will show you how to celebrate. But first, bow down, all of you, and let me examine your heads.' All the heads bowed before the ancient one. She clapped her hands and exclaimed: 'I thought as much! Now I know: it's not true that a pair of horns grows on the head of anyone who listens to a fable by day!'

They all laughed.

Out of the Fountain

» «

DORIS LESSING

I could begin, There was once a man called Ephraim who lived in . . . but for me this story begins with a fog. Fog in Paris delayed a flight to London by a couple of hours, and so a group of travellers sat around a table drinking coffee and entertaining each other.

A woman from Texas joked that a week before she had thrown coins into the fountain in Rome for luck – and had been dogged by minor ill-fortune ever since. A Canadian said she had spent far too much money on a holiday and at the same fountain three days ago had been tempted to lift coins out with a magnet when no one was looking. Someone said that in a Berlin theatre last night there had been a scene where a girl flung money all about the stage in a magnificently scornful gesture. Which led us on to where money is trampled on, burned, flung about or otherwise ritually scorned; which is odd, since such gestures never take place in life. Not at all, said a matron from New York – she had seen with her own eyes some Flower Children burning money on a sidewalk to show their contempt for it; but for her part what it showed was that they must have rich parents. (This dates the story, or at least the fog.)

All the same, considering the role money plays in all our lives, it *is* odd how often authors cause characters to insult dollar bills, roubles, pound notes. Which enables audience, readers, to go home, or to shut the book, feeling cleansed of the stuff? Above it?

Whereas we are told that in less surly days sultans on feast days flung gold coins into crowds happy to scramble for it; that kings caused showers of gold to descend on loved ministers; and that if jewels fell in showers from the sky no one would dream of asking suspicious questions.

The nearest any one of us could remember to this kingly stuff was a certain newspaper mogul in London who would reward a promising young journalist for an article which he (the mogul) liked, with an envelope stuffed full of five-pound notes sent around by special messenger – but this kind of thing is only too open to unkind interpretation; and the amount of ill-feeling aroused in the bosoms of fellow journalists, and the terror in that of the recipient for fear the thing might be talked about, is probably why we stage such scenes as it were in reverse, and why, on the edge of a magic fountain, we slide in a single coin, like a love letter into an envelope during an affair which one's better sense entirely deplores. Sympathetic magic – but a small magic, a mini-magic, a most furtive summoning of the Gods of Gold. And, if a hand rose from the fountain to throw us coins and jewels, it is more than likely that, schooled as we are by recent literature, we'd sneer and throw them back in its teeth – so to speak.

And now a man who had not spoken at all said that he knew of a case where jewels had been flung into the dust of a public square in Italy. No one had thrown them back. He took from his pocket a wallet, and from the wallet a fold of paper such as jewellers use, and on the paper lay a single spark or gleam of light. It was a slice of milk-and-rainbow opal. Yes, he said, he had been there. He had picked up the fragment and kept it. It wasn't valuable, of course. He would tell us the story if he thought there was time, but for some reason it was a tale so precious to him that he didn't want to bungle it through having to hurry. Here there was another swirl of silkily gleaming fog beyond the glass of the restaurant wall, and another announcement of unavoidable delay.

So he told the story. One day someone will introduce me to a young man called Nikki (perhaps, or what you will) who was born during the Second World War in Italy. His father was a hero, and his mother now the wife of the Ambassador to . . . Or perhaps in a bus, or at a dinner party, there will be a girl who has a pearl hanging around her neck on a chain, and when asked about it she will say: Imagine, my mother was given this pearl by a man who was practically a stranger, and when she gave it to me she said . . . Something like that will happen: and then this story will have a different beginning, not a fog at all . . .

There was a man called Ephraim who lived in Johannesburg. His father was to do with diamonds, as had been his father. The family were immigrants. This is still true of all people from Johannesburg, a city a century old. Ephraim was a middle son, not brilliant or stupid, not good or bad. He was nothing in particular. His brothers became diamond merchants, but Ephraim was not cut out for anything immediately obvious, and so at last he was apprenticed to an uncle to learn the trade of diamond-cutting.

To cut a diamond perfectly is an act like a samurai's sword-thrust, or a master archer's centred arrow. When an important diamond is shaped a man may spend a week, or even weeks, studying it, accumulating powers of attention, memory, intuition, till he has reached that moment when he finally knows that a tap, no more, at just *that* point of tension in the stone will split it exactly *so*.

While Ephraim learned to do this, he lived at home in a Johannesburg suburb; and his brothers and sisters married and had families. He was the son who took his time about getting married, and about whom the family first joked, saying that he was choosy; and then they remained silent when others talked of him with that edge on their voices, irritated, a little malicious, even frightened, which is caused by those men and women who refuse to fulfil the ordinary purposes of nature. The kind ones said he was a good son, working nicely under his uncle Ben, and living respectably at home, and on Sunday nights playing poker with bachelor friends. He was twenty-five, then thirty, thirty-five, forty. His parents became old and died, and he lived alone in the family house. People stopped noticing him. Nothing was expected of him.

Then a senior person became ill, and Ephraim was asked to fly in his stead to Alexandria for a special job. A certain rich merchant of Alexandria had purchased an uncut diamond as a present for his daughter, who was to be married shortly. He wished only the best for the diamond. Ephraim, revealed by this happening as one of the world's master diamond-cutters, flew to Egypt, spent some days in communion with the stone in a quiet room in the merchant's house, and then caused it to fall apart into three lovely pieces. These were for a ring and earrings.

Now he should have flown home again; but the merchant asked him to dinner. An odd chance that – unusual. Not many people got inside that rich closed world. But perhaps the merchant had become infected by the week of rising tension while Ephraim became one with the diamond in a quiet room.

At dinner Ephraim met the girl for whom the jewels were destined.

And now – but what can be said about the fortnight that followed? Certainly not that Ephraim, the little artisan from Johannesburg, fell in love with Mihrène, daughter of a modern merchant prince. Nothing so simple. And that the affair had about it a quality out of the ordinary was shown by the reaction of the merchant himself, Mihrène's conventional papa.

Conventional, commonplace, banal – these are the words for the members of the set, or class, to which Mihrène Kantannis belonged. In all the cities about the Mediterranean they live in a scattered community, very rich, but tastefully so, following international fashions, approving Paris when they should and London when they should, making trips to New York or Rome, summering on whichever shore they have chosen, by a kind of group instinct, to be the right one for the year, and sharing comfortably tolerant opinions. They were people, are people, with nothing remarkable about them but their wealth, and the enchanting Mihrène, whom Ephraim first saw in a mist of white embroidered muslin standing by a fountain, was a girl neither more pretty nor more gifted than, let's say, a dozen that evening in Alexandria, a thousand or so in Egypt, hundreds of thousands in the countries round about, all of which produce so plentifully her particular type – her beautiful type: small-boned, black-haired, black-eyed, apricot-skinned, lithe.

She had lived for twenty years in this atmosphere of well-chosen luxury; loved and bickered with her mother and her sisters; respected her papa; and was intending to marry Paulo, a young man from South America with whom she would continue to live exactly the same kind of life, only in Buenos Aires.

For her it was an ordinary evening, a family dinner at which a friend of Papa's was present. She did not know about the diamonds: they were to be a surprise. She was wearing last year's dress and a choker of false pearls: that season it was smart to wear 'costume' pearls, and to leave one's real pearls in a box on one's dressing-table.

Ephraim, son of jewellers, saw the false pearls around that neck and suffered.

Why, though? Johannesburg is full of pretty girls. But he had not travelled much, and Johannesburg, rough, built on gold, as it were breathing by the power of gold, a city waxing and waning with the fortunes of gold (as befits this story), may be exciting, violent, vibrant, but it has no mystery, nothing for the imagination, no invisible dimensions. Whereas Alexandria . . . This house, for instance, with its discreetly blank outer walls that might conceal anything, crime, or the hidden court of an exiled king, held inner gardens and fountains, and Mihrène, dressed appropriately in moonwhite and who . . . well, perhaps she wasn't entirely at her best that evening. There were those who said she had an ugly laugh. Sometimes the family joked that it was lucky she would never have to earn a living. At one point during dinner, perhaps feeling that she ought to contribute to the entertainment, she told a rather flat and slightly bitchy story about a friend. She was certainly bored, yawned once or twice, and did not try too hard to hide the yawns. The diamond-cutter from Johannesburg gazed at her, forgot to eat, and asked twice why she wore false pearls in a voice rough with complaint. He was gauche, she decided – and forgot him.

He did not return home, but wired for money. He had never spent any, and so had a great deal available for the single perfect pearl which he spent days looking for, and which he found at last in a back room in Cairo, where he sat bargaining over coffee cups for some days with an old Persian dealer who knew as much about gems as he did, and who would not trade in anything but the best.

With this jewel he arrived at the house of Mihrène's father, and when he was seated in a room opening on to an inner court where jasmine clothed a wall, and lily pads a pool, he asked permission to give the pearl to the young girl.

It had been strange that Papa had invited this tradesman to dinner. It was strange that now Papa did not get angry. He was shrewd: it was his life to be shrewd. There was no nuance of commercial implication in a glance, a tone of voice, a turn of phrase, that he was not certain to assess rightly. Opposite this fabulously rich man into whose house only the rich came as guests, sat a little diamond-cutter who proposed to give his daughter a small fortune in the shape of a pearl, and who wanted nothing in return for it.

They drank coffee, and then they drank whisky, and they talked of the world's jewels and of the forthcoming wedding, until for the second time Ephraim was asked to dinner.

At dinner Mihrène sat opposite the elderly gentleman (he was forty-five or so) who was Papa's business friend, and was ordinarily polite: then slightly more polite, because of a look from Papa. The party was Mihrène, her father, her fiancé Paulo, and Ephraim. The mother and sisters were visiting else-where. Nothing happened during the meal. The young couple were rather inattentive to the older pair. At the end, Ephraim took a screw of paper from his pocket, and emptied from it a single perfect pearl that had a gleam like the flesh of a rose, or of a twenty-year-old girl. This pearl he offered to Mihrène, with the remark that she oughtn't to wear false pearls. Again it was harshly inflected; a complaint, or a reproach for imperfect perfection.

The pearl lay on white damask in candlelight. Into the light above the pearl was thrust the face of Ephraim, whose features she could reconstruct from the last time she had seen him a couple of weeks before only with the greatest of difficulty.

It was, of course, an extraordinary moment. But not dramatic – no, it lacked that high apex of decisiveness as when Ephraim tapped a diamond, or an archer lets loose his bow. Mihrène looked at her father for an explanation. So, of course, did her fiancé. Her father did not look confused, or embar-rassed, so much as that he wore the air of somebody standing on one side because here is a situation which he has never professed himself competent to judge. And Mihrène had probably never before in her life been left free to make a decision.

She picked up the pearl from the damask, and let it lie in her palm. She, her fiancé, and her father, looked at the pearl whose value they were all well equipped to assess, and Ephraim looked sternly at the girl. Then she lifted long, feathery black lashes and looked at him – in inquiry? An appeal to be let off? His eyes were judging, disappointed; they said what his words had said: Why are you content with the second-rate?

Preposterous . . .

Impossible . . .

Finally Mihrène gave the slightest shrug of shoulders, tonight covered in pink organza, and said to Ephraim, 'Thank you, thank you very much.'

They rose from the table. The four drank coffee on the terrace over which rose a wildly evocative Alexandrian moon, two nights away from the full, a moon quite unlike any that might shine over strident Johannesburg. Mihrène let the pearl lie on her palm and reflect moonrays, while from time to time her black eyes engaged with Ephraim's – but what colour his were had never been, would never be, of interest to anyone – and, there was no doubt of it, he was like someone warning, or reminding, or even threatening.

Next day he went back to Johannesburg, and on Mihrène's dressing-table lay a small silver box in which was a single perfect pearl.

She was to marry in three weeks.

Immediately the incident became in the family: 'That crazy little Jew who fell for Mihrène . . .' Her acceptance of the pearl was talked of as an act of delicacy on her part, of kindness. 'Mihrène was so kind to the poor old thing . . .' Thus they smoothed over what had happened, made acceptable an incident which could have no place in their life, their thinking. But they knew, of course, and most particularly did Mihrène know, that something else had happened.

When she refused to marry Paulo, quite prettily and nicely, Papa and Mamma Kantannis made ritual remarks about her folly, her ingratitude, and so forth, but in engagements like these no hearts are expected to be broken, for the marriages are like the arranged marriages of dynasties. If she did not marry Paulo, she would marry someone like him – and she was very young.

They remarked that she had not been herself since the affair of the pearl. Papa said to himself that he would see to it no more fly-by-nights arrived at his dinner-table. They arranged for Mihrène a visit to cousins in Istanbul.

Meanwhile in Johannesburg a diamond-cutter worked at his trade, cutting diamonds for engagement rings, dress rings, tie pins, necklaces, bracelets. He imagined a flat bowl of crystal, which glittered like diamonds, in which were massed roses. But the roses were all white, shades of white. He saw roses which were cold marble white, white verging on coffee colour, greenish white, like the wings of certain butterflies, white that blushed, a creamy white, white that was nearly beige, white that was almost yellow. He imagined a hundred shades of white in rose shapes. These he pressed together, filled a crystal dish with them and gave them to – Mihrène? It is possible that already he scarcely thought of her. He imagined how he would collect stones in shades of white, and create a perfect jewel, bracelet, necklet, or crescent for the hair, and present this jewel to – Mihrène? Does it matter whom it was for? He bought opals, like mist held behind glass on which lights moved and faded, like milk where fire lay buried, like the congealed breath of a girl on a frosty night. He bought pearls, each one separately, each one perfect. He bought fragments of mother-of-pearl. He bought moonstones like clouded diamonds. He even bought lumps of glass that someone had shaped to reflect light perfectly. He bought white jade and crystals and collected chips of diamond to make the suppressed fires in pearl and opal flash out in reply to their glittering frost. These jewels he had in folded flat paper, and they were kept first in a small cigarette box, and then were transferred to a larger box that had been for throat lozenges, and then to an even larger box that had held cigars. He played with these gems, dreamed over them, arranged them in his mind in a thousand ways. Sometimes he remembered an exquisite girl dressed in moonmist: the memory was becoming more and more like a sentimental postcard or an old-fashioned calendar.

In Istanbul Mihrène married, without her family's approval, a young Italian engineer whom normally she would never have met. Her uncle was engaged in reconstructing a certain yacht; the engineer was in the uncle's office to discuss the reconstruction when Mihrène came in. It was she who made the first move: it would have to be. He was twenty-seven, with nothing but his salary, and no particular prospects. His name was Carlos. He was political. That is, precisely, he was revolutionary, a conspirator. Politics did not enter the world of Mihrène. Or rather, it could be said that such families *are* politics, politics in their aspect of wealth, but this becomes evident only when deals are made that are so vast that they have international cachet, and repute, like the alliances or rifts between countries.

Carlos called Mihrène 'a white goose' when she tried to impress him with her seriousness. He called her 'a little rich bitch'. He made a favour of taking her to meetings where desperately serious young men and women discussed the forthcoming war – the year was 1939. It was an affair absolutely within the traditions of such romances: her family were bound to think she was throwing herself away; he and his friends on the whole considered that it was he who was conferring the benefits.

To give herself courage in her determination to be worthy of this young hero, she would open a tiny silver box where a pearl lay on silk, and say to herself: *He* thought I was worth something . . .

She married her Carlos in the week Paulo married a girl from a French dynasty. Mihrène went to Rome and lived in a small villa without servants, and with nothing to fall back on but the memory of a nondescript elderly man who had sat opposite her throughout two long, dull dinners and who had given her a pearl as if he were giving her a lesson. She thought that in all her life no one else had ever demanded anything of her, ever asked anything, ever taken her seriously.

The war began. In Buenos Aires the bride who had taken her place lived in luxury. Mihrène, a poor housewife, saw her husband who was a conspirator against the fascist Mussolini become a conscript in Mussolini's armies, then saw him go away to fight, while she waited for the birth of her first child.

The war swallowed her. When she was heard of again, her hero was dead, and her first child was dead, and her second, conceived on Carlos's final leave, was due to be born in a couple of months. She was in a small town in the centre of Italy with no resources at all but her pride: she had sworn she would not earn the approval of her parents on any terms but her own. The family she had married into had suffered badly: she had a room in the house of an aunt.

The Germans were retreating through Italy: after them chased the victorious armies of the Allies . . . but that sounds like an official war history.

To try again: over a peninsula that was shattered, ruinous, starved by war, two armies of men foreign to the natives of the place were in movement; one in retreat up towards the body of Europe, the other following it. There were places where these opposing bodies were geographically so intermingled that only uniforms distinguished them. Both armies were warm, well clothed, well fed, supplied with alcohol and cigarettes. The native inhabitants had no heat, no warm clothes, little food, no cigarettes. They had, however, a great deal of alcohol.

In one army was a man called Ephraim who, being elderly, was not a combatant, but part of the machinery which supplied it with food and goods. He was a sergeant, and as unremarkable in the army as he was in civilian life. For the four years he had been a soldier, for the most part in North Africa, he had pursued a private interest, or obsession, which was, when he arrived anywhere at all, to seek out the people and places that could add yet another fragment of iridescent or gleaming substance to the mass which he carried around in a flat tin in his pack.

The men he served with found him and his preoccupation mildly humorous. He was not disliked or liked enough to make a target for that concentration of unease caused by people who alarm others. They did not laugh at him, or call him madman. Perhaps he was more like that dog who is a regiment's pet. Once he mislaid his tin of loot and a couple of men went into a moderate danger to get it back: sometimes a comrade would bring him a bit of something or other picked up in a bazaar – amber, an amulet, a jade. He advised them how to make bargains; he went on expeditions with them to buy stones for wives and girls back home.

He was in Italy that week when – *everything disintegrated*. Anyone who has been in, or near, war (which means, by now, everyone, or at least everyone in Europe and Asia) knows that time – a week, days, sometimes hours – when everything falls apart, when all forms of order dissolve, including those which mark the difference between enemy and enemy.

During this time old scores of all kinds are settled. It is when unpopular officers get killed by 'accident'. It is when a man who has an antipathy for another will kill him, or beat him up. A man who wants a woman will rape her, if she is around, or rape another in her stead if she is not. Women get raped; and those who want to be will make sure they are where the raping is. A woman who hates another will harm her. In short, it is a time of anarchy, of looting, of arson and destruction for destruction's sake. There are those who believe that this time out of ordinary order is the reason of war, its hidden justification, its purpose and law, another pattern behind the one we see. Afterwards there are no records of what has happened. There is no one to keep records: everyone is engaged in participating, or in protecting himself.

Ephraim was in a small town near Florence when his war reached that phase. There was a certain corporal, also from Johannesburg, who always had a glitter in his look when they talked of Ephraim's tin full of jewels. On an evening when every human being in the place was hunter or hunted, manoeuvred for advantage, or followed scents of gain, this man, in civilian life a storekeeper, looked across a room at Ephraim and grinned. Ephraim knew what to expect. Everyone knew what to expect – at such moments much older knowledges come to the surface together with old instincts. Ephraim quietly left a schoolroom for that week converted into a mess, and went out into the early dark of streets emptied by fear, where walls still shook and dust fell in clouds because of near gunfire. But it was also very quiet. Terror's cold nausea silences, places invisible hands across mouths . . . The occasional person hurrying through those streets kept his eyes in front, and his mouth tight. Two such people meeting did not look at each other except for a moment when their eyes violently encountered in a hard clash of inquiry. Behind every shutter or pane or door people stood, or sat or crouched, waiting for the time out of order to end, and guns and sharp instruments stood near their hands.

Through these streets went Ephraim. The Corporal had not seen him go, but by now would certainly have found the scent. At any moment he would catch up with Ephraim who carried in his hand a flat tin, and who as he walked looked into holes in walls and in pavements, peered into a church half filled with rubble, investigated torn earth where bomb fragments had fallen and even looked up into the branches of trees as he passed and at the plants growing at doorways. Finally, as he passed a fountain clogged with debris, he knelt for a moment and slid his tin down into the mud. He walked away, fast, not looking back to see if he had been seen, and around the corner of the church he met Corporal Van der Merwe. As Ephraim came up to his enemy he held out empty hands and stood still. The Corporal was a big man and twenty years younger. Van der Merwe gave him a frowning look, indicative of his powers of shrewd assessment, rather like Mihrène's father's look when he heard how this little nonentity proposed to give his daughter a valuable pearl for no reason at all, and when Ephraim saw it, he at once raised his hands above his head like a prisoner surrendering, while Van der Merwe frisked him. There was a moment when Ephraim might very well have been killed: it hung in the balance. But down the street a rabble of soldiers were looting pictures and valuables from another church, and Van der Merwe, his attention caught by them, simply watched Ephraim walk away, and then ran off himself to join the looters.

By the time that season of anarchy had finished, Ephraim was a couple of hundred miles north. Six months later, in a town ten miles from the one where he had nearly been murdered by a man once again his military subordinate (but that incident had disappeared, had become buried in the foreign texture of another time, or dimension), Ephraim asked for an evening's leave and travelled as he could to V—, where he imagined, perhaps, that he would walk through deserted streets to a rubble-filled fountain and beside this fountain would kneel, and slide his hand into dirty water to retrieve his treasure.

But the square was full of people, and though this was not a time when a café served more than a cup of bad coffee or water flavoured with chemicals, the two cafés had people in them who were half starved but already inhabiting the forms of ordinary life. They served, of course, unlimited quantities of cheap wine. Everyone was drunken, or tipsy. In a wine country, when there is no food, wine becomes a kind of food, craved like food. Ephraim walked past the fountain and saw that the water was filthy, too dirty to let anyone see what was in it, or whether it had been cleared of rubble, and, with the rubble, his treasure.

He sat on the pavement under a torn awning, by a cracked wood table, and ordered coffee. He was the only soldier there; or at least, the only uniform. The main tide of soldiery was washing back and forth to one side of this little town. Uniforms meant barter, meant food, clothing, cigarettes. In a moment half a dozen little boys were at his elbow offering him girls. Women of all ages were sauntering past or making themselves visible, or trying to catch his eye, since the female population of the town were for the most part in that condition for which in our debased time we have the shorthand term: being prepared to sell themselves for a cigarette. Old women, old men, cripples, all kinds of person, stretched in front of him hands displaying various more or less useless objects – lighters, watches, old buckles or bottles or brooches – hoping to get chocolate or food in return. Ephraim sat on, sad with himself because he had not brought eggs or tinned stuffs or chocolate. He had not thought of it. He sat while hungry people with sharp faces that glittered with a winy fever pressed about him and the bodies of a dozen or so women arranged themselves in this or that pose for his inspection. He felt sick. He was almost ready to go away and forget his tin full of gems. Then a tired-looking woman in a much-washed print dress lifted high in front because of pregnancy came to sit at his table. He thought she was there to sell herself, and hardly looked at her, unable to bear it that a pregnant woman was brought to such a pass.

She said: 'Don't you remember me?'

And now he searched her face, and she searched his. He looked for Mihrène; and she tried to see in him what it was that changed her life, to find what it was that that pearl embodied which she carried with her in a bit of cloth sewn into her slip.

They sat trying to exchange news; but these two people had so little in common they could not even say: And how is so and so? What has happened to him, or to her?

The hungry inhabitants of the town withdrew a little way, because this soldier had become a person, a man who was a friend of Mihrène, who was their friend.

The two were there for a couple of hours. They were on the whole more embarrassed than anything. It was clear to both by now that whatever events had taken place between them, momentous or not (they were not equipped to say), these events were in some realm or on a level where their daylight selves were strangers. It was certainly not the point that she, the unforgettable girl of Alexandria, had become a rather drab young woman waiting to give birth in a war-shattered town; not the point that for her he had carried with him for four years of war a treasury of gems, some precious, some mildly valuable, some worthless, bits of substance with one thing in common: their value related to some other good which had had, arbitrarily and for a short time, the name *Mihrène*.

It had become intolerable to sit there, over coffee made of burned grain, while all round great hungry eyes focused on him, the soldier, who had come so cruelly to their starving town with empty hands. He had soon to leave. He had reached this town on the back boards of a peasant's cart, there being no other transport; and if he did not get another lift of the same kind, he would have to walk ten miles before midnight.

Over the square was rising a famished watery moon, unlike the moons of his own city, unlike the wild moons of Egypt. At last he simply got up and walked to the edge of the evil-smelling fountain. He kneeled down on its edge, plunged in his hand, encountered all sorts of slimy things, probably dead rats or cats or even bits of dead people, and, after some groping, felt the familiar shape of his tin. He pulled it out, wiped it dry on some old newspaper that had blown there, went back to the table, sat down, opened the tin. Pearls are fed on light and air. Opals don't like being shut away from light which makes their depths come alive. But no water had got in, and he emptied the glittering, gleaming heap on to the cracked wood of the table top.

All round pressed the hungry people who looked at the gems and thought of food.

She took from her breast a bit of cloth and untwisted her pearl. She held it out to him.

'I never sold it,' she said.

And now he looked at her – sternly, as he had done before.

She said, in the pretty English of those who have learned it from governesses: 'I have sometimes needed food, I've been hungry, you know! I've had no servants . . .'

He looked at her. Oh, how she knew that look, how she had studied it in memory! Irritation, annoyance, grief. All these, but above all disappointment. And more than these, a warning, or reminder. It said, she felt: Silly white goose! Rich little bitch! Poor little nothing! Why do you always get it wrong? Why are you stupid? What is a pearl compared with what it stands for? If you are hungry and need money, sell it, of course!

She sat in that sudden stillness that says a person is fighting not to weep. Her beautiful eyes brimmed. Then she said stubbornly: 'I'll never sell it. Never!'

As for him he was muttering: I should have brought food. I was a dummkopf. What's the use of these things . . .

But in the hungry eyes around him he read that they were thinking how even in times of famine there are always men and women who have food hidden away to be bought by gold or jewels.

'Take them,' he said to the children, to the women, to the old people.

They did not understand him, did not believe him.

He said again: 'Go on. Take them!'

No one moved. Then he stood up and began flinging into the air pearls, opals, moonstones, gems of all kinds, to fall as they would. For a few moments there was a mad scene of people bobbing and scrambling, and the square emptied as people raced back to the corners they lived in with what they had picked up out of the dust. It was not yet time for the myth to start, the story of how a soldier had walked into the town, and inexplicably pulled treasure out of the fountain which he flung into the air like a king or a sultan – treasure that was ambiguous and fertile like a king's, since one man might pick up the glitter of a diamond that later turned out to be worthless glass, and another be left with a smallish pearl that had nevertheless been so carefully chosen it was worth months of food, or even a house or small farm.

'I must go,' said Ephraim to his companion.

She inclined her head in farewell, as to an acquaintance re-encountered. She watched a greying, dumpy little man walk away past a fountain, past a church, then out of sight.

Later that night she took out the pearl and held it in her hand. If she sold it, she would remain comfortably independent of her own family. Here, in the circle of the family of her dead husband, she would marry again, another engineer or civil servant: she would be worth marrying, even as a widow with a child. Of course if she returned to her own family, she would also remarry, as a rich young widow with a small child from that dreadful war, luckily now over.

Such thoughts went through her head: at last she thought that it didn't make any difference what she did. Whatever function Ephraim's intervention had performed in her life was over when she refused to marry Paulo, had married Carlos, had come to Italy and given birth to two children, one dead from an unimportant children's disease that had been fatal only because of the quality of war-food, war-warmth. She had been wrenched out of her pattern, had been stamped, or claimed, by the pearl – by something else. Nothing she could do now would put her back where she had been. It did not matter whether she stayed in Italy or returned to the circles she had been born in.

As for Ephraim, he went back to Johannesburg when the war finished, and continued to cut diamonds and to play poker on Sunday nights.

This story ended more or less with the calling of the flight number. As we went to the tarmac where illuminated wisps of fog still lingered, the lady from Texas asked the man who had told the story if perhaps he was Ephraim?

'No,' said Dr Rosen, a man of sixty or so from Johannesburg, a brisk, well-dressed man with nothing much to notice about him – like most of the world's citizens.

No, he was most emphatically not Ephraim.

Then how did he know all this? Perhaps he was there?

Yes, he was there. But if he was to tell us how he came to be a hundred miles from where he should have been, in that chaotic, horrible week – it was horrible, horrible! – and in civvies, then that story would be even longer than the one he had already told us.

Couldn't he tell us *why* he was there?

Perhaps he was after that tin of Ephraim's too! We could think so if we liked. It would be excusable of us to think so. There was a fortune in that tin, and everyone in the regiment knew it.

He was a friend of Ephraim's then? He knew Ephraim?

Yes, he could say that. He had known Ephraim for, let's see, nearly fifty years. Yes, he thought he could say he was Ephraim's friend.

In the aircraft Dr Rosen sat reading, with nothing more to tell us.

But one day I'll meet a young man called Nikki, or Raffele; or a girl wearing a single pearl around her neck on a gold chain; or perhaps a middle-aged woman who says she thinks pearls are unlucky, she would never touch them herself: a man once gave her younger sister a pearl and it ruined her entire life. Something like that will happen, and this story will have a different shape.

Ekaterina

» «

JACK COPE

Coming into Athens. The man in the next seat tucked away some papers, looking bored.

'Air travel simply folds up one's idea of place, time, country,' I said to him. 'In fact there aren't countries any more, not in the old sense. No places are more than twenty-four hours apart. It's a matter of time before the borders just fade.'

He laughed.

'What's so strange about that?' I said. 'And yet where I came from there are still people who measure distance by days. "He lives two days off towards the sunset." Two days' walk, that is.'

'Sounds prehistoric to me.'

The man was an American and I had to explain what things were like in some parts of Africa. I'd been around the wilder places in my fifty years.

'We've shattered the fourth dimension,' I went on, 'but our minds haven't caught up. We don't know what's come over us, like juveniles, dangerous adolescents. The world's shrunk up.'

He thought me slightly off the beam. 'Coming from South Africa, I guess you should be black and speak Zulu,' he said.

'I do,' was my answer.

He was leaving the aircraft at Athens and we broke off without any regrets. He could not suspect that I was fighting against the anticlimax of a return to Johannesburg. Only twelve hours distant; but the place felt ten thousand leagues away. In Africa, time and dimensions held off stubbornly.

I had not before been through Athens and I ran down the steps to plant my feet for the first time on Greek soil. Here Euripides might have walked, or Aristophanes. It needed all the strength of faith. Back beyond the present, beyond the waste of an international airport, perhaps they saw from here these same white and gold hills, breathed in this air. I stepped on the little trolley and was hauled swiftly away. It was late afternoon and a luminous early summer glow enveloped the far-off white hills. Over the fumes of hot oil and engine gas, I had the illusion of spice-scented air. At the terminal entrance, marigolds and small papery plants survived in the dry, dusty beds. Athens itself lay miles distant, and now I felt this was a lost chance and I might never return. Greece and the sacred islands . . . girls leading a heifer to the festival, with ribbons about its horns; and the Athenians whose confession had blazed against all doubts for thousands of years: that man was the beauty of the world.

An undersized youth with decayed teeth and slicked-back dark hair plucked me by the sleeve to offer me sex pictures. Like the airport, the smell of oil and the faceless passengers, he was a world symbol. Could anyone say he was not from the blood of ancestors who fought at Marathon?

Then a little bewildered party came fluttering among the crowd across the wide airport vestibule. In poor best clothing, the big red hands of the men hung from overlong sleeves. Women with head-scarves carried small bundles and boxes and one trailed a flashy, cheap travelling-case. A young girl at their centre swept large eyes, dark and dazed, over the utter strangeness of everything. A light yellow costume hung uncomfortably new about her shoulders, and the pleated skirt swung to her sturdy walk. She looked direct at me with the same bewilderment, smiled and turned away. Her profile was almost soulless in its perfection – a short straight nose, a strict but soft modelling of the lips. She had sprinkled in the thick black swathes of her hair a ring of small flowers, white and starlike. The procession was swallowed at a gulp among the echoes and hurrying, the aseptic smells of the air terminal.

The light still caught on the ring of ancient hills, silver-green olives on the slopes, darkening as the sun sank lower. When the same sun rose again for me it would be red and wintry over the gold mines, the great pale yellow dumps and winding gears of the East Rand. Why not step off here like my air-mate from San Francisco; find some age-still village in the Plain of Thessaly or a hut in the hills? Maybe Greece never had lost its magic and there was a reconciliation, a way back and a way forward, and like a pilgrim you need reach it only once.

Warnings were echoing over the call system. I ran for the trolley and climbed on as it moved. Slants of sunlight streaked the concrete apron. As we came near, the smooth belly of the waiting aircraft flashed in our eyes. I ducked through the open hatch door, the last aboard.

At my place aft of the wing I found the next seat, left empty by the American, now taken by the girl of the little procession. She stood up at once, rosy and seeming to glow in the light through the portholes, and she gave me her hand. Each slight movement of hers had a fluency of nature, of some half-tame unobserved creature. Her greeting sounded with a charm of the unknown. There had been tears in her eyes.

Back in her seat, she was at once straining through the double window of the pressure cabin for a glimpse of the minute figures far away across the runway. A tightly squeezed handkerchief unfolded in her hand and fluttered at the porthole. Nobody would see that final gesture. A gritty shudder of the starting motors vibrated the airliner. The flowers in the girl's hair were orange blossoms and a finger of the hand at the window carried the shining gold band of a new wedding ring.

She cried in silence, and the whole giant stir of shipping off from her native ground was nothing to the turmoil inside herself. The machine rumbled out along the communicating strips, wheeled on a great arc and stood poised for flight, trembling under its power. We were skimming the ground, and spurts of black smoke coughed from the motors. The last upward heave came and then the sense of ease as we swung away towards the small salmon-coloured clouds beyond the edge of the land. The sea opened blue-dark below, and far off to the west, over a point of smoky land, the path of the setting sun lay on the water.

The wonder of this first flight broke suddenly on the girl. Her mouth was open. She looked around and touched the curtain and the window as if to confirm her own doubting senses. When she caught my eye, it was with a little burst of laughter, startled and greatly moved. She said something quietly, shaking her head. Tears glistened on her lashes but the weight had lifted from her heart, and a minute later she touched my arm and excitedly pointed out something on the land. I gazed past her through the porthole. Athens was going down in a blur into the sea and the night. Two ships, shrunk to leaves on a pond, trailed the faint streak of their wakes. Already we had topped the level of the clouds; in the enormous distance, they were strung out like a line of homing flamingos.

I thought I would get back to my magazine. There was no way of making polite talk, and to look at her simply because she was very good to look at seemed equally pointless. She was quite unconscious of the difficulty and, when she had dried her eyes and folded up her handkerchief in a tight wad and tucked it in her bosom, she seemed tranquil and ready to explore the strangeness around her.

'Ekaterina,' she said, tapping her chest.

I told her my name – Neil, Neil Gordon. This called for another handshake and she was delighted at so easily making herself understood. Using a range of gestures and expressions, I got across in answer to her questions that I was not an Englishman, a German or an American but a citizen of Johannesburg.

'A! Yoannisburg!' That was where she, too, was bound. How lucky, how wonderful, how strange – it was one of these, or maybe all of them, that fitted her look. She clapped her hands together and narrowed her eyes. We were fairly launched on a companionship at once intimate and warm, as if the same rocky hills had raised and sheltered us, if not the identical hut. She chattered away softly, her face changed, shadowed at times, and her lips glowed. Unthinkingly she turned the ring on her finger, looking downcast. Then she smiled mysteriously, remembering something, and went on talking. It did not matter that she was not understood at all. I could feel the flow in her words, consoling, inevitable, reaching out for strength. So a child talks to herself in the night or a mother tells her thoughts to her baby. I could not be wrong about her. For a moment she looked at me full, but with eyes that stayed dark and inward. As she paused I said she was like my idea of Andromache or Iphigenia.

No, she was neither Andromache nor Iphigenia. She was E-kat-er-i-na, vigorously shaking her head. I did not dare smile but the girl felt swiftly that she had said something comic and she burst out laughing.

'Neil . . . Yoannisburg,' she said at last, meaning – who could say – that someday I might tell her what it was all about.

The air hostess was passing, and I stopped her to ask if she understood Greek.

'Not a bloomin' word,' she said in a ripe Transvaal accent. But there was a gentleman down the aisle at the back who looked like a Greek and she would ask him. A minute later she was back. The passenger was not a Greek. He was an Italian. But he was quite willing to exchange places with me and entertain the young lady.

'Tell him,' I said, 'to go to hell, *à l'inferno, malebolge . . .*'

The lights had come on; from the height of seven miles, the horizon had receded to a luminous mauve band and a few faint stars were framed in the violet space of the window. The girl took off her jacket, revealing a delicately embroidered blouse or bodice of fine linen, and apparently no underwear. She invited me to admire the blouse, smiling, and turned about to display its points. Clearly it was made by her and into it had gone her endless hours of patience. Unlike the poor factory-made yellow costume, it was a garment of character and perhaps traditional taste. I praised her extravagantly, and she watched my expression keenly and with a slight flush. Her eyes had turned grave. She sat thinking, smoothed down her skirt and even bent to flick the dust off her flashy black shoes. She made up her mind and took from her bag a square notebook. Out of it came her passport, which she put in my hands. It was a passport of my own country with familiar wording in English and Afrikaans. A frightened little face, not remotely like the beautiful Ekaterina, peered out from the photograph. How did she come to be a citizen of South Africa? She had not been there, nor even set foot outside of her lovely and poverty-wracked Hellas.

But there was not much difficulty in getting this across to me. She had changed her nationality by the simple process of marrying a fellow citizen of mine. The marriage had taken place that morning. And her husband? He was in Yoannisburg. She would meet him there. She had never seen him; vehemently she shook her head. The marriage had been by proxy and her brother had stood in for the bridegroom. It had been arranged by her parents. I could piece it all together. The husband had paid for everything. He had paid for her. He had sent money for the air passage. Her clothes were her dowry. The consul had issued her the passport and immigration permit. Her face burnt and she gripped the documents tightly.

Dinner was coming up in half an hour but I called for a bottle of Beaujolais and drank to her happiness. The Italian passenger came and leaned over the seat. I told him Ekaterina had been married that morning and invited him to join in drinking her health. He tried Italian, Spanish and German on her; she only looked at him, startled. He raised his glass and insisted on kissing her hand, small and strong, toughened by work.

'Whatever may be her family, she ees too beautiful,' he said. 'Are you her chaperon?'

I said on the contrary that I was doing my best to carry her off and had a very good chance of success.

'She ees simply a child.'

'I know how old she is, I've just seen her passport. Do you still want to entertain her, *signor*?'

He shrugged with no sign of humour and wandered back to his seat. Ekaterina said something and smiled. She sipped at the wine and in a moment was back in her own thoughts. She was small in stature, not much above five feet, but this took nothing from an effect more striking because it was unstudied, timeless, inviolate. The faint visible beat of her pulse and a slight sheen of dark hair on her forearms alone brought her, for me, into the actual present.

She turned to me seriously, troubled. She had made up her mind to something, and this raised her doubt. It was a slow, firm gesture she made with her hands, as if she appealed for support in a sacred and grave cause, then she calmly unwrapped a photograph and handed it to me. The print, postcard size, was of a young man about twenty-eight or thirty. He had dark hair massed thickly over a broad, flat forehead; the face was generous in its way, rugged if not handsome, and the eyes had a gentle watchfulness that attracted me. The print had been trimmed, but enough was left to show the young man was leaning with his back to a shining new motor car.

Who? It was her husband, of course, whom she had never seen. She told me his name: Savvas Athanassiades. I had not glanced up from the portrait but I knew she was watching me, dead still and tense. Judging by the car, Savvas was unusually short, certainly not more than five feet. I had owned a car like that myself, before the war. Why the bridegroom wanted himself snapped propping up a thirty-year-old Chev was his own business, no doubt.

'Very good.' I wanted her to get the idea that I was pleased in a noncommittal way. '*Homme honnête, galantuomo*, a grand fellow. Here's to Savvas Athanassiades.'

I had avoided her eyes, splashing wine again into the two glasses, and when I raised mine to her I knew her intuition had been sharply aroused. Some power of belief in women can defy the outward laws of nature, of logic and the physical senses. Ekaterina's look said she was not believing. It was a kind of unflickering regard, her mouth set as if cut in Italian rose marble and her straight nose and brow smooth and static. Then she lowered her eyes and sighed. Very deliberately she wrapped and put away the picture of Savvas. She noticed her glass and raised it with a nod. 'Yoannisburg,' she said.

'Athena,' was my toast. She repeated it and added with a grave, sad smile, 'Vari.' I did not know Vari, and tried to picture it as a small and ancient town built around an amphitheatre of crumbling golden stone. But the image its name fished up was of a smoky industrial waste with a thousand huddled streets. Vari. But wherever or whatever it was, it still possessed a power and a mystery from the past and in it she had left her dreams.

The dinner was served on plastic trays with neat, hygienic containers and wrappings and capsules – the tasteless and characterless kind of meal anyone can start where he likes and end with the same sense of disillusion. Ekaterina got through it by watching and imitating. I showed her how to hold her knife and fork and she managed without any show of embarrassment. She was slightly flushed by the wine and glanced at me from time to time, beatifically. She was on cloud-bearing Olympus before a feast of ambrosia.

We came down at Khartoum and left the airliner while it was inspected and sprayed against flies or mosquitoes. The vivid African night folded about us, stifling and oppressive with unnameable scents. Ekaterina kept close as we trailed across the tarmac apron. Dazed flies staggered across the dirty tabletops of the restaurant. The passengers drank lukewarm lemonade that tasted of scented soap. The girl gazed at the tall white-robed waiters with red fezzes and sashes, carrying their tall glass jugs of nauseous liquid. A hawker draped before her a length of trashy Japanese rayon and her eyes lit with delight and regret. I offered to present it to her and she refused softly, shaking her head, no, no, no. She thanked me but no, it was impossible. Not because I was a stranger, that was not it. Why? Maybe because she could not give anything back. The heat was well up in the hundreds and she fanned herself with a limp handkerchief. The hawker slipped into her hand a bamboo fan. It was worth a few cents and I got no change out of a pound; but that was different, it was a necessity.

The aircraft took off again, lifting up and up over sleeping Africa. The last lights swam heavily into oblivion. For a while the Nile lay like spilt quicksilver, catching the moon's reflection until it, too, merged with the black earth, and we went on climbing alone into the milky-luminous sky. The cabin lights were switched down, and the whole human cargo shuffled restlessly, settling back in the cramped space to snatch at sleep. Ekaterina curled up facing the porthole and I dozed back, horribly uncomfortable, one knee jammed against the seat ahead and the other leg sprawled for space into the aisle. A huge African with three tiers of chins and a shaved head, a diplomat from one of the new states, snored in an ultra-basso behind me.

Maybe half an hour farther down the spine of the continent I woke drowsily. Like a newborn calf or puppy, Ekaterina had snuggled against me. One arm was flung round my neck and her face was half buried in my shoulder. A warm, sweet scent came from her like buttercups or the deep new loam behind a plough. She was fast asleep – and her soul had taken flight, back to Vari, back to a street of quiet little huts, to a single room full of sisters and brothers, with a goat on the floor, and a lamb, a dog or two maybe, and chickens roosting. I wondered if she had ever slept alone. Who was I in her sleep, who was held in her poor arms? A little brother who would not be consoled, or a sister restless with hunger? I could not think how this lovely child could have been sold, or sold herself, to an unknown groom – Savvas Athanassiades, possibly a worthy and honourable man who had earned his place in the privileged caste of a privileged state. And now he stretched back into the past, beyond the age of Byron, beyond the Turkish conquest, to the medieval darkness and took a bride of his own race, of the imperishable blood of Greece. Let him only be worthy – a damn Greek god and not, as the old joke goes, a goddam Greek. Half drugged with weariness and speed and the impacts on one's system of flight in the stratosphere, I could not check this dizzy spin of thoughts. It was not easy to say that the girl, Ekaterina, was nothing to me when she was actually asleep and warm and living against my body.

I had dozed off and, waking, I found Ekaterina had not moved. But she, too, was now wide awake and her full eyes were fixed darkly on me. How long had she stared at me like that?

'Hello, Ekaterina,' I said thickly.

'Ello.'

Then she closed her eyes and drawing her arms tighter settled her face back to sleep.

'Ekaterina, I'm talking to you.'

A faint movement of her head showed she was awake.

'Listen, it may be a good thing you don't understand. Listen, Ekaterina, you shouldn't be here. Go back, take the first chance to go back. This may turn out well, but it's a risk and a humiliation. It's a false step from the beginning and won't save anybody. You're not a piece of property, you're not a prisoner. No one knows what freedom is until they've had it taken away. Go back and learn to be free. They've taken the past from you and you are throwing aside the future. Ekaterina, don't run away; you must know it's better always and always to perish fighting.'

I was wandering along like this, talking almost to myself. She could not have understood a word and nobody else could have distinguished anything above the drone of the engines. Something in my tone may have entered her, and once again I had to realize how tense and alert and sensitive she was. She had begun crying.

The great airliner bored into the silken blackness. Under us lay Africa, a giant, snoring on the long night wind. A green light showed in the dark out along the wing, and from the pilot's cockpit away up forward I thought I could catch the monotony of a nasal human voice. What message was cutting up through the thin envelope of air? Far below, men and women slept in the heat as though dead; mosquitoes whined over them, and spiders and centipedes moved in the grass.

Ekaterina cried quietly, but not for long, as if weeping were too great a luxury for one so simple and used to suffering. She took my hand and kissed it before I could draw away, a modest and grateful little show of feeling, but to me almost unbearable. Then she wiped her eyes and nose innocently on the back of her hand, talking brightly like a playful child. She seemed shy that I might see in her grief a weakness and for a few minutes she sat up primly in her seat with her head high. Soon she was nodding to sleep again. Her body slackened, and her arms drowsily reached out again, instinctively protective and loving.

We came in over the Transvaal before dawn. A haze of tiny lights struggled up from some town on the veld; beyond it, like a thin red dagger, a veld fire crept somewhere over the hills. Then the horizon began to gather rose and lilac tints and soon the flat earth itself was coming up out of the void. The passengers began stirring. I went aft to shave. When I got back to my seat I found Ekaterina in a commotion. She had lost something; she was searching everywhere; the air hostess was drawn in, hunting too though she did not know what for. The Greek girl whimpered and fluttered her hands and tears stood bright in her big dark eyes. Nobody could make out what it was all about. The Italian passenger was there, chivalrously down on his hands and knees to help in the rummaging.

'What are you after, *signor*?' I asked him. 'You look like a Mussulman in search of his God.'

He got to his feet, looking furiously at me. 'The girl is in a state. What have you done to her?'

'*Signor*, you have not slept well?'

'Slept! I can never sleep on these . . . these aviation trips.'

'You should travel by camel.'

He went back to his seat. Ekaterina appealed to me, but I had no more idea than anyone else what she had lost. Whatever it was, perhaps it had gone at Khartoum.

'Khartoum!' She threw up her hands. She had been robbed, no doubt, by the Sudanese. She was beginning to lament this injustice when a passenger down the aisle held up a roll of newspapers tied with string. Ah, that was it – yesterday's Greek papers, for Savvas to read. Athena in the evening, Yoannisburg next morning. A miracle for the good Athanassiades.

I helped her down with her bags and packages. Her face was ivory in the frosty air and she hugged her thin overcoat around her, looking about fearfully. At the immigration barrier we became separated, and I did not see her again until I came out into the main concourse of the airport building. There were some palms in pots, a kiosk, groups of green leather lounge chairs and, beyond them, Ekaterina among a party of four or five. Her head was bowed and her face hidden in her hands. I could not make out which was Savvas; there was nobody answering to the likeness in the picture.

Ekaterina raised her head and stared around. Then she saw me and came running down the hall. She laid her forehead like a child against my chest, sobbing. The melancholy little group of strangers looked on from a distance. Now I saw that Savvas was there, the bridegroom himself. He was carrying a black hat in one hand and with the other he wiped a handkerchief over his head. It was unquestionably Athanassiades, and he was quite bald and aged and very stout, almost as fat as he was tall. I had half expected it.

'Ekaterina, I'll help you get back if you wish, to Athena, Vari . . .'

I gave her my card and she gazed at it through blurred eyes. She gripped my hand firmly for a moment, then she dried her eyes and, with a nod to me, walked back slowly, with great dignity.

My son and daughter-in-law found me there staring after Ekaterina's retreating back.

'Who's that beautiful little statue?' Loraine asked.

'Ekaterina.'

'Is it a romance?'

'I don't know. It looks to me more like an unhappy ending, Loraine, like Iphigenia.'

They were amused and joked with me about it over breakfast in the large, crudely cheerful restaurant.

'It's just possible you have it all wrong. After all, you could not understand, and you had to depend on your imagination to fill the gaps.'

'My instinct.'

'You can't trust to instinct. Only a woman can risk that.'

I should have spoken to Savvas Athanassiades and now I do not know where to find him. His name is not in the directory. I have waited to hear from Ekaterina, but nothing, not a word. Where is she? I remember how she walked away with her head up, calmly, but not defiantly. Her dark shining hair, the yellow of her costume – 'Freely now I sink in night . . .' Yet Loraine may be proved right.

I have heard nothing, and it is now four days.

The Goat

» «

INGRID JONKER

TRANSLATED FROM THE AFRIKAANS BY THE AUTHOR AND JACK COPE

From where she stood at the window Susan could see the stony hill looming through the morning mist. That was where the goat would be wandering around. By this time he would have come down, stepping white under the mistbank, from the upper ledge. If she turned her face upwind she was sure to see him standing there under the acacia tree just beyond the wire fence of her garden. But she kept her glance fixed no further than the nearest line of rose bushes. A few buds were bursting already into bloom. As the breeze touched and passed her again she turned away from the window and drew the blue silk kimono round her swollen stomach.

'Hein!'

He did not stir from his sleep. As if he had got used to that insistent voice forever calling his name. He lay on his side, one hand under his sun-tanned cheek and creasing up the leathery skin. His white pointed beard was flattened on the blanket. Susan remembered how those hands of his worked with the goats at milking, or digging and planting, the sure strength of his skinny wrists and the joy in his fingers. But he had begun lately to keep away from the house and things were running to neglect. When she brought in his early cup of coffee he heaved himself up with a shudder and began drinking with greedy little slurps and gulps. She stared straight out through the window now and over the rose garden searching under the acacia tree. But she could hardly make out the shape of the animal in the fog except for a denser white patch. Under her set gaze she could at last trace its faint outline. Gradually the mist cleared and as she watched the goat came forward with its careful, precise steps, to challenge her.

It butted insolently at the air a few times, the yellowish hair on its legs blowing in the breeze and its expressionless eyes fixed steadily on her. Behind it was the acacia tree with slender leaf-blades and yellow puffs of blossom against the pale blue of the sky.

The man got out of bed, his thin whitish body naked, a wrinkled stomach and knotty knees – 'What's that you're gaping at, woman?'

She saw the goat turn round and start grazing unconcernedly with its backside towards her. 'I'll murder that goat one of these fine days.' She swung towards the man as he stood there in the middle of the room chafing his hands tenderly over his chest.

'Who's that – the goat?'

'Yes, I'll cut his throat – I'm warning you.'

'But good grief, what've you got against the stinking thing?'

Impatiently she levelled her arm, pointing through the window – 'Me, against him? You've got to sell him, I say.'

'Ag, come off it.'

'What's he after here, anyway?'

'Well I don't know, it's our place and the goats roam around, why not?'

'Why not, why doesn't he stay with the others up on the hill? What does he want?'

'Good God, what sin has the goat done you?'

'He's trying to get into my yard.'

'You know he can't get into the back yard. With the gate shut.'

'Just let him.'

'Ag, now, woman . . .'

'I tell you, I'm ready for him . . . with his . . . his sinful eyes.'

'Well, I'll be damned!'

'Oh go and get dressed – standing there stark naked. Do you think I need the sight of you like that all day long? Get moving and chase that goat away up the hill where he belongs.'

He shrugged and picked up his khaki pants and woollen shirt from the heap in the chair, keeping his back to her while he dressed.

'It's hours since sunrise,' Susan said, and went on mumbling – 'Can't get to work, but still fancies himself as a father.'

He hurried getting his boots on and started out of the room, but she halted him – 'You can do without a wash, I suppose, being a man.' He scuttled out quickly through the door.

Her thoughts had lingered occasionally on his nervous embraces, or she would think of him walking away with something stiff and reserved in the slant of his shoulder-blades. And at other times when he lay quiet and his body slackened into the nest of his own warmth she reproached him with her nerveless silence. He was a stranger to her then and not even the coming child counted any more.

She had got dressed when she heard the lorry starting up in the silence. And suddenly it struck her how quiet the house was and no sound of Lena in the kitchen. The mist had all drifted away. Maybe Hein had driven the goat up the hill after all because its place under the acacia was empty.

The dishes lay stacked in the kitchen sink. Spotted by a few flies. Lena's blue-rimmed coffee mug had frothed over on the stove. Susan looked about and then from the kitchen door she saw the coloured girl come with a swinging step past the budding rose bushes. From the way she walked it seemed she was keeping time with some sad song in her heart; but as she came out into the sun you could see her smile. The sunlight cut across her shoulders and fell on her bosoms, free under the woollen bodice. At the garden gate she stopped, and resting her hand on it she turned her face as if to listen to that song fading away among the orchard trees.

'Lena!'

The girl opened the gate and hurried through.

'Have you been out to see Jager again? And all the dirty dishes left in the sink!'

As she slipped past, something in the woman's attitude made her glance up into the puffy face.

'Have you lost your tongue?'

'Missus?'

'I'm asking if you've been to Jager again.'

'Yes, Missus.'

'What for?'

'I took him his coffee.'

'And what about the housework? Listen, Lena, you're getting a bit out of hand. Jager can damn well fetch his own coffee if he wants it. Do I have to go on telling you?'

When Susan came back to the kitchen to collect the garden shears Lena in her quick deft way was drying the dishes. She stared a moment at the girl's back and noticed the movement of her shoulders.

'Yes, and I guess he lays you, eh?' She turned her back and reached up to the hook for the shears, muttering to herself. 'In any case he's too old for you. Early ripe, early rotten.' And then bursting out passionately—'I won't have any laying about here, d'you hear me!'

She got a glimpse as she passed of the young face, the mouth a little open as if waiting for a kiss. And over it the hurt eyes, dark brown and lightless.

The shears glinted in the garden and threw fire up the whitewashed walls of the house. She stooped heavily at the first rose bush and her hand searched carefully among the leaves, touched an open bud, the petals still lying folded softly in, and she shook her head: 'That these can still bloom in such an earth!'

The child strained and stirred under her heart. She squatted down comfortably among the roses. The sun on her bare head and the scent of the leaves and buds made her drowsy. Strange how much she had come to love working in the soil. She must have got it from Hein. Because she knew nothing whatever about gardening when she had come with him as a young creature to this stony patch of ground above the bay. She had grown up in the city with her large family and was a pink-cheeked girl when she met him. He was twenty years older than she but upright and quiet like a man used to the open veld.

The blood flushed in her cheeks the instant she picked up that acrid stale smell in the air. The goat was standing behind her. As she got quickly to her feet she buttoned her blouse up the front without taking her eyes off it. At first it made a few little jumps as if inviting her to come out and play, then it pawed the ground rhythmically with one front hoof.

She took a few long strides to the gate and jerked it open. The shears flashed in her hand. The goat came skipping towards her.

'Can't you see I'm going to slaughter you?' But it came up nearer, thrust out its tongue slavering, half playful, half provocative.

'Kill you,' she warned again, and it only butted its horns towards her insultingly and stood firm in all its gleaming white hair. She caught hold of it and the shears flew from her hand; and she gripped it so hard against her that a falsetto bleat was forced from its throat, before she let it go and ran back up the garden path to the kitchen.

Lena had stood the broom tidily in the corner, and she looked for a moment pityingly at the woman who had fallen into a chair at the kitchen table and sat with her head in her hands.

'Shall I start lunch for you, Missus?'

Susan stood up wearily.

'No . . . no thanks, Lena.' Dazed, she went off along the passage. She sat on the green wooden bench on the stoep and far off she could see the shining blue waters of the bay. Hein would be somewhere down there among the fishermen, drinking wine in one of the cool stone huts, or maybe on the slipway where they were working on their boats, or along the jetty with its smells of fish and bait in the very grain of the wood. She could almost see him sitting there right among the men with their wet brown legs; or he would stand and talk to one of the city men who came to fish, dressed in their anglers' outfits with their faces red and sunburnt under white straw hats.

It was late in the afternoon before she saw the lorry climbing up the winding road. She rolled up the pair of stockings she had been darning on her lap. At the door Hein stopped and climbed out and in the last glow of the day he came up a little uncertainly towards her.

'So – you've been sitting out on the stoep.'

'Uhu . . .' she responded, shifting her heavy body.

'Ah well . . .' He sighed and sat down next to her, stiffly, pulled up his khaki pants at the knees and began filling his pipe.

'Course it's too late now to start fixing the fence,' Susan said. 'One of these days the goat will get through.'

'Anyway, it's Saturday.'

'That's nothing. You promised to put it right.'

'All right, all right . . . I was helping the fishermen today, mending nets. They are going out tonight. And I showed a couple of newcomers the best place to cast. I couldn't really get away earlier.'

He felt awkward remembering how the men chaffed him about his wife and the coming baby. And he getting long in the tooth. They also had a kind of idea he was half a millionaire with his lorry and his piece of land. He wasn't really one of them, more a man of the veld than of the sea, and they looked up to him. He was a bit sorry for his wife, pregnant and so much alone in the house, but maybe she was thankful that he let her alone. And then with a child coming there was less need for him to exert himself and he could count on help in his old age.

In his left eye he caught sight of Jager walking between the blossoming pear trees to his shack. He felt like jumping up and shouting to the bastard what had he been doing today, but he sank back against the wooden support, suddenly ashamed, seeing he had taken the day off himself.

'Seems as if that Lena and Jager are sweet on each other,' he said by way of a joke. Susan, who had also watched the brown man sauntering along, stood up.

'Look, if lovemaking's all that funny to you just get me straight that I don't think so. You care nothing that I have to put up with them all day. Wasting your whole time down at the bay. And it never troubles you that you've got a wife and a kid on the way. No, that's damn all. But it won't be long before that slut's up in the guts and looking like me, swelling out for a man's pleasure, and then where's the sweet lovely stuff? No, then there's nothing . . .'

'What sort of a way is this to talk?' He stood up too, his white hair sharply etched against the rosy light, the beard trembling on his chin but his pale eyes blank.

'I'm telling you straight.'

'But my God, woman . . .'

'Listen, if you're too stupid to understand, why not shut up . . .'

She brushed past him down the steps from the stoep and trudged off round the corner of the house. She had got as far as the acacia tree and stopped and only then she caught sight of the goat in the garden greedily nibbling in the twilight at the new rose shoots. Those roses would never bloom again, not after a goat had eaten them off, so the saying went.

She threw back her head and the scream broke from her throat: 'Jager!'

Before Jager came out of his room all the shoots had been nibbled. His shirt was open to the navel and his trousers rolled up. A smirk twitched his full lips.

'Missus?'

'God, haven't you got eyes in your head? Look at that!' He turned to follow the direction of her finger, shrugged his shoulders and again fixed questioning eyes on her.

'Catch the bloody goat and shut him in the shed. Jump to it, man.' The goat stopped chewing for the first time and looked their way, and then it came straight towards her, shameless and deliberate.

'Get hold of the brute, Jager.'

He jumped the wire, landed lightly and caught it. He held it by one horn, the muscles knotted along his arm and under the thin shirt on his back, and he landed a few kicks in the animal's side before he could get it firmly by both horns. Then he started backing out and dragged the goat with him, and its hooves skidded the whole time on the pebbly ground. Lena had run to fling wide the shed door. Under the acacia tree the woman stood stiffly and in the half-light kept her eyes on the scuffling goat, seeing it turn its head towards her before Jager shoved it in the shed and slammed the door.

Susan pulled open the kitchen drawer without thinking what she was looking for; among the balls of string and matches and clutter the long blade of the butcher's knife gleamed and her fingers closed over the haft.

'What are you up to?'

She pushed the drawer shut and leaned against it, but her husband had seen. She was breathing open-mouthed and did not answer.

'I'm talking to you!'

He took a step forward, his hands cupped. A feeling of anxiety squeezed his throat. 'It never troubles you that you've got a wife,' she had said, 'and swelling out for a man's pleasure.' He looked around uneasily and into the shadows moving across the wall, sensing the accusation in her against him, surging in her big maternal breasts, a flood to overwhelm him.

She stood quite still but while she watched him she thought again of the making of her baby, the child that should have done away with the estrangement between them, that should have made them one. But now it was only her child, not theirs, not what she had thought it would be, different. And he, standing always on the outside and watching, from some cold rocky height.

Suddenly from the shed she heard the false abrupt bleat and she knew the goat was standing against the door; it seemed as if those eyes were still fixed steadily on her, demanding. Then she found she was staring into the pale eyes of the man facing her.

'What have you got there?' His voice was unsteady.

With a quick movement he pushed past her, ripped open the drawer, knocking her in the side. She fell against the table, caught her weight on her hands and stood there bent over with her head bowed to her chest. He snatched out the knife and stood behind her holding the blade raised in his fist. Then he let it fall nervelessly.

'What are you going to do with the knife?'

'I'm going to sharpen it, that's what.'

He backed away into the darkening passage, stood a moment, then swung round with something of his old agility and hurried out stumbling and a little grotesque to the front stoep. The bay stretched out dark below, and in the fishermen's huts the men would be sitting at their stoves with their bread and soup. Strange how warm he had felt that afternoon when the men had chaffed him: 'When's her time? It's sure to be a boy, you old ram.' Now he felt only the blade of that knife as if he had already bled cold.

When they sat down to supper she rested one arm on the table and her look strayed to the open window where the shed was. The man's jaws moved jerkily as he chewed on a piece of coarse bread. When she got up he started back slightly in his chair but she merely walked out at the kitchen door. At Jager's shack she paused before knocking. There was a creaking of the bed. She opened the door wide. Jager raised himself to his elbow and his eyes shone warm into hers. The girl who had woken with a fright turned towards him with a soft cry and pressed her face to his chest.

'What's going on here?'

'Missus?'

Lena suddenly sat up and drew the bedclothes round her.

'You can give me the sack, Missus.' A small hard line flickered round her mouth and her head was thrown back.

'If I kick her out, Jager, what will you do? Just get yourself another one?'

'Me? No, I'll go away with her, Missus.'

'And then? One, two, three and the fun's all over . . .'

'Missus?'

'Get up and go and bring the goat out of the shed.'

'Yes, Missus.'

'Tie him up to the tree.'

'I'll tie him up.'

The night air had a cold cut to it and a thin half-moon shone on the white blossom of the pear trees. When she got to the bedroom she found her man lying awake. The half-light fell grey on the well-worn furniture. She got undressed and climbed in and he shifted over and lay on the further edge of the bed. Just before he fell asleep, tired out, she saw the glisten of his eyes turned towards her.

A heavy wind came up in the trees, and though she could hear nothing she knew the goat was standing there fastened to the acacia. She lifted herself carefully on her elbow and the blankets fell from the man's naked chest. His little beard thrust stiffly up on the stubborn chin. She bent forward and drew the blankets off him until he lay there quite uncovered, whitish in the pale light, bleak and hard. She placed her hand gently on his stomach between the narrow hips.

He jerked up clumsily.

'Don't!' and one hand made a wild gesture, then gripped his chest as though he were bleeding from a wound there, but he had merely called out in his sleep and he lay back quiet again, the pitiable line of his mouth sunken in. She covered him carefully and climbed out of bed.

The wind outside blowing from the hills pressed the cold blade in the inner pocket of her kimono against her belly.

'Now you'll get it, you swine!' The goat stood alert as if it knew. She drew out the knife and caught the animal by one horn. An indolent figure emerged out of the shadows and leant against the tree trunk.

'What are you going to do, Missus?'

Jager flicked the burning cigarette-end away between his thumb and middle finger. It fell with a red spark over the garden gate. Then he looked away towards the hill.

'I just wanted to come and tell you, Missus, that I'm leaving with Lena. Seems to me there's a time for flowers and a time for the fall. But now I'm going along with her.'

He stood very still, and then looked down at the goat and said with real regret: 'Shame, and he looks just like the old man.'

The strong horn jerked in her grasp which had already relaxed. To her touch the hair felt silken and wavy like Hein's in his prime. She saw him all at once as if in an old snap, on a forgotten morning, leaning on his spade in the rose garden in the soft light, with a gentle secret smile, his glance frank, calm, unalterable.

The goat struggled under her hold. Then she cut it loose.

Long after it had made off, white in the half-dark, for the hill, Susan remained standing there. Only when the child in her began moving she walked back slowly through the garden gate. The hill lay dark and protecting behind her and ahead, the bay, just as it had been the first time she arrived to live here. The wind had died down and a singing silence came from the lifting night. She looked up at the white house where her husband lay asleep; then she stooped to touch the rose bushes.

Next summer there would be no roses.

Soup for the Sick

» «

HENNIE AUCAMP

TRANSLATED FROM THE AFRIKAANS BY IAN FERGUSON

Tant Rensie went to her rest years ago, but she remains one of the most fascinating people I remember from my childhood. Fascinating, not for what we knew of her, but for what we suspected about her. In reality she was not an exceptional person, she was retiring, although not a hermit. She regularly attended church functions and fêtes, and from time to time she visited the Scottish doctor or old Mr and Mrs Verwey. But this was very occasionally, and later not at all. Her health troubled her.

She would have no help from outside. Sofietjie, her life-long nurse and friend, was sufficient for her. Even when it began to look as if her end was near, no family came to visit. Twenty years before that, she and Sofietjie had arrived in our Karoo dorp and had moved into the tower house that stood on the edge of town. Even then she had received no family visits. Had she renounced her family, or had they disowned her? Perhaps they had parted by mutual agreement?

Whoever tried to talk to Tant Rensie about her past came up against the barrier of her mysterious smile, and anyone trying to break through that barrier laid himself open to insult or permanent dismissal.

It later became general knowledge in Klipkraal that one shouldn't pry into Tant Rensie's past. Only strangers fell into that trap. Nonetheless people remained inquisitive: Perhaps she had been born in another country? Perhaps she had come to South Africa for health reasons? Something in her speech and her way of keeping house marked her as different . . . Something – and here they whispered about the thing that vaguely disturbed the whole of Klipkraal – there was something different about her relationship with Sofietjie . . .

One shouldn't be so intimate with one's servant. It wasn't that they were familiar, or that they chattered to each other. It was just that each was so aware of the other. If Sofietjie appeared, as quietly as a cat, in the doorway, Tant Rensie knew it even if she sat with her back towards her. 'Tea,' she would say to Sofietjie, and Sofietjie would glide back into the dim passage as if absorbed into it. To tell the truth their exchanges were brief, even curt. Sofietjie knew her place, as the older people would say. Nevertheless there was something between them.

On one particular evening I became very aware of the silent relationship between Tant Rensie and Sofietjie. It was the occasion that I first saw Sofietjie step out of line. Tant Rensie had been ailing for some time, more frequently in bed than out of it. Ma, who was the district nurse, sent me with a pot of soup to Tant Rensie's house.

When nobody answered the door I simply walked in, since the front door was ajar. Tant Rensie's bedroom door was also open, and Sofietjie sat on the bed next to Tant Rensie with her brown hands folded protectively over Tant Rensie's. Two old people, both grey-haired, the one white and serene, the other brown. They were whispering confidentially to each other, but when they became aware of me they stopped talking and looked up calmly, innocently.

'Oh, Stevie, soup!' Tant Rensie tried to prop herself up against the pillows.

'Partridge soup,' I reported with pride. 'I shot it myself.'

Tant Rensie struggled against the cushions.

'Slowly now, your heart,' Sofietjie said sharply.

'Not my heart, yours, Sofie. You are not to lift me again!'

Sofietjie smiled gently. I had never seen her severe face look so beautiful. She was also wrinkled, she had many wrinkles if one looked closely, but she seemed much younger than Tant Rensie. She didn't look like any of the coloured people I knew. Her nose was delicately formed, her mouth proud, and her eyes, with dark shadows beneath them, glowed.

'Go and fetch plates and spoons for all of us, Sofie . . .'

Flustered, I protested when a short while later Sofie offered me a plate. I had already eaten.

'Just to be sociable,' coaxed Tant Rensie. 'Go on.'

Sofie sat once more on the bed, calmly holding a soup plate in her capable hand.

Why did Tant Rensie act so strangely? Had I become the embodiment of the social order that she had resisted so passively for so many years? A heavy burden for a twelve-year-old boy! Or did she want to 'educate' me? Or had she simply become too old and tired to bother about any social code?

That afternoon still holds timelessness for me in just the way that moments of revelation are timeless. Through the green curtains the light, cool as in an aquarium, filtered into Tant Rensie's room. Unexpectedly one smelt roses – in the room or outside in the garden? They must have been in the room. It was a heavy perfume, pervasive and almost like decay. Suddenly I knew that between these two people was a bond beyond my apprehension. I was strung taut, needing to push my intuition further than my years allowed.

Sofietjie died before Tant Rensie. I was staying with cousins in the Free State when it happened. It was on my return to Klipkraal that I first heard of the confusions over her burial. Tant Rensie wanted Sofietjie buried in the garden in front of her house. This was not allowed by the town council. Then Tant Rensie requested that Sofietjie should be buried among white people. The Women's Association and the MSA organized protest meetings, and finally poor Sofietjie was buried in the cemetery just the other side of the coloured location.

Oom Gawie, the town's only taxi driver, took Tant Rensie to Sofietjie's grave whenever her health allowed it. She would sit there for so long – a camp-stool went with her every time – that Oom Gawie developed the habit of popping back to town for a quick nip. One day, while he was away, Tant Rensie was caught in a thunderstorm that signalled her end: she developed pneumonia.

Oom Gawie gave up drinking for some time, from remorse, but the sacrifice was uncalled for: Tant Rensie didn't want to live any longer. Everyone said so.

Her will was an odd one. The town inherited her money to build a hospital, but she stipulated one condition: she wanted to be laid to rest next to Sofietjie.

Klipkraal has a beautiful hospital for such a small place. But someone, the missionary says, someone should care for those graves.

Drought

» «

JAN RABIE

TRANSLATED FROM THE AFRIKAANS BY THE AUTHOR

Whirling pillars of dust walk the brown floor of the earth. Trembling, the roots of the withered grass await the rain; thirsty for green love the vast and arid plain treks endlessly out to its horizon. One straight ruler-laid railway track shoots from under the midday sun's glare towards where a night will be velvet-cool with stars. The landscape is that of drought. Tiny as two grains of sand, a white man and a black man build a wall. Four walls. Then a roof. A house.

The black man carries blocks of stone and the white man lays them in place. The white man stands inside the walls where there is some shade. He says: 'You must work outside. You have a black skin, you can stand the sun better than I can.'

The black man laughs at his muscles glistening in the sun. A hundred years ago his ancestors reaped dark harvests with their assegais, and threshed out the fever of the black sun in their limbs with the Ngoma-dance. Now the black man laughs while he begins to frown.

'Why do you always talk of my black skin?' he asks.

'You are cursed,' the white man says. 'Long ago my God cursed you with darkness.'

'Your God is white,' the black man angrily replies. 'Your God lies! I love the sun and I fear the dark.'

The white man speaks dreamily on: 'Long ago my forefathers came across the sea. Far they came, in white ships tall as trees, and on the land they built them waggons and covered them with the sails of their ships. Far they travelled and spread their campfire ashes over this vast barbaric land. But now their children are tired, we want to build houses and teach you blacks how to live in peace with us. It is time, even if your skins will always be black . . .'

Proudly the black man counters: 'And my ancestors dipped their assegais in the blood of your forefathers and saw that it was red as blood. Red as the blood of the impala that our young men run to catch between the two red suns of the hills!'

'It's time you forgot the damned past,' the white man sadly says. 'Come, you must learn to work with me. We must build this house.'

'You come to teach me that God is white. That I should build a house for the white man.' The black man stands with folded arms.

'Kaffir!' the white man shouts, 'will you never understand anything at all! Do what I tell you!'

'Yes, Baas,' the black man mutters.

The black man carries blocks of stone and the white man lays them in place. He makes the walls strong. The sun glares down with its terrible eye. Far, as the only tree in the parched land, a pillar of dust walks the trembling horizon.

'This damned heat!' the white man mutters, 'if only it would rain.'

Irritably he wipes the sweat from his forehead before he says: 'Your ancestors are dead. It's time you forgot them.'

Silently the black man looks at him with eyes that answer: Your ancestors, too, are dead. We are alone here.

Alone in the dry and empty plain the white man and the black man build a house. They do not speak to each other. They build the four walls and then the roof. The black man works outside in the sun and the white man inside in the shade. Now the black man can only see the white man's head. They lay the roof.

'Baas,' the black man asks at last, 'why has your house no windows and no doors?'

The white man has become very sad. 'That, too, you cannot understand,' he says. 'Long ago in another country my forefathers built walls to keep out the sea. Thick, watertight walls. That's why my house, too, has no windows and no doors.'

'But there's no big water here!' the black man exclaims, 'the sand is dry as a skull!'

You're the sea, the white man thinks, but is too sad to explain.

They lay the roof. They nail the last plank, the last corrugated iron sheet, the black man outside and the white man inside. Then the black man can see the white man no more.

'Baas!' he calls, but hears no answer.

The Inkoos cannot get out, he thinks with fright, he cannot see the sky or know when it is day or night. The Inkoos will die inside his house!

The black man hammers with his fists on the house and calls: 'But Baas, no big water will ever come here! Here it will never rain for forty days and forty nights as the Book of your white God says!'

He hears no answer and he shouts: 'Come out, Baas!'

He hears no answer.

With his fists still raised as if to knock again, the black man raises his eyes bewilderedly to the sky empty of a single cloud, and stares around him at the horizon where red-hot pillars of dust dance the fearful Ngoma of the drought.

Alone and afraid, the black man stammers: 'Come out, Baas . . . Come out to me . . .'

Boy-Boy

» «

CASEY MOTSISI

Boy-Boy, the son of Esther, the prostitute and shebeen-keeper, was born crippled in the left leg, but when he was ten years old he was already earning his living. He sold newspapers in town. He hoarded his money like a miser and a year later he was able to buy himself a pair of long pants and a colourful windbreaker. He felt like a man as he hobbled around on one crutch in his long pants and windbreaker.

Esther was proud of her son. Although Boy-Boy left school when he was only nine, Esther felt she had no cause for worry because her son showed that he had the makings of a man who could make a success out of life without being saddled with the knowledge of the three Rs.

But as the years passed by and Boy-Boy grew older, Esther's pride in her son began to wane. In fact, she became apprehensive.

'Oh, MaSello, that boy worries me with so many silly questions, I don't know what's got into him,' Esther remarked to her neighbour. She looked so agitated that MaSello, in an attempt to dispel her fears, said, as light-heartedly as she could: 'Children at his age are all like that. My children were like that too.'

'Ma?'

'Yes, my boy?'

'You know those steps at Johannesburg Station that walk?'

'Yes, they call them escalators,' said Esther, wondering which of her many lovers had told her that word. Probably that matric student with the hairy chest, she thought to herself.

'Those steps are always walking up. Why don't they walk down?'

'There are others that walk down.'

'But those are always walking up. Can I walk down on them while they are walking up?'

'I don't know.'

184

'Have you tried it?'

'No.'

'Has anybody tried it?'

'I don't know. Please shut up!'

'I'm going to try it.'

Boy-Boy did try it and was as pleased as punch when he realized that it was possible to go down an escalator while it was moving up. It was the same thrill as a motorist must feel after safely taking a short cut going the wrong way along a one-way street.

'Ma, why do we have policemen?'

'We have policewomen, too,' said Esther, anticipating her son's next question.

'Why do we have them?'

'To arrest people.'

'I'm going to be a policeman.'

How and where he got them will for ever remain a mystery, but Boy-Boy managed to get himself a pair of handcuffs and a policewhistle. And how he loved blowing that whistle! And how it got on Esther's nerves!

'I'm a policeman. I'm going to arrest one of those people drinking skokiaan in the kitchen,' Boy-Boy told Esther with the light of his brand of justice shining in his eyes.

'I'm arresting you,' Boy-Boy said to one greyhead who had just taken a sip out of his tin.

'Owright, arrest me,' said the greyhead trying to humour the boy. He thrust out his hands.

Kraang, kraang, went the handcuffs.

Two hours later the greyhead was still pleading with Boy-Boy to remove the handcuffs. But Boy-Boy demanded five shillings first.

'Five bob,' he said for the umpteenth time.

The greyhead was furious.

'If you don't take them off I'm going to kick your bloody . . .'

Boy-Boy hit him over the head with his crutch before he could say another word.

'Esther!' The greyhead was almost in tears. There was a trickle of blood on his head.

Esther paid the greyhead's 'fine' and the handcuffs came off.

'I'm a policeman,' shouted Boy-Boy as he hobbled out of the house into the street.

'I'll never drink in this house any more,' said the greyhead. And so, one by one, Esther's customers dwindled.

Even her lovers dwindled. This was also Boy-Boy's doing. He would rush into the bedroom in the middle of the night and belabour whoever was in bed with Esther on the head with his crutch.

'There are too many flies in this house,' Boy-Boy said to his mother one day. Esther did not reply. She just shook her head sadly as she watched her son hobble out of the house.

A few minutes later Boy-Boy came back carrying a dozen boxes of matches. He sat on a bench, opened one box and pulled out one stick. He struck it and laughed as it burst into flames. He did this until the box was empty. Then he reached out for a second one. After some time, all the twelve boxes were empty.

'Now I've got twelve coffins,' Boy-Boy said, eyeing the twelve empty boxes of matches gleefully, 'I'm going to kill and bury twelve flies today.'

Twelve flies were buried that day.

The next day Esther found her son busy at work with pieces of plank and nails. He looked in such a happy mood that Esther, although she was never too keen to engage her son in conversation, could not help asking what he was doing.

'I'm building a coffin for Topsy.'

Topsy was the family pet dog.

'But Topsy's not dead!' Esther was shocked beyond words.

'I dreamt he was dead last night.'

She felt relieved. 'Well, it was a bad dream. He is not dead.'

Tap, tap, tap, went the hammer.

'Then I'm going to kill him. I must bury him in this coffin.'

Esther went out in search of the dog. 'Top, Topsy, *Topsy-y-y*!'

When she got hold of the dog she took it by taxi to the safety of her uncle's place in Alexandra.

It was about nine o'clock at night when she came back. The door was locked. She knocked.

'This is my house. Go away,' Boy-Boy shouted through the window.

'Boy-Boy! It's me, your mother!'

'My mother is not born yet. Go away! Go away!'

The Bench

» «

RICHARD RIVE

'We are part of a complex society further complicated by the fact that the vast majority of the population is denied the very basic privileges of citizenship. Our society condemns a man to an inferior status because he is born black. Our society can only retain its social and economic position at the expense of a large black working-class.'

Karlie was concentrating hard while trying to follow the speaker. Something at the back of his mind told him that these were great and true words, whatever they meant. The speaker was a huge black man with a rolling voice. He paused to sip water from a glass. Karlie sweated. The hot October sun beat down mercilessly on the gathering. A burning sky without the slightest vestige of cloud over Table Mountain. The trees on the Grand Parade, drooping and wilted, afforded hardly any shelter. His handkerchief was already soaking where he had placed it around his neck. Karlie looked cautiously at the sea of faces. Black, brown, olive, a few white faces and scattered red fezzes of Muslims. Near a parked car two detectives were taking notes. On the raised platform the rolling voice started again.

'It is up to every one of us to challenge the right of any law which wilfully condemns any person to an inferior position. We must challenge the right of any people to segregate any others on grounds of skin colour. You and your children are denied rights which are yours by virtue of your being South Africans. But you are segregated against politically, socially and economically.'

Karlie felt something stirring deep inside him, something he had never experienced before, had never known was there. The man on the platform seemed to be rolling out a new religion which said that he, Karlie, had certain rights, and his children would have certain rights. What sort of rights? Like a white man, for instance? To live as well as Oubaas Lategan at Bietjiesfontein? The idea took shape and started developing. A rush of feeling and an insight

187

he had never explored before. To sit at a table in the café at Bietjiesfontein. Nellie and himself ordering steak and eggs and coffee. Sitting downstairs in the local bioscope with the other farmers, and going out at interval to buy drinks at the Panorama. His children attending the Hoërskool and playing rugby and hockey against visiting teams. This was a picture that frightened but at the same time seduced. Now what would Ou Klaas think of that? Ou Klaas who always said that God in his wisdom made the white man white and the coloured man brown and the black man black. And they must know their place. What would Ou Klaas say to such things? Those ideas coming from the platform were far from Ou Klaas and Bietjiesfontein, but in a vague way they made sense.

Karlie knitted his brow while trying to make it all out. There were many others on the platform, black and white and brown. And they behaved as if there were no difference in colour. What would Ou Klaas say when he told him about it? Oubaas Lategan? A white woman in a blue dress offering a cigarette to the previous speaker who was a black man? He had been introduced as Mr Nxeli, a trade-union leader who had often been in jail. A white woman offering him a cigarette. Karlie also felt like smoking and took out a crumpled packet of Cavalla.

Imagine if Ou Klaas offered Annetjie Lategan a suck at his pipe. What would her father say? Oubaas Lategan would most probably get his gun and shoot him on the spot. The idea was so ludicrous that Karlie burst out laughing. One or two people looked round inquiringly. In a fit of embarrassment he converted the laugh into a cough and lit the mangled cigarette. But his mind refused to give up the picture. And Annetjie was nowhere near as pretty and had no such blue, shop-bought dress. When the lady on the platform moved, her dress was tight around her. He saw that when she offered Mr Nxeli a cigarette.

If all the things the speaker said were true, it meant that he, Karlie, was as good as any other man. His mouth played with the words, 'even a white man', but he quickly dispelled this notion. But the speaker seemed to be emphasizing just that. And why should he not accept those ideas? He remembered being shown a picture torn out of a newspaper of those people who defied laws which they said were unjust. He had asked Ou Klaas about it but the old man had merely shrugged his shoulders. The people in the newspaper were smiling as they went to prison. These things were confusing and strange.

The speaker with the rolling voice continued and Karlie listened intently. He seemed so sure and confident of himself as the words flowed out. Karlie felt sure that he was even greater than Oubaas Lategan or even the dominee of the whites-only church in Bietjiesfontein. The lady in the blue dress spoke next. The one who had given Mr Nxeli a cigarette. She said that one must challenge all discriminatory laws. It was one's duty to do so. All laws which said that one person was inferior to another. 'Sit anywhere you wish, whether in a train or a restaurant. Let them arrest you if they dare.' The white detectives were very busy taking notes. Why should she be telling them this? She could go to the best bioscopes, swim off the best beaches, live in the best areas. What made a white woman who could have everything say such words? And she was far more beautiful than Annetjie Lategan and had hair that gleamed with gold in the sun.

He had been worried before he left Bietjiesfontein that things would be different in Cape Town. He had seen the skollies in Hanover Street but they no longer held any terror for him, although he had been frightened at first. He now lived off Caledon Street near Star Bioscope. He had very few friends, one in Athlone whom he was going to visit when he saw the meeting on the Grand Parade. District Six proved a bit of a let-down, but no one, not even Ou Klaas, had warned him about the things he was now hearing. This was new. This set the mind racing. The lady emphasized that they should challenge these laws and suffer the consequences. Yes, he must challenge. The resolve started shaping in his mind but still seemed far too daring, far too ridiculous. But as the lady continued, a determination started creeping over the vagueness. Yes, he must challenge. He, Karlie, would challenge and suffer the consequences. He would astound Oubaas Lategan and Ou Klaas and Annetjie and Nellie when they saw his picture in the newspaper. And he would smile. He would even astound the lady in the blue dress. With the fervency of a new convert he determined that he was going to challenge, even if it meant prison. He would smile like those people in the newspaper.

The meeting passed a resolution, then sang 'Nkosi Sikelel' iAfrika' and they all raised their hands with the thumbs pointing up and shouted 'Afrika!' And then the crowd dispersed. Karlie threaded his way through the mass to get to the station. His friend would be waiting for him in Athlone. The words of all the speakers still milled in his head. Confusing somehow but at the same time quite clear. He must challenge. This could never have happened at Bietjiesfontein, or could it? The sudden screech of a car as brakes were applied. Karlie jumped out of the way just in time. A head was angrily thrust through the window.

'Look where you're going, you bloody baboon!'

Karlie stared dazed, momentarily too stunned to speak. Surely the driver could not have seen the white woman offering Mr Nxeli a cigarette? She would never have shouted at him like that and called him a baboon. She had said one must challenge. These things were all so confusing. Maybe best to catch a train and get to his friend in Athlone and tell him all about it. He had to speak to someone.

He saw the station through the eyes of a fresh convert. A mass of human beings, mostly white but with some blacks and a few browns like himself. Here they pushed and jostled but there seemed a cocoon around each person. Each one in his own world. Each moving in a narrow pattern of his own manufacture. But one must challenge these things, the woman had said. And the man with the rolling voice. Each in his own way. But how did one challenge? What did one challenge?

Then it dawned on him. Here was his chance. The bench. The railway bench with the legend WHITES ONLY neatly painted on it in white.

For a moment it symbolized all the misery of South African society. Here was his challenge to his rights as a man. Here it stood. A perfectly ordinary wooden bench like the hundreds of thousands of others all over South Africa. Benches on dusty stations in the Karoo; under ferns and subtropical foliage in Natal; benches all over the country each with its legend. His challenge. That bench now had concentrated in it all the evils of a system he could not understand. It was the obstacle between himself and his manhood. If he sat on it, he was a man. If he was afraid, he denied himself membership as a human in human society. He almost had visions of righting the system if only he sat on that bench. Here was his chance. He, Karlie, would challenge.

He seemed perfectly calm as he sat down, but his heart was thumping wildly. Two conflicting ideas now seeped through him. The one said, 'You have no right to sit on the bench.' The other questioned, 'Why have you no right to sit on the bench?' The first spoke of the past, of the life on the farm, of the servile figure of his father and Ou Klaas, his father's father who had said, 'God in his wisdom made the white man white and the black man black.' The other voice had promise of the future in it and said, 'Karlie, you are a man. You have dared what your father would not have dared. And his father. You will die like a man.'

Karlie took out a Cavalla from the crumpled packet and smoked. But nobody seemed to notice him sitting there. This was also a let-down. The world still pursued its natural way. People still lived, breathed and laughed. No voice shouted triumphantly, 'Karlie, you have conquered!' He was a perfectly ordinary human being sitting on a bench on a crowded station, smoking a cigarette. Or was this his victory? Being an ordinary human being sitting on a bench?

A well-dressed white lady walked down the platform. Would she sit on the bench? And the gnawing voice, 'You should stand up and let the white woman sit. This bench is not for you.' Karlie's eyes narrowed as he pulled more fiercely at his cigarette. She swept past with scarcely a glance at him. Was she afraid of challenging his rights to be a human being? Or couldn't she care less?

Karlie now realized that he was completely exhausted. He was used to physical work, but this was different. He was mentally and emotionally drained. A third conflicting thought now crept in, a compensatory one which said, 'You do not sit on the bench to challenge. You sit here because you are tired, therefore you are sitting here.' He would not move because he was tired. He wanted to rest. Or was it because he wanted to challenge?

People were now pouring from the Athlone train that had pulled in at the platform. There were so many pushing and jostling one another that nobody seemed to have time to notice him. When the train pulled out it would pass Athlone. It would be the easiest thing in the world to step into it and ride away from all this. He could rest because he was tired. Away from challenges, and benches one was not allowed to sit on. And meetings on the Grand Parade. And a white lady offering Mr Nxeli a cigarette. But that would be giving in, suffering a personal defeat, refusing to challenge. In fact it would be admitting that he was not a human being . . .

He sat on, smoking another cigarette and allowing his mind to wander. Far away from the station and the bench. Bietjiesfontein and that talk he had had with his grandfather when he had told Ou Klaas what he had on his mind. The glittering lights of Cape Town and better jobs and more money so that he could send some home. Ou Klaas had looked up quizzically while sucking at his pipe. Ou Klaas was wise and had lived long. He always insisted that one must learn through travelling. He had lived in Cape Town as a young man and would spit and laugh slyly when he told of the girls in District Six. Beautiful, olive-skinned and doe-eyed. Ou Klaas knew everything. He also said that God in his wisdom made the white man white and the black man black. And each must keep his place.

'You are sitting on the wrong seat.' Karlie did not notice the person speaking. Ou Klaas had a trick of spitting on the ground and pulling his mouth slyly when he made a strong point, especially about the women he had had.

'This is the wrong seat.'

Karlie whipped back to reality. He was going to get up instinctively when he realized who he was and why he was sitting there. He suddenly felt very tired and looked up slowly. A thin, gangling, pimple-faced white youth lugging an enormous suitcase.

'I'm sorry but you on the wrong seat. This is for whites only.'

Karlie stared at him, saying nothing.

'Are you deaf? You are sitting on the wrong bench. This is not for you people. It is for white people only.'

Slowly and deliberately Karlie puffed at his cigarette and examined it exaggeratedly. This was the test, or the contest? The white youth was sizing him up.

'If you don't move now you can get into serious trouble.'

Karlie maintained his obstinate silence. The youth was obviously not going to take the law into his own hands. For Karlie to speak now would be to break the spell, the supremacy he felt he was gaining.

'Well, you asking for it. I will have to report you.'

Karlie realized that the youth was brazening it out, afraid to take action himself. He went off, leaving his suitcase on the bench next to Karlie. He, Karlie, had won the first round of the bench dispute.

He took out another cigarette. Irresolution had now turned to determination. Under no circumstances was he going to give up his bench. They could do what they wanted. He stared hostilely at the suitcase.

'Come on, you're sitting on the wrong bench. There are seats further down for you people.' The policeman towered over him. Karlie could see thin red hairs on his neck. The white youth stood behind the officer. Karlie said nothing.

'I'm ordering you to move for the last time.'

Karlie remained seated.

'All right. Then I want your name and address and you will come with me.' Karlie maintained the obstinate silence. This took the policeman unawares. The crowd started growing and one joker shouted 'Afrika!' and then disappeared among the spectators.

'I will have to place you under arrest. Come on, get up.'

Karlie remained seated. The policeman grabbed him by the shoulders, assisted by the white youth. Karlie turned to resist, to cling to the bench, to his bench. He hit out wildly and then felt a dull pain as a fist rammed into his stomach. He rolled on to the ground, grazing his face against the rough tarmac. Then his arms were twisted behind him and handcuffs bit into his wrists. Suddenly he relaxed and struggled to his feet. It was senseless fighting any longer. Now it was his turn to smile. He had challenged and felt he had won. If not a victory over them, then one over himself. Who cared about the consequences? The white youth was dusting his trousers.

'Come on,' said the policeman, forcing Karlie through the crowd.

'Certainly,' said Karlie for the first time, and stared at the crowd with the arrogance of one who had dared to sit on a WHITES ONLY bench.

Mrs Plum

» «

ES'KIA MPHAHLELE

My madam's name was Mrs Plum. She loved dogs and Africans and said that everyone must follow the law even if it hurt. These were three big things in Madam's life.

I came to work for Mrs Plum in Greenside, not very far from the centre of Johannesburg, after leaving two white families. The first white people I worked for as a cook and laundry woman were a man and his wife in Parktown North. They drank too much and always forgot to pay me. After five months I said to myself No, I am going to leave these drunks. So that was it. That day I was as angry as a red-hot iron when it meets water. The second house I cooked and washed for had five children who were badly brought up. This was in Belgravia. Many times they called me You Black Girl and I kept quiet. Because their mother heard them and said nothing. Also I was only new from Phokeng my home, far away near Rustenburg, I wanted to learn and know the white people before I knew how far to go with the others I would work for afterwards. The thing that drove me mad and made me pack and go was a man who came to visit them often. They said he was a cousin or something like that. He came to the kitchen many times and tried to make me laugh. He patted me on the buttocks. I told the master. The man did it again and I asked the madam that very day to give me my money and let me go.

These were the first nine months after I had left Phokeng to work in Johannesburg. There were many of us girls and young women from Phokeng, from Zeerust, from Shuping, from Kosten, and many other places who came to work in the cities. So the suburbs were full of blackness. Most of us had already passed Standard Six and so we learned more English where we worked. None of us likes to work for white farmers, because we know too much about them on the farms near our homes. They do not pay well and they are cruel people.

At Easter time so many of us went home for a long weekend to see our people and to eat chicken and sour milk and morogo – wild spinach. We also took home sugar and condensed milk and tea and coffee and sweets and custard powder and tinned foods.

It was a home-girl of mine, Chimane, who called me to take a job in Mrs Plum's house, just next door to where she worked. This is the third year now. I have been quite happy with Mrs Plum and her daughter Kate. By this I mean that my place as a servant in Greenside is not as bad as that of many others. Chimane too does not complain much. We are paid six pounds a month with free food and free servant's room. No one can ever say that they are well paid, so we go on complaining somehow. Whenever we meet on Thursday afternoons, which is time-off for all of us black women in the suburbs, we talk and talk and talk: about our people at home and their letters; about their illnesses; about bad crops; about a sister who wanted a school uniform and books and school fees; about some of our madams and masters who are good, or stingy with money or food, or stupid or full of nonsense, or who kill themselves and each other, or who are dirty – and so many things I cannot count them all.

Thursday afternoons we go to town to look at the shops, to attend a women's club, to see our boyfriends, to go to bioscope some of us. We turn up smart, to show others the clothes we bought from the black men who sell soft goods to servants in the suburbs. We take a number of things and they come round every month for a bit of money until we finish paying. Then we dress the way of many white madams and girls. I think we look really smart. Sometimes we catch the eyes of a white woman looking at us and we laugh and laugh and laugh until we nearly drop on the ground because we feel good inside ourselves.

What did the girl next door call you? Mrs Plum asked me the first day I came to her. Jane, I replied. Was there not an African name? I said yes, Karabo. All right, Madam said. We'll call you Karabo, she said. She spoke as if she knew a name is a big thing. I knew so many whites who did not care what they called black people as long as it was all right for their tongue. This pleased me, I mean Mrs Plum's use of *Karabo*; because the only time I heard the name was when I was at home or when my friends spoke to me. Then she showed me what to do: meals, meal times, washing, and where all the things were that I was going to use.

My daughter will be here in the evening, Madam said. She is at school. When the daughter came, she added, she would tell me some of the things she wanted me to do for her every day.

Chimane, my friend next door, had told me about the daughter Kate, how wild she seemed to be, and about Mr Plum who had killed himself, with a gun in a house down the street. They had left the house and come to this one.

Madam is a tall woman. Not slender, not fat. She moves slowly, and speaks slowly. Her face looks very wise, her forehead seems to tell me she has a strong liver: she is not afraid of anything. Her eyes are always swollen at the lower eyelids like a white person who has not slept for many many nights or like a large frog. Perhaps it is because she smokes too much, like wet wood that will not know whether to go up in flames or stop burning. She looks me straight in the eyes when she talks to me, and I know she does this with other people too. At first this made me fear her, now I am used to her. She is not a lazy woman, and she does many things outside, in the city and in the suburbs.

This was the first thing her daughter Kate told me when she came and we met. Don't mind mother, Kate told me. She said, She is sometimes mad with people for very small things. She will soon be all right and speak nicely to you again.

Kate, I like her very much, and she likes me too. She tells me many things a white woman does not tell a black servant. I mean things about what she likes and does not like, what her mother does or does not do, all these. At first I was unhappy and wanted to stop her, but now I do not mind.

Kate looks very much like her mother in the face. I think her shoulders will be just as round and strong-looking. She moves faster than Madam. I asked her why she was still at school when she was so big. She laughed. Then she tried to tell me that the school where she was was for big people, who had finished with lower school. She was learning big things about cooking and food. She can explain better, me I cannot. She came home on weekends.

Since I came to work for Mrs Plum Kate has been teaching me plenty of cooking. I first learned from her and Madam the word *recipes*. When Kate was at the big school, Madam taught me how to read cookery books. I went on very slowly at first, slower than an ox-waggon. Now I know more. When Kate came home, she found I had read the recipe she left me. So we just cooked straightaway. Kate thinks I am fit to cook in a hotel, Madam thinks so too. Never never! I thought. Cooking in a hotel is like feeding oxen. No one can say thank you to you. After a few months I could cook the Sunday lunch and later I could cook specials for Madam's or Kate's guests.

Madam did not only teach me cooking. She taught me how to look after guests. She praised me when I did very well; not like the white people I had worked for before. I do not know what runs crooked in the heads of other people. Madam also had classes in the evenings for servants to teach them how to read and write. She and two other women in Greenside taught in a church hall.

As I say, Kate tells me plenty of things about Madam. She says to me she says, My mother goes to meetings many times. I ask her I say, What for? She says to me she says, For your people. I ask her I say, My people are in Phokeng far away. They have got mouths, I say. Why does she want to say something for them? Does she know what my mother and what my father want to say? They can speak when they want to. Kate raises her shoulders and drops them and says, How can I tell you Karabo? I don't say your people – your family only. I mean all the black people in this country. I say Oh! What do the black people want to say? Again she raises her shoulders and drops them, taking a deep breath.

I ask her I say, With whom is she in the meeting?

She says, With other people who think like her.

I ask her I say, Do you say there are people in the world who think the same things?

She nods her head.

I ask, What things?

So that a few of your people should one day be among those who rule this country, get more money for what they do for the white man, and – what did Kate say again? Yes, that Madam and those who think like her also wanted my people who have been to school to choose those who must speak for them in the – I think she said it looks like a kgotla at home who rule the villages.

I say to Kate I say, Oh I see now. I say, Tell me Kate why is madam always writing on the machine, all the time everyday nearly?

She replies she says, Oh my mother is writing books.

I ask, You mean a book like those? – pointing at the books on the shelves.

Yes, Kate says.

And she told me how Madam wrote books and other things for newspapers and she wrote for the newspapers and magazines to say things for the black people who should be treated well, be paid more money, for the black people who can read and write many things to choose those who want to speak for them.

Kate also told me she said, My mother and other women who think like her put on black belts over their shoulders when they are sad and they want to show the white government they do not like the things being done by whites to blacks. My mother and the others go and stand where the people in government are going to enter or go out of a building.

I ask her I say, Does the government and the white people listen and stop their sins? She says, No. But my mother is in another group of white people.

I ask, Do the people of the government give the women tea and cakes? Kate says, Karabo! How stupid; oh!

I say to her I say, Among my people if someone comes and stands in front of my house I tell him to come in and I give him food. You white people are wonderful. But they keep standing there and the government people do not give them anything.

She replies, You mean strange. How many times have I taught you not to say *wonderful* when you mean *strange*! Well, Kate says with a short heart and looking cross and she shouts, Well they do not stand there the whole day to ask for tea and cakes stupid. Oh dear!

Always when Madam finished to read her newspapers she gave them to me to read to help me speak and write better English. When I had read she asked me to tell her some of the things in it. In this way, I did better and better and my mind was opening and opening and I was learning and learning many things about the black people inside and outside the towns which I did not know in the least. When I found words that were too difficult or I did not understand some of the things I asked Madam. She always told me You see this, you see that, eh? with a heart that can carry on a long way. Yes, Madam writes many letters to the papers. She is always sore about the way the white police beat up black people; about the way black people who work for whites are made to sit at the Zoo Lake with their hearts hanging, because the white people say our people are making noise on Sunday afternoon when they want to rest in their houses and gardens; about many ugly things that happen when some white people meet a black man on the pavement or street. So Madam writes to the papers to let others know, to ask the government to be kind to us.

In the first year Mrs Plum wanted me to eat at table with her. It was very hard, one because I was not used to eating at table with a fork and knife, two because I heard of no other kitchen worker who was handled like this. I was afraid. Afraid of everybody, of Madam's guests if they found me doing this. Madam said I must not be silly. I must show that African servants can also eat at table. Number three, I could not eat some of the things I loved very much: mealie-meal porridge with sour milk or morogo, stamped mealies mixed with butter beans, sour porridge for breakfast and other things. Also, except for morning porridge, our food is nice when you eat with the hand. So nice that it does not stop in the mouth or the throat to greet anyone before it passes smoothly down.

We often had lunch together with Chimane next door and our garden boy – Ha! I must remember never to say *boy* again when I talk about a man. This makes me think of a day during the first few weeks in Mrs Plum's house. I was talking about Dick her garden man and I said 'garden boy'. And she says to me she says Stop talking about a 'boy', Karabo. Now listen here, she says, You Africans must learn to speak properly about each other. And she says

White people won't talk kindly about you if you look down upon each other.

I say to her I say Madam, I learned the word from the white people I worked for, and all the kitchen maids say 'boy'.

She replies she says to me, Those are white people who know nothing, just low-class whites. I say to her I say I thought white people know everything.

She said, You'll learn my girl and you must start in this house, hear? She left me there thinking, my mind mixed up.

I learned. I grew up.

If any woman or girl does not know the Black Crow Club in Bree Street, she does not know anything. I think nearly everything takes place inside and outside that house. It is just where the dirty part of the City begins, with factories and the market. After the market is the place where Indians and Coloured people live. It is also at the Black Crow that the buses turn round and back to the black townships. Noise, noise, noise all the time. There are women who sell hot sweet potatoes and fruit and monkey nuts and boiled eggs in the winter, boiled mealies and the other things in the summer, all these on the pavements. The streets are always full of potato and fruit skins and monkey nut shells. There is always a strong smell of roast pork. I think it is because of Piel's cold storage down Bree Street.

Madam said she knew the black people who work in the Black Crow. She was happy that I was spending my afternoon on Thursdays in such a club. You will learn sewing, knitting, she said, and other things that you like. Do you like to dance? I told her I said, Yes, I want to learn. She paid the two shillings fee for me each month.

We waited on the first floor, we the ones who were learning sewing; waiting for the teacher. We talked and laughed about madams and masters, and their children and their dogs and birds and whispered about our boyfriends.

Sies! My Madam you do not know – mojuta oa'nete – a real miser . . .

Jo – jo – jo! you should see our new dog. A big thing like this. People! Big in a foolish way . . .

What! Me, I take a master's bitch by the leg, me, and throw it away so that it keeps howling, tjwe – tjwe! ngo – wu ngo – wu! I don't play about with them, me . . .

Shame, poor thing! God sees you, true . . . !

They wanted me to take their dog out for a walk every afternoon and I told them I said It is not my work in other houses the garden man does it. I just said to myself I said they can go to the chickens. Let them bite their elbow before I take out a dog, I am not so mad yet . . .

Hei! It is not like the child of my white people who keeps a big white rat and you know what? He puts it on his bed when he goes to school. And let the blankets just begin to smell of urine and all the nonsense and they tell me to wash them. Hei, people! . . .

Did you hear about Rebone, people? Her Madam put her out, because her master was always tapping her buttocks with his fingers. And yesterday the madam saw the master press Rebone against himself . . .

Jo – jo – jo! people . . . !

Dirty white man!

No, not dirty. The madam smells too old for him.

Hei! Go and wash your mouth with soap, this girl's mouth is dirty . . .

Jo, Rebone, daughter of the people! We must help her to find a job before she thinks of going back home.

The teacher came. A woman with strong legs, a strong face, and kind eyes. She had short hair and dressed in a simple but lovely floral frock. She stood well on her legs and hips. She had a black mark between the two top front teeth. She smiled as if we were her children. Our group began with games, and then Lilian Ngoyi took us for sewing. After this she gave a brief talk to all of us from the different classes.

I can never forget the things this woman said and how she put them to us. She told us that the time had passed for black girls and women in the suburbs to be satisfied with working, sending money to our people and going to see them once a year. We were to learn, she said, that the world would never be safe for black people until they were in the government with the power to make laws. The power should be given by the Africans who were more than the whites.

We asked her questions and she answered them with wisdom. I shall put some of them down in my own words as I remember them.

Shall we take the place of the white people in the government?

Some yes. But we shall be more than they as we are more in the country. But also the people of all colours will come together and there are good white men we can choose and there are Africans some white people will choose to be in the government.

There are good madams and masters and bad ones. Should we take the good ones for friends?

A master and a servant can never be friends. Never, so put that out of your head, will you! You are not even sure if the ones you say are good are not like that because they cannot breathe or live without the work of your hands. As long as you need their money, face them with respect. But you must know that many sad things are happening in our country and you, all of you, must always be learning, adding to what you already know, and obey us when we ask you to help us.

At other times Lilian Ngoyi told us she said, Remember your poor people at home and the way in which the whites are moving them from place to place like sheep and cattle. And at other times again she told us she said, Remember that a hand cannot wash itself, it needs another to do it.

I always thought of Madam when Lilian Ngoyi spoke. I asked myself, What would she say if she knew that I was listening to such words. Words like: A white man is looked after by his black nanny and his mother when he is a baby. When he grows up the white government looks after him, sends him to school, makes it impossible for him to suffer from the great hunger, keeps a job ready and open for him as soon as he wants to leave school. Now Lilian Ngoyi asked she said, How many white people can be born in a white hospital, grow up in white streets be clothed in lovely cotton, lie on white cushions; how many whites can live all their lives in a fenced place away from people of other colours and then, as men and women, learn quickly the correct ways of thinking, learn quickly to ask questions in their minds, big questions that will throw over all the nice things of a white man's life? How many? Very very few! For those whites who have not begun to ask, it is too late. For those who have begun and are joining us with both feet in our house, we can only say Welcome!

I was learning. I was growing up. Every time I thought of Madam, she became more and more like a dark forest which one fears to enter, and which one will never know. But there were several times when I thought, This woman is easy to understand, she is like all other white women.

What else are they teaching you at the Black Crow, Karabo?

I tell her I say, nothing, Madam. I ask her I say Why does Madam ask?

You are changing.

What does Madam mean?

Well, you are changing.

But we are always changing Madam.

And she left me standing in the kitchen. This was a few days after I had told her that I did not want to read more than one white paper a day. The only magazines I wanted to read, I said to her, were those from overseas, if she had them. I told her that white papers had pictures of white people most of the time. They talked mostly about white people and their gardens, dogs, weddings and parties. I asked her if she could buy me a Sunday paper that spoke about my people. Madam bought it for me. I did not think she would do it.

There were mornings when, after hanging the white people's washing on the line Chimane and I stole a little time to stand at the fence and talk. We always stood where we could be hidden by our rooms.

Hei, Karabo, you know what? That was Chimane.

No – what? Before you start, tell me, has Timi come back to you?

Ach, I do not care. He is still angry. But boys are fools they always come back dragging themselves on their empty bellies. Hei you know what?

Yes?

The Thursday past I saw Moruti K.K. I laughed until I dropped on the ground. He is standing in front of the Black Crow. I believe his big stomach was crying from hunger. Now he has a small dog in his armpit, and is standing before a woman selling boiled eggs and – hei home-girl! – tripe and intestines are boiling in a pot – oh, the smell! you could fill a hungry belly with it, the way it was good. I think Moruti K.K. is waiting for the woman to buy a boiled egg. I do not know what the woman was still doing. I am standing nearby. The dog keeps wriggling and pushing out its nose, looking at the boiling tripe. Moruti keeps patting it with his free hand, not so? Again the dog wants to spill out of Moruti's hand and it gives a few sounds through the nose. Hei man, home-girl! One two three the dog spills out to catch some of the good meat! It misses falling into the hot gravy in which the tripe is swimming I do not know how. Moruti K.K. tries to chase it. It has tumbled on to the women's eggs and potatoes and all are in the dust. She stands up and goes after K.K. She is shouting to him to pay, not so? Where am I at that time? I am nearly dead with laughter the tears are coming down so far.

I was myself holding tight on the fence so as not to fall through laughing. I held my stomach to keep back a pain in the side.

I ask her I say, Did Moruti K.K. come back to pay for the wasted food?

Yes, he paid.

The dog?

He caught it. That is a good African dog. A dog must look for its own food when it is not time for meals. Not these stupid spoiled angels the whites keep giving tea and biscuits.

Hmm.

Dick our garden man joined us, as he often did. When the story was repeated to him the man nearly rolled on the ground laughing.

He asks who is Reverend K.K.?

I say he is the owner of the Black Crow.

Oh!

We reminded each other, Chimane and I, of the round minister. He would come into the club, look at us with a smooth smile on his smooth round face. He would look at each one of us, with that smile on all the time, as if he had forgotten that it was there. Perhaps he had, because as he looked at us, almost stripping us naked with his watery shining eyes – funny – he could have been a farmer looking at his ripe corn, thinking many things.

K.K. often spoke without shame about what he called ripe girls – matjitjana – with good firm breasts. He said such girls were pure without any nonsense in their heads and bodies. Everybody talked a great deal about him and what they thought he must be doing in his office whenever he called in so-and-so.

The Reverend K.K. did not belong to any church. He baptized, married, and buried people for a fee, who had no church to do such things for them. They said he had been driven out of the Presbyterian Church. He had formed his own, but it did not go far. Then he later came and opened the Black Crow. He knew just how far to go with Lilian Ngoyi. She said although she used his club to teach us things that would help us in life, she could not go on if he was doing any wicked things with the girls in his office. Moruti K.K. feared her, and kept his place.

When I began to tell my story I thought I was going to tell you mostly about Mrs Plum's two dogs. But I have been talking about people. I think Dick is right when he says What is a dog! And there are so many dogs cats and parrots in Greenside and other places that Mrs Plum's dogs do not look special. But there was something special in the dog business in Madam's house. The way in which she loved them, maybe.

Monty is a tiny animal with long hair and small black eyes and a face nearly like that of an old woman. The other, Malan, is a bit bigger, with brown and white colours. It has small hair and looks naked by the side of the friend. They sleep in two separate baskets which stay in Madam's bedroom. They are to be washed often and brushed and sprayed and they sleep on pink linen. Monty has a pink ribbon which stays on his neck most of the time. They both carry a cover on their backs. They make me fed up when I see them in their baskets, looking fat, and as if they knew all that was going on everywhere.

It was Dick's work to look after Monty and Malan, to feed them, and to do everything for them. He did this together with garden work and cleaning of the house. He came at the beginning of this year. He just came, as if from nowhere, and Madam gave him the job as she had chased away two before him, she told me. In both those cases, she said that they could not look after Monty and Malan.

Dick had a long heart, even although he told me and Chimane that European dogs were stupid, spoiled. He said One day those white people will put ear-rings and toe-rings and bangles on their dogs. That would be the day he would leave Mrs Plum. For, he said, he was sure that she would want him to polish the rings and bangles with Brasso.

Although he had a long heart, Madam was still not sure of him. She often went to the dogs after a meal or after a cleaning and said to them Did Dick give you food sweethearts? Or, Did Dick wash you sweethearts? Let me see. And I could see that Dick was blowing up like a balloon with anger. These things called white people! he said to me. Talking to dogs!

I say to him I say, People talk to oxen at home do I not say so?

Yes, he says, but at home do you not know that a man speaks to an ox because he wants to make it pull the plough or the waggon or to stop or to stand still for a person to inspan it. No one simply goes to an ox looking at him with eyes far apart and speaks to it. Let me ask you, do you ever see a person where we come from take a cow and press it to his stomach or his cheek? Tell me!

And I say to Dick I say, We were talking about an ox, not a cow.

He laughed with his broad mouth until tears came out of his eyes. At a certain point I laughed aloud too.

One day when you have time, Dick says to me, he says, you should look into Madam's bedroom when she has put a notice outside her door.

Dick, what are you saying? I ask.

I do not talk, me. I know deep inside me.

Dick was about our age, I and Chimane. So we always said moshiman'o when we spoke about his tricks. Because he was not too big to be a boy to us. He also said to us Hei, lona banyana kelona – Hey you girls, you! His large mouth always seemed to be making ready to laugh. I think Madam did not like this. Many times she would say What is there to make you laugh here? Or in the garden she would say This is a flower and when it wants water that is not funny! Or again, If you did more work and stopped trying to water my plants with your smile you would be more useful. Even when Dick did not mean to smile. What Madam did not get tired of saying was, If I left you to look after my dogs without anyone to look after you at the same time you would drown the poor things.

Dick smiled at Mrs Plum. Dick hurt Mrs Plum's dogs? Then cows can fly. He was really – really afraid of white people, Dick. I think he tried very hard not to feel afraid. For he was always showing me and Chimane in private how Mrs Plum walked, and spoke. He took two bowls and pressed them to his chest, speaking softly to them as Madam speaks to Monty and Malan. Or he sat at Madam's table and acted the way she sits when writing. Now and again he looked back over his shoulder, pulled his face long like a horse's making as if he were looking over his glasses while telling me something to do. Then he would sit on one of the armchairs, cross his legs and act the way Madam drank her tea; he held the cup he was thinking about between his thumb and the pointing finger, only letting their nails meet. And he laughed after every act. He did these things of course, when Madam was not home. And where was I at such times? Almost flat on my stomach, laughing.

But oh how Dick trembled when Mrs Plum scolded him! He did his house-cleaning very well. Whatever mistake he made, it was mostly with the dogs; their linen, their food. One white man came into the house one afternoon to tell Madam that Dick had been very careless when taking the dogs out for a walk. His own dog was waiting on Madam's stoep. He repeated that he had been driving down our street; and Dick had let loose Monty and Malan to cross the street. The white man made plenty of noise about this and I think wanted to let Madam know how useful he had been. He kept on saying Just one inch, *just* one inch. It was lucky I put on my brakes quick enough . . . But your boy kept on smiling – Why? Strange. My boy would only do it twice and only twice and then . . . ! His pass. The man moved his hand like one writing, to mean that he would sign his servant's pass for him to go and never come back. When he left, the white man said Come on Rusty, the boy is waiting to clean you. Dogs with names, men without, I thought.

Madam climbed on top of Dick for this, as we say.

Once one of the dogs, I don't know which – Malan or Monty – took my stocking – brand new, you hear – and tore it with its teeth and paws. When I told Madam about it, my anger as high as my throat, she gave me money to buy another pair. It happened again. This time she said she was not going to give me money because I must also keep my stockings where the two gentlemen would not reach them. Mrs Plum did not want us ever to say Voetsek when we wanted the dogs to go away. Me I said this when they came sniffing at my legs or fingers. I hate it.

In my third year in Mrs Plum's house, many things happened, most of them all bad for her. There was trouble with Kate; Chimane had big trouble; my heart was twisted by two loves; and Monty and Malan became real dogs for a few days.

Madam had a number of suppers and parties. She invited Africans to some of them. Kate told me the reasons for some of the parties. Like her mother's books when finished, a visitor from across the seas and so on. I did not like the black people who came here to drink and eat. They spoke such difficult English like people who were full of all the books in the world. They looked at me as if I were right down there whom they thought little of – me a black person like them.

One day I heard Kate speak to her mother. She says I don't know why you ask so many Africans to the house. A few will do at a time. She said something about the government which I could not hear well. Madam replies she says to her You know some of them do not meet white people often, so far away in their dark houses. And she says to Kate that they do not come because they want her as a friend but they just want a drink for nothing.

I simply felt that I could not be the servant of white people and of blacks at the same time. At my home or in my room I could serve them without a feeling of shame. And now, if they were only coming to drink!

But one of the black men and his sister always came to the kitchen to talk to me. I must have looked unfriendly the first time, for Kate talked to me about it afterwards as she was in the kitchen when they came. I know that at that time I was not easy at all. I was ashamed and I felt that a white person's house was not the place for me to look happy in front of other black people while the white man looked on.

Another time it was easier. The man was alone. I shall never forget that night, as long as I live. He spoke kind words and I felt my heart grow big inside me. It caused me to tremble. There were several other visits. I knew that I loved him, I could never know what he really thought of me, I mean as a woman and he as a man. But I loved him, and I still think of him with a sore heart. Slowly I came to know the pain of it. Because he was a doctor and so full of knowledge and English I could not reach him. So I knew he could not stoop down to see me as someone who wanted him to love me.

Kate turned very wild. Mrs Plum was very much worried. Suddenly it looked as if she were a new person, with new ways and new everything. I do not know what was wrong or right. She began to play the big gramophone aloud, as if the music were for the whole of Greenside. The music was wild and she twisted her waist all the time, with her mouth half-open. She did the same things in her room. She left the big school and every Saturday night now she went out. When I looked at her face, there was something deep and wild there on it, and when I thought she looked young she looked old, and when I thought she looked old she was young. We were both twenty-two years of age. I think that I could see the reason why her mother was so worried, why she was suffering.

Worse was to come.

They were now openly screaming at each other. They began in the sitting room and went upstairs together, speaking fast hot biting words, some of which I did not grasp. One day Madam comes to me and says You know Kate loves an African, you know the doctor who comes to supper here often. She says he loves her too and they will leave the country and marry outside. Tell me, Karabo, what do your people think of this kind of thing between a white woman and a black man? It *cannot* be right is it?

I reply and I say to her We have never seen it happen before where I come from.

That's right, Karabo, it is just madness.

Madam left. She looked like a hunted person.

These white women, I say to myself I say these white women, why do not they love their own men and leave us to love ours!

From that minute I knew that I would never want to speak to Kate. She appeared to me as a thief, as a fox that falls upon a flock of sheep at night. I hated her. To make it worse, he would never be allowed to come to the house again.

Whenever she was home there was silence between us. I no longer wanted to know anything about what she was doing, where or how.

I lay awake for hours on my bed. Lying like that, I seemed to feel parts of my body beat and throb inside me, the way I have seen big machines doing, pounding and pounding and pushing and pulling and pouring some water into one hole which came out at another end. I stretched myself so many times so as to feel tired and sleepy.

When I did sleep, my dreams were full of painful things.

One evening I made up my mind, after putting it off many times. I told my boyfriend that I did not want him any longer. He looked hurt, and that hurt me too. He left.

The thought of the African doctor was still with me and it pained me to know that I should never see him again; unless I met him in the street on a Thursday afternoon. But he had a car. Even if I did meet him by luck, how could I make him see that I loved him? Ach, I do not believe he would even stop to think what kind of woman I am. Part of that winter was a time of longing and burning for me. I say part because there are always things to keep servants busy whose white people go to the sea for the winter.

To tell the truth, winter was the time for servants; not nannies, because they went with their madams so as to look after the children. Those like me stayed behind to look after the house and dogs. In winter so many families went away that the dogs remained the masters and madams. You could see them walk like white people in the streets. Silent but with plenty of power. And when you saw them you knew that they were full of more nonsense and fancies in the house.

There was so little work to do.

One week word was whispered round that a home-boy of ours was going to hold a party in his room on Saturday. I think we all took it for a joke. How could the man be so bold and stupid? The police were always driving about at night looking for black people; and if the whites next door heard the party noise – oho! But still, we were full of joy and wanted to go. As for Dick, he opened his big mouth and nearly fainted when he heard of it and that I was really going.

During the day on the big Saturday Kate came.

She seemed a little less wild. But I was not ready to talk to her. I was surprised to hear myself answer her when she said to me Mother says you do not like a marriage between a white girl and a black man, Karabo.

Then she was silent.

She says But I want to help him, Karabo.

I ask her I say You want to help him to do what?

To go higher and higher, to the top.

I knew I wanted to say so much that was boiling in my chest. I could not say it. I thought of Lilian Ngoyi at the Black Crow, what she said to us. But I was mixed up in my head and in my blood.

You still agree with my mother?

All I could say was I said to your mother I had never seen a black man and a white woman marrying, you hear me? What I think about it is my business.

I remembered that I wanted to iron my party dress and so I left her. My mind was full of the party again and I was glad because Kate and the doctor would not worry my peace that day. And the next day the sun would shine for all of us, Kate or no Kate, doctor or no doctor.

The house where our home-boy worked was hidden from the main road by a number of trees. But although we asked a number of questions and counted many fingers of bad luck until we had no more hands for fingers, we put on our best pay-while-you-wear dresses and suits and clothes bought from boys who had stolen them, and went to our home-boy's party. We whispered all the way while we climbed up to the house. Someone who knew told us that the white people next door were away for the winter. Oh, so that is the thing! we said.

We poured into the garden through the back and stood in front of his room laughing quietly. He came from the big house behind us, and were we not struck dumb when he told us to go into the white people's house! Was he mad? We walked in with slow footsteps that seemed to be sniffing at the floor, not sure of anything. Soon we were standing and sitting all over on the nice warm cushions and the heaters were on. Our home-boy turned the lights low. I counted fifteen people inside. We saw how we loved one another's evening dress. The boys were smart too.

Our home-boy's girlfriend Naomi was busy in the kitchen preparing food.

He took out glasses and cold drinks – fruit juice, tomato juice, ginger beers, and so many other kinds of soft drink. It was just too nice. The tarts, the biscuits, the snacks, the cakes, woo, that was a party, I tell you. I think I ate more ginger cake than I had ever done in my life. Naomi had baked some of the things. Our home-boy came to me and said I do not want the police to come here and have reason to arrest us, so I am not serving hot drinks, not even beer. There is no law that we cannot have parties, is there? So we can feel free. Our use of this house is the master's business. If I had asked him he would have thought me mad.

I say to him I say, You have a strong liver to do such a thing.

He laughed.

He played pennywhistle music on gramophone records – Miriam Makeba, Dorothy Masuka and other African singers and players. We danced and the party became more and more noisy and more happy. Hai, those girls Miriam and Dorothy, they can sing, I tell you! We ate more and laughed more and told more stories. In the middle of the party, our home-boy called us to listen to what he was going to say. Then he told us how he and a friend of his in Orlando collected money to bet on a horse for the July Handicap in Durban. They did this each year but lost. Now they had won two hundred pounds. We all clapped hands and cheered. Two hundred pounds woo!

You should go and sit at home and just eat time, I say to him. He laughs and says You have no understanding not one little bit.

To all of us he says Now my brothers and sisters enjoy yourselves. At home I should slaughter a goat for us to feast and thank our ancestors. But this is town life and we must thank them with tea and cake and all those sweet things. I know some people think I must be so bold that I could be midwife to a lion that is giving birth, but enjoy yourselves and have no fear.

Madam came back looking strong and fresh.

The very week she arrived the police had begun again to search servants' rooms. They were looking for what they called loafers and men without passes who they said were living with friends in the suburbs against the law. Our dog's meat boys became scarce because of the police. A boy who had a girlfriend in the kitchens, as we say, always told his friends that he was coming for dog's meat when he meant he was visiting his girl. This was because we gave our boyfriends part of the meat the white people bought for the dogs and us.

One night a white and a black policeman entered Mrs Plum's yard. They said they had come to search. She says no, they cannot. They say Yes, they must do it. She answers No. They forced their way to the back, to Dick's room and mine. Mrs Plum took the hose that was running in the front garden and quickly went round to the back. I cut across the floor to see what she was going to say to the men. They were talking to Dick, using dirty words. Mrs Plum did not wait, she just pointed the hose at the two policemen. This seemed to surprise them. They turned round and she pointed it into their faces. Without their seeing me I went to the tap at the corner of the house and opened it more. I could see Dick, like me, was trying to keep down his laughter. They shouted and tried to wave the water away, but she kept the hose pointing at them, now moving it up and down. They turned and ran through the back gate, swearing the while.

That fixes them, Mrs Plum said.

The next day the morning paper reported it.

They arrived in the afternoon – the two policemen – with another. They pointed out Mrs Plum and she was led to the police station. They took her away to answer for stopping the police while they were doing their work.

She came back and said she had paid bail.

At the magistrate's court, Madam was told that she had done a bad thing. She would have to pay a fine or else go to prison for fourteen days. She said she would go to jail to show that she felt she was not in the wrong.

Kate came and tried to tell her that she was doing something silly going to jail for a small thing like that. She tells Madam she says This is not even a thing to take to a high court. Pay the money. What is £5?

Madam went to jail.

She looked very sad when she came out. I thought of what Lilian Ngoyi often said to us: You must be ready to go to jail for the things you believe are true and for which you are taken by the police. What did Mrs Plum really believe about me, Chimane, Dick and all the other black people? I asked myself. I did not know. But from all those things she was writing for the papers and all those meetings she was going to where white people talked about black people and the way they are treated by the government, from what those white women with black bands over their shoulders were doing standing where a white government man was going to pass, I said to myself I said This woman, hai, I do not know she seems to think very much of us black people. But why was she so sad?

Kate came back home to stay after this. She still played the big gramophone loud-loud-loud and twisted her body at her waist until I thought it was going to break. Then I saw a young white man come often to see her. I watched them through the opening near the hinges of the door between the kitchen and the sitting room where they sat. I saw them kiss each other for a long long time. I saw him lift up Kate's dress and her white-white legs begin to tremble, and – oh I am afraid to say more, my heart was beating hard. She called him Jim. I thought it was funny because white people in the shops call black men Jim.

Kate had begun to play with Jim when I met a boy who loved me and I loved. He was much stronger than the one I sent away and I loved him more, much more. The face of the doctor came to my mind often, but it did not hurt me so any more. I stopped looking at Kate and her Jim through openings. We spoke to each other, Kate and I, almost as freely as before but not quite. She and her mother were friends again.

Hello, Karabo, I heard Chimane call me one morning as I was starching my apron. I answered. I went to the line to hang it. I saw she was standing at the fence, so I knew she had something to tell me. I went to her.

Hello!

Hello, Chimane!

O kae?

Ke teng. Wena?

At that moment a woman came out through the back door of the house where Chimane was working.

I have not seen that one before, I say, pointing with my head.

Chimane looked back. Oh, that one. Hei, daughter-of-the-people, hei, you have not seen miracles. You know this is Madam's mother-in-law as you see her there. Did I never tell you about her?

No, never.

White people, nonsense. You know what? That poor woman is here now for two days. She has to cook for herself and I cook for the family.

On the same stove?

Yes, she comes after me when I have finished.

She has her own food to cook?

Yes, Karabo. White people have no heart no sense.

What will eat them up if they share their food?

Ask me, just ask me. God! She clapped her hands to show that only God knew, and it was His business, not ours.

Chimane asks me she says, Have you heard from home?

I tell her I say, Oh daughter-of-the-people, more and more deaths. Something is finishing the people at home. My mother has written. She says they are all right, my father too and my sisters, except for the people who have died. Malebo, the one who lived alone in the house I showed you last year, a white house, he is gone. Then teacher Sedimo. He was very thin and looked sick all the time. He taught my sisters not me. His mother-in-law you remember I told you died last year – no, the year before. Mother says also there is a woman she does not think I remember because I last saw her when I was a small girl she passed away in Zeerust she was my mother's greatest friend when they were girls. She would have gone to her burial if it was not because she has swollen feet.

How are the feet?

She says they are still giving her trouble. I ask Chimane, How are your people at Nokaneng? They have not written?

She shook her head.

I could see from her eyes that her mind was on another thing and not her people at that moment.

Wait for me Chimane eh, forgive me, I have scones in the oven, eh! I will just take them out and come back, eh!

When I came back to her Chimane was wiping her eyes. They were wet.

Karabo, you know what?

E – e. I shook my head.

I am heavy with child.

Hau!

There was a moment of silence.

Who is it, Chimane?

Timi. He came back only to give me this.

But he loves you. What does he say have you told him?

I told him yesterday. We met in town.

I remembered I had not seen her at the Black Crow.

Are you sure, Chimane? You have missed a month?

She nodded her head.

Timi himself – he did not use the thing?

I only saw after he finished, that he had not.

Why? What does he say?

He tells me he says I should not worry I can be his wife.

Timi is a good boy, Chimane. How many of these boys with town ways who know too much will even say Yes it is my child?

Hai, Karabo, you are telling me other things now. Do you not see that I have not worked long enough for my people? If I marry now who will look after them when I am the only child?

Hm, I hear your words. It is true. I tried to think of something soothing to say.

Then I say You can talk it over with Timi. You can go home and when the child is born you look after it for three months and when you are married you come to town to work and can put your money together to help the old people while they are looking after the child.

What shall we be eating all the time I am at home? It is not like those days gone past when we had land and our mother could go to the fields until the child was ready to arrive.

The light goes out in my mind and I cannot think of the right answer. How many times have I feared the same thing! Luck and the mercy of the gods that is all I live by. That is all we live by – all of us.

Listen, Karabo. I must be going to make tea for Madam. It will soon strike half-past ten.

I went back to the house. As Madam was not in yet, I threw myself on the divan in the sitting room. Malan came sniffing at my legs. I put my foot under its fat belly and shoved it up and away from me so that it cried tjunk – tjunk – tjunk as it went out. I say to it I say Go and tell your brother what I have done to you and tell him to try it and see what I will do. Tell your grandmother when she comes home too.

When I lifted my eyes he was standing in the kitchen door, Dick. He says to me he says Hau! now you have also begun to speak to dogs!

I did not reply. I just looked at him, his mouth ever stretched out like the mouth of a bag, and I passed to my room.

I sat on my bed and looked at my face in the mirror. Since the morning I had been feeling as if a black cloud were hanging over me, pressing on my head and shoulders. I do not know how long I sat there. Then I smelled Madam. What was it? Where was she? After a few moments I knew what it was. My perfume and scent. I used the same cosmetics as Mrs Plum's. I should have been used to it by now. But this morning – why did I smell Mrs Plum like this? Then, without knowing why, I asked myself I said, Why have I been using the same cosmetics as Madam? I wanted to throw them all out. I stopped. And then I took all the things and threw them into the dustbin. I was going to buy other kinds on Thursday; finished!

I could not sit down. I went out and into the white people's house. I walked through and the smell of the house made me sick and seemed to fill up my throat. I went to the bathroom without knowing why. It was full of the smell of Madam. Dick was cleaning the bath. I stood at the door and looked at him cleaning the dirt out of the bath, dirt from Madam's body. Sies! I said aloud. To myself I said, Why cannot people wash the dirt of their own bodies out of the bath? Before Dick knew I was near I went out. Ach, I said again to myself, why should I think about it now when I have been doing their washing for so long and cleaned the bath many times when Dick was ill. I had held worse things from her body times without number . . .

I went out and stood midway between the house and my room, looking into the next yard. The three-legged grey cat next door came to the fence and our eyes met. I do not know how long we stood like that looking at each other. I was thinking, Why don't you go and look at your grandmother like that? when it turned away and mewed hopping on the three legs. Just like someone who feels pity for you.

In my room I looked into the mirror on the chest of drawers. I thought Is this Karabo this?

Thursday came, and the afternoon off. At the Black Crow I did not see Chimane. I wondered about her. In the evening I found a note under my door. It told me if Chimane was not back that evening I should know that she was at 660 3rd Avenue, Alexandra Township. I was not to tell the white people.

I asked Dick if he could not go to Alexandra with me after I had washed the dishes. At first he was unwilling. But I said to him I said, Chimane will not believe that you refused to come with me when she sees me alone. He agreed.

On the bus Dick told me much about his younger sister whom he was helping with money to stay at school until she finished; so that she could become a nurse and a midwife. He was very fond of her, as far as I could find out. He said he prayed always that he should not lose his job, as he had done many times before, after staying a few weeks only at each job; because of this he had to borrow monies from people to pay his sister's school fees, to buy her clothes and books. He spoke of her as if she were his sweetheart. She was clever at school, pretty (she was this in the photo Dick had shown me before). She was in Orlando Township. She looked after his old people, although she was only thirteen years of age. He said to me he said Today I still owe many people because I keep losing my job. You must try to stay with Mrs Plum, I said.

I cannot say that I had all my mind on what Dick was telling me. I was thinking of Chimane: what could she be doing? Why that note?

We found her in bed. In that terrible township where night and day are full of knives and bicycle chains and guns and the barking of hungry dogs and of people in trouble. I held my heart in my hands. She was in pain and her face, even in the candlelight, was grey. She turned her eyes at me. A fat woman was sitting in a chair. One arm rested on the other and held her chin in its palm. She had hardly opened the door for us after we had shouted our names when she was on her bench again as if there were nothing else to do.

She snorted, as if to let us know that she was going to speak. She said There is your friend. There she is my own-own niece who comes from the womb of my own sister, my sister who was made to spit out my mother's breast to give way for me. Why does she go and do such an evil thing. Ao! you young girls of today you do not know children die so fast these days that you have to thank God for sowing a seed in your womb to grow into a child. If she had let the child be born I should have looked after it or my sister would have been so happy to hold a grandchild on her lap, but what does it help? She has allowed a worm to cut the roots, I don't know.

Then I saw that Chimane's aunt was crying. Not once did she mention her niece by her name, so sore her heart must have been. Chimane only moaned.

Her aunt continued to talk, as if she was never going to stop for breath, until her voice seemed to move behind me, not one of the things I was thinking: trying to remember signs, however small, that could tell me more about this moment in a dim little room in a cruel township without street lights, near Chimane. Then I remembered the three-legged cat, its grey-green eyes, its miaou. What was this shadow that seemed to walk about us but was not coming right in front of us?

I thanked the gods when Chimane came to work at the end of the week. She still looked weak, but that shadow was no longer there. I wondered Chimane had never told me about her aunt before. Even now I did not ask her.

I told her I told her white people that she was ill and had been fetched to Nokaneng by a brother. They would never try to find out. They seldom did, these people. Give them any lie, and it will do. For they seldom believe you whatever you say. And how can a black person work for white people and be afraid to tell them lies. They are always asking the questions, you are always the one to give the answers.

Chimane told me all about it. She had gone to a woman who did these things. Her way was to hold a sharp needle, cover the point with the finger, and guide it into the womb. She then fumbled in the womb until she found the egg and then pierced it. She gave you something to ease the bleeding. But the pain, spirits of our forefathers!

Mrs Plum and Kate were talking about dogs one evening at dinner. Every time I brought something to table I tried to catch their words. Kate seemed to find it funny, because she laughed aloud. There was a word I could not hear well which began with sem– : whatever it was, it was to be for dogs. This I understood by putting a few words together. Mrs Plum said it was something that was common in the big cities of America, like New York. It was also something Mrs Plum wanted and Kate laughed at the thought. Then later I was to hear that Monty and Malan could be sure of a nice burial.

Chimane's voice came up to me in my room the next morning, across the fence. When I come out she tells me she says Hei child-of-my-father, here is something to tickle your ears. You know what? What? I say. She says, These white people can do things that make the gods angry. More godless people I have not seen. The madam of our house says the people of Greenside want to buy ground where they can bury their dogs. I heard them talk about it in the sitting room when I was giving them coffee last night. Hei, people, let our forefathers come and save us!

Yes, I say, I also heard the madam of our house talk about it with her daughter. I just heard it in pieces. By my mother one day these dogs will sit at table and use knife and fork. These things are to be treated like people now, like children who are never going to grow up.

Chimane sighed and she says Hela batho, why do they not give me some of that money they will spend on the ground and on gravestones to buy stockings! I have nothing to put on, by my mother.

Over her shoulder I saw the cat with three legs. I pointed with my head. When Chimane looked back and saw it she said Hm, even *they* live like kings. The mother-in-law found it on a chair and the madam said the woman should not drive it away. And there was no other chair, so the woman went to her room.

Hela!

I was going to leave when I remembered what I wanted to tell Chimane. It was that five of us had collected £1 each to lend her so that she could pay the woman of Alexandra for having done that thing for her. When Chimane's time came to receive money we collected each month and which we took in turns, she would pay us back. We were ten women and each gave £2 at a time. So one waited ten months to receive £20. Chimane thanked us for helping her.

I went to wake up Mrs Plum as she had asked me. She was sleeping late this morning. I was going to knock at the door when I heard strange noises in the bedroom. What is the matter with Mrs Plum? I asked myself. Should I call her, in case she is ill? No, the noises were not those of a sick person. They were happy noises but like those a person makes in a dream, the voice full of sleep. I bent a little to peep through the keyhole. What is this? I kept asking myself. Mrs Plum! Malan! What is she doing this one? Her arm was round Malan's belly and pressing its back against her stomach at the navel, Mrs Plum's body in a nightdress moving in jerks like someone in fits . . . her leg rising and falling . . . Malan silent like a thing to be owned without any choice it can make to belong to another.

The gods save me! I heard myself saying, the words sounding like wind rushing out of my mouth. So this is what Dick said I would find out for myself!

No one could say where it all started; who talked about it first; whether the police wanted to make a reason for taking people without passes and people living with servants and working in town or not working at all. But the story rushed through Johannesburg that servants were going to poison the white people's dogs. Because they were too much work for us: that was the reason.

We heard that letters were sent to the newspapers by white people asking the police to watch over the dogs to stop any wicked things. Some said that we the servants were not really bad, we were being made to think of doing these things by evil people in town and in the locations. Others said the police should watch out lest we poison madams and masters because black people did not know right from wrong when they were angry. We were still children at heart, others said. Mrs Plum said that she had also written to the papers.

Then it was the police came down on the suburbs like locusts on a cornfield. There were lines and lines of men who were arrested hour by hour in the day. They liked this very much, the police. Everybody they took, everybody who was working was asked, Where's the poison eh? Where did you hide it? Who told you to poison the dogs eh? If you tell us we'll leave you to go free, you hear? and so many other things.

Dick kept saying It is wrong this thing they want to do to kill poor dogs. What have these things of God done to be killed for? Is it the dogs that make us carry passes? Is it dogs that make the laws that give us pain? People are just mad they do not know what they want, stupid! But when a white policeman spoke to him, Dick trembled and lost his tongue and the things he thought. He just shook his head. A few moments after they had gone through his pockets he still held his arms stretched out, like the man of straw who frightens away birds in a field. Only when I hissed and gave him a sign did he drop his arms. He rushed to a corner of the garden to go on with his work.

Mrs Plum had put Monty and Malan in the sitting room, next to her. She looked very much worried. She called me. She asked me she said Karabo, you think Dick is a boy we can trust? I did not know how to answer. I did not know whom she was talking about when she said *we*. Then I said I do not know, Madam. You know! she said. I looked at her. I said I do not know what Madam thinks. She said she did not think anything, that was why she asked. I nearly laughed because she was telling a lie this time and not I.

At another time I should have been angry if she lied to me, perhaps. She and I often told each other lies, as Kate and I also did. Like when she came back from jail, after that day when she turned a hosepipe on two policemen. She said life had been good in jail. And yet I could see she was ashamed to have been there. Not like our black people who are always being put in jail and only look at it as the white man's evil game. Lilian Ngoyi often told us this, and Mrs Plum showed me how true those words are. I am sure that we have kept to each other by lying to each other.

There was something in Mrs Plum's face as she was speaking which made me fear her and pity her at the same time. I have seen her when she had come from prison; I had seen her when she was shouting at Kate and the girl left the house; now there was this thing about dog poisoning. But never had I seen her face like this before. The eyes, the nostrils, the lips, the teeth seemed to be full of hate, tired, fixed on doing something bad; and yet there was something on that face that told me she wanted me on her side.

Dick is all right madam, I found myself saying. She took Malan and Monty in her arms and pressed them to herself, running her hands over their heads. They looked so safe, like a child in a mother's arm.

Mrs Plum said All right you may go. She said Do not tell anybody what I have asked about Dick eh?

When I told Dick about it, he seemed worried.

It is nothing, I told him.

I had been thinking before that I did not stand with those who wanted to poison the dogs, Dick said. But the police have come out, I do not care what happens to the dumb things, now.

I asked him I said Would you poison them if you were told by someone to do it?

No. But I do not care, he replied.

The police came again and again. They were having a good holiday, everyone could see that. A day later Mrs Plum told Dick to go because she would not need his work any more.

Dick was almost crying when he left. Is madam so unsure of me? he asked. I never thought a white person could fear me! And he left.

Chimane shouted from the other yard. She said, Hei ngoana'rona, the boers are fire-hot eh!

Mrs Plum said she would hire a man after the trouble was over.

A letter came from my parents in Phokeng. In it they told me my uncle had passed away. He was my mother's brother. The letter also told me of other deaths. They said I would not remember some, I was sure to know the others. There were also names of sick people.

I went to Mrs Plum to ask her if I could go home. She asks she says When did he die? I answer I say It is three days, madam. She says So that they have buried him? I reply Yes Madam. Why do you want to go home then? Because my uncle loved me very much madam. But what are you going to do there? To take my tears and words of grief to his grave and to my old aunt, madam. No you cannot go, Karabo. You are working for me you know? Yes, madam. I, and not your people pay you. I must go madam, that is how we do it among my people, madam. She paused. She walked into the kitchen and came out again. If you want to go, Karabo, you must lose the money for the days you will be away. Lose my pay, madam? Yes, Karabo.

The next day I went to Mrs Plum and told her I was leaving for Phokeng and was not coming back to her. Could she give me a letter to say that I worked for her. She did, with her lips shut tight. I could feel that something between us was burning like raw chillies. The letter simply said that I had worked for Mrs Plum for three years. Nothing more. The memory of Dick being sent away was still an open sore in my heart.

The night before the day I left, Chimane came to see me in my room. She had her own story to tell me. Timi, her boyfriend, had left her – for good. Why? Because I killed his baby. Had he not agreed that you should do it? No. Did he show he was worried when you told him you were heavy? He was worried, like me as you saw me, Karabo. Now he says if I kill one I shall eat all his children up when we are married. You think he means what he says? Yes, Karabo. He says his parents would have been very happy to know that the woman he was going to marry can make his seed grow.

Chimane was crying, softly.

I tried to speak to her, to tell her that if Timi left her just like that, he had not wanted to marry her in the first place. But I could not, no, I could not. All I could say was Do not cry, my sister, do not cry. I gave her my handkerchief.

Kate came back the morning I was leaving, from somewhere very far I cannot remember where. Her mother took no notice of what Kate said asking her to keep me, and I was not interested either.

One hour later I was on the Railway bus to Phokeng. During the early part of the journey I did not feel anything about the Greenside house I had worked in. I was not really myself, my thoughts dancing between Mrs Plum, my uncle, my parents, and Phokeng, my home. I slept and woke up many times during the bus ride. Right through the ride I seemed to see, sometimes in sleep, sometimes between sleep and waking, a red car passing our bus, then running behind us. Each time I looked out it was not there.

Dreams came and passed. He tells me he says You have killed my seed I wanted my mother to know you are a woman in whom my seed can grow . . . Before you make the police take you to jail make sure that it is for something big you should go to jail for, otherwise you will come out with a heart and mind that will bleed inside you and poison you . . .

The bus stopped for a short while, which made me wake up.

The Black Crow, the club women . . . Hei, listen! I lie to the madam of our house and I say I had a telegram from my mother telling me she is very very sick. I show her a telegram my sister sent me as if mother were writing. So I went home for a nice weekend . . .

The laughter of the women woke me up, just in time for me to stop a line of saliva coming out over my lower lip. The bus was making plenty of dust now as it was running over part of the road they were digging up. I was sure the red car was just behind us, but it was not there when I woke.

Any one of you here who wants to be baptized or has a relative without a church who needs to be can come and see me in the office . . . A round man with a fat tummy and sharp hungry eyes, a smile that goes a long, long way . . .

The bus was going uphill, heavily and noisily.

I kick a white man's dog, me, or throw it there if it has not been told the black people's law . . . This is Mister Monty and this is Mister Malan. Now get up you lazy boys and meet Mister Kate. Hold out your hands and say hello to him . . . Karabo, bring two glasses there . . . Wait a bit – What will you chew boys while Mister Kate and I have a drink? Nothing? Sure?

We were now going nicely on a straight tarred road and the trees rushed back. Mister Kate. What nonsense, I thought.

Look Karabo, madam's dogs are dead. What? Poison. I killed them. She drove me out of a job did she not? For nothing. Now I want her to feel she drove me out for something. I came back when you were in your room and took the things and poisoned them . . . And you know what? She has buried them in clean pink sheets in the garden. Ao, clean clean good sheets. I am going to dig them out and take one sheet do you want the other one? Yes, give me the other one I will send it to my mother . . . Hei, Karabo, see here they come. Monty and Malan. The bloody fools they do not want to stay in their hole. Go back you silly fools. Oh you do not want to move eh? Come here, now I am going to throw you in the big pool. No, Dick! No Dick! no, no! Dick! They cannot speak do not kill things that cannot speak. Madam can speak for them she always does. No! Dick . . . !

I woke up with a jump after I had screamed Dick's name, almost hitting the window. My forehead was full of sweat. The red car also shot out of my sleep and was gone. I remembered a friend of ours who told us how she and the garden man had saved two white sheets in which their white master had buried their two dogs. They went to throw the dogs in a dam.

When I told my parents my story Father says to me he says, So long as you are in good health my child, it is good. The worker dies, work does not. There is always work. I know when I was a boy a strong sound body and a good mind were the biggest things in life. Work was always there, and the lazy man could never say there was no work. But today people see work as something bigger than everything else, bigger than health, because of money.

I reply I say, Those days are gone Papa. I must go back to the city after resting a little to look for work. I must look after you. Today people are too poor to be able to help you.

I knew when I left Greenside that I was going to return to Johannesburg to work. Money was little, but life was full and it was better than sitting in Phokeng and watching the sun rise and set. So I told Chimane to keep her eyes and ears open for a job.

I had been at Phokeng for one week when a red car arrived. Somebody was sitting in front with the driver, a white woman. At once I knew it to be that of Mrs Plum. The man sitting beside her was showing her the way, for he pointed towards our house in front of which I was sitting. My heart missed a few beats. Both came out of the car. The white woman said Thank you to the man after he had spoken a few words to me.

I did not know what to do and how to look at her as she spoke to me. So I looked at the piece of cloth I was sewing pictures on. There was a tired but soft smile on her face. Then I remembered that she might want to sit. I went inside to fetch a low bench for her. When I remembered it afterwards, the thought came to me that there are things I never think white people can want to do at our homes when they visit for the first time: like sitting, drinking water or entering the house. This is how I thought when the white priest came to see us. One year at Easter Kate drove me home as she was going to the north. In the same way I was at a loss what to do for a few minutes.

Then Mrs Plum says, I have come to ask you to come back to me, Karabo. Would you like to?

I say I do not know, I must think about it first.

She says, Can you think about it today? I can sleep at the town hotel and come back tomorrow morning, and if you want to you can return with me.

I wanted her to say she was sorry to have sent me away, I did not know how to make her say it because I know white people find it too much for them to say Sorry to a black person. As she was not saying it, I thought of two things to make it hard for her to get me back and maybe even lose me in the end.

I say, You must ask my father first, I do not know, should I call him?

Mrs Plum says, Yes.

I fetched both Father and Mother. They greeted her while I brought benches. Then I told them what she wanted.

Father asks Mother and Mother asks Father. Father asks me. I say if they agree, I will think about it and tell her the next day.

Father says, It goes by what you feel my child.

I tell Mrs Plum I say, If you want me to think about it I must know if you will want to put my wages up from £6 because it is too little.

She asks me, How much will you want?

Up by £4.

She looked down for a few moments.

And then I want two weeks at Easter and not just the weekend. I thought if she really wanted me she would want to pay for it. This would also show how sorry she was to lose me.

Mrs Plum says, I can give you one week. You see you already have something like a rest when I am in Durban in the winter.

I tell her I say I shall think about it.

She left.

The next day she found me packed and ready to return with her. She was very much pleased and looked kinder than I had ever known her. And me, I felt sure of myself, more than I had ever done.

Mrs Plum says to me, You will not find Monty and Malan.

Oh?

Yes, they were stolen the day after you left. The police have not found them yet. I think they are dead myself.

I thought of Dick . . . my dream. Could he? And she . . . did this woman come to ask me to return because she had lost two animals she loved?

Mrs Plum says to me she says, You know, I like your people, Karabo, the Africans.

And Dick and Me? I wondered.

The Lovers

» «

BESSIE HEAD

The love affair began in the summer. The love affair began in those dim dark days when young men and women did not have love affairs. It was one of those summers when it rained in torrents. Almost every afternoon towards sunset the low-hanging, rain-filled clouds would sweep across the sky in packed masses and suddenly, with barely a warning, the rain would pour down in blinding sheets.

The young women and little girls were still out in the forest gathering wood that afternoon when the first warning signs of rain appeared in the sky. They hastily gathered up their bundles of wood and began running home to escape the approaching storm. Suddenly, one of the young women halted painfully. In her haste she had trodden on a large thorn.

'Hurry on home, Monosi!' she cried to a little girl panting behind her. 'I have to get this thorn out of my foot. If the rain catches me I shall find some shelter and come home once it is over.'

Without a backward glance the little girl sped on after the hard-running group of wood gatherers. The young woman was quite alone with the approaching storm. The thorn proved difficult to extract. It had broken off and embedded itself deeply in her heel. A few drops of rain beat down on her back. The sky darkened.

Anxiously she looked around for the nearest shelter and saw a cavern in some rocks at the base of a hill nearby. She picked up her bundle of wood and limped hastily towards it, with the drops of rain pounding down faster and faster. She had barely entered the cavern when the torrent un-leashed itself in a violent downpour. Her immediate concern was to seek its sanctuary but a moment later her heart lurched in fear as she realized that she was not alone. The warmth of another human filled the interior. She swung around swiftly and found herself almost face to face with a young man.

222

'We can shelter here together from the storm,' he said with a quiet authority.

His face was as kind and protective as his words. Reassured, the young woman set down her bundle of sticks in the roomy interior of the cavern and together they seated themselves near its entrance. The roar of the rain was deafening so that even the thunder and lightning was muffled by its intensity. With quiet, harmonious movements the young man undid a leather pouch tied at his waist. He spent all his time cattle-herding and to while away the long hours he busied himself with all kinds of leather work, assembling skins into all kinds of clothes and blankets. He had a large number of sharpened implements in his pouch. He indicated to the young woman that he wished to extract the thorn. She extended her foot towards him and for some time he busied himself with this task, gently whittling away the skin around the thorn until he had exposed it sufficiently enough to extract it.

The young woman looked at his face with interest and marvelled at the ease and comfort she felt in his presence. In their world men and women lived strictly apart, especially the young and unmarried. This sense of apartness and separateness continued even throughout married life and marriage itself seemed to have no significance beyond a union for the production of children. This wide gap between the sexes created embarrassment on the level of personal contact; the young men often slid their eyes away uneasily or giggled at the sight of a woman. The young man did none of this. He had stared her directly in the eyes; all his movements were natural and unaffected. He was also very pleasing to look at. She thanked him with a smile once he had extracted the thorn and folded her extended foot beneath her. The violence of the storm abated a little but the heavily-laden sky continued to pour forth a steady downpour.

She had seen the young man around the village; she could vaguely place his family connections.

'Aren't you the son of Rra-Keaja?' she asked. She had a light chatty voice with an undertone of laughter in it, very expressive of her personality. She liked above all to be happy.

'I am the very Keaja he is named after,' the young man replied with a smile. 'I am the first-born in the family.'

'I am the first-born in the family, too,' she said. 'I am Tselane, the daughter of Mma-Tselane.'

His family ramifications were more complicated than hers. His father had three wives. All the first born of the first, second and third house were boys. The children totalled eight in number, three boys and five girls, he explained. It was only when the conversation moved into deep water that Tselane realized that a whole area of the young man's speech had eluded her. He was the extreme opposite of her light chatty tone. He talked from deep rhythms within himself as though he had specifically invented language for his own use. He had an immense range of expression and feeling at his command; now his eyes lit up with humour, then they were absolutely serious and in earnest. He swayed almost imperceptibly as he talked. He talked like no one she had ever heard talking before, yet all his utterances were direct, simple and forthright. She bent forward and listened more attentively to his peculiar manner of speech.

'I don't like my mother,' he said, shocking her. 'I am her only son simply because my father stopped cohabiting with her after I was born. My father and I are alike. We don't like to be controlled by anyone and she made his life a misery when they were newly married. It was as if she had been born with a worm eating at her heart because she is satisfied with nothing. The only way my father could control the situation was to ignore her completely . . .'

He remained silent a while, concentrating on his own thoughts. 'I don't think I approve of all the arranged marriages we have here,' he said finally. 'My father would never have married her had he had his own choice. He was merely presented with her one day by his family and told that they were to be married and there was nothing he could do about it.'

He kept silent about the torture he endured from his mother. She hated him deeply and bitterly. She had hurled stones at him and scratched him on the arms and legs in her wild frustration. Like his father he eluded her. He rarely spent time at home but kept the cattle-post as his permanent residence. When he approached home it was always with some gift of clothes or blankets. On that particular day he had an enormous gourd filled with milk.

The young woman, Tselane, floundered out of her depth in the face of such stark revelations. They lived the strictest of traditional ways of life; all children were under the control of their parents until they married, therefore it was taboo to discuss their elders. In her impulsive chatty way and partly out of embarrassment, it had been on the tip of her tongue to say that she liked her mother, that her mother was very kind-hearted. But there was a disturbing undertone in her household too. Her mother and father – and she was sure of it due to her detailed knowledge of her mother's way of life – had not cohabited for years either. A few years ago her father had taken another wife. She was her mother's only child. Oh, the surface of their household was polite and harmonious but her father was rarely at home. He was always irritable and morose when he was home.

'I am sorry about all the trouble in your home,' she said at last, in a softer, more thoughtful tone. She was shaken at having been abruptly jolted into completely new ways of thought.

The young man smiled and then quite deliberately turned and stared at her. She stared back at him with friendly interest. She did not mind his close scrutiny of her person; he was easy to associate with, comfortable, truthful and open in his every gesture.

'Do you approve of arranged marriages?' he asked, still smiling.

'I have not thought of anything,' she replied truthfully.

The dark was approaching rapidly. The rain had trickled down to a fine drizzle. Tselane stood up and picked up her bundle of wood. The young man picked up his gourd of milk. They were barely visible as they walked home together in the dark. Tselane's home was not too far from the hill. She lived on the extreme western side of the village, he on the extreme eastern side.

A bright fire burned in the hut they used as a cooking place on rainy days. Tselane's mother was sitting bent forward on her low stool, listening attentively to a visitor's tale. It was always like this – her mother was permanently surrounded by women who confided in her. The whole story of life unfolded daily around her stool: the ailments of children, women who had just had miscarriages, women undergoing treatment for barren wombs – the story was endless. It was the great pleasure of Tselane to seat herself quietly behind her mother's stool and listen with fascinated ears to this endless tale of woe. Her mother's visitor that evening was on the tail-end of a description of one of her children's ailments; chronic epilepsy, which seemed beyond cure. The child seemed in her death throes and the mother was just at the point of demonstrating the violent seizures when Tselane entered. Tselane quietly set her bundle of wood down in a corner and the conversation continued uninterrupted. She took her favoured place behind her mother's stool. Her father's second wife, Mma-Monosi, was seated on the opposite side of the fire, her face composed and serious. Her child, the little girl, Monosi, fed and attended to, lay fast asleep on a sleeping mat in one corner of the hut.

Tselane loved the two women of the household equally. They were both powerful independent women but with sharply differing personalities. Mma-Tselane was a queen who vaguely surveyed the kingdom she ruled, with an abstracted, absent-minded air. Over the years of her married life she had built up a way of life for herself that filled her with content. She was reputed to be very delicate in health as after the birth of Tselane she had suffered a number of miscarriages and seemed incapable of bearing any more children. Her delicate health was a source of extreme irritation to her husband and at some stage he had abandoned her completely and taken Mma-Monosi as his second wife, intending to perpetuate his line and name through her healthy body.

The arrangement suited Mma-Tselane. She was big-hearted and broad-minded and yet, conversely, she prided herself in being the meticulous upholder of all the traditions the community adhered to. Once Mma-Monosi became a part of the household, Mma-Tselane did no work but entertained and paid calls the day long. Mma-Monosi ran the entire household.

The two women complemented each other, for, if Mma-Tselane was a queen, then Mma-Monosi was a humble worker. On the surface, Mma-Monosi appeared as sane and balanced as Mma-Tselane, but there was another side of her personality that was very precariously balanced. Mma-Monosi took her trembling way through life. If all was stable and peaceful, then Mma-Monosi was stable and peaceful. If there was any disruption or disorder, Mma-Monosi's precarious inner balance registered every wave and upheaval. She hungered for approval of her every action and could be upset for days if criticized or reprimanded.

So, between them, the two women achieved a very harmonious household. Both were entirely absorbed in their full busy daily round; both were unconcerned that they received scant attention from the man of the household for Rra-Tselane was entirely concerned with his own affairs. He was a prominent member of the chief's court and he divided his time between the chief's court and his cattle-post. He was rich in cattle and his herds were taken care of by servants. He was away at his cattle-post at that time.

It was with Mma-Monosi that the young girl, Tselane, enjoyed a free and happy relationship. They treated each other as equals, they both enjoyed hard work and whenever they were alone together, they laughed and joked all the time. Her own mother regarded Tselane as an object to whom she lowered her voice and issued commands between clenched teeth. Very soon Mma-Tselane stirred in her chair and said in that lowered voice: 'Tselane, fetch me my bag of herbs.'

Tselane obediently stood up and hurried to her mother's living-quarters for the bag of herbs. Then another interval followed during which her mother and the visitor discussed the medicinal properties of the herbs. Then Mma-Monosi served the evening meal. Then the visitor departed with assurances that Mma-Tselane would call on her the following day. Then they sat for a while in companionable silence. At one stage, seeing that the fire was burning low, Mma-Tselane arose and selected a few pieces of wood from Tselane's bundle to stoke up the fire.

'Er, Tselane,' she said. 'Your wood is quite dry. Did you shelter from the storm?'

'There is a cave in the hill not far from here, mother,' Tselane replied. 'And I sheltered there.' She did not think it wise to add that she had shared the shelter with a young man; a lot of awkward questions of the wrong kind might have followed.

The mother cast her eyes vaguely over her daughter as if to say all was in order in her world; she always established simple facts about any matter and turned peacefully to the next task at hand. She suddenly decided that she was tired and would retire. Tselane and Mma-Monosi were left alone seated near the fire. Tselane was still elated by her encounter with the young man; so many pleasant thoughts were flying through her head.

'I want to ask you some questions, Mma-Monosi,' she said eagerly.

'What is it you want to say, my child?' Mma-Monosi said, stirring out of a reverie.

'Do you approve of arranged marriages, Mma-Monosi?' she asked earnestly.

Mma-Monosi drew in her breath between her teeth with a sharp, hissing sound, then she lowered her voice in horror and said: 'Tselane, you know quite well that I am your friend but if anyone else heard you talking like that you would be in trouble! Such things are never discussed here! What put that idea into your head because it is totally unknown to me?'

'But you question life when you begin to grow up,' Tselane said defensively.

'That is what you never, never do,' Mma-Monosi said severely. 'If you question life you will upset it. Life is always in order.' She looked thoroughly startled and agitated. 'I know of something terrible that once happened to someone who questioned life,' she added grimly.

'Who was it? What terrible thing happened?' Tselane asked, in her turn agitated.

'I can't tell you,' Mma-Monosi said firmly. 'It is too terrible to mention.'

Tselane subsided into silence with a speculative look in her eye. She understood Mma-Monosi well. She couldn't keep a secret. She could always be tempted into telling a secret, if not today then on some other day. She decided to find out the terrible story.

When Keaja arrived home his family was eating the evening meal. He first approached the women's quarters and offered them the gourd of milk.

'The cows are calving heavily,' he explained. 'There is a lot of milk and I can bring some home every day.'

He was greeted joyously by the second and third wife of his father who anxiously inquired after their sons who lived with him at the cattle-post.

'They are quite well,' he said politely. 'I settled them and the cattle before I left. I shall return again in the early morning because I am worried about the young calves.'

He avoided his mother's baleful stare and tight, deprived mouth. She never had anything to say to him, although, on his approach to the women's quarters, he had heard her voice, shrill and harsh, dominating the conversation. His meal was handed to him and he retreated to his father's quarters. He ate alone and apart from the women. A bright fire burned in his father's living-quarters.

'Hello, Father-Of-Me,' his father greeted him, making affectionate play on the name Keaja. Keaja meant: I am eating now because I have a son to take care of me.

His father doted on him. In his eyes there was no greater son than Keaja. After an exchange of greetings his father asked: 'And what is your news?'

He gave his father the same information about the cows calving heavily and the rich supply of milk; that his other two sons were quite well. They ate for a while in companionable silence. His mother's voice rose shrill and penetrating in the silent night. Quite unexpectedly his father looked up with a twinkle in his eye and said: 'Those extra calves will stand us in good stead, Father-Of-Me. I have just started negotiations about your marriage.'

A spasm of chill, cold fear almost constricted Keaja's heart. 'Who am I to marry, father?' he asked, alarmed.

'I cannot mention the family name just yet,' his father replied cheerfully, not sensing his son's alarm. 'The negotiations are still at a very delicate stage.'

'Have you committed yourself in this matter, father?' he asked, a sharp angry note in his voice.

'Oh, yes,' his father replied. 'I have given my honour in this matter. It is just that these things take a long time to arrange as there are many courtesies to be observed.'

'How long?' the son asked.

'About six new moons may have to pass,' his father replied. 'It may even be longer than that. I cannot say at this stage.'

'I could choose a wife for myself,' the son said with deadly quietude. 'I could choose my own wife and then inform you of my choice.'

His father stared at him in surprise.

'You cannot be different from everyone else,' he said. 'I must be a parent with a weakness that you can talk to me so.'

His father knew that he indulged his son, that they had free and easy exchanges beyond what was socially permissible; even that brief exchange was more than most parents allowed their children. They arranged all details of their children's future and on the fatal day merely informed them that they were to be married to so-and-so. There was no point in saying: 'I might not be able to live with so-and-so. She might be unsuited to me,' so that when Keaja lapsed into silence, his father merely smiled indulgently and engaged him in small talk.

Keaja was certainly of a marriageable age. The previous year he had gone through his initiation ceremony. Apart from other trials endured during the ceremony, detailed instruction had been given to the young men of his age group about sexual relations between men and women. They were hardly private and personal but affected by a large number of social regulations and taboos. If he broke the taboos at a personal and private level, death, sickness and great misfortune would fall upon his family. If he broke the taboos at a social level, death and disaster would fall upon the community. There were many periods in a man's life when abstinence from sexual relations was required; often this abstinence had to be practised communally as in the period preceding the harvest of crops and only broken on the day of the harvest thanksgiving ceremony.

These regulations and taboos applied to men and women alike but the initiation ceremony for women, which Tselane had also experienced the previous year, was much more complex in their instruction. A delicate balance had to be preserved between a woman's reproductive cycle and the safety of the community; at almost every stage in her life a woman was a potential source of danger to the community. All women were given careful instruction in precautions to be observed during times of menstruation, childbirth and accidental miscarriages. Failure to observe the taboos could bring harm to animal life, crops and the community.

It could be seen then that the community held no place for people wildly carried away by their passions, that there was a logic and order in the carefully arranged sterile emotional and physical relationships between men and women. There was no one to challenge the established order of things; if people felt any personal unhappiness it was smothered and subdued and so life for the community proceeded from day to day in peace and harmony.

As all lovers do, they began a personal and emotional dialogue that excluded all life around them. Perhaps its pattern and direction was the same for all lovers, painful and maddening by turns in its initial insecurity. Who looked for who? They could not say, except that the far-western unpolluted end of the river where women drew water and the forests where they gathered firewood became Keaja's favoured hunting grounds. Their work periods coincided at that time. The corn had just been sowed and the women were idling in the village until the heavy soaking rains raised the weeds in their fields, then their next busy period would follow when they hoed out the weed between their corn.

Keaja returned every day to the village with gourds of milk for his family and it did not take Tselane long to note that he delayed and lingered in her work areas until he had caught some glimpse of her. She was always in a crowd of gaily chattering young women. The memory of their first encounter had been so fresh and stimulating, so full of unexpected surprises in dialogue that she longed to approach him. One afternoon, while out wood gathering with her companions, she noticed him among the distant bushes and contrived to remove herself from her companions. As she walked towards him, he quite directly approached her and took hold of her hand. She made no effort to pull her hand free. It rested in his as though it belonged there. They walked on some distance, then he paused, and turning to face her told her all he had on his mind in his direct, simple way. This time he did not smile at all.

'My father will arrange a marriage for me after about six new moons have passed,' he said. 'I do not want that. I want a wife of my own choosing but all the things I want can only cause trouble.'

She looked away into the distance, not immediately knowing what she ought to say. Her own parents had given her no clue of their plans for her future; indeed she had not had cause to think about it but she did not like most of the young men of the village. They had a hang-dog air as though the society and its oppressive ways had broken their will. She liked everything about Keaja and she felt safe with him as on that stormy afternoon in the cavern when he had said: 'We can shelter here together from the storm . . .'

'My own thoughts are not complicated,' he went on, still holding on to her hand. 'I thought I would find out how you felt about this matter. I thought I would like to choose you as my wife. If you do not want to choose me in turn, I shall not pursue my own wants any longer. I might even marry the wife my father chooses for me.'

She turned around and faced him and spoke with a clarity of thought that startled her.

'I am afraid of nothing,' she said. 'Not even trouble or death but I need some time to find out what I am thinking.'

Of his own accord, he let go of her hand and so they parted and went their separate ways. From that point onwards right until the following day, she lived in a state of high elation. Her thought processes were not all coherent; indeed she had not a thought in her head. Then the illogic of love took over. Just as she was about to pick up the pitcher in the late afternoon, she suddenly felt desperately ill, so ill that she was almost brought to the point of death. She experienced a paralysing lameness in her arms and legs. The weight of the pitcher with which she was to draw water was too heavy for her to endure.

She appealed to Mma-Monosi.

'I feel faint and ill today,' she said. 'I cannot draw water.'

Mma-Monosi was only too happy to take over her chores but at the same time consulted anxiously with her mother about this sudden illness. Mma-Tselane, after some deliberation, decided that it was the illness young girls get in the limbs when they are growing too rapidly. She spent a happy three days doctoring her daughter with warm herb drinks, for Mma-Tselane liked nothing better than to concentrate on illness. Still, the physical turmoil the young girl felt continued unabated; at night she trembled violently from head to toe. It was so shocking and new that for two days she succumbed completely to the blow. It wasn't any coherent thought processes that made her struggle desperately to her feet on the third day but a need to quieten the anguish. She convinced her mother and Mma-Monosi that she felt well enough to perform her wood gathering chores. Towards the afternoon she hurried to the forest area, carefully avoiding her gathering companions.

She was relieved, on meeting Keaja, to see that his face bore the same anguished look that she felt. He spoke first.

'I felt so ill and disturbed,' he said. 'I could do nothing but wait for your appearance.'

They sat down on the ground together. She was so exhausted by her two-day struggle that for a moment she leaned forward and rested her head on his knee. Her thought processes seemed to awaken once more because she smiled peacefully and said: 'I want to think.'

Eventually, she raised herself and looked at the young man with shining eyes.

'I felt so ill,' she said. 'My mother kept on giving me herb drinks. She said it was normal to feel faint and dizzy when one is growing. I know now what made me feel so ill. I was fighting my training. My training has told me that people are not important in themselves but you so suddenly became import-ant to me, as a person. I did not know how to tell my mother all this. I did not know how to tell her anything yet she was kind and took care of me. Eventually I thought I would lose my mind so I came here to find you . . .'

It was as if, from that moment onwards, they quietly and of their own willing, married each other. They began to plan together how they should meet and when they should meet. The young man was full of forethought and planning. He knew that, in the terms of his own society, he was starting a terrible mess, but then his society only calculated along the lines of human helplessness in the face of overwhelming odds. It did not calculate for human inventiveness and initiative. He only needed the young girl's pledge and from then onwards he took the initiative in all things. He was to startle and please her from that very day with his forethought. It was as if he knew that she would come at some time, that they would linger in joy with their love-making, so that when Tselane eventually expressed agitation at the lateness of the hour, he, with a superior smile, indicated a large bundle of wood nearby that he had collected for her to take home.

A peaceful interlude followed and the community innocently lived out its day-by-day life, unaware of the disruption and upheaval that would soon fall upon it. The women were soon out in the fields, hoeing weeds and tending their crops, Tselane among them, working side by side with Mma-Monosi, as she had always done. There was not even a ripple of the secret life she now lived; if anything, she worked harder and with greater contentment. She laughed and joked as usual with Mma-Monosi but sound instinct made her keep her private affair to herself.

When the corn was already high in the fields and about to ripen, Tselane realized that she was expecting a child. A matter that had been secret could be a secret no longer. When she confided this news to Keaja, he quite happily accepted it as a part of all the plans he had made, for as he said to her at that time: 'I am not planning for death when we are so happy. I want it that we should live.'

He had only one part of all his planning secure, a safe escape route outside the village and on to a new and unknown life they would make for themselves. They had made themselves outcasts from the acceptable order of village life and he presented her with two alternatives from which she could choose. The one alternative was simpler for them. They could leave the village at any moment and without informing anyone of their intentions. The world was very wide for a man. He had travelled great distances, both alone and in the company of other men, while on his hunting and herding duties. The area was safe for travel for some distance. He had sat around firesides and heard stories about wars and fugitives and other hospitable tribes who lived distances away and whose customs differed from theirs. Keaja had not been idle all this while. He had prepared all they would need for their journey and hidden their provisions in a secret place.

The alternative was more difficult for the lovers. They could inform their parents of their love and ask that they be married. He was not sure of the outcome but it was to invite death or worse. It might still lead to the escape route out of the village as he was not planning for death.

So after some thought Tselane decided to tell her parents because as she pointed out the first plan would be too heartbreaking for their parents. They therefore decided on that very day to inform their parents of their love and name the date on which they wished to marry.

It was nearing dusk when Tselane arrived home with her bundle of wood.

Her mother and Mma-Monosi were seated out in the courtyard, engaged in some quiet conversation of their own. Tselane set down her bundle, approached the two women and knelt down quietly by her mother's side. Her mother turned towards her, expecting some request or message from a friend. There was no other way except for Tselane to convey her own message in the most direct way possible.

'Mother,' she said. 'I am expecting a child by the son of Rra-Keaja. We wish to be married by the next moon. We love each other . . .'

For a moment her mother frowned as though her child's words did not make sense. Mma-Monosi's body shuddered several times as though she were cold but she maintained a deathly silence. Eventually Tselane's mother lowered her voice and said between clenched teeth: 'You are to go to your hut and remain there. On no account are you to leave it without the supervision of Mma-Monosi.'

For a time Mma-Tselane sat looking into the distance, a broken woman. Her social prestige, her kingdom, her self-esteem crumbled around her.

A short while later her husband entered the yard. He had spent an enjoyable day at the chief's court with other men. He now wished for his evening meal and retirement for the night. The last thing he wanted was conversation with women, so he looked up irritably as his wife appeared without his evening meal. She explained herself with as much dignity as she could muster. She was almost collapsing with shock. He listened in disbelief and gave a sharp exclamation of anger.

Just at this moment Keaja's father announced himself in the yard. 'Rra-Tselane, I have just heard from my own son the offence he has committed against your house, but he desires nothing more than to marry your child. If this would remove some of the offence, then I am agreeable to it.'

'Rra-Keaja,' Tselane's father replied. 'You know as well as I that this marriage isn't in the interests of your family or mine.' He stood up and walked violently into the night.

Brokenly, Keaja's father also stood up and walked out of the yard.

It was her husband's words that shook Mma-Tselane out of her stupor of self-pity. She hurried to her living quarters for her skin shawl, whispered a few words to Mma-Monosi about her mission. Mma-Monosi too sped off into the night after Rra-Keaja. On catching up with him she whispered urgently: 'Rra-Keaja! You may not know me. I approach you because we now share this trouble which has come upon us. This matter will never be secret. Tomorrow it will be a public affair. I therefore urge you to do as Mma-Tselane has done and make an appeal for your child at once. She has gone to the woman's compound of the chief's house as she has many friends there.'

Her words lightened the old man's heavy heart. With a promise to send her his news, he turned and walked in the direction of the chief's yard.

Mma-Monosi sped back to her own yard.

'Tselane,' she said, earnestly. 'It is no light matter to break custom. You pay for it with your life. I should have told you the story that night we discussed custom. When I was a young girl we had a case such as this but not such a deep mess. The young man had taken a fancy to a girl and she to him. He therefore refused the girl his parents had chosen for him. They could not break him and so they killed him. They killed even though he had not touched the girl. But there is one thing I want you to know. I am your friend and I will die for you. No one will injure you while I am alive.'

Their easy, affectionate relationship returned to them. They talked for some time about the love affair, Mma-Monosi absorbing every word with delight. A while later Mma-Tselane re-entered the yard. She was still too angry to talk to her own child but she called Mma-Monosi to one side and informed her that she had won an assurance in high places that no harm would come to her child.

And so began a week of raging storms and wild irrational deliberations. It was a family affair. It was a public affair. As a public affair, it would bring ruin and disaster upon the community and public anger was high. Two parents showed themselves up in a bad light, the father of Tselane and the mother of Keaja. Rra-Tselane was adamant that the marriage would never take place. He preferred to sound death warnings all the time. The worm that had been eating at the heart of Keaja's mother all this while finally arose and devoured her heart. She too could be heard to sound death warnings. Then a curious and temporary solution was handed down from high places. It was said that if the lovers removed themselves from the community for a certain number of days, it would make allowance for public anger to die down. Then the marriage of the lovers would be considered.

So appalling was the drama to the community that on the day Keaja was released from his home and allowed to approach the home of Tselane, all the people withdrew to their own homes so as not to witness the fearful sight. Only Mma-Monosi, who had supervised the last details of the departure, stood openly watching the direction in which the young lovers left the village. She saw them begin to ascend the hill not far from the home of Tselane. As darkness was approaching, she turned and walked back to her yard. To Mma-Tselane, who lay in a state of nervous collapse in her hut, Mma-Monosi made her last, sane pronouncement on the whole affair.

'The young man is no fool,' she said. 'They have taken the direction of the hill. He knows that the hilltop is superior to any other. People are angry and someone might think of attacking them. An attacker will find it a difficult task as the young man will hurtle stones down on him before he ever gets near. Our child is quite safe with him.'

Then the story took a horrible turn. Tension built up towards the day the lovers were supposed to return to community life. Days went by and they did not return. Eventually search parties were sent out to look for them but they had disappeared. Not even their footmarks were visible on the bare rock faces and tufts of grass on the hillside. At first the searchers returned and did not report having seen any abnormal phenomena, only a baffled surprise. Then Mma-Monosi's precarious imaginative balance tipped over into chaos. She was seen walking grief-stricken towards the hill. As she reached its base she stood still and the whole drama of the disappearance of the lovers was re-created before her eyes. She first heard loud groans of anguish that made her blood run cold. She saw that as soon as Tselane and Keaja set foot on the hill, the rocks parted and a gaping hole appeared. The lovers sank into its depths and the rocks closed over them. As she called, 'Tselane! Keaja!' their spirits arose and floated soundlessly with unseeing eyes to the top of the hill.

Mma-Monosi returned to the village and told a solemn and convincing story of all the phenomena she had seen. People only had to be informed that such phenomena existed and they all began seeing them too. Then Mma-Tselane, maddened and distraught by the loss of her daughter, slowly made her way to the hill. With sorrowful eyes she watched the drama re-create itself before her. She returned home and died. The hill from then onwards became an unpleasant embodiment of sinister forces which destroy life. It was no longer considered a safe dwelling place for the tribe. They packed up their belongings on the backs of their animals, destroyed the village and migrated to a safer area.

The deserted area remained unoccupied from then onwards until 1875 when people of the Bamalete tribe settled there. Although strangers to the area, they saw the same phenomena, they heard the loud groans of anguish and saw the silent floating spirits of the lovers. The legend was kept alive from generation unto generation and so the hill stands until this day in the village of Otse in southern Botswana as an eternal legend of love. Letswe La Baratani, The Hill of the Lovers, it is called.

Exile

» «

ROSE MOSS

Stephen Katela dozed at the back of the car. Occasionally he opened his eyes to look at the two dark heads in front of him, the kind white couple who were taking him to their home. Yesterday he had been at another college and had given a talk on African music, and another kind white couple had taken him home as their guest, and he had talked about South Africa. He closed his eyes. A theme kept palpitating under the surface of his attention, its outline blurred like a cat in a bag, like his own young body when he crept down to the bottom of his mother's bed and thought that no one could see him because it was dark under the blanket. His brother played with him there, a touch and move game in the shapeless dark, a hiding-go-seek without rules, until they started to wrestle and wriggled so fast they rolled off the bed on to the humourless floor. Then their mother scolded them while she fed another baby mealie pap with one hand and attended to the tea and remaining mealie pap on the stove with the other. Stephen and his brother went out to play until she called them in to breakfast. They ignored her injunctions to take soap and wash under the tap in the yard. Winter was too cold for washing. She would come out when the baby was fed and give them a slap and another scolding, would oversee their mutual lathering and squirming at the tap, and when the relics of their brief exploration had been washed off them – cinders of a brazier in which they had poked for coal, gritty smears if they had been examining the rubbish in the street – she would fold them into the bosomy warmth of the room. The reminiscent smell of early morning fires, the grey blue haze of the township, bit like an acrid, toxic gas into the tissue of Stephen's memory. He opened his eyes again to fill them with the two silhouettes in front of him, the white couple driving home through a heavy mist that the headlights held pale and solid, close to the car.

The road twisted and heaved. They had come off the smooth turnpike, homogeneous from Virginia to Maine, that made Stephen feel that his whole

236

lecture tour was an hallucination in which distance had no more dimension than in a dream. Episodes that repeated the same obsessional pattern followed each other arbitrarily in settings that differed only like the scenery of an impoverished theatrical company. Every road was the same road. The arrangement played with slightly differing signs and overpasses, discreet banks of grass, and trees that only gradually and reluctantly admitted the grey agglomeration of cities whose suburbs had long been suppressed by the same green uniform as the countryside. At last, off the highway, an idiosyncratic thrust from the land moulded the road into a pliant index of fields and streams, pulled straight over flats, packed more densely in steep valleys and rises. The mist was so thick he could hardly see the vegetation. From the dancing swell of the road he could imagine himself back on the stretch between Mooi River and Pietermaritzburg where frequent mists nourished the land, and cattle condensed the airy whiteness into substances richly edible – for those who could afford to buy them.

But every now and then a leafy intrusion over the road caught his eye, the uneven bars of a wooden fence, or irregular stone globules of a wall, and Stephen was reminded by these foreign shapes and colours that he was not on that Natal road, he was somewhere in New England, going to spend the night in a strange house among strangers. These sights, like foreign substances grafted among the tissues of what he had seen, lived, and compounded into organic constituents of his own self, set up a resistance. Each reminder that he was not home accelerated an irritation, a process of rejection. His body, his perception, the accumulated chemicals of his own being barred these alien elements and tried to seal their pernicious proximity off from himself, to cast them off like a foreign skin or organ, to expel all toxic strangeness. He shut his eyes. He tried to lull himself. Let him not think that if he did not learn how to assimilate America there would be nothing left for him to see, no place where he could retain that dwindling self he felt to be his own. He thought of his brother and the dusty soccer field where they used to play when their mother went off with the baby and a bundle of washing wrapped in a sheet, to the white city where she worked until night came. How did that theme shape?

His host was also a composer. Stephen had heard a quartet by him. It had been played at one of the colleges where Stephen had contributed to a symposium on modern music. There had been lectures and workshops during the day. In the evening there was a concert and Ken Radley's String Quartet, cited as an example of some of the finest composition in the United States, was played to instruct an audience that might find such compositions hard to come by. To Stephen the quartet seemed unintelligible, thin, and boring, but he blamed his response on his own ignorance. Ken's quartet was one of the many signs, like billboards on the road, that said to Stephen, 'We don't speak to you. We are not written in your language. You have nothing to say to us.'

The car slowed, turned up a driveway, and they had come. 'We're here,' Janet announced smiling. This was her home. Stephen smiled to her. They were so kind. Ken opened the door and light flared out of the amber hall over damp steps. Inside there was more light.

'Why don't we wash and have a drink while Janet's preparing supper?' Ken suggested. 'I'll show you your room,' and he took Stephen's suitcase, which he had already fetched from the car. Stephen wondered whether it was right to let Ken carry his suitcase; or did he feel uncomfortable because Ken was white? 'I'll take it.' He reached for the handle. Ken let him take it and picked up another suitcase. He led the way up carpeted stairs, pointed out the bathroom, and gestured inside the doorway of a room at the end of the passage, 'This is yours. See you downstairs.' With a quick smile he indicated his confidence that Stephen could manage from this point. He could, in a manner of speaking. He had done it before. He took the smaller of two towels neatly waiting for him at the foot of the bed, and the cake of soap, still wrapped, and went to the bathroom. It retained the old-fashioned tub of an old house, but a combed sheepskin on the floor and a shelf over the tub for an ashtray, two detective stories and a small vase of brightly dyed star flowers indicated that it was not a room where Ken and Janet expected austere behaviour.

When he came back to the room they had given him Stephen noted the artefacts of someone else's life. A childhood unimaginably unlike his own surrounded him. Behind the bed hung a drawing of the beach. The sea was a properly undulating blue on whose conventional waves there sailed the black outline of a yacht, innocent of the relatively immense fish whose profile stood mute, motionless, and symbolic between it and the yellow and purple sand, where a green scribble suggested grass. In a low bookcase under the window, children's books about shells and birds, adventure stories, Webster's illustrated dictionary, a microscope under a plastic cover, indicated another layer of the American boy's life. The most recent stratum was evidenced near the dressing table where a poster of Humphrey Bogart ignored college pennants and the image of the alien in the mirror.

Stephen sat on the bed. He felt his knees under his palms. He insisted on his own undeniable life, on his own childhood in and out of the dusty location and the dusty mission school, on his skill to be as slick as a tsotsi who wore tight trousers and carried knives. He had been as mocking as a mosquito when he played the pennywhistle on street corners, when he demanded a penny, a tickey, a sixpence, baas. He went downstairs for a drink.

Janet was busy in the kitchen that was separated from the dining area and lounge by a wooden counter. He noticed that she was wearing a string of those grey seeds that white women didn't think smart in South Africa. Here they were favoured by the wives of college professors, like Janet, and girl students from good homes.

It was fine to sit in the same room as a busy woman preparing food. 'Haven't you got some vegetables to peel?' he offered. In America it was all right to help like a piccanin.

'It's all done, frozen and sliced,' she laughed, 'very American.' She untied her apron and hung it over a rail. 'Come and have a drink.'

How casually legal it seemed to her to offer him a drink. How legal and unremarkable to be alone with a black man. In South Africa when white women offered him drinks, he was wary. Even at mixed parties he felt his safety as sharp as a blade's edge. With Cynthia Barton he would drink; after dinner, meat and wine, she offered him brandy and liqueur. After slow talk and darkness he would wake to hear his heart slamming, police banging the door, and his brother crying, sick. When the police arrested David Msimang with a white woman and found out that he was a musician, they broke his eardrums, just for fun. After that, Stephen would not visit Cynthia alone any more, and on the phone she said, 'For goodness' sake, don't *explain*. There's nothing to *explain*. If you don't want to come, don't come. You don't owe me anything. I'm not your white madam.' She never allowed him to tell her about David Msimang.

In New York he went to some mixed parties given by Andrew Mohone. South Africans who had left with the cast of *King Kong*, after Sharpeville, after Mandela, after Sobukwe, after waves of arrests under the sabotage laws, after Vorster, on scholarships, on exit permits, on passports and family money, met each other at mixed parties and felt that the old risk and thrill could be recaptured. They repeated the gestures of defiance that here did not defy, and knew again that they were singly brave and free. Some of the whites at Andrew's parties were Americans – young reporters, instructors at Columbia and the Free School, churchmen with missionary acquaintances – a miscellaneous lot who, like the South Africans themselves, of different generations and concerns, seemed to have little in common but a geographically named node of feeling. By two o'clock in the morning the parties had usually divided into Siamese twin parties, one black, one white. In South Africa the mixture would have lasted all night. Mixed parties here missed the police.

Once or twice black separatists came instead of whites. They made remarks to Stephen like, 'I can see you come from Africa. Your face is so proud.' They had never heard his music. The mixed parties were easier. At first, the old South Africans asked him for news and gossip. 'Do you know Diana Zindberg? . . . What's she doing now?'

'Didn't she marry an Englishman? I think she married an Oxford don,' someone would supply. Or she was 'on the West Coast now', or she had remained in South Africa.

A few people knew Cynthia Barton, and asked whether he knew her. 'Yes, I think she's still in Johannesburg.'

'Goli, hey! Good old Goli! Man, I still miss the place. Well Cynthia was a great gal,' as though she had partially died, 'just a great kid! I wish she'd come here.'

Why? Stephen wondered, why did anyone wish that?

He imagined that in New York there were such parties given by White Russians, Serbians, Spanish anarchists, Palestinian Arabs, Ghanaians and Czechs. All exiles, all dying. When all his oxygen was exhausted he would also relish thin gossip about South Africa and the people of his generation, become a comfortable exile, a cell in the specific tissue of exiles and cosmopolitans who had by now become organically accepted and integral in the American metabolism.

Ken entered from another room. 'There's a letter from Christopher. He says he'll stop by on his way to New York,' he told Janet.

'Good. When'll that be?'

'Any time.'

'Christopher's our son,' she explained to Stephen. 'He's been summering in the Hudson Bay area. He says there are some interesting algae there. Algae are his thing.' She smiled fondly, indulgently.

The remoteness of these lives that he saw in midstream pressed in on Stephen. There was none of his own air left, none of the spacious sunlight, naïve and simple, by which he had learned to read the world. Here, existence was compounded into individual complex studies and specialized fields. Each man saw his own topic, noted its intricate interrelationships and structures, and guessed at the intricacies known by others. In South Africa he had written music, it seemed to him now, like a child. He had composed as though he could pour sound simply into the heart of another man, a heart unobstructed by perceptions evolved to assimilate incommunicable knowledge. Here his communications were defined. He was a practising composer, and an authority on the music of Southern Africa. He had become a curiosity devoted to curiosities, the speaker of an arcane language – composer, consequently, to no ear but his own. The longer he stayed the more arcane his music must become; it must breed into itself to retain that exotic worth that was supposed to give it value. It could not mate again with the sounds of his daily life, now American – that would breed an impurity into his sound, a new idiom into his voice. And then he would lose that now ghostly audience in South Africa who, when they listened to his music, thought that the earth sang and the cicadas chorused together, and did not know that their unique earth was quaint veld, their noon remote from others'.

Each of these Americans with his intricate knowledge constituted one cell of this complex society whose function was a life other than Stephen's, whose purpose was something he did not know, and could not, without destroying himself, adopt. If he did not adopt its purpose, America would shake him off as an intrusion, a piece of a foreign body, a cell or organ that lived by the principles of some other body born under the Southern Cross.

Something of Stephen's loneliness emanated through to Janet. It prompted her to the inbred courtesy that required her to turn the topic of conversation to her guest's interests rather than her own. She reserved the subject of Christopher and his letter for later, for that conjugal conversation whose even tenor is like the even conversation a man conducts with the sights and texture of his belongings and his people. She would deal with Christopher in a time and a language from which Stephen felt sealed off as if from the air of life. She asked him questions about South Africa while they sipped gin and tonic with wedges of lime – a drink he had never known in South Africa, even at the mixed parties of Houghton and Northcliff, and certainly never in the shebeens. At last she came to the question that all these polite, interested Americans asked.

'Will you ever go back?'

'I can't. I got out illegally, without a passport. I'm a refugee.'

'You mean they wouldn't give you a passport. Why on earth not?'

'They've had some bad experiences with the wrong people getting out and making propaganda against the government overseas. We Africans talk too much.'

Ken liked his dryness. 'And have you talked too much here?'

'I've been on a lecture tour.' They laughed.

'Your topic's not very incendiary,' Ken pursued.

'No,' Stephen agreed, 'but I do some damage in ordinary conversations like this. And then, most Afrikaners, especially those who deal with us, are ignorant. They're afraid of people like me because I'm not a simple kaffir.'

'How did you get out?' Janet wanted to know.

'Oh, there's a sort of underground railroad, and a refugee centre in Dar-es-Salaam.'

'Will you go back there?'

'I don't know what will happen to me.' After he had spoken he heard the passive helplessness he had revealed. Ken heard it too.

'Why do you want to go back to South Africa?'

'I don't.' But Ken ignored this reply. His waiting silence was as heavily palpable as a waking sensation that presses into sleep and breaks its integuments. And like a sleeper who begins to talk before he has quite shaken off sleep, and talks as truthfully as in a dream, Stephen continued.

'I can't work here. I say to myself that tomorrow, or next week I'll be able to, but I can't. I compose, but it's all false. I can't bear to listen to it. I don't think I can write outside South Africa.'

'Then you must go back.' Ken spoke the imperative that Stephen feared. He brought into it the auditory reality of an American accent with a resolute inflection that Stephen would never have invented in his own mind, the instruction that, like the ground bass of a passacaglia, had sounded without interruption in Stephen's feelings for weeks.

Stephen repeated, 'I can't.' Ken and Janet said nothing. 'If I go back I'll be in prison within a year – not a nice comfortable prison where people can write their memoirs. I'll be in a South African jail where people get beaten up and tortured and go mad. I've been in prison. A pass offender gets kicked around. Sometimes he's sent to work on potato farms where he wears a potato sack, winter and summer. Sometimes he's beaten for not working hard enough. They knocked the eardrums out of a friend of mine because he was a musician. Some people get beaten to death. In the jail they put ten men in one cell, and give you one bucket that gets full long before morning. There are no beds. You sleep on the floor, as far away from the bucket as you can. And I'm not a pass offender. I can't expect such good treatment. I'm not likely to write much music there.'

'Then you must learn how to write here.'

'How? How can I learn anything like that?' Stephen breathed hard on his rage. These Americans thought they could solve everything. They had no respect for boulder weight, for things too heavy for a man to lift.

'I don't know. I guess it's easier to say than to do. Just give yourself time to hear what this country sounds like. You probably just need time.'

'Yes,' seconded Janet. 'After all, you haven't been here very long.'

Their unsuffering sympathy fed Stephen's rage. 'I want to write in my own language. In South Africa that isn't allowed. An African has to speak English or Afrikaans, a composer has to learn the sonata form and the instruments of the European orchestra. They are what he must write for. There's an instrument we have in Lesotho – a bow and a string, and a gourd for resonance. It plays two notes. The person who plays it can hardly hear it himself, it's like a whisper, like a lover. In a world that's so quiet, there's room for an instrument like that. There are nothing but mountains, and one bad road. It keeps the cars out. The people are too poor for radios. All they can afford is the sound of a gourd, like the earth, like the sunlight, like being poor, like being black. You can't hear it in Johannesburg – even the Africans are too rich there, or their being poor is a cramping vice. That bow and gourd says what I want – but where could I play something like that in America? No one would hear it. Everything's so loud here, the cars, the radios, the fire trucks, planes. I can't hear anything human, alive. And even if anyone could hear my bow and gourd, what would they make of it? Two simple notes over and over, so monotonous. Not at all . . . psychedelic.' He smiled at this disparaged word of praise, as if to overcome squeamishness at having used it. 'I sound angry, but I'm not angry at Americans for being what they are. That's what they are. It's incurable. Like being an African. But it's at the other end of the world, and I can't make myself learn what to be again, like a baby. I don't start from nothing. I'm a man already.'

Ken and Janet were embarrassed at this outburst. Their habitual withdrawal from involvement with strangers, especially strangers whose insoluble problems could grieve and fester in those whose pity held no power to remedy; an accepted training rooted in the manners of ancestors who knew that what is delicate must be protected (sometimes by deliberate ignorance), who would not mention rape, drunkenness or money in front of women; and a traditional stoicism that would not weep but fastened troubles to the self like a brace to keep men upright – all made them withdraw from Stephen's demand.

Ken spoke first. 'I hope you'll take advantage of the musical opportunities in these parts. There'll be some interesting concerts in New York this fall, and other things too. I've got a notice from Hunter College. I'll look for it after supper. You will be in New York, won't you?'

'Yes.' Stephen didn't tell him that he received his own notices, invitations, introductions.

'And I've got programmes for Lincoln Center. I can often get complimentary tickets . . .'

Stephen saw how the problems of the boy Christopher must have been kindly finessed away until he grew up into, not quite a man – for he was allowed no human, intractable troubles, only those his society could digest – but an expert on algae.

Christopher came home that night. Stephen heard him arrive, and the noise of welcome and explanation that a guest was sleeping in his room. 'Then you must go back,' Ken had said in an American voice with an unforeseen inflexion. 'Then you must go back.' The initial staccatos of greeting sank into long blurred sentences, and Stephen tried to fuse the reawakened rhythm of family discourse in his ear with the theme that had struggled forward during the drive through the mist, the song of playing with his brother in the morning. But he could not achieve the fusion, and fell asleep again.

He met Christopher at the breakfast table. Ken introduced him to the bony youth. 'Steve's giving a paper on African music at Fenmore Hall this afternoon, and going to New York tomorrow.'

'I think I'm in your room,' Stephen said tentatively.

'I'm only camping here,' Christopher assured him. 'I'm going on to New York myself.'

'Perhaps Chris can give you a ride down,' Ken suggested. 'Unless you'd rather fly . . .'

During the meal Christopher accompanied firm gestures that reached for butter or toast on the well-known table with stories about his summer. He talked about what his expedition had accomplished. 'We collected hundreds of specimens that are probably new. How'd you like an alga named after you, Mother?'

'I'd have to see it first,' she joked.

'I've got slides. Are you free tonight? Can we look at them?'

Janet drew him back to arrangements for the day. 'I've been waiting all summer for you to help your father clear out the cellar.'

'That'll be great,' Christopher assented before Ken could protest.

Stephen wondered whether his help would be welcome or obtrusive. No, he'd work on the location theme, even though nothing would come of it.

While he was sitting at the desk the boy Christopher must have used, Stephen saw them walking through the grounds. Sometimes they stopped to examine a change or permanence. The two men walking among trees, their heads flickering among bright foliage, who lived in that world inhabited by squirrels and jays that he had sometimes read about in northern storybooks, were indeed men, not plastic surrogates produced by a society that forbade suffering and wanted only organs of perception, units of intelligence, consumers. These two were men, father and son, archetypal, and as mythical to Stephen as woods that harboured plentiful creatures, as strange as snows and blueberries and maples. Such familial affluence was unknown to him. His father had been one of the men who lived with his mother for a few years and then disappeared into the jails, into the labyrinth of townships around Johannesburg, or into the reserves. A series of men had played with him and the other children, in idle friendliness. Nostalgic for a life some of them had never known, they assessed him as a candidate for initiation, and told him stories to inspire warlike heroism, sagas of Zulu impis led by Chaka and

Dingaan. But often they were irritable. The children seemed always under-
foot, Sarah wanted more money to buy them clothes, and Stephen was always
wasting candles at night when a man wanted darkness and Sarah's hard
breathing.

Stephen and his brother knew the world directly, not by the mediation of
fathers. There were not discrete worlds, one filled with talking animals and
fairies for children, another with money and taxes and politics for adults. It
was all one world. Grown men as frightened as children of policemen who, as
irresistible as witchcraft, might bang on the door in the middle of the night to
ask for a pass, or dig up the floor to look for skokiaan. It was all one world. In
an acid dawn as pink as millions of pounds, neighbours climbed on to bicycles
and rode into the city; on the way to the long queue at the bus-stop they
stepped on the hoar that clung to wisps of dry grass and paper; some who had
slept with braziers in closed rooms breathed the warm air too long and did not
wake up in time for life. Nothing was omitted except this other world,
inconceivable – the house set among wild trees and lavish grass, this world
that the father and the son were revisiting, and had never altogether left, and
this kind of humanity that grew among them. Stephen could never revisit his
childhood. Now he must live in a world that his childhood had never guessed
existed.

That night Christopher showed them slides of his expedition to the Hudson
Bay. Beyond sight or sound of any other human life small villages grasped
tight in dour friendliness. Granite boulders grew lichens like birthmarks, and
in their brief summer thronged with silky flowers that looked like Karoo
vygies. Pane after pane of light offered visions that Stephen could understand
– emptiness, light, virginity – where he had expected only more that was alien,
unassimilable. In a landscape like this one could play an instrument with two
notes. But he was afraid to think of what he saw. Would he go to the Hudson
Bay to try another kind of exile?

Being driven to New York, he asked about the expedition. 'Didn't you feel
lonely?'

'No. There were seven of us on the ship, and we got to know some of the
village people quite well. Strangers are very welcome. And it's not as if there
aren't any phones. I called my girl in New York twice a week. It's not half as
bad as it'll be next year when we go to Lake Baikal, if we can arrange it. We
might go to Antarctica instead. What's Cape Town like? They say it's
beautiful.'

'I've never been there. The government tries to keep us Africans out of
Cape Town.'

'Oh, I thought most of the population was Negro.'

'In Cape Town there are a lot of people of mixed blood. They're called coloureds and are treated differently from us. Every shade of whiteness deserves a special degree of privilege.'

'You must be really glad to be out of it.'

'I am. Don't you ever get homesick when you go to these strange places?'

'I guess I've never been away long enough. It's no problem really. I could come back any time.' They seemed to have come to a dead end. 'Do you ever get homesick?'

'Sometimes.'

'I guess people get homesick for the strangest things. One of our research team comes from Anatolia. He longs for sheep's eyes. Look for *that* in a supermarket!' Christopher laughed.

Stephen was silent.

'Mind if I turn on the radio?'

'Go ahead.'

Sometimes they let the clamour of baroque music substitute for conversation. Sometimes they spoke through it.

'Why did you come to the States? To get out of South Africa?'

'Partly. And people always told me I should go overseas to finish my education. They said my composing needed to be finished.' He smiled at the private irony.

'But your family's still there?'

'My mother.'

'Have you got brothers, or sisters?'

'Most of them died as babies. One brother grew up with me, but he died when I was in high school.'

'Your mother must miss you.'

'I don't know. I wrote, but didn't get an answer. And I asked someone I knew to look for her, but I haven't heard from him either.'

'Why don't you phone.'

'We haven't got phones. In the locations, only white officials have phones.'

Vivaldi gave way to Cimarosa by way of a commercial. How must it be to live in Christopher's world, where there was no sensual space, distance, silence, darkness? Stephen remembered reading that a night of darkness had come upon New York like a disaster. How must it be to live like that, deprived of any sense of the given light, and the given earth's autonomous being? How would it be to live in America and lose all stillness, loneliness, man-otherness, to live in a world where the whisper of a string in a gourd could never be heard, imagined? Christopher could hardly be five years younger than himself, but Stephen felt old, old-fashioned, old as the chameleon who first allowed the news of death to be brought into the world, old as death, incomprehensible to Christopher. Christopher lived in the new world. Was there any music Stephen could write for him? What was there in Christopher's life he could understand?

'What does your girl do?'

Christopher answered in sentences whose individual words were intelligible. It was the syntax, the meaning, that fled.

When they came to New York, the road lost all connection with the shape or look of the land. It dived, swung, curved, twisted back on itself, over other roads and under them. Buildings crowded nearer and nearer as in a kinetic hallucination of suffocation, claustrophobia and spacelessness. The commercials between symphonies gave way to a long newscast about Vietnam, New York, Turkey, Israel, Lindsay, Rockefeller and people whose roles and names Stephen could not identify. As usual there was nothing about South Africa. From here it seemed an almost non-existent country. The few Americans who had heard of it refracted it, distorted it, saw it as an image of their own problems. If they cared at all, it was not for a country that had an independent existence, it was for a symbol of their own conflicts. The little of South Africa that survived had been absorbed into the bloodstream of another system. And if he were to survive, he must learn who all these people were, must learn to become interested in them, must tutor himself in this system, this Vietnam, CORE, LSD, FBI, CIA, UCLA, this system of symbols and personalities in whom he had no interest. He must give up his self, and must become a self who could subsist in this vast artefact that offered hardly a blade of grass he could recognize from his own life.

They drove through Harlem. The stores advertised foods he had never eaten. Children played games with rules and passwords he had never known. He had been here, in a black world as foreign as the white, where people didn't understand his English and stared at his strangeness, this black Harlem whose language was as opaque as Spanish Harlem's, as whiteness, as the intelligent assurance of a youth like Christopher.

They left Central Park behind them and the big stores, and came to Stephen's hotel. When Andrew Mohone and Ester Matimba had come to meet him at the airport and offered to help him find accommodation, they had been careful not to take him to Harlem. Andrew wore a loose, flowered costume that he had never worn in South Africa. He carried an airmail edition of the London *Times* under his arm. Later he explained that many had to masquerade to get a respect they could not otherwise achieve.

'Don't you feel funny to be an African pretending to be an African so that Americans will recognize you as the kind of African they recognize?'

'What sort of game is that, man? You've got to do it. Believe me, there are lots of tricks to learn.'

Ester wore the expensive clothes of a performer offstage. Her bearing neither expected nor brooked contempt. And in their aura, Stephen had been able to rent a room out of Harlem.

When Christopher left him, with vaguely friendly American remarks about being glad to meet him, Stephen wondered whether to phone Ester. Or should he wait until this sombre mood lightened? He felt lethargic, almost inanimate. He opened the window of his room. It gave on to a dark airshaft. In a corner a heap of crates and cartons rotted and waited for someone to dispose of them. Lights from other rooms in the hotel glowed anonymously. A pale sky sagged against the building's dark bulk. The city's flaccid roar sank towards the rotting corners of the airshaft. Its hoarse wheeze breathed into his face. The outside air, like the air in his room and in the passages of the hotel, had been used so often that an impalpable grime hung in it, like wear in the face of an old prostitute. Any man who took comfort in its warmth breathed dying, as if he slept in a closed room where a brazier breathed.

He took out his notes for the theme of the game under the blanket. The whole affair seemed pitifully thin and worthless, but he tried to work on it. Every new idea seemed banal, false, either involuntarily reminiscent of a commercial, or masquerading like Andrew as an Africa he had never experienced, unnaturally bright and vigorous. Ai! the winter mornings had been cold, the air outside fierce, the water from the tap outside blinding. He and his brother in torn vests hid from the windy sun. Did Andrew tell stories about living in a jungle? Did he wear a different country in his memory and forget the location winters and the cracked European jackets of his native past? Stephen juggled the thin souvenir of those winters he dared not forget, devised harmonies and variations, and eventually put the sheets away. He phoned Ester.

'Stephen! It's good to hear you, man. How *are* you?'

'Okay. How're you?'

'I'm giving a party. Come.'

'When? Now?'

'Yes now. I've got two people from Columbia who've heard your music and want to meet you. Have you done anything new?'

'No.'

'Well, they like what they've heard.'

'Okay.'

'Are you all right, Stephen?'

'Yes. Why not?'

'I must be imagining. Too long since I've seen you. I'd like to see you myself, not just hand you over to those people from Columbia.'

'Drop the party and come with me.'

'I can't. TV people and journalists are here too. I want you to meet them, Stephen.'

'I've just come back. I'm tired. Some other time.'

'Stephen, you sound awfully depressed.'

'Good-bye, Ester.'

He was surprised to find Ester giving a party. Parties were one of Andrew Mohone's tricks, a habit of the exile community. Ester was surely not one of these. She did not make a special, trivial virtue of being South African and different. She met New York on its own terms. She worked. She did not talk about how much she had suffered at home, how rare and sensational her escape had been. She worked. Ken worked. Christopher worked. That was how they survived. But he could not work. He had lost a gear. He had become junk. He was like the rest of the South African clique. He might as well not despise their party.

He showered and changed. He looked in the mirror cynically. What had been the matter, man. He could still live.

He walked through the airless corridor into the streets. Stores offered enticements to millions of people with incomprehensible needs. Windows showed copper pots and wooden bowls, dyed hammocks, coloured glass spheres, ceramic fungus, leather waistcoats, books about Zen, posters, and records of Indian ragas. At best his music would cling to this sea ledge with other monstrous forms, curiosities, fads, psychedelia, and would be heard by these bedecked hermaphrodites whose fantastic forms pressed past him with insinuations of contempt, either at his clothes or blackness. This transient hallucination was yet another world, another language. He was lost in an infinity of variations, unconceived possibilities. They all extinguished him. All pressed suffocation. He was nothing. South Africa was nothing. What he had taken as the world omitted a world, an infinity of worlds.

He mounted a bus and rode it passively until the driver told him that he'd have to pay another fare – the bus had completed its route. He climbed off and walked among shabby and indefinite stores. Some screaming children ran in front of him and were rebuked by a screaming woman whose words he could not interpret. He stopped to stare at a window that displayed a French Provincial dining room and bar. Then he walked on again. A man who might have been drunk leaned towards him and asked the time, brother, but he didn't answer, and the man said, 'Fuck you, nigger.' He didn't answer that either. He was near another incessant highway. It roared without rhythm. He came to an overpass. He stopped to stare at the rapid cars, the inhuman speed, the implacable concrete legs of another overpass, the din of America. There was only one way. He would accept America. He would throw himself into it, into the breathless air, the machine light. He tightened his hand on the railing and pulled up. The freeway rushed and fled beneath him. He leapt into it.

My Cousin Comes to Jo'burg

» «

MBULELO MZAMANE

Township kids are incredibly good in tracing a man's origin. They can usually tell by his speech and deportment. They seldom pounce upon the swaggerer who crosses a busy intersection without pausing, even before the traffic lights turn green. But they'll not hesitate to taunt the man they hear humming a tribal ditty instead of whistling a jazz tune.

My cousin, Jola, comes from Tsolo in the Transkei. He has the stature of an adult gorilla and walks with his arms flung far out and his hands curving in, like a cowboy ready to draw. He has a protruding chest which seems to lead him wherever he goes. Overall, he gives the impression of a well-constructed tower. He can carry both our rubbish bins, full, with the ease and dignity of an educated man carrying a newspaper. His is not the delicate walking-cane amble of office workers who walk for relaxation, but the easy gait of one to whom walking is as customary as it is necessary.

He's been in the city for years now. But there was a time when he was as green and raw as a cabbage.

One day Mzal' uJola went to buy some cold drink. Shops are usually where street urchins 'rank', so they spotted him at a distance, carrying an empty family-size bottle.

'Where can I refill this bottle, makwedini?'

The boys laughed derisively at being called piccaninnies. Did he think he could lick them all, single-handed?

'He thinks we get cold drink from a tap?' one asked facetiously.

'Just because he's used to getting milk freely from a cow,' added another.

They laughed.

Mzal' uJola was more surprised than annoyed by this unexpected outburst from boys who should have been looking after cattle in the veld. He left them

251

and walked up to an elderly woman carrying a child on her back, who directed him to Mzimba's Native Eating Bazaar.

He came out of the shop with a bottle of raspberry. This again sent the boys into peals of laughter – red and green are favourites with country folk where people of the city will buy Fanta or Coke.

The boys had decided on a scheme to harass him. They stood in his path and pretended not to notice him. When he changed direction, they shifted to be directly in line with him.

His anger was mounting. He charged straight for the centre like an uncompromising rhino.

The boys found courage in numbers and stood their ground.

His eyes met those of the boy in the middle. The boy returned his stare. Mzal' uJola headed straight for him.

'Move out of my way, wena,' he said to the boy in the middle.

He was now dangerously close. Mouths stood agape as the contest assumed the form of a duel. He'd picked on the boss of the gang – feared, begrudged and, if the truth be told, hated by the rest.

The boss's bravado melted. He moved aside. The rest broke rank and Mzal' uJola passed.

My father once hitchhiked from Natalspruit because his car had been stolen there while he was visiting a friend's house.

'But couldn't they approach you decently and borrow the car if they needed it that badly?' Mzal' uJola asked.

We all gaped.

The phone rang. It was the police. The car had been found abandoned near New Market in Alberton. Except for a broken side-window the car didn't appear damaged in any way.

'I can't understand the mentality of a man who takes another's car, or even a horse that belongs to another, only to dump it elsewhere,' Mzal' uJola said.

My younger brother, Soso, once offered to take Mzal' uJola to the movies. They were showing Richard Widmark in *Street with no Name*, a great favourite with township audiences. Most of us had seen the film twice or three times before but we didn't mind seeing it again.

We had a transistor radio of which Mzal' uJola was inordinately fond. He played it even when we were listening to the radiogram. Its batteries were replaced daily. No matter how many times I told him to switch it off before going to bed, I always had to reach under his pillow and kill the music myself. He would never learn, that one. I remember threatening to break it once when he switched it on as I was listening to the news, and wondering if I could teach him how to use the earphones. I believe he even carried that transistor radio with him to the toilet.

In the evening we went to the movies. Nobody saw him hide the transistor under his overcoat.

The film offered plenty of action. But the dialogue was even more captivating. Most of us knew stretches of it off by heart, but we wanted to hear it all the same.

'There's only one guy who's the brains of this outfit, and that's me.'

'All these barbarians are under my command.'

'No shooting till I say so.'

'Friends, Romans, countrymen, lend me your ears . . .'

Suddenly a roaring noise from Mzal' uJola's overcoat. It was Lloyd Price's hit song, 'Personality'.

I dug my elbows into his ribs but only met with layers of cloth.

There was an uproar of hisses, catcalls and invective from the audience.

'Switch off that blerry gramophone.'

'Who's that f . . . m . . . ?'

'What are you up to?' Soso asked.

'Switch off that thing,' I whispered through clenched teeth.

He fumbled with the radio. I grabbed it and promptly switched it off.

'Mzala, please give it to me. I was going to insert the thing of the ear,' he said.

'Don't give it to him,' Soso said. 'Ufun' ukusibethisa ngabantu? Hoekom het ek die spy hier gebring?'

I kept the transistor. At the end of the film, not long before the lights came on, I walked out to wait for them outside. I didn't care to be identified with a chap who played a radio during a film show.

My father had several outstations, mostly on the mines. At Crown Mines there were several migrant labourers who came from Tsolo. My father knew many of these men, whom he introduced to Mzal' uJola. When he went to Crown Mines he always took Mzal' uJola with him. Among the old friends Mzal' uJola met were Hlubi and Mbele, his former classmates – they'd all left school after standard four.

During weekends Hlubi and Mbele sometimes visited Mzal' uJola, too, and took him to their favourite shebeens in the township where they drank mbhambha. But on most occasions it was my father who drove Mzal' uJola to Crown Mines, till he had learnt the way back home, more or less.

One Sunday they went to Crown Mines, as usual. Mzal' uJola asked my father to leave him behind. It was the first time he'd ever made such a request and so my father was worried. Hlubi and Mbele promised to take care of him and my father reluctantly left, alone. They remained drinking mbhambha until it was time for Mzal' uJola to return home. There was really no problem because the bus would drop him almost on our doorstep. They accompanied him to the bus-stop and pointed out the right bus to him.

Darkness was fast descending. Heavy smoke hung over the township like a canopy. In the bus Mzal' uJola had to keep his face glued to the misty window to be able to see outside. The bus was packed to capacity and Mzal' uJola was seated at the back. A group of Zionists returning from a baptismal retreat sang lustily and danced spiritedly along the length of the bus. When Mzal' uJola recognized the bus-stop nearest home the bus was already moving off. He edged his way to the front, over cursing folk's corns, through layers of human flesh, mostly feminine, until he reached the door. But by this time the bus had passed another stop so that he got off two stages beyond his intended alighting point.

To reach home he had to go through the shopping centre. Near the shops he heard someone saying, 'There's that Xhosa mampara,' but he took no notice. He began to sing softly to himself 'Ulo Thixo Omkhulu', a traditional hymn of praise.

A brick whizzed through the air, another found its mark. Mzal' uJola held his ribs in pain but walked on. He could hear the swift tread of footsteps retreating in the opposite direction.

Soso, coming from the shops, overheard a group of jubilant boys talking about how they had fixed that Xhosa mampara, but paid little attention. When he got home he found Mzal' uJola massaging his ribs in the privacy of the bathroom and asked him what had happened.

'Shh . . . Mzala.' He pulled Soso into the bathroom and shut the door. 'Don't tell anybody. I bumped into a brick.'

'Did you get beaten up by a group of boys near the shops?'

'How did you know?'

'I met a group of boys talking about someone they'd just fixed.'

'Mzala wam', if you know them, just take me to where I may lay my hands on them.'

'Hey, ndoda, I haven't as yet grown tired of eating sorghum in this world.'

Around this time Mzal' uJola struck up a few significant acquaintances, significant because they were later to turn into valuable allies. The first was Jikida, a sly man who could make his way out of a hungry crocodile's mouth with ease, a man of infinite resources and vast experience. He'd been a constable once, just in order to establish contacts with the police force. He also served two terms as a member of the township advisory board, during which period he made a small fortune by charging people who came to consult him, as though he were a lawyer. At the time when Mzal' uJola got to know him he described himself as a herbalist and a landlord.

Jikida came to our house to see my father on some business. He found my father out and decided to wait for him for a while. While he waited he began to chat with Mzal' uJola.

'D'you also stay here,' he asked.

'Yes,' Mzal' uJola replied. 'This is my uncle's place.'

'Have we met before?'

'No. I came here last Christmas.'

'Liphi ikhaya?'

'In the Transkei.'

'What part?'

It turned out Jikida was very familiar with Mzal' uJola's part of the Transkei, having himself trained at St Cuthbert's as a carpenter. He'd originally come from Cofimvaba more than twenty years before. His wife still lived there and occasionally came to Johannesburg 'to fetch a child'.

'You should visit me some day to see what we do in this land,' Jikida said.

'What do you do for a living?' Mzal' uJola asked.

'I'm what you might call a herbalist.'

'Oh! You're just the man who might help. I've a pain here that's causing me sleepless nights.' He pointed at his ribs.

'I know just the right ointment for you. Got it during my last visit to the zoo. There's nothing more potent than the waste matter from some of these strong, wild animals.'

A definite appointment was fixed.

Thereafter Jikida's house became Mzal' uJola's second home.

It was at Jikida's that Mzal' uJola met his first girlfriend, one of Jikida's tenants. Jikida occupied a four-roomed municipality house and rented three of the rooms to different families. He meddled with the feminine members of his tenancy more than was appreciated by their male counterparts. It was the unavailability of alternative accommodation which kept them at Jikida's.

Mzal' uJola's woman – her husband was actually a nightwatchman in town – was stout in a pleasantly feminine way and bowlegged. Her breasts were two watermelons and her buttocks gave an equally succulent and corpulent impression. Her dresses sat loosely on her like an eiderdown on a double bed.

Mzal' uJola slept out for the first time during this period, something which became a habit with him and drew an endless volley of curses from my mother.

'The first thing you'll learn here,' she said, 'is to choose your friends with greater circumspection. You'll find that out the day you and that Jikida of yours land in prison. I know of everything that goes on at that den of iniquity. Yours won't be the first corpse to be found in that yard.'

Although in slightly milder terms, my father also expressed his disapproval of Mzal' uJola's association with Jikida.

'One other thing,' my father added, 'you shouldn't move about the township so much. We're still trying to get you a pass. Don't spoil your chances at this stage.'

'One of these days he'll see for himself,' my mother said. 'He'll bump into Mawulawula and his police gang. Let him continue roaming the streets.'

It didn't happen as my mother had predicted. For one thing he wasn't roaming the streets but was actually in our yard, leaning against the gate and watching traffic, when a few policemen on bicycles stopped just opposite our house.

'Can you lend us some matches, mfowethu?' one of them asked.

'I don't smoke but I think I can get it for you from the house.' He disappeared into the house and came back with a box of matches.

The policemen remained on their bicycles in the street so that Mzal' uJola had to walk up to them to give them matches.

'Do you stay here?' asked the policeman who'd sent him for matches.

'Yes.'

'But I don't know you.'

'Let him produce his pass to prove it,' another policeman suggested.

'Where's your pass?'

'It's not here.'

'We can pull him in for failing to produce,' said the one with the bright ideas.

Mzal' uJola's trousers were now doing the jitterbug.

Another policeman put his bicycle down and approached Mzal' uJola with handcuffs. But before he could fasten them a second group of policemen appeared round the corner.

'Wenzeni?' one of them asked.

'He hasn't got a pass, sajeni,' the policeman with the handcuffs answered.

'Wait a minute, I think I've seen this chap before. Aren't you mfundisi's nephew?'

Mzal' uJola nodded.

'That's right, leave him alone, chaps. He's our mfundisi's nephew. Recently arrived from the Transkei?'

Mzal' uJola again nodded.

'Pasop,' the policeman with the handcuffs said. 'You must thank your stars for Sergeant Mawulawula's timely intervention. We don't want vagrants in this location.'

The other policeman gave him back the box of matches. They cycled away.

Mzal' uJola could never forget Sergeant Mawulawula. The longer he remained in our township the more his admiration for him increased. The sergeant was essentially a man of the world.

It was days before Mzal' uJola could summon enough courage to venture out of our yard. But even then he travelled with my father to Crown Mines.

Hlubi and Mbele had good news for him. They'd been talking to their foreman, a most understanding white man. There was a job he could get which didn't require him to carry a pass. They discussed the matter with my father who agreed that Mzal' uJola should take up the job.

Mzal' uJola thus started work on the mines as a compound cleaner. He stayed there and only came home over the weekend.

When he eventually got a pass he left his job at the mines and went to work as a hotel cleaner. He was later promoted to cook.

His pass gave him a sense of space. He refused to be confined to any one job, so that in his many years in the city he's worked as a doctor, a painter, a priest and a prophet.

He's been arrested and deported to the Transkei several times. Once the police managed to guard him as far as Bloemfontein. He came back to Johannesburg on a goods train.

These experiences have revealed rather more to Mzal' uJola than a landscape shows to a bat's eyes. 'Uvulekile manje', as everybody acknowledges: he's as wide-awake as an owl. He has remained in the township, where his wits have sharpened with exposure to the vicissitudes of life. What's more, he's lived so long under the shadow of the vagrancy laws, the Influx Control regulations and the rest that he has come to consider such hazards as a shield and an umbrella. I also happen to know that the twenty-third psalm is his personal favourite. He lives, as township folk never fail to point out, by 'Nkosi Sikelela'.

Two Sisters

» «

AHMED ESSOP

'When I want to baat den dey want to baat, when I want to go to lavatry den dey want to go also. Dey so shelfish in everything dey do. My stepmader and my fader dey jus lock demselves in de room, sometimes de whole day. I don't know wat dey do in dere. Dere is no food in de house and if dere is den we must cook. And den dey jus come out of dere room and eat all de food up.'

'Why didn't you speak to your father?'

'He don't listen to us since he marry dat woman. He very nice man, but when he marry dat woman all niceness disappear. She spoil him and he don't care for us anymore. Den I tell my sister Habiba we go away. Dat not true, Habiba?'

'It true.'

'A friend tell us dere's room in dis yard. Dat's how we come here.'

Rookeya was talking to me and my friend Omar. The two sisters caused a sensation the day they arrived to live in the yard. They wore robe-like dresses with ijars (trousers). But there was nothing unusual in this. What was unusual was the colour of their hair. It was dyed blonde. They looked rather odd as blonde hair did not accord with Eastern features. They were both very hairy and waged a constant battle with the hair on their faces. 'Their hairiness,' my friend Omar said, 'indicates that they are sweet-time girls.' Rookeya was in her thirties and Habiba a few years younger.

Before long a change occurred in their mode of dress. Either because of some feminine quirk or the dictates of fashion the two sisters shed their Eastern garments (much to the consternation of Aziz Khan) and began to wear Western clothing.

Soon Omar and I were making love to the two sisters. I took the younger, Habiba. There was no real selection on our part: we gravitated towards them and indulged in some light-hearted love-making.

I found Habiba to be a woman who performed everything in jerks, as though her body were a wound-up mechanical toy. Her very walk was jerky and toy-like. She would look left, then right, and now and then look back as though fearing pursuit. Her arms would be bent almost at ninety-degree angles and she would tread the ground as though she were treading on a spike bed. When I kissed her I had the queer sensation that I was kissing a mobile skeleton.

After some time Omar and I tired of the company of the two sisters. Free of us they hitched themselves to other men.

In the morning one saw them emerge from their apartment, sprucely dressed, and descend the stairs, Rookeya always preceding Habiba protectively. They would go to Main Road and take the tram to their place of work. Both sisters worked as shop-assistants. They would return in the late afternoon, prepare food, eat, wash the dishes, and dress, sometimes in shimmering saris, and wait. Invariably men would come for them and they would be driven away in cars.

The attitude of the women in the yard towards the two sisters varied between frigid contempt and outright hostility. The married men in the yard, watched by their wives, were unable to approach them, but the unmarried ones fluttered around them despite Aziz Khan's prophecy that the 'two sisters and their lovers would go hand in hand into hell'.

On Saturday afternoons or Sunday mornings the two sisters, dressed in short pants or brief skirts, could be seen leaning on the iron balustrade of the balcony, talking to a group of young men gathered below, and laughing with them whenever anyone made a risqué remark or cracked a joke.

And then, as anyone could have predicted, the two sisters were impregnated. At first they became alarmed and made random accusations. Omar was one of those charged by Rookeya as being responsible for her pregnancy.

She sent for me.

'Please tell Omar dat I pregnant and he fader of child. I marry him anytime. I frighten to tell him because he little bit young.'

'And how do you know?'

'We women we know who de fader. Is dat not so, Habiba?'

'It so.'

'Habiba, who is the father of your child?'

'He Hamid Majid of Newtown. He got shop.'

'And does he know?'

'I already tell him of baby, but he say he married and has six children. He say he look after baby.'

'You are lucky.'

'I also lucky,' Rookeya said, smiling.

I left to convey to Omar the allegation of paternity.

'How does that woman know that I made her pregnant?'

'Feminine intuition perhaps.'

'She thinks I am some stupid joker.'

Omar refused to face Rookeya. He feared that she might have some irrefutable evidence. What would his parents say? What would all the people say? Father of a harlot's child! He would be taunted by schoolchildren; his teachers would point him out as an example of degenerate youth.

After a few days he decided to face Rookeya and 'settle things' with her.

They quarrelled. There were 'tears, tantrums and hysterics' (according to Omar) but nothing was settled.

Rookeya sent for me again.

'Tell Omar it my baby. I make it and no man make it. Tell Omar I love him and he not worry.'

'But surely the child must have a father?'

'My child need no fader. It glad it has no fader, it tell me so. I feel it inside me, telling me so. My own fader not care for us, derefore my baby need no fader.'

'And Habiba?'

'Habiba also not worry about fader of baby. Dat not true, Habiba?'

'It true.'

And as the days passed the two sisters' wombs swelled. This provoked the anger and outraged the sense of morality of the people in the yard.

'Fine example they set our young girls,' said Mrs Musa to my landlady. 'Can't they see I have growing girls.'

'Lucky I got no girls to worry about.'

'I must tell my husband to do something. I cannot go on living alongside two pregnant unmarried women. And my eldest daughter is so friendly with them.'

Mrs Cassim, who was half-Chinese, said: 'My mother used to tell me that in China unmarried girls never become pregnant.'

'Yes, that is true,' agreed Halima, the Malay woman. 'Even in Cape Town the women are better behaved. They go out with men but they behave themselves.'

'I wonder how they managed to get pregnant together,' said Mrs Cassim.

'Perhaps one man sleep with both during the same night,' suggested my landlady, and for a moment the seriousness of the discussion was forgotten in laughter.

'They practise polygamy,' said Dorothy, the builder Solomon's wife, trying to raise another laugh.

'I beg your pardon, Mrs Solomon,' Mrs Musa retorted, annoyed that her religion should be misunderstood. 'That is not polygamy. They are not married to one man.'

Hajji Fatima, who had been to Mecca the previous year, stated that in an Islamic country such as Arabia the two women would be stoned to death.

'They should cut off their pudenda,' said Dorothy (she was an avid reader of cheap novels), and although no one had heard the word before they understood what she meant. But it was something too bloody to contemplate. There was something more decent and clean in stoning.

While other women talked, Aziz Khan's wife decided to act. One afternoon she glided out of her house, looked up at the apartment of the two sisters and stationed herself at the bottom of the stairs. Excitement flared through the yard and people gathered around her. When the two sisters arrived, she scrutinized their bulging bellies, spat and screamed: 'O Muslim women! O Muslim women! What have you done! What have you done! O Allah punish the women who call themselves Muslims and sin before you. O Muslims! O how you have fallen!'

And she fell down and wept. The two sisters looked at her in fear, hurried up the stairs and locked themselves in their apartment.

There was something so tragic in Mrs Khan's performance that gloom spread through the yard. Children were constantly reminded to keep quiet. People would emerge from their houses and look at the apartment of the two sisters as though something tragic was happening in there.

Aziz Khan, a whipcord-lean man in oversized clothing with the face of an overfed baby, said to us: 'If I had the time I would write a book on the nefarious activities of the two sisters. They pre-eminently exemplify the moral degeneration into which present-day Muslims are falling. They should be locked up in prison and starved to death.'

When someone suggested that they were not wholly responsible for their pregnancies, he answered: 'Are you suggesting that they were unable to guard their most sacred private places? Islam would never have attained its ineffable heights if it had allowed its daughters to run wild, to indulge in all sorts of acts of concupiscence.'

After a few months the two sisters gave birth to two girls.

There was much talk in the yard about the birth of the babies. Some felt sorry for the babies and wished to adopt them; others suggested that they be given to the carnivores in the zoo; others wanted to set fire to the apartment.

Aziz Khan felt that the time had come for action and that the two sisters and their babies should be 'ousted' from the yard. 'For their continued residence is a threat to the moral fibre of the people living in the yard and a blot on the fair name and fame of our religion and our holy Prophet.'

First he went to the gangster Gool, approaching him at his house immediately after noon prayers on Friday. But Gool, perhaps more interested in satisfying his hunger or finding moral talk odious, briskly disposed of him, shutting the door contemptuously.

His next call was on Molvi Haroon, priest at the Newtown mosque and head of the Islamic Academy. Abdulla, a disciple of Aziz Khan, accompanied him and gave us the following account of the interview: 'Aziz informed the Molvi of the serious moral problem facing us, and do you know what he said? He said that the punishment of the two women rested in the hands of Allah! Aziz, incensed at his cowardly fence-sitting, called him a "stupid dwarf". The Molvi grabbed his staff and Aziz thrust his left fist at him. I dragged Aziz out of the house.'

Aziz Khan's next call was on Mr Joosub, the landlord of the tenements in the yard. Mr Joosub was an eccentric who was always clad in koortah (white cotton smock), even on cold days. His head was always shaved and his beard bushy and long. He was obsessed by religion and would pray to Allah anywhere, even at street intersections. Once during the festival of Eid he came into the yard with a monkey. The monkey had a tasselled red fez strapped to its head. 'This monkey Muslim! This monkey Muslim!' he shouted to the spectators, especially directing his remarks to the servants. 'But you no Muslim, you no Muslim.' Then he scattered handfuls of coins – which turned out to be cents.

Mr Joosub expressed his willingness to oust the 'two bitches' from the yard. He would do so personally. He was king of several backyards in Fordsburg and would not tolerate the presence of 'bitches' on his domains.

He came one Sunday afternoon in his chauffeur-driven Mercedes. He stood at the foot of the stairs leading to the apartment of the two sisters and made several threatening pugilistic gestures. Excited people gathered around him. He struggled up the stairs, breathing hard and clutching the railing. When he reached the landing he paused to rest for a few minutes. The sisters were standing near the doorway. First he approached Rookeya and smacked her resoundingly on the cheek, shouting, 'Pig! Bitch! Pig!' in Gujarati. Habiba, who tried to escape past him, received a blow on the head. She fell and nearly came tumbling down the stairs. Mr Joosub then entered the apartment. The two sisters, shivering with fright, went towards the door to see what he would do next. Soon he appeared in the doorway, holding a primus stove in his hands, the brass contraption glinting in the sunlight, and he flung it over the railing. It fell with a clanging sound and several parts were shattered by the impact. Next a chair came hurtling down, followed by a pot and a bath. Other household articles followed in quick succession as the mania for destruction gripped Mr Joosub: crockery, linen, clothing. The two sisters, frightened, impotent, watched through the doorway as their landlord entered the apartment and gave way like marionettes as he emerged with some article.

Then, suddenly, Rookeya and Habiba screamed as Mr Joosub appeared in the doorway, holding one of the infants. They flung themselves on him. Mr Joosub tried to fend them off with one hand, while with the other he clutched the screaming infant.

At this stage Solomon made his way through the crowd and climbed the stairs. When he reached the landing he gently pushed the sisters aside, held Mr Joosub by the neck, shook him, took the infant and gave it to its mother, then gave Mr Joosub a hard push against the door-frame so that his face bumped painfully against it. Retaining a firm hold of Mr Joosub he dragged him down the stairs. When they reached the ground the crowd gave way for them and the children burst into applause. Solomon conducted Mr Joosub to his Mercedes, opened the door and without any ceremony pushed him into the car. The chauffeur, knowing his cue, reversed the car out of the yard and drove off.

We didn't see Mr Joosub again for some time. But the sisters decided it was dangerous living in premises belonging to a madman. They found another apartment in Newtown and moved away.

A Strange Romance

» «

ACHMAT DANGOR

Although it is November, the August winds still blow strongly. One's eyes burn like warm pee, and there is nothing to do. Especially on Sundays. Except get drunk on the watery (doped?) brandy which is all that the shebeen has left in stock, and shelter from this damnable wind. And avoid that new priest. Blerrie busybody. Always poking into the affairs of others, young as he is.

Intervening in perfectly normal and legitimate marital quarrels, as if there aren't nosy people digging into our lives already.

Men from the Department of the Interior. 'What was your father? And his father's father's father's . . .' Oh, we are still a mixed community. Well, you know, white and black. Never made any difference to us.

'We want you people to live in decent homes. Get you out of these slums.'

'Thank you for your blerrie kindness, sir, but the sun still rises over Beit Street.'

Oh ho! Here he comes. Slip-slap.

The priest, decorated like a corpse, black and white, with a deadly earnest expression. His pants, regulation Roman Catholic issue, a few folds too large, clap in the wind as he walks.

Slip-slap, slip-slap.

He pauses here and there to deliver a terse admonishment to some blushing victim who has absented himself from the early morning Mass. Although he was an assistant priest at the Saratoga Avenue Cathedral – a huge place as churches go, with a congregation of thousands – Father Stanley knew almost every one of its Doornfontein congregants.

Such was his dedication, Blerrie Bible-drunk zealotry, if you ask me. Never bothers with the fish-and-chips belt in Hillbrow, where you are likely to find thousands of Latin immigrants, piety dripping from their iconed noses. Just we happy half-castes and down-at-the-soul whites. For every sinner a saviour.

Anyway, here he comes, walking hastily across and glancing from side to side, even though there isn't a damn car in sight. George, who works night shift replacing the street bulbs that his and our children destroy during the day, warily observes the priest's progress. George continues cleaning his nails with an over-large 'apple-knife', his hooded eyes watching to see if Father Stanley has any intention of stopping at their gate.

'Arra! Here he comes!' George whispers to his wife and hastily retreats indoors. George's spouse rises from her recliner like a rocket, in spite of her burden of huge, rolling thighs. She makes it indoors, bumping and painfully scraping herself. 'Eina, die blerrie hond!'

Father Stanley stands sombre and sad where the woman has, a moment ago, abandoned her beer. He shakes his head and continues his journey, leaving George's gate open behind him. George emerges from the house and cautiously peers at the priest's receding figure before shutting the gate with a vehement curse.

Father Stanley judiciously skirts the corner of Beit Street and Sivewright Avenue, where a group of young 'ouens' are indulging in their favourite sport, innocent but raucous molesting of anything in a skirt.

'Hey, look at that lekker boud!'

He now approaches the section of Sivewright Avenue where the last of the great terraced houses stand. Crumbling, seedy reminders of the heady age of Barnato and of Cecil Rhodes, ghosts of opulence and shameless pleasure.

Five sleepy whores relax on the terrace of a once-magnificent mansion. The top part of the house is boarded up. A skull-and-crossbones presides over a chilling notice.

CONDEMNED. ENTER AT YOUR OWN RISK.

One of the whores, Marie, rises and runs an emaciated hand through her hair.

'Hey, here comes Father Stanley.'

Immediately a girl known only as Adele rises and, muttering to herself, goes indoors.

'Hey, Della, why are you running away?' Marie asks.

Susanna, a deep laugh already rising from her huge, heaving breasts, exclaims: 'Hey Della, I hear he asked you for a stukkie now the other day.'

'Haai voetsek,' Adele retorts from inside.

'Hey! Come and look at the party pants he's wearing today. Father, Father, when are your shoes going to invite your pants down for a party?' Marie says while the priest is still out of earshot. Her audience bursts into laughter.

Father Stanley, aware that he is the object of their mirth, greets the girls, and blushingly walks by, his head held a bit higher.

Now you must not get the impression that Doornfontein is infested with prostitutes or that it abounds with hoboes and other such prosaic flotsam of our national character, even though the venerable Father Stanley tripped over the outstretched legs of an inebriated layabout, this after lifting his eyes to heaven in embarrassment at being the butt of whorish laughter.

In the name of 'urban renewal' the city fathers had demolished our large houses, creating immensely overgrown lots that attracted these undesirables; dereliction invites derelicts.

Anyway, there lies Father Stanley, flat on his face, blood pouring from his nose.

The hobo shifts his legs and falls asleep again. Father Stanley manages to raise himself to his hands and knees, and begins to collect his dazed wits.

The whores, their natural sympathy for fallen people aroused, come to his aid. More precisely, it is Adele, who only a moment ago has spurned with curses the merest suggestion of any liaison with the priest, who now places her arm around Father Stanley and helps him to his feet.

Thus we all see him on this windy Sabbath, standing in Sivewright Avenue, his arms around the slimness of Adele the whore, his head resting on her shoulder.

We are a simple folk, not given to scratching beneath the surface. We accept things at face value. And Father Stanley's face is a picture of bloodied bliss. What's more, he is clutching *that* woman in broad daylight, and that, mister, is enough.

There is one perplexing question.

Why did Adele, who had fled indoors when the priest approached, subsequently dash past her colleagues to help him? Was there more to it than the eye could see? For the moment we do not know. We do know that right now she is plying her dubious trade outside Joubert Park, her merchandise bared for maximum exposure by a very tight and revealing dress. She walks, her arms draped around her slim, girlish body, inadequately braced against the merciless wind. Adele, although she has turned twenty-one only the year before, is already the mother of a five-year-old boy. Perhaps this is the reason for her affinity with Father Stanley. Perhaps his extreme sympathy for her recalls his own upbringing in these very same streets.

These are speculations unworthy of incurious people like ourselves. A hoer child is a hoer child, so what!

Right now the poor man is undergoing his own excruciating ordeal. Father Stanley foolhardily insists upon going through with the evening Mass, despite his obvious injury and discomfort. He now stands at the altar, uncharacteristi-cally nervous, delivering his sermon in a thick, hoarse voice, the obvious result of snot collecting within his extremely swollen snout.

The congregants from Hillbrow and elsewhere are sympathetic, but not Doory's folk. Oh, no! The upright members of our community, the business-men and professional people who inhabit the Smit Street periphery of our area, regard Father Stanley with glances of hostility. These dikbekke are invariably members of the parish council – a situation that we merest mortals allow by the default of our interest. Already they are planning Father Stanley's demise.

For our part, we also enjoy his predicament in the same way that we learn to laugh at our own. In any case, one of the young flerries remarked earlier that it was not natural for a man to deny himself the ecstatic pleasures that someone like Adele has to offer.

The young flerrie who lives up the road from Adele does not understand our admittedly sketchy explanation of Father Stanley's aesthetic calling, solemnly declaring, 'So what if he is a Catholic priest, he's got a tool, hasn't he?'

So the battle-lines are drawn – between those who believe that a priest, once he accepts his calling, must be above human reproach, and those who accept that such indiscretions are part of the human calling. No airy notions of justice and all that are involved. It is a simple case of whether to forgive him or not. We, on this side of Smit Street, will soon forget, and thereby forgive. But the dikbekke, they are out for blood.

'It is because he wanders the streets trying to save everybody.'

'Yes, he wants to be a saviour instead of doing his work as a priest.'

The ministrants of our moral law are hard at work. Father Stanley is rapidly disappearing from sight and, as is the woeful nature of man, disappearing from our memory. Our few and disinterested inquiries are easily satisfied.

'He has gone into seclusion.' Or, more succinctly, 'He is doing penance.'

The ageing Monsignor, who on the few occasions he has been seen has scarcely been able to keep his eyes open, does not want the burden of responsibility for the doings of a meddlesome priest. After all, the venerated old man is very close to retirement. He wants to keep Father Stanley on ice – the new Monsignor can de-freeze him if the young priest survives the hazardous task of searching his soul.

It was December. The August wind had finally subsided, or perhaps returned to its native Karoo – with our blessings. The gardens bloomed again, and the bougainvillaea that gnarls the house across the road gleamed with glorious green decay. So did the empty plots and their colonists, a one-armed or one-legged miscellany who returned each evening, gay-spirited after a day's successful begging in the city.

As Christmas neared, their opulence and numbers seemed to increase. The whores, too, were doing a roaring trade. The immigrant intake, it seemed, had improved dramatically.

But the days of Adele and her colleagues were numbered. A new Monsignor had been installed. The old one, with a weary sigh, had doffed the heavy burden of his cloak and returned to his native Ireland – there, the IRA permitting, to die in peace.

The new regional spiritual leader, a youngish man as priests go, ruffled his short-cropped hair and pronounced: 'We are not only here to minister to the healthy and the virtuous. We are here to bring back to the path those who have strayed. Sin and sinfulness are not irrevocable.'

This won't affect our lekkerhuis community, we thought. Prostitution is not a sin, it's a vice.

Little did we know our Monsignor. He walked about with the same urgent gait as Father Stanley, but with more expertise and poise. Then, as predicted, the volume of churchly work became too much for him. To the horror of the already disturbed dikbekke, he thawed out Father Stanley and sent him into the streets, armed with a licence to reform. Now the priest who once scrambled across empty streets and stumbled over sleeping hoboes entered the new year with a jauntiness in his step.

'You have a chance to redeem yourself in the eyes of the community. Work among those who have strayed from the path of decency. Save yourself,' he was told. And, out to save, Father Stanley was imbued with a fire that either cleanses the world or guts it.

He wandered in and out of the houses of decay, pleading here and praying there. He was seen at the police station putting up bail for prostitutes who had inadvertently sold their wares on the wrong side of the law. At hospitals he could also be seen whispering words of comfort to pale and fevered girls who had succumbed to the occupational disease of whores.

The whores regarded Father Stanley's efforts indulgently and did not spurn him, for he provided very real benefits. Little clubs where the children were entertained and cared for while their mothers 'went about their work' at night. He created a choir appropriately named 'The Angels of the Night' whose velvety sounds could be heard streaming like light into the dark streets.

Father Stanley was fond of one boy in particular – John, five-year-old son of Adele. The poor girl was in and out of hospital, her constitution not being robust enough for the rigours of her occupation.

The rains came. Wet and dirty. Loneliness flowed through the streets. The festive season was over. The revellers had gone back to their homes. Back to the security of inertia and normality. It was field season again for wives, and the whores were back to scratching (mostly each other) for a living.

The hours were longer, the police less indulgent, and the weather worsened. Winter came, cold and blustery. The gardens were dry, and the tree outside stood naked and without disguise.

Whores, like most people who are forced to live speculatively, are beset by superstition and petty phobias. Susanna, Marie and the others domiciled in Sivewright Avenue believed that Adele, because of her constant illness, was the root cause of their growing misfortunes. Police harassment was increasing and the exceptional cold weather kept the clients away.

'She's bad luck.' 'Because of her they think we've all got V D.'

Adele was therefore evicted from the house by majority consent. Not wishing to incur any further ill-luck, they mitigated their heartlessness by sending a message to Father Stanley. He found her and the boy shivering in a squatter colony whose inhabitants fixed beady, lustful eyes on the attractive young woman.

He led them back to their house, but despite his numerous pleas and threats, the other whores would not relent. They even barred Father Stanley from the house, thus depriving him of the greater portion of his congregation.

He walked the streets with the fevered woman, her son asleep in his arms. Finally, after resorting to tactics more strenuous than cajoling, he found temporary lodging for Adele and the child in a seedy boarding-house off Rockey Street.

'You come take her away tomorrow. I don't want thees badness in my house. I could lose my permit, you know. Thees is a white area.'

Father Stanley returned to his lodgings and spent a sleepless night racking his conscience whether to confide in the Monsignor and risk exposing the fact of his fragmented congregation. And the boy! They would certainly send him away. This would be extremely cruel to Adele who, in Father Stanley's opinion, had not many months to live.

Needless to say Father Stanley did not confide in his superior.

He returned to the boarding-house where an irate proprietor greeted him.

'Ah, Mr Priest, what kind of trouble you bring to my house? Thees girl she scream and shout all night like mad woman. Twice I had to silence her. She upset my other guests. The priest, he bring her here, I say to them, and I do not fight with priests. She is prostitute, they say. How I know collar make you priest, they ask. I do not know, I say. Now please Mr Priest, you tek away your friend, eh?'

Together they walked down the corridor. Doors creaked, eyes peered maliciously.

'I believe you are a priest, I tell them. How many of them they believe me? How many they will leave, eh? Now please you tek her away, eh?' Somewhere a cistern struggled and then gushed into life. 'If not for the boy I put them in the street last night. And because you are a priest.'

Father Stanley drew the curtains open. Pale sunlight filtered on to Adele's face. One look at her inflamed, sunken cheeks spurred the priest into action.

'Call a doctor.' He silenced the proprietor's protests with a curt wave of the hand. 'Here's the number. Tell the doctor Father Stanley asked you to phone. He must come at once!' he shouted after the cursing man.

The doctor fussed expertly about the girl while he clucked sorrowfully. Finally, after administering a fearsome-looking injection, he announced that she would live – for the moment.

'Father, whatever this girl's occupation, I do not want to know.'

'Shh!' he put his finger to his lips and silenced Father Stanley's attempt to explain. 'This VD is in an advanced stage. Get her to a hospital, and after that . . . Well, perhaps God knows? *You* ask Him.'

'How much . . . ?'

'You owe me nothing. Some services I render without payment. Perhaps you can pray for my soul.'

At the door the doctor stopped. 'Stanley, forgive me if I discard the "Father" for the moment. You are as old as my son, let alone my father. I've known you since you were a child. How come you became a priest? How come a priest in Doornfontein?'

'Fate. Fate and my mother.'

'Ah! Your mother. Well, goodbye, Father.'

The proprietor poked his head into the doorway expectantly.

Father Stanley had subsided. 'I'm sorry to be such a nuisance, Mr Patel, but we need an ambulance.'

'No, no, no! Ambulance brings people. They stare. They talk. That's no good for my reputation. Not so good for you too, eh?'

Father Stanley emitted a weary sigh.

'Look, Father,' Mr Patel said, imitating the doctor. 'I have a car, not too fancy, but it will get your friend to the hospital. She is your friend, no?' There was a wicked and warm gleam in his eye.

Outside it was raining; in Afrikaans it is called a 'motreën', a soft, unceasing downpour. Mr Patel hummed to himself as he steered the car through the narrow streets. Occasionally he glanced in his rearview mirror or at Father Stanley who cradled the sick woman's head in his lap.

He stopped at the hospital entrance, where Adele was lifted on to a stretcher. Father Stanley hastily deposited a handful of notes in Mr Patel's palm.

'Hey, Mr Priest.'

'Is that enough?'

Mr Patel shook his head sadly.

'It is too much. I have a conscience, Father, even though I am black. Besides, you are a priest. Good luck!'

Father Stanley spent the ensuing months caring for Adele's son and, unsuccessfully, attempting to rebuild his congregation. The fragile thread of allegiance that had bound him and the whores of Sivewright Avenue had snapped. For all their gaudy faces and other trappings of emotionalism, prostitutes are cynical people, and cynically believed that the priest's benevolence had a selfish intent – the possession of Adele.

'Got! If that blerrie priest wants a piece from that maargat, that's his business, but he mustn't come and preach to me!' said Susanna.

Father Stanley trudged through the streets of Doornfontein talking to every loafer he could find, to no avail.

'Hey! G'wan man, can't you leave a man in peace to drink liquor, heh?'

Each night he returned to the cathedral weary and disillusioned, not daring to confide his failure to any of his fellow priests for fear that the whole preposterous campaign would be abandoned. What would happen to Adele's child, and to Adele who was improving slowly, but steadily, in hospital? He believed that he was a source of comfort and strength to the woman. He had placed her son in a Catholic orphanage with an arrangement that nothing be reported to the authorities. This had cost him a great deal of wheedling and begging, and the major proportion of his measly stipend each month.

Father Stanley paid for his many deceptions with a tortured conscience. He prayed for hours on his knees, begging the Lord for forgiveness and guidance, and was rewarded with stiff and cramped limbs and such utter exhaustion that he was finally able to sleep.

The only glimmer of cheer in his life was provided by Adele's son, whose eyes had such a reckless glint that he charmed even the orphanage's austere Mother Superior.

Adele, now stripped of her garish and crusty prostitute's mask, was found to be quite an intelligent and decent woman. Almost daily he would sit and talk to her in the drab, whitewashed hospital ward. With childlike innocence he would make plans for her future. He had found a house for her and her child and he would find her a job. Breathlessly he fecundated his own mind with illusions and hope, while she lay still, pale and feckless, propped up on pillows, smiling beautifully at him.

What stirring times Father Stanley lived in. It was an age of prolonged agonies, prolonged August winds, prolonged winters, prolonged rains, prolonged and vain hopefulness.

Adele was discharged from hospital when the winter had ended, but summer had not yet come. Father Stanley and young John waited for her at the gate, their faces streaming with rain. How different she looked now! Without any make-up, without that shapeless hospital gown he had seen her in for three months. Her once girlish beauty had been melted down by her illness and had been transformed into a sculptured, emaciated loveliness.

A shadow of fear flickered across his mind, and Father Stanley expunged these wayward thoughts. He ushered the embracing mother and child into the waiting taxi and directed the driver to an address in Berea.

The wind, once again locked out of the Karoo, rattled the window panes in their wooden frames. Father Stanley and Adele had just had their supper. John was asleep in his own bed for the first time in his life. Adele's eyes moved about the small but neat cottage. She rose and embraced Father Stanley.

'I don't know how to thank you!'

In the beginning of his priestly days he had savagely suppressed any sensual desires. He would pay for one wayward thought by uttering a thousand 'Hail Marys'. Prayer and penance had quelled any further emotional riots. Thereafter his carnal instincts lay locked up within an iron box somewhere in his soul. Now, after ten years of festering and secret germination they seeped out of their iron prison and ran quiveringly through his veins.

'Father, you are hurting me.'

He raised his head from her shoulder and released her.

'Forgive me, forgive me.' Shame and anger in his scarlet face.

Adele looked in bewilderment at the red-faced, quivering priest.

'Stanley, Stanley, why didn't you tell me?'

She took his head gently and kissed him on the mouth, drawing his body close to her. Ten years of passion exploded in his pants.

Adele stroked his hair.

'There, there, I understand. It's been a long time. There will be another time.'

'No! No!' he screamed and collapsed with a heavy sob on to the couch.

Adele touched his shuddering back. He rose and, savagely pushing her aside, he fled. Father Stanley ran all the way back to his quarters as if pursued by the devil, the wasted semen wet and sticky in his pants.

For days thereafter he was observed scrubbing himself harshly with a brush used for scrubbing the vestry floors. His back was sore and lacerated, but he still persisted as if afflicted with a fatal and dire filth. He would lie completely naked on the floor of his room and pray incessantly.

The Monsignor, although fearing for the young priest's sanity, did not intervene. Whatever his transgression, he himself would have to devise his own penance and find forgiveness in his own way.

One day a fellow priest shook him from the stupor of the prayer he was incessantly intoning.

'Father Stanley, Father Stanley, there is a young boy to see you.'

Still dazed, he stumbled towards the garden, supporting his enfeebled legs by leaning against the walls of the corridor.

'John.'

'Hello Oomie.'

The child looked as dirty and as unkempt as ever.

'What are you doing here?'

'Came to see you, Oomie.'

'Why do you look like this? Where is your mother?'

The boy looked down shamefully and did not answer.

'Oh Lord, not again.'

Father Stanley had forgotten to pay the rent. They had probably been evicted. The rest was easy to guess. Adele had resumed her old profession.

'I haven't seen Ma for a week.'

Father Stanley washed and dressed hastily, restoring a modicum of composure to his gaunt, wild-eyed face. They searched the hospitals and police stations, and all the other familiar haunts, but there was no sign of Adele.

Wearily they returned to Father Stanley's quarters, where they had supper. The voracious manner in which his guest ate told Father Stanley of the boy's suffering, far more arduous and real than his own. He understood the real meaning of guilt.

Father Stanley sat outside his superior's office, the boy on his knee. Opposite him, stern in their black suits, sat a group of dikbekke. One of them paced up and down the corridor in creaking shoes.

Father Stanley understood why he had been summoned.

The door opened and the delegation entered the Monsignor's office.

'Oomie, why do they look so cross?'

'They are also in a kind of prison.'

'Oh.'

Outside the wind blew coldly, rain washed upon the window pane. Tears on a painted cheek, like the surface of a wound. A man walked by, then stopped, peering in through the window. He desires this clammy warmth. Perhaps he too was sired by awkward fumbling in a lane. As mysterious and satisfying as rain on dry, virgin land. Now he shuffles his life away between Rockey, Beit and Curry Streets.

Father Stanley thought of his own beginnings here in these streets. There under a tree, perhaps, its leaves dripping with starlight and raindrops, an unknown man driven by the hunger in his loins sowed my seed. My mother a young servant from the unknown Karoo.

The door opened and the delegation swept out, smiling broadly, as if someone had slit their ungodly throats. 'Stormbloeding'. A remedy his forefathers in the Karoo had used to exorcize the devil from obsessed souls. The remedy was strong, too strong for the poor patient. But the devil, his powers of survival are remarkable. Here he walks now, complete with black suit, his shoes creaking down the corridor.

'Oomie, I'm raining wet.' Ping, pang the rain resounded on the low roofs around them.

'Why did you not confide in us?'

'I confided in God.'

'Father! You border on the blasphemous!'

'No, it borders on me!'

'You are disturbed, my son?'

'No more and no less than the world. No more than the seeds in me.'

'They know that you are coloured.'

'I never denied it, and life is discoloured.'

'Do not play with words, Father. They used it to get rid of you.'

'I am not rid of myself.'

'And the woman?'

'She is a woman. A fallen angel.'

'The child?'

'He is my memory.'

'Father Stanley, have you sinned?'

'With my first cry, and my last.'

The Road to Migowi

»«

KEN LIPENGA

At Chitakale the bus, although already packed to capacity, picks up a few more passengers and continues on its way. The road is wet and a persistent March rain hammers gently but endlessly upon the roof of the bus. Outside, the already ripe maize in the fields stands listless, intoxicated by too much rain. The rainy season, dark, long and heavy, is coming to an end, and soon people will be harvesting.

But neither the muddy road nor the approaching harvest presents anything new or interesting to me. For nine years I have been a bus conductor, and there is no reckoning how many times during those nine years I have been on the road. Whether it is the rainy season as now, or a dusty September afternoon, or a cold June morning, it is all the same to me.

I always – invariably – wish for one thing only: to get to the end of the journey as quickly as possible. And somehow my wish never seems to be granted. I feel as though I have always been assigned to this same route every day since I started work. I swear I know the life history of every bridge, every stone and every tree on the road from Limbe to Migowi. My past is on the road, so is my present, and I can hardly imagine a future away from this road, the road to Migowi and back to Limbe, and back again to Migowi . . .

I find little pleasure in thinking about my past before I became a conductor. I know I once had a father and a mother. We once lived in a little hut on one of the large tea estates in Mulanje. But of this part of the past there remains in my memory only something vague and fluid like a dream. My father died when I was a little boy, having been bitten by a snake while working on the plantation. My mother lived on, selling kachasu to see me through primary school. Having completed that task, she then drank herself to death just the day I was going home with my first pay. The piece of cloth I had brought for her chirundu was used to cover her coffin.

I also had an elder brother who went to work in the mines in South Africa.

At first we used to write each other; then my brother stopped answering my letters and I gave up writing him.

The bus stops at one of the many stages, and I loudly ask if there is anyone getting out here. There is no answer, so the driver starts his engine and the bus moves on. But a moment later someone rings the bell and again the bus stops.

'I'm dropping here,' says a man rising up from a seat not far away from me.

Several passengers loudly voice their anger, addressing some unprintable words to the man as he struggles his way to the exit. I say nothing to him and as a result some of the ugly words are hurled at me too.

Before I became a conductor I worked as an assistant in the laboratory of a tea research station. My job was to sit all day and record the readings of a strange and complicated machine which, I was told, measured the brownness of made tea. I never got to understand the significance of those readings, let alone how the machine arrived at them, but my boss repeatedly assured me that my job was of great importance in the advancement of tea. I did not understand this either, although it gave me some pride to know that I was making a contribution to some great cause. However, I quickly grew tired of sitting at the same spot and recording the same figures day after day. The monotony of it all threatened to drive me mad, and I quit the job after only a year. 'I want an interesting job,' I told my friends as I left. 'I'm going to be a conductor; there is variety there, different people, different places every day.'

The bell once again rings and the bus stops for some passengers to get off.

'I have a bicycle on the roof-rack,' says one of those getting out.

'And I have a bag of maize,' says another.

I swear I know the reason why I am growing so thin: my ears have grown tired of hearing such things. I have heard them hundreds, no, thousands, of times, and I always pray for the day when the passengers will be considerate enough to spare me those words.

The bus has reached the worst part of the road and is moving at a walking pace. The driver swings it from one side of the road to another as he tries to keep to the less muddy parts. Many a time the wheels sink deeply in, and all the passengers have to help in pushing the bus out.

'I wonder what time we'll get to Migowi,' I say aloud without meaning to.

The driver, hearing me, guiltily looks at his watch and says: 'By five o'clock we should be there.'

The driver is a very old man, has been a driver for over thirty years, and has long passed retiring age, although all attempts by the National Transport Company to get him to retire have failed. No one understands why this queer old man, who is said to be very rich, prefers hardship to the comfort of resting at home, although I suspect that he will die the moment he is taken off the road.

Behind the steering wheel he looks graceful and vigorous, yet in his eyes one sees a being already touched by the tentacles of decay, a being kept alive only by the road. Wrenching him off the road will be like forcing him into a coffin before his death.

The bus lurches violently and is on the point of upsetting. There is a steep ascent uphill through the slippery clay. Several rivulets gurgle down the winding ditches where the water has gnawed the road.

'Everyone come out and push . . .'

It seems to me that not only the driver, but all the passengers I have met are sustained by the road. The road has done to them something from which they can never recover. This thought provokes pity in me, but also causes me much discomfort.

I became a conductor in order to escape from boredom, to run away from the cold impersonality of a machine that measured the brownness of made tea. But after nine years I do not find much variety in the brownness of men. Indeed it seems to me that these are the same passengers I set out with from Limbe that rainy morning nine years ago.

That rude talkative man at the back has been on that same seat since nine years ago, and he is still recounting the story of his success with some business. So too that other man near the window, who smokes all the time while insisting that all the windows be closed. That crying child seems never to grow up. And there is that fat woman, who cleverly pushes off everyone attempting to share the seat with her . . . Yes, these are the same passengers, and it is same road, the same journey without end.

'Everyone come out and push!'

The rain continues to fall and the driver keeps swinging from one side of the road to another, to avoid the muddy puddles. The bus groans continuously, as if complaining against the appalling state of the road, or against the weight of its load, which remains the same in spite of the passengers getting off. This bus is always packed, the passengers seem to multiply all the time.

At Kambenje the bus stops to pick up a few rain-soaked passengers. Among them is a man wearing a tattered yellow raincoat. I eye him intently as he enters. Yes indeed! My father! My father had just that hardened look on his face, just that slight stoop resulting from his tea picking. And with incredible distinctiveness, for the first time in these nine years, there arises before me a vivid picture of my father, my mother, my brother, our little house on the tea plantation, the avocado and pawpaw trees in front of the house, the red roof of the factory in the distance and the black smoke coming out of it, everything to the last detail.

I hear the singing of the workers as they pick tea leaves in the fields. I see them in their coarse yellow raincoats, with the bamboo baskets flung on their backs. I feel now as I felt then: admiration for these labourers who, with their songs, make toil and hardship seem so charming and attractive. A feeling of joy suddenly overcomes me. I move over to where the man is standing and pat him in ecstasy.

'Father!' I exclaim, and I feel the tears coming out of my eyes. I turn and smile at everyone in the bus, and I see my joy reflected on all the faces around me. Oh, what a beautiful world! The spattering of the rain on the roof and the groaning of the engine are transformed into sounds of joy, the old man at the steering wheel has become the very incarnation of happiness. The voices of the passengers and the continuous crying of the child combine to fill me with intense and extraordinary pleasure.

'Father!'

So my father and mother have never died after all, my brother has never had to go to South Africa, and I myself have never had to record the readings of a machine that measures the brownness of tea . . .

But suddenly the driver puts on the brakes, the bus violently jerks to a stop, and all the standing passengers fall over one another. I try to steady myself by holding on to the man I had called my father, but the man himself is already falling and he pulls me down with him. Everything in my dream vanishes, and I feel as though I am returning from the dead as I and the man I had called my father help each other to our feet.

'Everyone get out and push.'

The bus has once again got stuck in the mud; the two front wheels have sunk so deep that it is going to take hours before we can continue.

'By seven o'clock we should be at Migowi,' says the driver, when we have eventually succeeded in pulling the bus out.

Once those words had the effect of reassuring me. But now as I hear them I feel cold all over. The prospect of arrival has now begun to frighten me. I say nothing, and instead look at the ripening maize outside.

The Slow Sound of His Feet

» «

DAMBUDZO MARECHERA

> But someday if I sit
> Quietly at this corner listening, there
> May come this way the slow sound of his feet.
> – J. D. C. Pellow

I dreamt last night that the Prussian surgeon Johann Friedrich Dieffenbach had decided that I stuttered because my tongue was too large; and he cut my large organ down to size by snipping of chunks from the tip and the sides. Mother woke me up to tell me that father had been struck down by a speeding car at the roundabout; I went to the mortuary to see him, and they had sewn back his head to the trunk and his eyes were open. I tried to close them but they would not shut, and later we buried him with his eyes still staring upwards.

It was raining when we buried him.

It was raining when I woke up looking for him. His pipe lay where it had always been, on the mantelpiece. When I looked at it the rain came down strongly and rattled the tin roof of my memories of him. His leatherbound books were upright and very still in the bookcase. One of them was Oliver Bloodstein's *A Handbook on Stuttering*. There was also a cuneiform tablet – a replica of the original – on which was written, several centuries before Christ, an earnest prayer for release from the anguish of stuttering. He had told me that Moses, Demosthenes and Aristotle also had a speech impediment; that Prince Battus, advised by the oracle, cured himself of stuttering by conquering the North Africans; and that Demosthenes taught himself to speak without blocks by outshouting the surf through a mouthful of pebbles.

It was still raining when I lay down and closed my eyes, and I could see him stretched out in the sodden grave and trying to move his mandibles. When I woke up I could feel him inside me; and he was trying to speak, but I could not. Aristotle muttered something about my tongue being abnormally thick and hard. Hippocrates then forced my mouth open and stuck blistering substances to my tongue to drain away the dark fluid. Celsus shook his head and said: 'All that the tongue needs is a good gargle and a massage.' But Galen, who would not be left out, said my tongue was merely too cold and wet. And Francis Bacon suggested a glass of hot wine.

As I walked down to the beerhall I saw a long line of troop-carriers drawn up at the gates of the township. They were all white soldiers. One of them jumped down and prodded me with his rifle and demanded to see my papers. I had only my University student card. He scrutinized it for such a long time that I wondered what was wrong with it.

'Why are you sweating?' he asked.

I took out my paper and pencil and wrote something and showed it to him.

'Dumb, eh?'

I nodded.

'And you think I'm dumb too, eh?'

I shook my head. But before I could finish shaking my head, his hand came up fast and smacked my jaw. I brought up my hand to wipe away the blood, but he blocked it and hit me again. My false teeth cracked and I was afraid I would swallow the jagged fragments. I spat them out without bringing up my hand to my mouth.

'False teeth too, eh?'

My eyes were stinging. I couldn't see him clearly. But I nodded.

'False identity too, eh?'

I had an overwhelming desire to move my jaws and force my tongue to repeat what my student card had told him. But I only managed to croak out unintelligible sounds. I pointed to my paper and pencil which had fallen to the ground.

He nodded.

But as I bent down to pick them up, he brought up his knee suddenly and almost broke my neck.

'Looking for a stone, were you, eh?'

I shook my head and it hurt so much I couldn't stop shaking my head any more. There were running feet behind me; my mother's and my sister's voices. There was the sharp report of firing. Mother, struck in mid-stride, her body held rigid by the acrid air, was staring straight through her eyes. A second later, something broke inside her and she toppled over. My sister's outstretched hand, coming up to touch my face, flew to her opening mouth and I could see her straining her vocal muscles to scream through my mouth.

Mother died in the ambulance.

The sun was screaming soundlessly when I buried her. There were hot and cold rings around its wet brightness. My sister and I, we walked the four miles back home, passing the Africans Only hospital, the Europeans Only hospital, the British South Africa Police camp, the Post Office, the railway station, and walked across the mile-wide green belt, and walked into the black township.

The room was so silent I could feel it trying to move its tongue and its mandibles, trying to speak to me. I was staring up at the wooden beams of the roof. I could hear my sister pacing up and down in her room which was next to mine. I could feel her strongly inside me. My room contained nothing but my iron bed, my desk, my books, and the canvases upon which I had for so long tried to paint the feeling of the silent but desperate voices inside me. I stung back the tears and felt her so strongly inside me I could not bear it. But the door mercifully opened and they came in leading her by the hand. She was dressed in pure white. A pale blue light was emanating from her. On her slender feet were the sandals of gleaming white leather. But the magnet of her fleshless face, the two empty eye-sockets, the sharp grinning teeth (one of her teeth was slightly chipped), and high cheekbones, and the cruelly missing nose – the magnet of them held my gaze until, it seemed, my straining eyes were abruptly sucked into her rigid stillness.

He was dressed in black. Her fleshless hand lay still in his fleshless fingers. His head had not been sewn back properly; it was precariously leaning to one side and it seemed as if it would fall off any moment. His skull had a jagged crack running down from the centre of the forehead to the tip of the lower jaw; the skull had been crudely welded back into shape, so much so it looked as though it would fall apart any moment.

The pain in my eyes was unbearable. I blinked. When I opened my eyes they had gone. My sister was standing in their place. She was breathing heavily and that made my chest ache. I held out my hand and touched her: she was warm and alive and her very breath was painfully anxious in my voice. I had to speak! but before I could utter a single sound she bent down over me and kissed me. The hot flush of it shook us in each other's arms. Outside, the night was making a muffled gibberish upon the roof and the wind had tightened its hold upon the windows. We could hear, in the distance, the brass and strings of a distant military band.

Sunlight in Trebizond Street

» «

ALAN PATON

Today the Lieutenant said to me, *I'm going to do you a favour*. I don't answer him. I don't want his favours. *I'm not supposed to do it*, he said. *If I were caught I'd be in trouble.* He looks at me as though he wanted me to say something, and I could have said, *that'd break my heart*, but I don't say it. I don't speak unless I think it will pay me. That's my one fast rule.

Don't you want me to do you a favour? he asks. *I don't care*, I said, *if you do me a favour or you don't. But if you want to do it, that's your own affair.*

You're a stubborn devil, aren't you? I don't answer that, but I watch him. I have been watching Caspar for a long time, and I have come to the conclusion that he has a grudging respect for me. If the major knew his job, he'd take Caspar away, give me someone more exciting, more dangerous.

Don't you want to get out? I don't answer. There are two kinds of questions I don't answer, and he knows it. One is the kind he needs the answers to. The other is the kind to which he knows the answers already. Of course I want to get out, away from those hard staring eyes, whose look you can bear only if your own are hard and staring too. And I want to eat some tasty food, and drink some wine, in some place with soft music and hidden lights. And I want . . . but I do not think of that. I have made a rule.

How many days have you been here? I don't answer that, because I don't know any more. And I don't want Caspar to know that I don't. When they took away the first bible, it was 81. By an effort of will that exhausted me, I counted up to 105. And I was right, up to 100 at any rate, for on that day they came to inform me, with almost a kind of ceremony, that duly empowered under Act so-and-so, Section so-and-so, they were going to keep me another 100, and would release me when I 'answered satisfactorily'. That shook me, though I tried to hide it from them. But I lost my head a little, and called out quite loudly, 'Hooray for the rule of law.' It was foolish. It achieved exactly nothing. After 105 I nearly went to pieces. The next morning I couldn't remember if it were 106 or 107. After that you can't remember any more. You lose your certitude. You're like a blind man who falls over a stool in the well-known house. There's no birthday, no trip to town, no letter from abroad, by which to remember. If you try going back, it's like going back to look for something you dropped yesterday in the desert, or in the forest, or in the water of the lake. Something is gone from you that you'll never find again.

It took me several days to convince myself that it didn't matter all that much. Only one thing mattered, and that was to give them no access to my private self. Our heroic model was B. B. B. He would not speak, or cry out, or stand up, or do anything they told him to do. He would not even look at them, if such a thing is possible. Solitude did not affect him, for he could withdraw into a solitude of his own, a kind of state of suspended being. He died in one such solitude. Some say he withdrew too far and could not come back. Others say he was tortured to death, that in the end the pain stabbed its way into the solitude. No one knows.

So far they haven't touched me. And if they touched me, what would I do? Pain might open the door to that private self. It's my fear of that that keeps me from being arrogant. I have a kind of superstition that pride gets punished sooner than anything else. It's a relic of my lost religion.

You're thinking deep, said Caspar, *I'll come tomorrow. I expect to bring you interesting news.*

Caspar said to me, *Rafael Swartz has been taken in.* It's all I can do to hide from him that for the first time I stand before him in my private and naked self. I dare not pull the clothes round me, for he would know what he had done. Why doesn't he bring instruments, to measure the sudden uncontrollable kick of the heart, and the sudden tensing of the muscles of the face, and the contraction of the pupils? Or does he think he can tell without them? He doesn't appear to be watching me closely. Perhaps he puts down the bait carelessly, confident that the prey will come. But does he not know that the prey is already a thousand times aware? I am still standing naked, but I try to look as though I am wearing clothes.

Rafael Swartz. Is he brave? Will he keep them waiting 1,000 days, till in anger they let him go? Or will he break as soon as one of them casually picks up the poker that has been left carelessly in the coals?

He's a rat, says Caspar. *He has already ratted on you.* I say foolishly, *How can he rat on me? I'm here already.*

You're here, Caspar agreed. He said complainingly, *But you don't tell us anything. Swartz is going to tell us things that you won't tell. Things you don't want us to know. Tell me, doctor, who's the boss?*

I don't answer him. I begin to feel my clothes stealing back on me. I could now look at Caspar confidently, but that I mustn't do. I must wait till I can do it casually.

I don't know when I'll see you again, he said, quite like conversation. *I'll be spending time with Swartz. I expect to have interesting talks with him. And if there's anything I think you ought to know, I'll be right back. Goodbye, doctor.*

He stops at the door. *There's one thing you might like to know. Swartz thinks you brought him in.*

He looks at me. *He thinks that,* he says, *because we told him so.*

John Forrester always said to me when parting, *Have courage.* Have I any courage? Have I any more courage than Rafael Swartz? And who am I to know the extent of his courage? Perhaps they are lying to me. Perhaps when they told him I had brought him in, he laughed at them and said, *It's an old trick but you can't catch an old dog with it.*

Don't believe them, Rafael. And I shan't believe them either. Have courage, Rafael, and I shall have courage too.

Caspar doesn't come. It's five days now. At least I think it's five. I can't even be sure of that now. Have courage, Rafael.

It must be ten days now. I am not myself. My stomach is upset. I go to and fro the whole day, and it leaves me weak and drained. But though my body is listless, my imagination works incessantly. What is happening there, in some other room like this, perhaps in this building too? I know it is useless imagining it, but I go on with it. I've stopped saying, *Have courage, Rafael,* on the grounds that if he has lost his courage, it's too late, and if he hasn't lost his courage, it's superfluous. But I'm afraid. It's coming too close.

Who's your boss? asks Caspar, and of course I don't reply. He talks about Rafael Swartz and Lofty Coombe and Helen Columbus, desultory talk, with now and then desultory questions. The talk and the questions are quite pointless. Is the lieutenant a fool or is he not?

He says to me, *You're a dark horse, aren't you, doctor? Leading a double life, and we didn't know.*

I am full of fear. It's coming too close. I can see John Forrester now, white-haired and benevolent, what they call a man of distinction, the most miraculous blend of tenderness and steel that any of us will ever know. He smiles at me as though to say, *Keep up your courage, we're thinking of you every minute of the day.*

What does Caspar mean, my double life? Of course I led a double life, that's why I'm here. Does he mean some other double life? And how would they know? Could Rafael have known?

Can't you get away, my love? I'm afraid for you, I'm afraid for us all. What did I tell you? I can't remember. I swore an oath to tell no one. But with you I can't remember. And I swore an oath that there would never be any woman at all. That was my crime.

When I first came here, I allowed myself to remember you once a day, for about one minute. But now I am thinking of you more and more. Not just love, fear too. Did I tell you who we were?

Love, why don't you go? Tell them you didn't know I was a revolutionary. Tell them anything, but go.

As for myself, my opinion of myself is unspeakable. I thought I was superior, that I could love a woman, and still be remote and unknowable. We take up this work like children. We plot and plan and are full of secrets. Everything is secret except our secrecy.

What is happening now? Today the major comes with the lieutenant, and the mere sight of him sets my heart pounding. The major's not like Caspar. He does not treat me as superior or inferior. He says *Sit down*, and I sit. He says to me, *So you won't co-operate.* Such is my foolish state that I say to him, *Why should I co-operate? There's no law which says I must co-operate. In fact the law allows for my not co-operating, and gives you the power to detain me until I do.*

The major speaks to me quite evenly. He says, *Yes, I can detain you, but I can do more than that, I can break you. I can send you out of here an old broken man, going about with your head down, mumbling to yourself, like Samuelson.*

He talks to me as though I were an old man already. *You wouldn't like that, doctor. You like being looked up to by others. You like to pity others, it gives you a boost, but it would be hell to be pitied by them. In Fordsville they thought the sun shone out your eyes. Our name stinks down there because we took you away.*

We can break you, doctor, he said. *We don't need to give you shock treatment, or hang you up by the feet, or put a vice on your testicles. There are many other ways. But it isn't convenient. We don't want you drooling round Fordsville.* He adds sardonically, *It would spoil our image.*

He looks at me judicially, but there's a hard note in his voice. *It's inconvenient, but there may be no other way. And if there's no other way, we'll break you. Now listen carefully. I'm going to ask you a question.*

He keeps quiet for a minute, perhaps longer. He wants me to think over his threat earnestly. He says, *Who's your boss?*

After five minutes he stands up. He turns to Caspar. *All right, lieutenant, you can go ahead.*

What can Caspar go ahead with? Torture? for me? or for Rafael Swartz? My mind shies away from the possibility that it might be for you. But what did he mean by the double life? Their cleverness, which might some other time have filled me with admiration, fills me now with despair. They drop a fear into your mind, and then they go away. They're busy with other things, intent on their job of breaking, but you sit alone for days and think about the last thing they said. Ah, I am filled with fear for you. There are 3,000 million people in the world, and I can't get one of them to go to you and say, *Get out, this day, this very minute.*

Barbara Trevelyan, says Caspar, *it's a smart name. You covered it up well, doctor, so we're angry at you. But there's someone angrier than us. Didn't you promise on oath to have no friendship outside the People's League, more especially with a woman? What is your boss going to say?*

Yes, I promised. But I couldn't go on living like that, cut off from all love, from all persons, from all endearment. I wanted to mean something to somebody, a live person, not a cause. I am filled with shame, not so much that I broke my promise, but because I couldn't make an island where there was only our love, only you and me. But the world had to come in, and the great plan for the transformation of the world, and forbidden knowledge, dangerous knowledge, and . . . I don't like to say it, perhaps boasting came in too, dangerous boasting. My head aches with pain, and I try to remember what I told you.

You are having your last chance today, says Caspar. *If you don't talk today, you won't need to talk any more. Take your choice. Do you want her to tell us, or will you?*

I don't know. If I talk, then what was the use of these 100 days? Some will go to prison, some may die. If I don't tell, if I let her tell, then they will suffer just the same. And the shame will be just as terrible.

It doesn't matter, says Caspar, *if you tell or she tells. They'll kill you either way. Because we're going to let you go.*

He launches another bolt at me. *You see, doctor, she doesn't believe in the cause, she believes only in you. Tomorrow she won't even do that. Because we're going to tell her that you brought her in.*

Now he is watching me closely. Something is moving on my face. Is it an insect? or a drop of sweat? Don't tell them, my love. Listen, my love, I am sending a message to you. Don't tell them, my love.

Do you remember what Rafael Swartz used to boast at those meetings in the good old days, that he'd follow you to hell? Well, he'd better start soon, hadn't he? Because that's where you are now.

He takes off his watch and puts it on the table. *I give you five minutes*, he said, *and they're the last you'll ever get. Who's your boss?* He puts his hands on the table too, and rests his forehead on them. Tired he is, tired with breaking men. He lifts his head and puts on his watch and stands up. There is a look on his face I haven't seen before, hating and vicious.

You're all the same, aren't you? Subversion most of the time, and women in between. Marriage, children, family, that's for the birds, that's for our decadent society. You want to be free, don't you? You paint FREEDOM all over the damn town. Well you'll be free soon, and by God it'll be the end of you.

Lofty and Helen and Le Grange. And now Rafael. Is there anyone they can't break? Does one grow stronger or weaker as the days go by? I say a prayer for you tonight, to whatever God may be . . .

Did I say Rafael's name? I'm sorry, Rafael, I'm not myself today. Have courage, Rafael. Don't believe what they say. And I shan't believe either.

5 days? 7 days? More? I can't remember. I hardly sleep now. I think of you and wonder what they are doing to you. I try to remember what I told you. Did I tell you I was deep in? Did I tell you how deep? Did I tell you any of their names? It's a useless question, because I don't know the answer to it. If the answer came suddenly into my mind, I wouldn't know it for what it was.

Ah, never believe that I brought you in. It's an old trick, the cruellest trick of the cruellest profession in the world. Have courage, my love. Look at them out of your grey honest eyes and tell them you don't know anything at all, that you were just a woman in love.

Caspar says to me, *You're free*. What am I supposed to do? Should my face light up with joy? It might have done, only a few days ago. *Do you know why we're letting you go?* Is there point in not answering? I shake my head.

Because we've found your boss, that's why. When he sees I am wary, not knowing whether to believe or disbelieve, he says, *John Forrester's the name. He doesn't know what to believe either, especially when we told him you had brought him in. Doctor, don't come back here any more. You're not made for this game. You've only lasted this long because of orders received. Don't ask me why. Come, I'll take you home.*

Outside in the crowded street the sun is shining. The sunlight falls on the sooty trees in Trebizond Street, and the black leaves dance in the breeze. The city is full of noise and life, and laughter too, as though no one cared what might go on behind those barricaded walls. There is an illusion of freedom in the air.

The Butcher Shop

» «

SHEILA ROBERTS

I was maar walking up and down, sometimes on the sunny side of the street
and sometimes on the shady side. I would of stayed on the sunny side all the
time because there was this coldish May wind and our uniforms are not all that
thick hey, but I had to cross over to the shady side to check the meters there.
Ag it's not a bad job. It gives you time to do a bit of window shopping even
though you got no moela to spend with. And you get a chance to swot up the
people as they do what they got to do. You get the moerin with them though
too specially when they run up and put five cents in the meter just as you're
getting your pen ready to write out the ticket. I hate going back to the depot,
man, without a good cupla tickets. I think this maroon uniform suits me too.
It hides my big arse. Hennie said to me the other day, listen here Betty, either
you lose some of that weight you're carrying on your bee-hind or I'm cutting
out your usual Saturday night love-up. He was making a joke I know, but
still, I could see he was eyeing my arse as if he had just bitten off a piece of
dried bread that wouldn't mush up in his mouth. Actually, this walking
up and down should get some of the weight off, and I think the cap looks
jolly dee on my hair. At least there's no grey in my hair yet. Hennie has a
funny blob of grey at the back as if a pigeon shat on him from a dizzy
height.

So I was walking up and down when I saw him. He was locking his car at a
meter with still thirty minutes in it. I walked quickly up to him feeling a funny
kind of pleasure, you know that kind you get when it seems like Somebody-
up-there, God or whatever, is moving you and your old friends so that you
meet again after years.

'Chris Deventer!' I called as he was about to walk away. 'Howzit?'

He turned.

'Oh . . . hello,' he said.

'I haven't seen you for ages,' I said, smiling and taking him by the hand. I would of kissed him but he didn't bend as if he expected it. But his hand was warm, man, almost hot, and the palm was wet. He let my hand drop after giving it a sort of dishcloth touch.

'Ja, it's been a long time,' he said. Shading his eyes against the bright cool sun with the hand he had pulled away from mine, he added, 'I've got the hell of a bladdy hangover . . .'

'Let's get you a cuppa tea,' I suggested, still happy at the sight of him in his nice striped suit and a broad matching tie.

It was then that I noticed that the back seat of his car was stashed with suitcases and things thrown in, hats, jackets, books, a camera, binoculars or something, an old tennis racquet, and a portable record-player. And there were all his country-and-westerns in their old bright covers lying on the front left-hand seat.

We walked towards the tearoom.

'How you been keeping?' I asked, tugging at his arm like it was a bell-rope.

'Ag, man, okay . . . I . . . I just didn't get much sleep last night, so I'm . . .'

'Poeped out hey? Been painting ol' Pretoria all colours of red again hey?' I said, smiling up at him. Jesus, it's about twenty years ago now, but still he and his mates used to be wild ous when we were all at the Tech. It was one gewolt after the other, and the girls! Jissie but the girls liked them. Me too. But today he looked different. He didn't have that look I remembered of, you know, hey look at me, I've done it again, which he always used to have. He looked worried and maybe frightened, but I'm not sure of this. A ou with a hangover can look like a dozen things at once. You should see Hennie's face and he's got sweet fanny to worry about specially now that I got this job.

We took seats in a darkish corner of the tearoom and he told the waitress to bring black coffee for him and tea for me. I thought for a minute but shook my head when he offered me cake.

'You're looking well, Betty,' he said, really trying to make normal talk. 'How's Hennie?'

'Ag he's well,' I said. 'And how's Annetjie?'

'Well . . . you see . . . actually . . . she threw me out this morning . . .'

'Threw you out?'

'Ja, told me to bugger-off. So I packed my things.'

Then he did try to smile in his old fok-jou crooked fashion, but it didn't quite work. His mouth just stretched across his yellowish teeth (he smokes too much) in a stiff, corpsish way.

'What did you do this time?' I asked.

'Ag it's a long story . . .'

'And you don't want to tell me now, I suppose, what with a hangover and all,' I said, 'but I'm damn sorry . . .'

'You see, she just can't understand that a person just sometimes doesn't come home at night . . . you see. She just can't understand that. It's the way she was brought up, the church and all that. But sometimes a person *doesn't* come home at night . . . It can happen . . .'

He lit a cigarette in that lammetjie-lil sort of silence which happens when you're thinking of something intelligent to say to a man but as a woman you feel to yourself that he's a bladdy bastard anyway.

'Another cherry, hey?' I said at last.

'Ag Jesus, no! My days of keeping more than one woman happy at the same time are definitely over, Betty. I'm getting on, you know.'

So he did manage to grin at me in the ghost of his old way.

'No, it was something that happened in the *Office* . . .'

'Oh? Then for sure you won't want to talk about it!'

'Well you won't tell anyone, will you, Betty? You're still about the only woman I know who can keep a secret and who can suck . . .'

'Shut up, man,' I said, touching him lightly on the shoulder. But we had a good smile into each other's eyes and we both remembered certain things.

'Well, you see . . . it was like this . . . I shot up a butcher shop.'

'*What?*'

'Ja. I shot up this butcher shop . . .'

'Why? Why a butcher shop, for Chris' sake?'

'Man the butcher was there. He didn't mind.'

'But why? Why did you do such a stupid, gomgat thing?' I asked. 'Why a flipping, bladdy butcher shop?'

He looked at me and we both laughed a little but there was no warmth there I can tell you.

'It all started at the *Office*. As you know, Betty, the *Office* cares about one thing only, *one* thing, and that's total, but total efficiency. That's all they care about. Lately they been firing people. If *they* think you're not thinking the right way, their way, they fire you. Even if you're doing your job as best you can. You got to bladdy dream their way. The other day, a while back, they demoted an ex-Police Colonel! How about that? An ex-Police *Colonel*, and they set him in a back office and let him sort the post. A bladdy ex-Police Colonel!'

'Jis-like!' I whispered.

'Anyway,' he continued after he had let that sink in, 'you remember ol' Kees Brink? A fat, red-faced fellow, always busy laughing?'

'N-no . . . I don't think I remember him . . .'

'Man you do remember him. He was at the Police College with me after the Tech. He had this very light hair and a red face, and he was always sweating, poespiring, he called it. So someone nicknamed him Poes-Oom-Kees, and the name stuck. But he was really a lekker ou, and we stayed friends through the years, man, even though he went up higher than me. He wasn't stupid, even though you wouldn't think he was bright to look at him. But he made his matric at the Tech and then after Police College he joined the *Office*. Then they paid for him to go to university and he bladdy *passed* man, he passed and got his B. Mil. grade.'

'*B. Mil?*' I asked, not quite sure of what it was.

'Ja, *B. Mil.*, man.'

'Oh . . .'

'Anyway, yesterday morning he came into the *Office* as usual looking uitgepiets in a new suit, and his little bit of yellow hair brushed to one side, and a big grin on his bakkies. He came in making jokes and laughing, and just as he was taking this nice fresh clean hankie out of his pocket to wipe his forehead with, one of the clerks told him the big boss wanted to see him. So, still holding his hankie neatly in his hand, he walked off to see the big boss. Man, it wasn't ten minutes later when he walked back into our room, and that hankie of his was screwed up into a tight wet ball in his right fist. Like this!'

Ol' Chris gripped his fist under my nose to show how Poes-Oom-Kees had screwed up his clean handkerchief. There were tears in ol' Chris's already red eyes.

'The hankie was in a tight wet ball,' he said again.

'Why?' I asked, but had guessed already.

'They'd fired him. They'd bladdy fired him!'

'Why?' I asked.

Just then the waitress brought our cups and pots, and milk in little jugs, and spoons and paper serviettes, and set them out so slowly as if they had been made of egg-shells while we watched in silence. Just like a native girl. When you want them to be quick, they take their time. When you want them to do something carefully, they make it a bladdy rush-job. As she walked away, Chris said as if he had finished his story: 'I'm beginning to get pissed off by the Afrikaner, you know. I don't even want to read Afrikaans stories any more.'

'But, *Here*, jong, you're an Afrikaner!'

'I'm still pissed off by them. Do you know what's happening?' he said, almost grinding his teeth, and turning towards me in his seat until I had leant right back and my head was touching the wall, pushing my cap all wrong. 'Do you know what's happening? There's the wipneus upper-class Afrikaner who only cares for money and all the goeters it can buy. They don't care for nothing else. The English in this country mean nothing to them, and the country means nothing to them. So what's left? Just all us other poephols, what they call the man-in-the-street. And *he* knows nothing. He knows nothing about what's going on. And then there's the *Office*. And, you know something else? All the ideas and . . . and ideals and things that men think up are just so much kak because, I tell you, other men just balls them up. I myself don't believe in *nothing* any more. Nothing. And I tell you they don't believe in nothing!'

'But how can you work for the Office if you don't *believe*? You must believe. They *must* believe in it. You'll be the next to be fired if they get the idea that you don't *believe*!'

'Ag they won't fire me. I'm not important. I'm a backroom boy. I just sort information and that. And I keep my big mouth shut. But let them fire me! They can fire me!'

He took a sip of his coffee with a lit-up look in his eyes as if he would enjoy smashing something.

'I don't believe in nothing any more,' he said again in a low voice. 'I won't even talk about politics and that shit with anyone any more. And I won't stick my neck out for nothing . . . maybe for a tjommie but not for any idea. I'll maar just go along without thinking, doing my job . . .'

'But how can you do your job without believing that it's importantish for us and the country? It doesn't make sense to me!'

'But, Betty, nothing makes sense. Life's just a bladdy pissing competition all the bladdy time.'

So we both sipped from our cups without talking for a while. I felt the donder-in for my old friend. I'm only fifty per cent Afrikaans and I never could get my pee in a froth about neither the Nats nor the Youpees, but ol' Chris always used to be so full of loyalty for his language and his country. He would have died for it and he would talk about it with his eyes shining (sometimes from too much brandy, but still shining). He used to say that if we had a united South Africa we could take on the whole bladdy outside world. He wanted the English in too and even maybe the coloureds.

I looked at him sideways. Ag, *Here*, the ou had aged. The skin round his eyes was like old leather and his neck had gone loose and soft over his collar. He was going bald and there was stripes of grey here and there. At least not one silly blob like ol' Hennie has. And they say you never find a bald-headed donkey, so it goes to show.

'So they fired ol' Kees . . .' I said.

'Yes,' said Chris. 'An' there he stood screwing his bladdy hankie up in his hand. And I knew what he was thinking. He was thinking, what am I going to tell the wife? What am I going to do tomorrow when everybody gets up to go to work an' I got no job to go to? And what am I going to do with a fokken *B. Mil.* now that the *Office* has thrown me out?'

'But why the hell did they fire him? Or don't you know?'

He turned to me again, forcing me back against the wall, and spread his hands out palms upwards as if begging me to be reasonable.

'Man, this is what they did to him. Listen . . .'

I was listening.

'They send him to university, okay? He gets his *B. Mil.* Okay. They give him a nice car and tell him to buy nice suits. They give him a briefcase. Then they send him out and tell him to catch communists. Now what bladdy experience has he had in catching communists? Nothing! No bladdy experience whatsoever. So, what does he do? He makes a bladdy balls up. He gets taken for a hell of a bladdy ride and led up all the bladdy garden paths by a group of students and then by a group of blacks. So? So they fire him!'

'So you felt bad and went and shot up this butcher shop hey?'

'Ja. But not immediately, of course.'

'What did you do?'

'Well when I saw his hankie screwed up in his hand like that, I said to Kees, I said, ag come old tjommie, let's go and get us a drink. So we left the office and went to the Columbus and sat there the whole day from when the bar opened. We were both getting nicely arseholes when this Greek, Costa Costakis, comes in. I know him. He owns a butcher shop and runs a poker school. Anyway, I called him to come and join us. It was Wednesday, so the lucky bugger had already closed his butcher shop by twelve and was free for the day. So the three of us sat drinking and talking shit and enjoying ourselves until they threw us out at midnight . . .'

'And you hadn't eaten a damn thing all day?' I asked, feeling slightly sick myself.

'Ag ja. They'd served us chips and peanuts and then we asked them to send us up some sausages from the kitchen. But still we were all three lekker canned. And we got talking about shooting at targets and how good we were, and so on. We were still talking about this when they threw us out, and on the way home we passed Costa's butchery, and he said he'd give us some biltong to take. We went inside and then Costa said that we could never ever shoot out the top layer of tiles along the one wall. They were those pretty blue tiles, old-fashioned sort of with a blue pattern . . .'

'And so?'

'I shot them. One by one. All the blue ones. Right out.'

'But wasn't it dangerous. I mean, don't the bullets sort of bounce and hit something else?'

'Ricochet? No. Not lead bullets. The tile shatters and the bullet just drops, you see.'

'I see.'

'You should've seen ol' Costa's face as I knocked off the tiles one by one. He thought I was too canned to aim. But not *me*!'

'And Kees? Did he also shoot at the tiles?'

'No. He just sat on the floor with his legs spread and his head hanging down. Every time I pulled the trigger, he called out *skiet hom dood*!'

Chris half laughed.

'And then, Chris?'

'I told Costa he had better take Kees home. I couldn't trust myself to drive. I got that sudden feeling I might pass out. I found my car, but when I got into it, I just fell asleep in it, and woke up at about six this morning. And the world sure looked shit grey, you know. No colour. Just grey buildings and grey roads and grey sky and grey everything. So I drove home . . .'

'Are you going to be in trouble with Costa for shooting out all the blue tiles?'

'Ag no. He gave me a nice big parcel of biltong when we left. I gave them all to Annetjie to prove to her that I hadn't been with another woman, but she just threw them all on the floor and I had to pick the lot up again.'

'She must of been upset. Any woman would be, you know, Chris.'

'Ag, kak, Betty! She's been married to me long enough to . . . to *know*. And we've all been under strain these last months. Since after the riots we've had such a lot of work . . . and they think we're just machines . . . not humans hey . . . an' when I walked in the house this morning, there was the same grey light shining through Annetjie's curtains, and she hadn't slept and looked grey and when she started yelling at me, and her pale blue dressing gown looked grey, I just hadn't the strength to argue with her. When she said I must pack and leave I went and pulled down the bladdy suitcases and threw my things into them.'

'And now?'

'Now what?'

'Where are you going to live?'

'I don't know. I'm still thinking . . .'

'I'd invite you to our place, but Hennie knows I was keen on you in the old days . . .'

'No, no, no . . .'

'And you haven't been back to the *Office* this morning?'

'No.'

'So that's two days you've missed work. What will *they* say to that?'

'Bugger them!' he said, downing the last of his coffee, but he said it sort of frightenedish.

'Chris,' I insisted, 'what will you do if they fire you?'

He leaned back in his chair, stretched out his legs, plunged his hands in his pockets and let his head fall forward thoughtfully.

'You're not trained for anything except the *Office* . . .'

'I was at the Police College, remember,' he said. 'I'll spend the rest of my days investigating (and he began ticking the items off on his fingers) theft off washing line, theft by garden-boy of empty Coca-Cola bottles, theft of kid's bicycle out of the driveway, arrest of Bantoes without passes, arrest of hoboes in parks, arrest of noisy Bantoes outside kaffees, and even helping ol' tannies across streets. That's what I'll do!'

I had to laugh.

'More coffee?' I asked.

'No thanks, Betty. I'd better start thinking where I'm going to live.'

'And I'd better go'n check the bladdy meters to see who needs a ticket.'

We got up. He paid the bill and we left the tearoom. I walked with him to his car, a fairly new Datsun but with many little dents in the bodywork, as if he didn't worry about it. I saw that his meter had expired, but it was just a passing glance.

'We must keep in touch,' he said as he opened his door, but I knew he didn't really mean it.

'Here, you better have this,' he said, putting a brown paper parcel into my hands. I could feel it was biltong.

'Thanks,' I said, glad at first. Then the thought flashed through my brain. What would I tell Hennie? A pile of biltong like that costs rands and rands. But ol' Chris was already reversing out of the parking bay. He waved at me.

'Tjeers!' I called back. 'Give my love to . . . to . . . the butcher shop!'

At the Rendezvous of Victory

» «

NADINE GORDIMER

A young black boy used to brave the dogs in white men's suburbs to deliver telegrams; Sinclair 'General Giant' Zwedu has those bite scars on his legs to this day.

So goes the opening paragraph of a 'profile' copyrighted by a British Sunday paper, reprinted by reciprocal agreement with papers in New York and Washington, syndicated as far as Australia and translated in both *Le Monde* and *Neue Züricher Zeitung*.

But like everything else he was to read about himself, it was not quite like that. No. Ever since he was a kid he loved dogs, and those dogs who chased the bicycle – he just used to whistle in his way at them, and they would stand there wagging their long tails and feeling silly. The scars on his legs were from wounds received when the white commando almost captured him, blew up one of his hideouts in the bush. But he understood why the journalist had decided to paint the wounds over as dog-bites – it made a kind of novel opening to the story, and it showed at once that the journalist wasn't on the side of the whites. It was true that he who became Sinclair 'General Giant' Zwedu was born in the blacks' compound on a white man's sugar farm in the hottest and most backward part of the country, and that, after only a few years at a school where children drew their sums in the dust, he was the post office messenger in the farmers' town. It was in that two-street town, with the whites' Central Hotel, Main Road Garage, Buyrite Stores, Snooker Club and railhead, that he first heard the voice of the brother who was to become Prime Minister and President, a voice from a big trumpet on the top of a shabby van. It summoned him (there were others, but they didn't become anybody) to a meeting in the Catholic Mission Hall in Goodwill Township – which was what the white farmers called the black shanty town outside their own. And it was here, in Goodwill Township, that the young post office messenger took away the local Boy Scout troop organized by but segregated from the white Boy

Scout troop in the farmers' town, and transformed the scouts into the Youth Group of the National Independence Party. Yes – he told them – you will be prepared. The Party will teach you how to make a fire the government can't put out.

It was he who, when the leaders of the party were detained for the first time, was imprisoned with the future Prime Minister and became one of his chief lieutenants. He, in fact, who in jail made up defiance songs that soon were being sung at mass meetings, who imitated the warders, made pregnant one of the women prisoners who polished the cell floors (though no one believed her when she proudly displayed the child as his, he would have known *that* was true), and finally, when he was sent to another prison in order to remove his invigorating influence from fellow political detainees, overpowered three warders and escaped across the border.

It was this exploit that earned him the title 'General Giant' as prophets, saints, rogues and heroes receive theirs: named by the anonymous talk of ordinary people. He did not come back until he had wintered in the unimaginable cold of countries that offer refuge and military training, gone to rich desert cities to ask for money from the descendants of people who had sold Africans as slaves, and to the island where sugar-cane workers, as his mother and father had been, were now powerful enough to supply arms. He was with the first band of men who had left home with empty hands, on bare feet, and came back with A K M assault rifles, heat-guided missiles and limpet mines.

The future Prime Minister was imprisoned again and again and finally fled the country and established the Party's leadership in exile. When Sinclair 'General Giant' met him in London or Algiers, the future Prime Minister wore a dark suit whose close weave was midnight blue in the light. He himself wore a bush outfit that originally had been put together by men who lived less like men than prides of lion, tick-ridden, thirsty, waiting in thickets of thorn. As these men increased in numbers and boldness, and he rose in command of them, the outfit elaborated into a combat uniform befitting his style, title and achievement. At the beginning of the war, he had led a ragged hit-and-run group; after four years and the deaths of many, which emphasized his giant indestructibility, his men controlled a third of the country and he was the man the white army wanted most to capture.

Before the future Prime Minister talked to the Organization of African Unity or United Nations he had now to send for and consult with his commander-in-chief of the liberation army, Sinclair 'General Giant' Zwedu. General Giant came from the bush in his Czech jeep, in a series of tiny planes from secret airstrips, and at last would board a scheduled jet liner among oil and mineral men who thought they were sitting beside just another dolled-up black official from some unheard-of state whose possibilities they might have to look into sometime. When the consultation in the foreign capital was over, General Giant did not fidget long in the putter of official cocktail parties, but would disappear to find for himself whatever that particular capital could offer to meet his high capacities – for leading men to fight without fear, exciting people to caper, shout with pleasure, drink and argue; for touching women. After a night in a bar and a bed with girls (he never had to pay professionals, always found well-off, respectable women, black or white, whose need for delights simply matched his own) he would take a plane back to Africa. He never wanted to linger. He never envied his brother, the future Prime Minister, his flat in London and the invitations to country houses to discuss the future of the country. He went back imperatively as birds migrate to Africa to mate and assure the survival of their kind, journeying thousands of miles, just as he flew and drove deeper and deeper into where he belonged until he reached again his headquarters – that the white commandos often claimed to have destroyed but could not be destroyed because his head-quarters were the bush itself.

The war would not have been won without General Giant. At the Peace Conference he took no part in the deliberations but was there at his brother's, the future Prime Minister's side: a deterrent weapon, a threat to the defeated white government of what would happen if peace were not made. Now and then he cleared his throat of a constriction of boredom; the white delegates were alarmed as if he had roared.

Constitutional talks went on for many weeks; there was a ceasefire, of course. He wanted to go back – to his headquarters – home – but one of the conditions of the ceasefire had been that he should be withdrawn 'from the field' as the official term, coined in wars fought over poppy-meadows, phrased it. He wandered about London. He went to nightclubs and was invited to join parties of Arabs who, he found, had no idea where the country he had fought for, and won for his people, was; this time he really did roar – with laughter. He walked through Soho but couldn't understand why anyone would like to watch couples making the movements of love-making on the cinema screen instead of doing it themselves. He came upon the Natural History Museum in South Kensington and was entranced by the life that existed anterior to his own unthinking familiarity with ancient nature hiding the squat limpet mines, the iron clutches of offensive and defensive hand-grenades, the angular A K Ms, metal blue with heat. He sent postcards of mammoths and gasteropods to his children, who were still where they had been with his wife all through the war – in the black location of the capital of his home country.

Since she was his wife, she had been under police surveillance, and detained several times, but had survived by saying she and her husband were separated. Which was true, in a way; a man leading a guerrilla war has no family, he must forget about meals cooked for him by a woman, nights in a bed with two places hollowed by their bodies, and the snuffle of a baby close by. He made love to a black singer from Jamaica, not young, whose style was a red-head wig rather than fashionable rigid pigtails. She composed a song about his bravery in the war in a country she imagined but had never seen, and sang it at a victory rally where all the brothers in exile, as well as the white sympathizers with their cause, applauded her. In her flat she had a case of special Scotch whisky, twelve years old, sent by an admirer. She said – sang to him – Let's not let it get any older. As she worked only at night, they spent whole days indoors making love when the weather was bad – the big man, General Giant, was like a poor stray cat, in the cold rain: he would walk on the balls of shoe-soles, shaking each foot as he lifted it out of the wet.

He was waiting for the okay, as he said to his brother, the future Prime Minister, to go back to their country and take up his position as commander-in-chief of the new state's Defence Force. His title would become an official rank, the highest, like that of army chiefs in Britain and the United States – General Zwedu.

His brother turned solemn, dark in his mind; couldn't be followed there. He said the future of the army was a tremendous problem at present under discussion. The two armies, black and white, who had fought each other, would have to be made one. What the discussions were also about remained in the dark: the defeated white government, the European powers by whom the new black state was promised loans for reconstruction, had insisted that Sinclair 'General Giant' Zwedu be relieved of all military authority. His personality was too strong and too strongly associated with the triumph of the freedom fighter army for him to be anything but a divisive reminder of the past, in the new, regular army. Let him stand for parliament in the first peace-time election, his legend would guarantee that he win the seat. Then the Prime Minister could find him some safe portfolio.

What portfolio? What? This was in the future Prime Minister's mind when General Giant couldn't follow him. 'What he knows how to do is defend our country, that he fought for,' the future Prime Minister said to the trusted advisers, British lawyers and African experts from American universities. And while he was saying it, the others knew he did not want, could not have his brother Sinclair 'General Giant' Zwedu, that master of the wilderness, breaking the confinement of peace-time barracks.

He left him in Europe on some hastily-invented mission until the independence celebrations. Then he brought him home to the old colonial capital that was now theirs, and at the airport wept with triumph and anguish in his arms, while schoolchildren sang. He gave him a portfolio – Sport and Recreation; harmless.

General Giant looked at his big hands as if the appointment were an actual object, held there. What was he supposed to do with it? The great lungs that pumped his organ-voice failed; he spoke flatly, kindly, almost pityingly to his brother, the Prime Minister.

Now they both wore dark blue suits. At first, he appeared prominently at the Prime Minister's side as a tacit recompense, to show the people that he was still acknowledged by the Prime Minister as a co-founder of the nation, and its popular hero. He had played football on a patch of bare earth between wattle-branch goalposts on the sugar farm, as a child, and as a youth on a stretch of waste ground near the Catholic Mission Hall; as a man he had been at war, without time for games. In the first few months he rather enjoyed attending important matches in his official capacity, watching from a special box and later seeing himself sitting there, on a TV newsreel. It was a Sunday, a holiday amusement; the holiday went on too long. There was not much obligation to make speeches, in his cabinet post, but because his was a name known over the world, his place reserved in the mountain stronghold Valhalla of guerrilla wars, journalists went to him for statements on all kinds of issues. Besides, he was splendid copy, talkative, honest, indiscreet and emotional. Again and again, he embarrassed his government by giving an outrageous opinion, that contradicted government policy, on problems that were none of his business. The Party caucus reprimanded him again and again. He responded by seldom turning up at caucus meetings. The caucus members said that Zwedu (it was time his 'title' was dropped) thought too much of himself and had taken offence. Again, he knew that what was assumed was not quite true. He was bored with the caucus. He wanted to yawn all the time, he said, like a hippopotamus with its huge jaws open in the sun, half asleep, in the thick brown water of the river near his last headquarters. The Prime Minister laughed at this, and they drank together with arms round one another – as they did in the old days in the Youth Group. The Prime Minister told him – 'But seriously, sport and recreation are very important in building up our nation. For the next budget, I'll see that there's a bigger grant to your department, you'll be able to plan. You know how to inspire young men . . . I'm told a local team has adapted one of the freedom songs you made up, they sang it on TV.'

The Minister of Sport and Recreation sent his deputy to officiate at sports meetings these days and he didn't hear his war song become a football fans' chant. The Jamaican singer had arrived on an engagement at the Hilton that had just opened conference rooms, bars, a casino and nightclub on a site above the town where the old colonial prison used to be (the new prison was on the site of the former Peace Corps camp). He was there in the nightclub every night, drinking the brand of Scotch she had had in her London flat, tilting his head while she sang. The hotel staff pointed him out to overseas visitors – Sinclair 'General Giant' Zwedu, the General Giap, the Che Guevara of a terrible war there'd been in this country. The tourists had spent the day, taken by private plane, viewing game in what the travel brochure described as the country's magnificent game park but – the famous freedom fighter could have told them – wasn't quite that; was in fact his territory, his headquarters. Sometimes he danced with one of the women, their white teeth contrasting with shiny sunburned skin almost as if they had been black. Once there was some sort of a row; he danced too many times with a woman who appeared to be enjoying this intimately, and her husband objected. The 'convivial Minister' had laughed, taken the man by the scruff of his white linen jacket and dropped him back in his chair, a local journalist reported, but the government-owned local press did not print his story or picture. An overseas journalist interviewed 'General Giant' on the pretext of the incident, and got from him (the Minister was indeed convivial, entertaining the journalist to excellent whisky in the house he had rented for the Jamaican singer) some opinions on matters far removed from nightclub scandal.

When questions were asked in parliament about an article in an American weekly on the country's international alliances, 'General Giant' stood up and, again, gave expression to convictions the local press could not print. He said that the defence of the country might have been put in the hands of neo-colonialists who had been the country's enemies during the war – and he was powerless to do anything about that. But he would take the law into his own hands to protect the National Independence Party's principles of a people's democracy (he used the old name, on this occasion, although it had been shortened to National Party). Hadn't he fought, hadn't the brothers spilled their blood to get rid of the old laws and the old bosses, that made them *nothing*? Hadn't they fought for new laws under which they would be men? He would shed blood rather than see the Party betrayed in the name of so-called rational alliances and national unity.

International advisers to the government thought the speech, if inflammatory, so confused it might best be ignored. Members of the cabinet and Members of Parliament wanted the Prime Minister to get rid of him. General Giant Zwedu? How? Where to? Extreme anger was always expressed by the Prime Minister in the form of extreme sorrow. He was angry with both his cabinet members and his comrade, without whom they would never have been sitting in the House of Assembly. He sent for Zwedu. (He must accept that name now; he simply refused to accommodate himself to anything, he illogically wouldn't even drop the 'Sinclair' though *that* was the name of the white sugar farmer his parents had worked for, and nobody kept those slave names any more.)

Zwedu: so at ease and handsome in his cabinet minister's suit (it was not the old blue, but a pin-stripe flannel the Jamaican singer had ordered at his request, and brought from London), one could not believe wild and dangerous words could come out of his mouth. He looked good enough for a diplomatic post somewhere . . . Unthinkable. The Prime Minister, full of sorrow and silences, told him he must stop drinking. He must stop giving interviews. There was no mention of the Ministry; the Prime Minister did not tell his brother he would not give in to pressure to take that away from him, the cabinet post he had never wanted but that was all there was to offer. He would not take it away – at least not until this could be done decently under cover of a cabinet reshuffle. The Prime Minister had to say to his brother, you mustn't let me down. What he wanted to say was: What have I done to you?

There was a crop failure and trouble with the unions on the coal mines; by the time the cabinet reshuffle came the press hardly noticed that a Minister of Sport and Recreation had been replaced. Mr Sinclair Zwedu was not given an alternative portfolio, but he was referred to as a former Minister when his name was added to the boards of multinational industrial firms instructed by their principals to Africanize. He could be counted upon not to appear at those meetings, either. His director's fees paid for cases of whisky, but sometimes went to his wife, to whom he had never returned, and the teenage children with whom he would suddenly appear in the best stores of the town, buying whatever they silently pointed at. His old friends blamed the Jamaican woman, not the Prime Minister, for his disappearance from public life. She went back to England – her reasons were sexual and honest, she realized she was too old for him – but his way of life did not recover; could not recover the war, the third of the country's territory that had been his domain when the white government had lost control to him, and the black government did not yet exist.

The country is open to political and trade missions from both East and West, now, instead of these being confined to allies of the old white government. The airport has been extended. The new departure lounge is a sculpture gallery with reclining figures among potted plants, wearily waiting for connections to places whose directions criss-cross the colonial North–

South compass of communication. A former Chief-of-Staff of the white army, who, since the black government came to power, has been retained as chief military adviser to the Defence Ministry, recently spent some hours in the lounge waiting for a plane that was to take him on a government mission to Europe. He was joined by a journalist booked on the same flight home to London, after a rather disappointing return visit to the country. Well, he remarked to the military man as they drank vodka-and-tonic together, who wants to read about rice-growing schemes instead of seek-and-destroy raids? This was a graceful reference to the ex-Chief-of-Staff's successes with that strategy at the beginning of the war, a reference safe in the cosy no-man's-land of a departure lounge, out of earshot of the new black security officials alert to any hint of encouragement of an old-guard white coup.

A musical gong preceded announcements of the new estimated departure time of the delayed British Airways plane. A swami found sweets somewhere in his saffron robes and went among the travellers handing out comfits with a message of peace and love. Businessmen used the opportunity to write reports on briefcases opened on their knees. Black children were spores attached to maternal skirts. White children ran back and forth to the bar counter, buying potato crisps and peanuts. The journalist insisted on another round of drinks.

Every now and then the departure of some other flight was called and the display of groups and single figures would change; some would leave, while a fresh surge would be let in through the emigration barriers and settle in a new composition. Those who were still waiting for delayed planes became part of the permanent collection, so to speak; they included a Canadian evangelical party who read their gospels with the absorption other people gave to paperback thrillers, a very old black woman dry as the fish in her woven carrier, and a prosperous black couple, elegantly dressed. The ex-Chief-of-Staff and his companion were sitting not far behind these two, who flirted and caressed, like whites – it was quite unusual to see those people behaving that way in public. Both the white men noticed this although they were able to observe only the back of the man's head and the profile of the girl, pretty, painted, shameless as she licked his tiny black ear and lazily tickled, with long fingers on the stilts of purple nails, the roll of his neck.

The ex-Chief-of-Staff made no remark, was not interested – what did one *not* see, in the country, now that they had taken over. The journalist was the man who had written a profile, just after the war: *a young black boy used to brave the dogs in white men's suburbs* . . . Suddenly he leant forward, staring at the back of the black man's head. 'That's General Giant! I know those ears!' He got up and went over to the bar, turning casually at the counter to examine the couple from the front. He bought two more vodka-and-tonics, swiftly was back to his companion, the ice chuntering in the glasses. 'It's him. I thought so. I used to know him well. Him, all right. Fat! Wearing suède shoes. And the tart . . . where'd he find her!'

The ex-Chief-of-Staff's uniform, his thick wad of campaign ribbons over the chest and cap thrust down to his fine eyebrows, seemed to defend him against the heat rather than make him suffer, but the journalist felt confused and stifled as the vodka came out distilled once again in sweat and he did not know whether he should or should not simply walk up to 'General Giant' (no secretaries or security men to get past, now) and ask for an interview. Would anyone want to read it? Could he sell it anywhere? A distraction that made it difficult for him to make up his mind was the public address system nagging that the two passengers holding up flight something-or-other were requested to board the aircraft immediately. No one stirred. 'General Giant' (no mistaking him) simply signalled, a big hand snapping in the air, when he wanted fresh drinks for himself and his girl, and the barman hopped to it, although the bar was self-service. Before the journalist could come to a decision an air hostess ran in with the swish of stockings chafing thigh past thigh and stopped angrily, looking down at the black couple. The journalist could not hear what was said, but she stood firm while the couple took their time getting up, the girl letting her arm slide languidly off the man; laughing, arranging their hand luggage on each other's shoulders.

Where was he *taking* her?

The girl put one high-heeled sandal down in front of the other, as a model negotiates a catwalk. Sinclair 'General Giant' Zwedu followed her backside the way a man follows a paid woman, with no thought of her in his closed, shiny face, and the ex-Chief-of-Staff and the journalist did not know whether he recognized them, even saw them, as he passed without haste, letting the plane wait for him.

MILK

» «

ELSA JOUBERT

TRANSLATED FROM THE AFRIKAANS BY MARK SWIFT

The man with dust embedded in the grooves of his face spoke slowly. Occasionally he ran a hand over his head in an attempt to flatten his sparse hair. The interpreter followed on the heels of his words, and someone – a reporter? – scribbled them down.

The words were dragged out of him. They couldn't get enough. At intervals he swallowed hard; then continued:

He had pressed his pistol against my temple. How he had come to be beside me in the car, I do not know. By then they had already dragged my wife from the car. He had said: Move and you're dead.

I did not hear her scream – or utter any sound. Behind me – the seats were folded down – the children slept.

I sat still. What could I have done? The barrel of the pistol was biting into my skin. When the second one took the pistol, he had slid a hand over the other's, squeezing his body in next to mine while the other edged out.

There was not a moment in which the barrel was not pressed against my temple. I think five or six of them raped my wife.

When they were finished with her, they wanted to leave her alongside the road. But I would not drive without my wife. We were part of a long convoy of cars which had ground to a halt, and I was delaying it.

They wrenched the door open again and flung her back into the car. Her hair hung loose, her bloodied lips were swollen. Her eyes wore a strange expression.

She attempted to rearrange her torn clothes, for she was raised very correctly. All she said to me was: Drive.

When I switched on the ignition, the convoy also began to move. I inched forward in first gear. Later, when we picked up more speed, I was able to change to second and then to third gear. In the distance – and directly behind us – I could hear gunfire, but we were not stopped again.

When we reached the South African border post, there was little delay. A young soldier with clean fatigues and a clean-shaven face merely waved us by and said: Don't stop driving, go through.

They spent that night in an emergency camp.

The military tents billowed in the darkness, the cars turned into the dusty tracks between the tents or were parked in the veld against the wire. There the couple made a bed and attempted to sleep. They lay between the wire and the car, on a thin mattress allocated them by the soldiers.

Tears ran down his cheeks as his hands traversed her body. She swept greying hair from her damp forehead and talked quietly to the man: Try to come to terms with it. It is past.

He entered her torn body as a man would enter his house after a fire had ravaged it.

Did he wish to heal her?

Or was it fear that he spilled? Or doubt, or guilt?

He discovered her condition three months later. He gazed at her as though he were weighing something up and said: You're expecting a child?

And later he asked: Is it my child?

How can I know? she replied.

For as long as she could, she concealed it, here in the new cottage in the new township, in the new country. In the mornings when the children had left for their new school, the man to his new job, she gave herself over to nausea. It was a relief to be alone, to be able to lean over the bowl and allow the sickness to well up. The nausea persisted, her body deteriorated; the foetus clung to her spinal column like an alien growth.

He took her to the maternity home and filled in the forms, printed the name of his wife: Maria Margarida da Silva. His name, the name of his new medical fund, his religious denomination.

Because she was no longer young, they wheeled her in carefully.

The delivery was not that difficult. The body, which had nurtured the growing child for nine months, thrust it out with ease. With relief? And when the child was brought to the woman and she identified it and saw it resembled her other babies in skin and features, she wept.

The other women in the ward with her uttered comforting sounds: her weeping was natural. They recognized in her a stranger, fearful after flight. Allow the tears to fall. One woman raised herself on an elbow, and with her emptied belly resting heavily on the bed assured her: It's nature's way of getting rid of excess water, those tears.

Maria Margarida da Silva took the newborn child they brought her into the curve of her arm. She unbuttoned the nightdress and the blue-tinged lips closed greedily on the nipple and began to suck. She felt the tugging at her nipple and also how the moistness, not yet milk but mother-fluid which made the child still part of the mother-body, was painfully wrung from the reluctant nipple. She looked down and saw a hand grope free from its wrappings and stray blindly about until it encountered the soft swell of her breast and clamped to it. The fingers clawed so tightly that the flesh ballooned between them. The tugging at her nipple was so insistent that the nerve-ends throughout her body were aware of it.

Only on the second day did she examine the child closely. It resembled her other two children; only the lips were thicker, slightly more pursed – or was it merely craving for milk? – a little boy, even when covered and satiated in his blankets, still purses his mouth for milk. The nose, also, was different, but not noticeably so, and what baby's nose is fully formed? Are not noses all created as finger-marks in unworked clay?

The hand folded over her fingers with a convulsive grasp. The child was reluctant to release her, even when the smiling nurse attempted to unlock the little hand with her strong fingers.

Such a grip. The child would make his mark.

On the third day the small face peering from its covers showed a dark tint, as though a shadow had fallen over it. Maria da Silva glanced at the window, but the blind was not drawn. She looked at her own hand, which held the child in the crook of her arm, but the shadow had not fallen over her skin.

The child drank. It felt as if every swallow drained the life fluid from her marrow, her bones, from her deepest recesses. She attempted to tug the child from her breast, but the lips clung.

When the young nurse came to fetch the child, she handled him in a curious manner, as though she were keeping him at a distance – or, dear mother of God, was it her imagination that had created the impression? Was there revulsion for the baby in her eyes?

Her husband had visited her on the night of the second day.

He did not talk much about the child.

Things are going well, he said. The house is better than the one in Portugal, even the one in Angola. They are using me to the best of my ability at the factory. In the department I work in now, I know as much as the cleverest among them. And they know it. They need people with my training.

She was pleased by his confidence. She thought of the night when he had probed her wounds, when he had driven his guilt into her, when tears had coursed from his eyes.

Now his cheeks were clean and his hands lay still on the coverlet, or occasionally grasped her arm. He had brought flowers for her.

And the children? she asked.

They are well. The school helps them, even with the language.

That's good, she said. He ran a clumsy hand over her head, stroking flat the greying hair.

When the child was brought to her on the fourth day, the colour of his little face was grey, like ash, and in the armpits and the soft folds of his skin, black.

The nurse carried the child to her without a word, and laid it at her side. With the new black shadow that had spread over the skin, the structure of the nose was more apparent. It was wide, broad-flanged, like that of the man who had dragged her from the car, while her husband sat with the barrel of a pistol against his temple.

The child's mouth searched greedily for her breast, and when he encountered the milkiness of the nipple it began to nibble, to search, to clutch. The first drops oozed, giving her immediate relief.

She held the child's nose between thumb and finger. The baby struggled. Who would have thought there was so much strength in the tiny body? The feet pounded in fury against her belly, the hands beat against her full breasts. The mouth left her nipple and fought for breath in open confusion. The milk he had been drinking ran in white beads from the corners of his mouth.

She pushed the blanket into his open mouth, and shoved it deeper and deeper.

She held it there until the kicking against her abdomen subsided, until the grip on her breast relaxed and the hands with the dark-shadowed fingers fell away from her.

She rang and rang the bell until the nurse at last arrived; then she said: The child suffocated.

The reporter wanted a story. He approached Maria da Silva in the room. The nurse is my girlfriend, he said. She told me there's a story.

She gestured with a hand: I don't understand you.

He attempted to indicate: The child at your breast . . . did you fall asleep? He folded his hands together, held them at an angle, leant his head against them to mimic sleep. Did you fall asleep and smother the child beneath your breast?

She nods. She is tired.

The people want to know, the reporter urges. They take an interest. Tragedy in the new country.

Tears stream over the cheeks of the woman lying in the bed, the white coverlet pulled up to her chin over swollen breasts. The tears collect in the corners of her eyes. Unattractive eyes, for they are wrinkled and old and tired and her hair is streaked with grey. They collect in the corners of her eyes and run in rivulets down her cheeks. She does not wipe them away.

Her arms lie wide and brown and stocky on the coverlet. The streaked hank of hair lies at her left side, like a dead, dark animal beside her.

How does it feel to have smothered your baby? the reporter asks. He is over-hasty, he fears that it will all come to nothing. I want a caption for the picture.

Then even he falls silent before the tears which flow from the woman's eyes, down her cheeks.

She gestures at her breasts. The moisture seeps through the nightdress.

What do I do with the milk? she asks wordlessly. Who do I feed with the milk?

Space Invaders

» «

PETER WILHELM

OBJECTIVE: To stay alive as long as possible.

SCENARIO: You are standing alone on Earth, defending your civilization against attackers from outer space. They continually descend towards you, making threatening noises. They all shoot at you, and one hit will destroy you. If you let any of the attackers reach Earth, the world is lost. Talk about responsibility.

Discovering the deserted city together had several effects and served various functions. The deeper they penetrated into the vast subterranean shopping complexes, the more distant grew the grinding sounds of the aliens' levelling machines, now entirely ringing the city and closing in.

The fact of enclosure seemed less claustrophobic underground. Not quite a paradox: the artificially lit enclaves and malls (with their treasures of jewellery, electronic equipment, scheduled drugs and paperback novels) were as open to their predatory expeditions as a forest to a Romantic poet.

It was a labyrinthine underworld there, with interconnecting passageways and acre upon acre of consumer splendour; the abandoned monuments of a vanished society. And, down there, their ancient antagonisms were muted: the harshness of their relationship abated.

Lynda loved expensive furs and modish clothing. There was something approaching exultation in the way she looted the boutiques, spending hours trying on dresses and gowns that in her previous incarnation she would have despised as bourgeois. Now that all that luxury was laid out before her, she took a remorseless delight in modelling the latest fashion – for herself; she was her only witness in the glittering salons, turning about and about to catch every angle of her gaudiness, diamonds and gold trinkets clustered over her like bright insects.

She spent hours like that, while Paul was elsewhere, playing Space Invaders, Pac-man, Stargate, Asteroids and Defender. He had moved the machines from an arcade in Commissioner Street, wiring them up in the lobby of the Carlton Hotel, near the glittering wreckage of the Clock Bar; and he spent much of his time feeding 20c. coins into the consoles, money that he filched from the tills of the silent banks and building societies.

Entranced by the video machines, Paul found a sense of human fulfilment he had never believed possible: certainly, it transcended the ambiguous pleasures of being a Professor of History.

There were moments when a furtive sense of duty crept in; the heritage, doubtless, of his puritan upbringing. At such times – usually in the evening, when he and Lynda had parted acrimoniously for the day, or he was bored by the challenges of the machines – he abstractedly made marks in notebooks with a Parker fibre-tip pen. Invariably, what began as notes on the end of the world turned into childlike depictions of naked women. Since he was not a proficient artist, and was in any case drawing from memory, the details were far from clear: dots for nipples, scribbles for pubic hair. They were neither satisfactory as pornography, nor anatomically correct. He no longer knew what women looked like without clothes.

But the idea that he should keep some kind of record lingered like an unprepared lesson, and he could not shake free of it. But then: a record for whom? The alien advance would finally engulf him, Lynda, the room, the paper: everything would go. Using a telescope from the observation post at the top of the Carlton Centre, he had witnessed the profound efficiency of the transformation process. The alien machines at the perimeter – resembling vast beetles the colour of anthracite – scooped up everything in their path, leaving behind them a totally flat plain, dark and etched with lines of obscure purpose. Dotted about the plain at the various intersections of the etched lines, mile-high monoliths appeared from time to time. They were utterly without ornamentation, their surface a grey reflecting abstraction.

There was no indication of the purpose of the monoliths, nor evidence of the aliens. Paul, in fact, had never seen an alien. The most he could record was that the grinding contraction never ceased, and that the structures of the city were remorselessly engulfed and transformed into the dark plain and the gleaming monoliths. Since the process began, an indeterminate period past, the sky had been a deep violet colour in which stars were visible: hard and distant in the day, pulsating closer and more diffuse at night. The sun transected the sky with extreme slowness, taking far longer than it should. There was no rational explanation for this.

Once, rebuffed by Lynda, Paul used a derelict police car to broadcast poetry down the echoing corridors of empty streets, flanked by the dull façades of office blocks:

> O waar sal jy gaan
> En met watter skip?
> Die aarde is branding
> En oral is klip . . .

The words were sucked into darkness.

He thought of women: they burned brightly in his mind. Each night he and Lynda spent the hours before sleep alone, eating tinned food separately in their hotel rooms. The lights worked. Indeed, all electronic equipment continued to work, suggesting that the aliens were permitting power to flow unimpeded into the city, even as the encirclement continued. Did this indicate a knowledge of survivors? It was pointless to speculate.

Paul had his own vanities: he had allowed his beard to grow; it was threaded with silver, and made him feel distinguished. A burly man in his late thirties, he began to take on the appearance of a Professor of History with a comfortable share portfolio on the side. Like Lynda – since it was all there – he chose the best clothes in the shops. But unlike her he did it quickly, like a thief, with the sense that he was being watched.

Lynda watched him.

If Lynda was dressing for herself, who was he dressing for? He dreamed he was in a fashion parade for the aliens; they applauded his taste; but he swiftly repressed this intimation of something essential.

Even with no one around – to him, Lynda was not around as a witness – the act of removing an article from a store and not paying for it troubled him, at first. Lynda laughed at his hypocrisy: 'If you want to pay, take the money from a bank, like you do for your kids' games!' The truth and absurdity locked in his heart and he explored further and further with Lynda during the day; so like children, together and apart, in a mansion that the adults have left unlocked.

One night he drank too much. Half a bottle of Chivas Regal. The whisky burned throughout all his flesh and he found himself pacing restlessly to and fro. Pieces of paper were scattered about the room: sketchy women, random scrawls, notes on the situation that parodied academic study. In fact, he decided, what he wanted was a woman. That meant Lynda: at least, he persuaded himself, that meant Lynda.

He left his room and made his way down the deeply-carpeted corridor, weaving slightly and muttering self-justifications to himself. He came to Lynda's room: No. 1313. He knocked loudly.

'Who is it?' Her voice was fearful.

He laughed, or began to laugh. 'Who the fuck do you think it is?'

'Paul? What do you want?'

'Open up,' he said. 'I want to talk to you.'

'No. You've been drinking. Go to bed.'

'Open up!' He banged more loudly on the door, feeling anger and a consummate coldness of vision overtake him. He felt himself programmed to take certain steps.

Lynda flung the door back and retreated, hostile; she had a German Puma knife in her right hand, the edge ragged for gutting fish. He went in, ignoring her – and found a chair. He lit a Camel cigarette and watched her reactions. How pleasant to reassert – what was the word? – strategies.

'So?' She was dressed in a silk affair, blue and threaded with vertical lines of gold; she could have been a Dior model. Her dark hair was tugged back. She was small, aggressive and suspicious.

'Why don't we call it off,' he said slowly. 'This . . . antagonism. We need each other. I want to,' he considered, 'go to bed with you.'

'No.'

'Why not?'

'We've been through this before. You're invading my space. I don't find you attractive. You remind me of my husband.'

In his whisky gaze she became two people, separated out like images on a screen. One would accept him, the other not. He felt the need to humiliate both: 'So you're keeping yourself pure for some goddamn thing with eight eyes and tentacles?'

'Don't be disgusting. We don't even know what the Martians look like.'

'They're not Martians. They're from Cygnus RX 175. A distant and inscrutable star.'

She laughed and poured herself a glass of wine, the finest Bordeaux red from the hotel's cellar. 'You're so funny sometimes. So pedantic.'

'It's my training.' He brooded. 'Has it ever occurred to you that we may be the last people left alive? That in these circumstances your resistance to me is an absurdity.'

'We're not the last people left alive,' said Lynda. 'The aliens transported the entire population of Hong Kong to Cygnus; in fact, they took the buildings as well, the racecourse and the stock exchange.'

'To be in a zoo,' he said ponderously. 'The question is: can people breed in captivity?' He rose to his feet. 'The issue of Hong Kong is irrelevant to us: we're *here*. To stay.' He advanced on her, his heavy form taking on the furtive slouch of the rapist. 'Come on,' he said, somewhere between plaintiveness and anger. 'Let's go to bed.'

'This,' she said, tapping herself, 'is private property. I belong to me. And if you try something, I'll kill you.' She raised the Puma knife. The serrated edge fascinated him. He was uncertain. She stepped near to him. *Whisk whisk.* The knife made an ugly sound as it cut through his Pierre Cardin shirt and into his flesh. He staggered backwards, holding his hands up, very afraid. A large amount of blood was coming out of him. *That's me*, he thought. *That's me spilling out.* The two images of Lynda had come together.

In his own room he found the wound to be superficial. But it was frightening to consider Lynda's intensity. She – both of her – would have done it. And in the distance, the grinding sounds of the aliens advancing. On and on. Day and night. The world was ending, as an afterthought.

Paul cleaned himself and had another drink. He took a lift down to the hotel lobby and played several games of Space Invaders to calm himself. Entranced by the machine, he fired at the alien craft, detonating the threat to Earth. It was his responsibility to defend his entire civilization.

He had played the video game so often that he could anticipate the machine's moves: when, for example, a new menace would suddenly appear, what action to take. But as his score mounted higher and higher, he found something wrong. The electronic rules appeared to be changing. There were new craft appearing on the screen – craft he had never seen before. They were hexagonal in shape and moved randomly. As soon as he shot one down, two appeared in its place; and there was a geometrical progression of menace too. He felt as he had, faced with Lynda's knife. *Christ*, he thought. *The coding's been altered. I have no control here.*

He lost the game and a message flashed on the screen: TOUGH SHIT BUDDY. GO FUCK YOURSELF. The lights in the lobby dimmed and he had the impression of silvery shapes scuttling in remote corners, or just beyond the edges of vision. Behind his head. It became imperative to return to his room.

Utterly defeated, far from calm, he pressed a button for a lift. It was a long time coming, and as he waited he became aware of a vibration in the floor. Something was underneath the hotel, burrowing.

A gleaming rigid rod exploded upwards from the lobby carpet; it sent lines of disruption from its nexus. To Paul the thing appeared to be spinning incomprehensibly fast. It made a sound like a dentist's high-speed drill. For several seconds it probed the room, then retracted. The underground vibration died away, but like a sound falling below the threshold of audibility; he sensed intricate, senseless processes going on below the surface.

The lift came and opened like a mouth. His palms were sweating as he entered and pressed the button for the thirteenth floor. The door shut. The lift did not move. He pressed the button again. Nothing happened. He pressed the 'door open' button and the elevator's doors half opened and stuck. He was no longer on the lobby level. Instead, he faced out at an obsidian wall that, to his gaze, appeared to writhe and pulsate. The inward-bulging shape might have been made of dense tar or wax. Intricate symbols advanced from right to left across his field of vision, changing form as if what he faced was a computer display. It was no lettering or symbol system he understood. He was struck hot and cold with fear and ran his hand down the entire line of buttons, pressing everything in sight. The doors closed with some difficulty; the lift ascended.

At room 1313 he pressed his palms against the wooden panel and rested his head for a few seconds. With his eyelids closed, he saw the moving incomprehensible lettering in reversed colours. 'Lynda –' he called. 'Let me in. The aliens are here.'

The serrated edge of the Puma knife burst through the door panels, very close to his left eye. He was aware of the extraordinary force she must have used to drive the thing through the wood. 'I know,' he heard her cold voice say. 'Go home to your distant and inscrutable star. Leave me alone.'

Lynda heard Paul's footsteps retreat and sat back in a chair, trembling. In her right hand she held the German Puma knife. For a moment she had been tempted to drive it through the door as a warning, something that would have come from her in pity and despair. But she could not do it: it would only add to his delusional state, his belief that she hated him, rejected him, wished to wound him.

Violence, she considered, was being done to both of them. More than enough. If he had ever listened to her, they might have been able to transform the bitterness of the past into, at least, a common front against the Enemy. But he had never listened; she had no way of knowing what went on in his mind.

She took some lipstick and applied redness to her mouth, watching herself in a mirror, watching the redness smudge and blur behind her tears. Her hands shook. Outside, the grinding sounds of the aliens' levelling machines continued remorselessly, day and night. 'Paul,' she whispered, 'Paul: come back to me.'

In his room Paul double-locked the door, searched the cupboards, looked under the sumptuous bed. The covers had been drawn back, as if by an invisible maid; but he was alone. He looked in a mirror and saw his face monstrously deformed. Yet it was him.

The bottle of Chivas Regal stood beside a television set. He drank directly from it, unconsciously switching on the set as he did so.

A face formed on the screen. That, he considered, should not be happening. The face was that of a middle-aged man with silver hair, the kind of face you could trust. 'Good evening,' it said. 'Here is the late news.

'The Greater Magellanic Cloud is receding from the Home Galaxy at a velocity of 0·0663% of the speed of light. It is not yet known whether the movement is due to the expansion of the universe, or whether it represents a localized turbulence in the fabric of spacetime.'

Paul switched off the set. He drank more Chivas Regal. Beside his bed was a telephone. He lifted the receiver and dialled 1313. Lynda answered: 'Who is it?'

'Me.'

'Yes?'

'I love you, I need you,' Paul said.

There was a long silence.

'Well,' Lynda said, 'why didn't you say that before?'

'It seemed somehow inappropriate and outmoded.'

'You don't want to hurt me?' asked Lynda.

'On the contrary. I want to cherish you.'

'Oh God, how wonderful: I've waited so long. I'll come to your room at once.'

She did not. Paul waited morosely, feeling distant from his emotions, for an indeterminate period. Then he examined the phone and found, as he had half known, that it was not functioning. The earpiece gave back to him an electronic howling sound, like a far wind, interspersed with shouts, instructions, and lamentations in a strange language.

He took his Parker fibre-tip pen and made marks on a white pillow: dots for nipples, scribbles for pubic hair. The blue ink sank into the cloth and smudged. Then he switched off all the lights except a night-light that burned mutely in a corner in the centre of a display of artificial roses. He lay in his tangled bed, in red comforting gloom, until Lynda appeared to be beside him.

Her appearance was like that of the separate image he had seen earlier: alternate, unknown, yet present.

She ran a finger down his chest to where she had cut him. 'Sorry about that. You left me no choice.'

'It doesn't matter.'

'Nothing matters when you think about it,' said Lynda dispassionately.

She was wearing diamonds, rubies, gold and silver that glinted in the red light.

'When you think about it,' he concurred. He took from her a golden necklace and held it to his breast.

Outside the shelter of the room, the grinding sounds of the aliens' levelling machines continued and the Greater Magellanic Cloud receded from the Home Galaxy, from Paul and Lynda, and from all the planet transformed into a vast barren plain with geometrical etchings and the mile-high monoliths that were the major art form of the aliens.

Notes on Contributors

» «

PETER ABRAHAMS (b. 1919) in Vrededorp, Johannesburg. One of the forerunners of the African writing renaissance of the post-Second World War period, his first novel, *Mine Boy* (1946), remains staple reading about black–white relationships in an urban-industrial society, and his *Wreath for Udomo* (1956) deals with Pan-Africanism post-independence. His autobiography, *Tell Freedom* (1954), vividly recounts his ghetto origins, his (almost self-) education and his ambivalent relationship to South Africa, from which he emigrated to the UK in 1939. 'Lonesome', which is from his first collection of sketches and stories, *Dark Testament* (1942), defines the alienated intellectual dilemma and much of the depressed political activism of the 1930s in Southern Africa. Since 1959 he has lived in Jamaica.

HENNIE AUCAMP; critic and cabaret writer; born in the Cape and lectures in education at the University of Stellenbosch. To date, he has published eight collections of short pieces in Afrikaans, 'Soup for the Sick' being from *Spitsuur* (*Rush Hour*), his second volume of 1967. Acknowledged as the leading exponent of short fiction in Afrikaans literature, his achievement shows a technical inventiveness and outspokenness with regard to the private aches of South African experience which is without equal in the language. This translation is from a selection of his work, *House Visits* (1983).

STEPHEN BLACK (1880–1931); Cape Town-born journalist and dramatist, whose satirical play of 1908, *Love and the Hyphen*, about how all the ethnic groups of South Africa could unite, ran in his own repertory company season after season until 1929. Between seasons Black founded many short-lived polemical weeklies, including the scurrilous *The Sjambok* in Johannesburg (1929–31) which, while exposing capitalist scandals, also was the first journal to publish black writers like R. R. R. Dhlomo in its columns. Black's career began as a sketch-writer for the *Cape Argus Weekly*, where 'The Cloud Child' first appeared in 1908 – he was firmly encouraged by Rudyard Kipling on a visit to Cape Town to pursue the 'local colour' line. During the First World War Black worked for the *Daily Mail* in London, reporting from Belgium and Holland. He was of the union school of writers who proclaimed themselves the first South Africans.

WILHELM H. I. BLEEK (1827–75); born in Berlin and trained there as a philologist; with Bishop Colenso sailed for Zululand in 1853 to compile a Zulu grammar. For Governor Sir George Grey in the Cape he acted as official interpreter and collected folk material, resulting in the first of many publications, *Reynard the Fox in South Africa: Hottentot Fables and Tales* (1863), from which come 'The Origin of Death', one of many versions of the Khoikhoi myth of mortality, and 'The Unreasonable Child'. The latter, classified by Bleek as a 'household tale', and possibly the first recorded autochthonous short story, is from the Damara or Herero language of Namibia. Bleek enjoyed patronage from the South African Library and Cape Parliament, and particularly devoted himself to recording and preserving the San (Bushman) language and lore, working with Breakwater prisoners as informants. He was the first to research indigenous languages on a scientific basis and to compare them systematically.

HERMAN CHARLES BOSMAN (1905–51); editor, poet and novelist, born of an Afrikaans-speaking family in the Cape, trained as a teacher on the Rand and, after a period of incarceration in Pretoria for the murder of his step-brother, literary editor of Black's *Sjambok* and many subsequent scandal-sheets in Johannesburg. In exile in London for most of the 1930s, he was repatriated during the Second World War to a productive career as a short story writer. In his lifetime the state of publishing within South Africa was such that he published only three works, the most popular of which is *Mafeking Road* (1947), which included 'The Rooinek', originally serialized in *The Touleier* in 1931. It is the most developed of his stories using Oom Schalk (Uncle Schalk), the backveld Boer, as a mouthpiece, and reproduced here in its full, original version. Posthumously published were three further story collections, a novel (*Willemsdorp*, 1977), and collections of essays and sketches. Of all Southern African writers he is the most widely read at present for his humour and pathos, and his unique blending of history into allegory.

FRANK BROWNLEE (1876–1952); Eastern Cape and Transkei magistrate, whose novel, *Cattle Thief: The Story of Ntsukumbini* (1929), talked of the impact of the Depression on tribal reserves. Most of his creative work was devoted to presenting Xhosa experience in English, frequently in direct translation from oral informants. 'Dove and Jackal' is from *Lion and Jackal* (1938), which includes tales set down 'as nearly as may be in the words in which they were related to me'. The publication of this collection was facilitated by a Carnegie Research Grant which maintained Brownlee for several years. He notes that the Xhosa version of the fable of the Dove and the Jackal has a Khoisan original.

JACK COPE (b. 1913 in Natal); author of half a dozen novels, from *The Fair House* (1955) to *The Student of Zend* (1972), and several collections of short stories, including *The Man who Doubted and Other Stories* (1967) from which 'Ekaterina' is taken. From the early 1960s to the early 1980s from Cape Town he edited *Contrast*, South Africa's most enduring literary journal. In 1968, with Uys Krige, he edited the influential *Penguin Book of South African Verse*, the first extensive anthology to bring together South African poetry in many languages. Recently he has published *The Adversary Within: Dissident Writers in Afrikaans* which charts an alternative, anti-establishment strain within that literature. He now lives near Oxford.

ARTHUR SHEARLY CRIPPS (1869–1952); born in Kent, graduated from Oxford in 1891 and ordained as an Anglican missionary in Mashonaland from 1901; author of *An Africa for Africans* (1927), which asserted black rights within the Rhodesian colonial system. A Georgian poet and novelist, beautifully depicting Black Christianity, whose stories dealt openly with land rights, the pass and labour-control laws and other means of social control. 'Fuel of Fire' is from his collection, *Cinderella of the South*, first published in Britain in 1918. He died, blind and poverty-stricken, in his own hospital at Enkeldoorn.

ACHMAT DANGOR (b. 1948); born and educated in Johannesburg, and works for a cosmetics company. His first collection of poems, *Bulldozer*, appeared in 1983. 'A Strange Romance', set in the once-fashionable, now mostly demolished area of Doornfontein in Johannesburg, is from his first collection of short fiction, *Waiting for Leila* (1981).

ANTHONY DELIUS (b. 1916) in Simonstown; poet and journalist. In 1959 his epic-length satire of Nationalist Party apartheid policy was not only a bestseller, but was a factor in his expulsion from Parliament as a reporter. Resident in London for the last two decades, he has worked on the Africa desk of the BBC and as a syndicated columnist. 'Hannie's Journal' is a discrete part of his historical novel, *Border* (1976), which uses many nineteenth-century British colonial narrative forms. The journal is kept by the protagonist's son, from June to August 1828, while on campaign.

ROLFES REGINALD RAYMOND DHLOMO (1901–71); born near Pietermaritzburg of Zulu parents. While a mine clerk on the Rand he wrote the first novella in English by a black man, *An African Tragedy* (1928), and the earliest black literary short stories, of which 'The Death of Masaba', first published in *The Sjambok* in 1929, is one. From 1943 he was editor of the Zulu newspaper, *Ilanga Lase Natal*, and back in Natal he wrote many biographical novels of Zulu dynastic rulers. This story is one of the first to report black life from the inside, retaining certain features of the fireside tale, while issuing a caution about labour conditions so as to discourage migration to the gold mines.

AHMED ESSOP (b. 1931 in Johannesburg); teacher and satirist; his first collection of short stories, from which 'Two Sisters' is taken, was *The Hajji and Other Stories* (1978), which chronicled much of the life of the near-demolished Fordsburg–Vrededorp multiracial complex of Johannesburg. More recently he has published two novels, *The Visitation* (1980) and *The Emperor* (1984).

J. PERCY FITZPATRICK (b. 1862 in Kingwilliamstown – d. 1931 on his estate near Uitenhage); author of the bestselling work of the colonial period (after H. Rider Haggard's *King Solomon's Mines*), his memoir, *Jock of the Bushveld* (1907), which records his early life as a transport-rider in the Eastern Transvaal, also the setting for 'The Outspan' of 1897. This compendium of fireside tales, arranged as an interchange of oral narratives, includes all the strains of the high colonial story and, throughout, Fitzpatrick acts as mere amanuensis of the compilation. The story, perhaps unconsciously, reveals all the camaraderie and casual brutality, closed ranks and racism, of much high colonial fiction in Africa, and deserves study for its psychology of the conqueror. Many of the later stories in this anthology, intentionally or fortuitously, dismantle many of Fitzpatrick's assumptions, releasing the short story into nature and into a society from which his characters held themselves apart.

NADINE GORDIMER (b. of Jewish immigrant parents on the East Rand in 1923); resident in Johannesburg. Her first collection of short stories was published in South Africa in 1949, and her first novel in Britain in 1953 (*The Lying Days*), since when she has alternated novels and story collections, including the influential *A Guest of Honour* (a novel about a post-independent African country) and *Burger's Daughter* (1979) (about contemporary politicized relationships within a dissident radical South African family). Her *Selected Stories* (*No Place Like*, 1975) is drawn from five previous volumes. Her novellas include *July's People* (1981) and *Something Out There* (1984) which lends its title to the collection from which 'At the Rendezvous of Victory' is taken. Gordimer's analyses of society in Southern Africa have been touchstones of the interests of fiction in the subcontinent, and her sustained career makes her one of the most influential figures to have emerged in the arts. With Lionel Abrahams in 1967 she edited the Penguin *South African Writing Today*.

BESSIE HEAD (b. 1937) in Pietermaritzburg, Natal; has lived in exile from South Africa in Botswana since the 1960s, and has made her home in Serowe, the village she has chronicled in *Serowe: Village of the Rain Wind* (1981). Her three novels, all concerned with the exile experience, are *When Rain Clouds Gather* (1969), *Maru* (1971) and *A Question of Power* (1974), hailed as one of the first accounts of interiority of a black woman's experience. *The Collector of Treasures and Other Botswana Village Tales* (1977) is a sequence of interconnected short stories, similar in subject matter to the more recent 'The Lovers', which is one of many uncollected stories.

INGRID JONKER (1933–65); born in the Cape of an Afrikaner establishment family; her first collection of Afrikaans poems, *Ontvlugting* (*Escape*, 1953), and her second, *Rook en Oker* (*Smoke and Ochre*, 1963), established her as a major, and dissenting, voice in lyric poetry. Her work gave much of the impetus to the Sestiger movement, which was somewhat dissipated by her early death by drowning. 'Die Bok' first appeared in *Contrast* in December 1961, and her translation of it as 'The Goat' was completed and revised by Jack Cope for publication in *The London Magazine* in December 1966.

ARCHIBALD CAMPBELL JORDAN (1906–68); born in the Mpondomise district of Transkei, Lovedale educated and with a masters in African Languages at the University of South Africa (1942). Professor of African Languages and Literature at the University of Madison, Wisconsin, until his death. His classic Xhosa novel, *Ingqumbo Yeminyanya* (1940) appeared posthumously in English as *The Wrath of the Ancestors* (1980). His *Towards an African Literature: The Emergence of Literary Form in Xhosa*, drawn mainly from articles which appeared in *Africa South* in the 1950s, is a leading text in Southern African literary criticism. 'The King of the Waters' is from *Tales from Southern Africa*, and drawn from the Bhaca group's use of the ntsomi epic tradition.

ELSA JOUBERT (b. 1922 in the Cape); she has written several novels in Afrikaans, and travelogues of Angola and the Indian Ocean islands. When in 1978 she published *Die Swerfjare van Poppie Nongena*, a documentary novel telling the story of a black domestic servant and that of her clan, it was thought to be unsaleable, but rapidly became a bestseller in the original Afrikaans, winning the three major awards of the year. Translated into English as *Poppie* by the author, it won an award from the Royal Society of Literature in London, and has subsequently been translated widely. *Poppie* has also been dramatized in both English and Afrikaans, and adapted into a musical. 'Milk' is the title-story of a collection published in 1980.

DORIS LESSING (b. 1919 of British parents in Iran); grew up in the then Southern Rhodesia, now Zimbabwe. Author of over twenty-five books, including the novels *The Grass is Singing* (1950), the *Children of Violence* cycle and *The Golden Notebook* (1962); currently engaged on the *Canopus in Argos* cycle. Her collected short stories in four volumes date from the 1940s to the present. Although Lessing's career has at various times been sub-divided into focal areas – colonialism and the colour-bar, communism, feminism, mysticism and science fiction – her project remains one of the most extensively integrated in Western literature. From a Southern African perspective, one might say that she has made the most detailed use of local material in endlessly inventive contexts. 'Out of the Fountain', with its Decameronian story-telling format, uses much typically Lessing material in startlingly fresh combinations, showing a formal ingenuity at work that is the hallmark of her creative fictions.

KEN LIPENGA (born in Mulanje, Southern Malawi); in 1971 he entered the University of Malawi, graduating in 1976; he now teaches literature and language at Chancellor College, Zomba. His distinguished collection of short stories, *Waiting for a Turn*, appeared in the Malawian Writers Series in 1981, and deals with Malawian myths, legends and history in its pre-contact, colonial (Nyasaland) and independent phases. 'The Road to Migowi', from this collection, is a rare first-person biography dealing with the rural labour situation.

EUGÈNE N. MARAIS (1871–1936); naturalist and one of the first major Afrikaans poets. Born in the Transvaal and a student in London, he wrote many of his nature studies of a more technical kind in English, and actively furthered the development of Afrikaans in short stories and articles. One series of sketches, *Die Siel van die Mier* (1937), is translated as *The Soul of the White Ant* (1971), and another, *Burgers van die Berge* (1938), as *My Friends the Baboons* (1939). While doing field-work, particularly in the depopulated Waterberg region after the South African War, and following the example of Dr Bleek, Marais collected Khoisan tales, particularly from an Afrikaans-speaking informant called Ou Hendrik, who died in the 1910s aged over a hundred. Another of his famous storyteller informants was Outa Flip, in the service of a certain Grobler farming family. In 1927 he published *Dwaalstories* (literally 'Wandering' or 'Lost' Stories), which became children's favourites; 'Little Reed-Alone-in-the-Whirlpool' is the first literal translation into English of the first of these.

DAMBUDZO MARECHERA grew up in Zimbabwe, was thrown out of the University of Rhodesia and attended New College, Oxford. His first collection of fiction, which included the title novella, *The House of Hunger*, and from which 'The Slow Sound of His Feet' is taken, was first published in 1978 and was a winner of the *Guardian* Fiction Prize. He has since published a novel, *Black Sunlight* (1980).

C. E. MOIKANGOA (b. 1879 – date of death unknown); born in Lesotho (then the Kingdom of Basutoland), educated at Morija mission, a near contemporary of Thomas Mofolo, whose *Chaka* of 1925 achieved early fame for the novel in the vernacular. Moikangoa became the first African principal of the Lovedale Practising School and one of the first two African Inspectors of Education. In 1943 in Southern Sotho he published three novellas entitled *Sebogoli sa Ntsoana-Tsatsi (The Sentinel of Ntsoana-Tsatsi)*, with the Mazenod Institute; 'Sebolelo Comes Home' is his own condensation and literal translation of one of these, and was a prizewinner in a competition organized by *South African Outlook* in the early 1940s to promote literature in the black indigenous languages with a Christian theme. It was first published in *African New Writing* in London in 1947, an anthology which featured the early stories of many African writers in English, like Cyprian Ekwensi, who were to achieve post-war renown.

ROSE MOSS was born and educated in South Africa, and emigrated to the USA in 1961. In 1971 she won the American Quill Prize for Fiction with 'Exile', first published in *The Massachusetts Review*, and subsequently in *The Purple Renoster*, Johannesburg. She has published two novels: *The Family Reunion* (1974) and *The Terrorist* (1979), which is marketed in South Africa under the title *The Schoolmaster*. She teaches Creative Writing at Wellesley College in Massachusetts.

CASEY 'KID' MOTSISI (1931–77); went to Madibane High School in Western Township, Johannesburg, and Pretoria Normal College; on the staff of *Drum* magazine from the late 1950s until his death, where he enjoyed a huge readership for his column, On the Beat, which created an on-going fictionalization of 'shebeen culture'. Of the generation of Nat Nakasa and Can Themba, who both died in exile, Motsisi seemed to be a lone joker of a school which had come into prominence as the Sophiatown renaissance in Johannesburg in the 1950s, and which briefly included writers such as Es'kia Mphahlele, Todd Matshikiza, Richard Rive and James Matthews. 'Boy-Boy' is one of his few short stories.

ES'KIA (EZEKIEL) MPHAHLELE (b. 1919); published his first collection of short stories in 1947, and in 1957 went into exile in Nigeria from where he published the now-classic autobiography of his early life, *Down Second Avenue* (1959). Editor of the Penguin *African Writing Today* (1967) which brought much new English African writing into the spotlight. *The African Image* (1962, revised 1974), his Africa-wide survey of literature, is a standard critical work. His twenty-year odyssey in exile, including teaching in Paris, Nairobi, Denver, Lusaka and Philadelphia, is well chronicled. His novels include *The Wanderers* (1971) and *Chirundu* (1979), and *Exiles and Homecomings* (1983) is an experimental documentary towards a further autobiography. Currently the first Professor of African Literature in South Africa, at the University of the Witwatersrand. His long short story, 'Mrs Plum', from *In Corner B*, published by the East African Publishing House in 1967, contains all the characteristic themes and preoccupations of 1960s' literature in South Africa.

MBULELO MZAMANE (b. 1948); born of an Anglican priest father and a nurse mother on the East Rand; has lectured in English in Lesotho, Botswana and Nigeria; doctorate on Black South African poetry at Sheffield. His first novel, *The Children of Soweto* (1982), is currently banned in South Africa. As a critic Mzamane has monitored the development of black South African writing, particularly in short forms, and this is evident in the spoof title of 'My Cousin Comes to Jo'burg', which parodies the sombre, tragic 'Jim Comes to Jo'burg' strain of earlier writers. This is the opening story of an interconnected sequence (in *Mzala*, 1981).

D. B. Z. NTULI; Zulu scholar who wrote an influential survey of modern Zulu literature, published in *Limi* (June 1968), and a Zulu novel, *uBheka* (*The Observant One*, 1962). Recently he has published a pioneering work on modern Zulu poetry, *The Poetry of B. W. Vilakazi* (1984), for which he gained his doctorate at the University of South Africa.

ALAN PATON (b. 1903); born in Pietermaritzburg, whose *Cry, the Beloved Country* of 1948, perhaps the single most famous novel produced in Southern Africa, paralleled white and black family relationships in an epic-tragic framework. His *Too Late the Phalarope* (1953) followed, on the theme of inter-ethnic sexual taboos, and in 1981 his next novel, *Ah, but Your Land is Beautiful*, bridged the social history of apartheid South Africa since *Cry, the Beloved Country* launched him into prominence as a liberal spokesperson. 'Sunlight in Trebizond Street', written during the 1960s when Paton was President of the South African Liberal Party, now prohibited, and published first in 1970, reflects an increasing concern in South African writing, the theme of detention without trial. Other short stories are collected in *Debbie Go Home* (1961) and *Knocking on the Door* (1975). His recent autobiography is *Towards the Mountain* (1980).

SOLOMON T. PLAATJE (1876–1932); born in the Orange Free State of mission-educated parents of the Barolong tribe; newspaper editor, pamphleteer and translator, whose novel, *Mhudi: An Epic of South African Native Life a Hundred Years Ago*, when it was first published in 1930 by the Lovedale Press, was the first Southern African black novel in English. *Mhudi* itself, and several other of Plaatje's ventures, were attempts to record and transpose oral literature, notably Tswana tales and myth, into print. 'Gokatweng and the Buffaloes' is one such rendering, made in London for the orthographer Daniel Jones, who together with Plaatje published *A Sechuana Reader* in 1916. Plaatje was at the time on a delegation of the South African Native National Congress (forerunner of the African National Congress) to restore black land rights in South Africa, as recounted in *Native Life in South Africa* (1916). His recently discovered and published *Boer War Diary* of the siege of Mafeking shows his polyglot versatility.

WILLIAM PLOMER (1903–73); born in the Transvaal of British parents; novelist, poet and librettist. With Roy Campbell and Laurens van der Post in the 1920s in Natal, he formed the '*Voorslag* group', dedicated to exposing colonial English culture to international trends in the arts; 'When the Sardines Came' derives from this period, although it was not first published until 1933. His controversial first novel, *Turbott Wolfe*, published by Leonard and Virgina Woolf in 1926, set a trend for liberal thinking on the inter-ethnic love theme, as well as dramatizing backwater colonial conservatism and

Black African political aspirations. His novella of the same date, 'Ula Masondo', was an early example of the 'Jim Comes to Jo'burg' strain, which deals with the tribesman's encounter with mining and urban crime. Plomer published four other novels and collections of short fiction, although his *Selected Stories* has been published only recently.

JAN RABIE (b. 1920); born in the Cape where, after several years in Paris and Crete, he is settled; critic, short story writer and novelist, prominent among the Sestigers group of Afrikaans prose writers who effected a renewal in the 1960s and which includes Etienne Leroux and André P. Brink. In 1969 he published the novel, *A Man Apart*, translated by himself from *Waar Jy Sterwe* (1966), an historical work tendentiously dealing with racial issues and togetherness. A polemicist, Rabie is given to bald statements about the value and usefulness of other than white Afrikaans cultures, and to internationalizing the interests of Afrikaans literature. 'Drought', which dates from the the early 1960s, has been frequently anthologized and included in schools' syllabuses.

RICHARD RIVE (b. 1931); born in Cape Town, educated at the University of Cape Town and Oxford – his doctoral studies were on the life and work of Olive Schreiner – educationalist and critic. Rive's early stories, notably in *African Songs* (1963), achieved a far-flung readership, and 'The Bench' is probably the most widely anthologized of 'protest against apartheid' pieces. The story itself was written specifically in response to the South African Defiance of Unjust Laws Campaign of 1952–3. As an editor and anthologizer (*Modern African Prose*, 1964), Rive has set trends in much African writing in general, and is often associated with the *Drum* school of writing (Mphahlele, Motsisi) and the exiled generation of the 1960s (Alex La Guma, Lewis Nkosi, Nat Nakasa and Bloke Modisane). His novel, *Emergency* (1964), was banned in South Africa for a long period. Recently he has published an autobiography, *Writing Black* (1981).

SHEILA ROBERTS was born in Johannesburg during the Second World War; poet and lecturer on African and Commonwealth Literatures at Michigan State University. Her collections of short stories include *Outside Life's Feast* (1975) and *This Time of Year* (1983), and she has written three novels. 'The Butcher Shop' first appeared in *New Classic* in 1978.

OLIVE SCHREINER (1855–1920); born of a German missionary father and English mother on the Eastern Cape frontier; self-educated while governessing on remote Karoo farms, out of which experience grew her *The Story of an African Farm* (1883), the first colonial novel in English to gain a widespread metropolitan readership and classic status. Her *From Man to Man* (1926), which deals more ambitiously with marriage and colour problems, was published posthumously. In the 1890s she wrote many short stories, in the mode of dream-allegory or of memoir, which enjoyed a considerable vogue – 'The Woman's Rose' from *Dream Life and Real Life* (1893) is one of these. Her feminist manifesto of 1911, *Woman and Labour*, is perhaps her most influential text today, though much of her political commentary about South African affairs around the Second Anglo-Boer War, notably in *Thoughts on South Africa* (1923), remains provocative. Schreiner single-handedly moved Southern African literature into the world of

European letters, primarily through giving testimony of the human dilemmas of the colonial personality.

PAULINE SMITH (1882–1959); born of British parents in Oudtshoorn in the Little Karoo, of which she was to write almost exclusively; schooled in Scotland, where she first published sketches in *The Aberdeen Gazette* in 1902; under the tutelage of Arnold Bennett she produced short stories of *The Little Karoo* sequence, from which 'The Schoolmaster' was first published in *The Adelphi* in 1923. In 1926 Jonathan Cape published her only novel, *The Beadle*, also about the Oudtshoorn region in the 1890s. Smith occasionally returned from England to South Africa, keeping diaries and writing astute articles about her birthplace. A year before her death, many South African writers honoured her with a scroll paying tribute to the pioneering way in which she had written across racial groups, particularly in *The Little Karoo* (1925), to create a distinctive diction in the literature, rendering Dutch and other languages in a functional and poetic English.

TOON (F. P.) VAN DEN HEEVER (1894–1956); born in Heidelberg, Transvaal, and died in Bloemfontein, Orange Free State; lawyer and judge; principally a poet who wrote in Dutch and Afrikaans, first publishing in 1919, to become a leader of the Afrikaans lyric poetry movement of the 1920s. In 1948 he collected together his prose pieces under the title, *Gerwe uit die Erfpag van Skoppensboer (Sheaves from the Inheritance of the Knave of Spades)*, from which 'Outa Sem and Father Christmas' is taken. This English version was first published in 1964 as part of a project in translation undertaken by the South African Academy for Science and Art.

PETER WILHELM (b. 1943); journalist and poet, resident in Johannesburg; his first collection, *LM and Other Stories* (1975), was followed by a novel, *The Dark Wood* (1977), and *At the End of a War* (1981), the title of which derives from a novella, a form in which Wilhelm is one of Southern Africa's few practitioners. He has also written a science fiction novel for teenage readers, *Summer's End* (1984).

Acknowledgements

For permission to include the stories in this anthology, acknowledgement is made to the authors themselves and to the following copyright-holders:

for Frank Brownlee to the National English Literary Museum, Grahamstown; for A. C. Jordan to the University of California Press; for Eugène N. Marais to Human and Rousseau (Pty), Ltd, and to David Schalkwyk for the translation; for Anthony Delius to David Philip, Publisher; for Pauline Smith to Jonathan Cape, Ltd; for Toon van den Heever to Perskor Books for the original and to Tafelberg Publishers for the translation; for Herman Charles Bosman to Human and Rousseau (Pty), Ltd and Mrs H. R. Lake; for Arthur Shearly Cripps to Mambo Press, Gwelo; for William Plomer to the author's estate; for R. R. R. Dhlomo to the author's estate; for Peter Abrahams reprinted by permission of Faber and Faber, Ltd, from *Dark Testament*; for C. E. Moikangoa to the Mazenod Institute; for D. B. Z. Ntuli to the author and C. S. Z. Ntuli for the translation; for Doris Lessing © 1972 Doris Lessing, reprinted by permission of Jonathan Clowes, Ltd, London, on behalf of the Doris Lessing Trust; for Jack Cope to the author and International Press Agency; for Ingrid Jonker to the author's estate, Jack Cope and International Press Agency; for Hennie Aucamp, translated by Ian Ferguson, to Tafelberg Publishers, Ltd; for Jan Rabie to the author; for Casey Motsisi to the author's estate and Ravan Press (Pty), Ltd; for Richard Rive to David Philip, Publisher; for Es'kia Mphahlele to the author; for Bessie Head to John Johnson (Authors' Agent), Ltd; for Rose Moss to the author, reprinted from the *Massachusetts Review*, © 1960, The Massachusetts Review, Inc.; for Mbulelo Mzamane to the author and International Press Agency; for Ahmed Essop to the author and Ravan Press (Pty), Ltd; for Achmat Dangor to the author and Ravan Press (Pty), Ltd; for Ken Lipenga to Montfort Press, from Malawian Writers Series No. 6, *Waiting for a Turn*, published by Popular Publications, Malawi, 1981; for Dambudzo Marechera to Heinemann Educational Books, Ltd; for Alan Paton to David Philip, Publisher; for Sheila Roberts to the author; for Nadine Gordimer, by permission of the author, © Nadine Gordimer, 1984; for Elsa Joubert to the author and to Mark Swift for the translation; and for Peter Wilhelm to the author.

FOR THE BEST IN PAPERBACKS, LOOK FOR THE

In every corner of the world, on every subject under the sun, Penguin represents quality and variety – the very best in publishing today.

For complete information about books available from Penguin – including Pelicans, Puffins, Peregrines and Penguin Classics – and how to order them, write to us at the appropriate address below. Please note that for copyright reasons the selection of books varies from country to country.

In the United Kingdom: For a complete list of books available from Penguin in the U.K., please write to *Dept E.P., Penguin Books Ltd, Harmondsworth, Middlesex, UB7 0DA*

In the United States: For a complete list of books available from Penguin in the U.S., please write to *Dept BA, Penguin, 299 Murray Hill Parkway, East Rutherford, New Jersey 07073*

In Canada: For a complete list of books available from Penguin in Canada, please write to *Penguin Books Canada Ltd, 2801 John Street, Markham, Ontario L3R 1B4*

In Australia: For a complete list of books available from Penguin in Australia, please write to the *Marketing Department, Penguin Books Australia Ltd, P.O. Box 257, Ringwood, Victoria 3134*

In New Zealand: For a complete list of books available from Penguin in New Zealand, please write to the *Marketing Department, Penguin Books (NZ) Ltd, Private Bag, Takapuna, Auckland 9*

In India: For a complete list of books available from Penguin, please write to *Penguin Overseas Ltd, 706 Eros Apartments, 56 Nehru Place, New Delhi, 110019*

In Holland: For a complete list of books available from Penguin in Holland, please write to *Penguin Books Nederland B.V., Postbus 195, NL–1380AD Weesp, Netherlands*

In Germany: For a complete list of books available from Penguin, please write to *Penguin Books Ltd, Friedrichstrasse 10 – 12, D–6000 Frankfurt Main 1, Federal Republic of Germany*

In Spain: For a complete list of books available from Penguin in Spain, please write to *Longman Penguin España, Calle San Nicolas 15, E–28013 Madrid, Spain*

A CHOICE OF PENGUIN FICTION

Monsignor Quixote Graham Greene

Now filmed for television, Graham Greene's novel, like Cervantes' seventeenth-century classic, is a brilliant fable for its times. 'A deliciously funny novel' – *The Times*

The Dearest and the Best Leslie Thomas

In the spring of 1940 the spectre of war turned into grim reality – and for all the inhabitants of the historic villages of the New Forest it was the beginning of the most bizarre, funny and tragic episode of their lives. 'Excellent' – *Sunday Times*

Earthly Powers Anthony Burgess

Anthony Burgess's magnificent masterpiece, an enthralling, epic narrative spanning six decades and spotlighting some of the most vivid events and characters of our times. 'Enormous imagination and vitality . . . a huge book in every way' – Bernard Levin in the *Sunday Times*

The Penitent Isaac Bashevis Singer

From the Nobel Prize-winning author comes a powerful story of a man who has material wealth but feels spiritually impoverished. 'Singer . . . restates with dignity the spiritual aspirations and the cultural complexities of a lifetime, and it must be said that in doing so he gives the Evil One no quarter and precious little advantage' – Anita Brookner in the *Sunday Times*

Paradise Postponed John Mortimer

'Hats off to John Mortimer. He's done it again' – *Spectator*. A rumbustious, hilarious new novel from the creator of Rumpole, *Paradise Postponed* is now a major Thames Television series.

Animal Farm George Orwell

The classic political fable of the twentieth century.

A CHOICE OF PENGUIN FICTION

Maia Richard Adams

The heroic romance of love and war in an ancient empire from one of our greatest storytellers. 'Enormous and powerful' – *Financial Times*

The Warning Bell Lynne Reid Banks

A wonderfully involving, truthful novel about the choices a woman must make in her life – and the price she must pay for ignoring the counsel of her own heart. 'Lynne Reid Banks knows how to get to her reader: this novel grips like Super Glue' – *Observer*

Doctor Slaughter Paul Theroux

Provocative and menacing – a brilliant dissection of lust, ambition and betrayal in 'civilized' London. 'Witty, chilly, exuberant, graphic' – *The Times Literary Supplement*

July's People Nadine Gordimer

Set in South Africa, this novel gives us an unforgettable look at the terrifying, tacit understanding and misunderstandings between blacks and whites. 'This is the best novel that Miss Gordimer has ever written' – Alan Paton in the *Saturday Review*

Wise Virgin A. N. Wilson

Giles Fox's work on the Pottle manuscript, a little-known thirteenth-century tract on virginity, leads him to some innovative research on the subject that takes even his breath away. 'A most elegant and chilling comedy' – *Observer* Books of the Year

Last Resorts Clare Boylan

Harriet loved Joe Fischer for his ordinariness – for his ordinary suits and hats, his ordinary money and his ordinary mind, even for his ordinary wife. 'An unmitigated delight' – *Time Out*

A CHOICE OF PENGUIN FICTION

Stanley and the Women   Kingsley Amis

Just when Stanley Duke thinks it safe to sink into middle age, his son goes insane – and Stanley finds himself beset on all sides by women, each of whom seems to have an intimate acquaintance with madness. 'Very good, very powerful . . . beautifully written' – Anthony Burgess in the *Observer*

The Girls of Slender Means   Muriel Spark

A world and a war are winding up with a bang, and in what is left of London all the nice people are poor – and about to discover how different the new world will be. 'Britain's finest post-war novelist' – *The Times*

Him with His Foot in His Mouth   Saul Bellow

A collection of first-class short stories. 'If there is a better living writer of fiction, I'd very much like to know who he or she is' – *The Times*

Mother's Helper   Maureen Freely

A superbly biting and breathtakingly fluent attack on certain libertarian views, blending laughter, delight, rage and amazement, this is a novel you won't forget. 'A winner' – *The Times Literary Supplement*

Decline and Fall   Evelyn Waugh

A comic yet curiously touching account of an innocent plunged into the sham, brittle world of high society. Evelyn Waugh's first novel brought him immediate public acclaim and is still a classic of its kind.

Stars and Bars   William Boyd

Well-dressed, quite handsome, unfailingly polite and charming, who would guess that Henderson Dores, the innocent Englishman abroad in wicked America, has a guilty secret? 'Without doubt his best book so far . . . made me laugh out loud' – *The Times*

A CHOICE OF PENGUIN FICTION

Trade Wind   M. M. Kaye

An enthralling blend of history, adventure and romance from the author of the bestselling *The Far Pavilions*

The Ghost Writer   Philip Roth

Philip Roth's celebrated novel about a young writer who meets and falls in love with Anne Frank in New England – or so he thinks. 'Brilliant, witty and extremely elegant' – *Guardian*

Small World   David Lodge

Shortlisted for the 1984 Booker Prize, *Small World* brings back Philip Swallow and Maurice Zapp for a jet-propelled journey into hilarity. 'The most brilliant and also the funniest novel that he has written' – *London Review of Books*

Village Christmas   'Miss Read'

The village of Fairacre finds its peace disrupted by the arrival in its midst of the noisy, cheerful Emery family – and only the advent of a Christmas baby brings things back to normal. 'A sheer joy' – *Glasgow Evening Times*

Treasures of Time   Penelope Lively

Beautifully written, acutely observed, and filled with Penelope Lively's sharp but compassionate wit, *Treasures of Time* explores the relationship between the lives we live and the lives we think we live.

Absolute Beginners   Colin MacInnes

The first 'teenage' novel, the classic of youth and disenchantment, *Absolute Beginners* is part of MacInnes's famous London trilogy – and now a brilliant film. 'MacInnes caught it first – and best' – *Harpers and Queen*

A CHOICE OF PENGUIN FICTION

Money   Martin Amis

Savage, audacious and demonically witty – a story of urban excess.
'Terribly, terminally funny: laughter in the dark, if ever I heard it'
– *Guardian*

Lolita   Vladimir Nabokov

Shot through with Nabokov's mercurial wit, quicksilver prose and intox-
icating sensuality, *Lolita* is one of the world's great love stories. 'A great
book' – Dorothy Parker

Dinner at the Homesick Restaurant   Anne Tyler

Through every family run memories which bind them together – in spite of
everything. 'She is a witch. Witty, civilized, curious, with her radar ears
and her quill pen dipped on one page in acid and on the next in orange
liqueur . . . a wonderful writer' – John Leonard in *The New York Times*

Glitz   Elmore Leonard

Underneath the Boardwalk, a lot of insects creep. But the creepiest of all
was Teddy. 'After finishing *Glitz*, I went out to the bookstore and bought
everything else of Elmore Leonard I could find' – Stephen King

The Battle of Pollocks Crossing   J. L. Carr

Nominated for the Booker McConnell Prize, this is a moving, comic
masterpiece. 'Wayward, ambiguous, eccentric . . . a fascinatingly out-
landish novel' – *Guardian*

The Dreams of an Average Man   Dyan Sheldon

Tony Rivera is lost. Sandy Grossman Rivera is leaving. And Maggie Kelly
is giving up. In the steamy streets of summertime Manhattan, the refugees
of the sixties generation wonder what went wrong. 'Satire, dramatic irony
and feminist fun . . . lively, forceful and funny' – *Listener*